A Secret Love

Love

Love and the Intern

J Matheny

J Matheny

This is a work of fiction. Names, characters, places, and incidents either are the product of the author's imagination or are used fictitiously. Any resemblance to actual persons, living or dead, events or locales, is entirely coincidental.

ISBN: 978-0-9858166-2-9

DEDICATION

To all of those who have supported me as I have written
and for all of those whose lives need some romance.

CONTENTS

❦Chapter 1 – Monday❧

The spring day was a little brisk, but not too brisk for the woman on her knees in the garden, her gown protected by a feed-sack doubled and thrown over the bare earth. This was a time for planting and she did not intend to miss a single moment of it. Her part-time gardener, Joe, had prepared the soil, but he knew that she preferred to set many of the plants herself and he had left her half of them to work with.

Her enthusiasm was evident in the intensity with which she attended to her task and it was this that made her fail to notice that she had a visitor.

Unbeknownst to her, a young man had walked around the side of the house and into the garden. He stood there for some time watching her on her knees, derriere occasionally lifted to the sky, digging holes and patting the soil in around her plants once she had placed them. He found the scene altogether pleasant --- especially the derriere.

Eventually, she sensed that she was being watched and turned to look. Seeing him, she quickly asked, "Are you come about the posting?" Then, seeing his confusion, she said, "No, you aren't, are you? Pity. I could use one such as you," looking at the long muscular arms straining to be released from his jacket. "Well, what is it you have come about, then?"

"I…. That is….. Is your husband to house, ma'am," he asked.

"Not these many years. Have you business?" she queried.

"No….. That is, yes. I had hoped to speak with Doctor Gray," he stammered.

"Oh, but Doctor Gray is my father," she clarified.

"Then, is he to house?"

"Sadly, no, having been dead these fifteen years."

"Oh. I didn't know. I thought he was still alive."

"Presumably, but, why did you want to see him?" she said, continuing to plant her flowers, for by this time he had come to stand beside her.

"I read a volume he wrote --- 'Medicine as a Calling' --- it seemed so new and forward thinking that I thought it was a recent publication."

"And?"

"I had hoped to study with him. I haven't enough for one of the colleges and his book seemed so sincere and honest..... and well written..... That is, I was hoping to exchange work for knowledge."

"Ah, I see..... What do you plan to do now? .....knowing that he is no longer able to help you."

"I have very little money, so I'm not able to return to the United States until I've earned some. Do you know of anyone needing a strong man to work in the fields or with their livestock?"

Sizing him up, with a lingering look, and rubbing a knuckle against her chin, leaving a dark mark, she made a swift decision, saying, "Actually, I have a position that needs filling. The wage is moderate and the duties are quite varied. Do you know anything besides farm work, Yank?"

"Yes ma'am, I've had good schooling as well as farming experience. I can do the managing of a business and the accounting thereof --- also carpentry and some joinery. I'm too large for a sweep, but I know how to hire a good one and I've also done masonry work and know some about waterworks."

Sounds like a posting, she thought, wondering if he would live up to his advertisement --- or his physique.....

"In that case, help me with this bit of gardening and we'll go from there. I am Elisabeth Hastings. Do you have a name?"

"Oh, yes, ma'am," he answered, "I'm John Bishop."

Smiling, she said, "I am Elisabeth Hastings, Mister Bishop."

As they worked, a pleasant camaraderie sprang up as if from nowhere. Elisabeth found herself enjoying the planting much more than she had alone. When his hand brushed her glove, as he passed her a trowel, it was as though a sudden shock went through her like lightning, startling her into dropping the trowel. He quickly scooped it up and handed it to her again, without even a comment. Taciturn man! she thought to herself.....

The gardening went faster with two working at it and soon they had finished. Elisabeth rose from her knees and, brushed herself off, saying," Would you care to accompany me into the house to discuss your employment, John Bishop?"

"Indeed, ma'am," he answered, then followed her into the kitchen, where they washed their hands, much to her maidservant's surprise, for the mistress usually washed with water from a barrel in the garden, then he followed her into the library, a room she used as a sort of study, where she conducted business at a desk of somewhat feminine proportions, surrounded by her father's best-loved books. Gesturing toward a chair, she pulled up her own favorite as John sat in the one she'd indicated was for him.

She could see that he felt uncomfortable sitting while she arranged her own seating, and said, in explanation, "No one can do it quite like oneself....."

He nodded assent and waited for her to begin, wondering if he dared tell her that she'd missed the smudge she'd put on her chin when she touched it with her glove outside. Finally, reasoning that she'd likely be more put out if she found it herself and realised he'd said nothing, he ventured, "Ma'am, you have a spot of soil on your chin from the gloves."

Startled by this, she opened a drawer and withdrew a large, folded man's handkerchief and wiped her face with it, then turned toward him, saying, "Has that got it all?"

"No, ma'am," he answered, "If I may?" then held his hand out for the cloth.

She tilted her head slightly to the left, as if thinking, then held it to him. Getting up, he took it from her fingers, engendering another jolt through her body, and began to wipe away the garden grime. She closed her eyes savoring the feel of a man touching her face and the little tingles it sent to every part of her anatomy. In a moment --- too short a moment --- he had finished and, once again, her face was clean. As he returned to his seat, she looked at him, slightly bemused, wondering what was happening here.

John Bishop seated himself and looked at her expectantly. Putting the tips of her fingers together as children do to make the steeple of a church, she began to speak. "When my father died, he left me a number of properties having income. They became my sole property, not under the control of my husband, and have seen me through the raising of my children when my husband's brother inherited the estate and all of his funds. You see, he didn't get around to making provision for our children or for me --- it was always something he would do tomorrow and, unfortunately, tomorrow came before he had done it."

She sat quietly for a few moments, then, continued, slowly, and sometimes with hesitation, as though she was remembering, "This is the house I was brought up in. I leased it out and lived in the Dower House on the estate until my eldest son, who would inherit the estate from his uncle, was old enough to be sent off to school at his uncle's expense. Then, I moved back here to finish the raising of the other four children. The younger boys are away at school, now, and my brother-in-law has kindly paid for their tuition as well, seeing that they were apt students under my tutelage. I taught the girls, of course, and my husband's spinster aunt has taken them under her wing --- not because she especially loves children, but they are twins, you see, and having two of them brings notice to her..... She loves it and they, being almost sixteen and very pretty, bring more than a little attention and activity to her household. Thus, I find myself alone here and in a renovating frame of mind." At this point, she paused, made as if to speak further, then folded her hands in her lap and sat there for a few minutes --- as though thinking about her decision.

Finally, noticing that John Bishop had not moved a muscle, she went on to say, "I am not rich, merely somewhat comfortable, but I have a proposition for you, Mr. Bishop. I was trained by my father and I am as competent a nurse as you will find --- 'better than many doctors', he always said. His surgery, which passed to me, is still open as an infirmary, serving the countryside hereabouts, and I supervise it and work in it as I am available. My father had a very high reputation with both the well-to-do and the poor in this district and, knowing he trained me, they trust me as they trusted him --- even the men. As a woman, I find very little of the prejudice one sees in the larger communities, possibly on my deceased husband's account as well as my father's, in truth. Now, then, I propose to undertake your training, give you room and board, an expense allowance and, in exchange, you will work in the infirmary with me and either complete, or arrange for the completion of, the renovations I have in mind. Does this suit you?"

The man before her drew in a deep breath, held it a moment, then let it release. He continued to sit there, obviously deep in thought and wrestling with the issue. A number of times he made as though to speak, then seemed to have another thought which must be taken into account in the ledger of his mind..... Finally, he asked, "Would this training suffice for me to practice on my own eventually?"

"Most assuredly in your country, where I understand things are a bit more casual, especially in the wilder places, but, if you learn well and give a good accounting of yourself, you will be able to practice here in due time. If you are good --- and I suspect that you are or you would not have come this far --- a doctor, male of a certainty, will likely pick you up as a protégé; perhaps a research assistant or something of that nature..... Would you like some time to think on it?" Then, she continued. "There is no hurry, and should you decide to accept, you can always cease your efforts later if you find them too tedious."

John Bishop made his decision at that moment, realizing that he had nothing to lose and everything to gain and said, "I'll do it, ma'am..... I'll do it."

"Good, then. Did you bring much clothing?"

"I have two valises, but I left them at the coaching inn behind the bar --- the woman who owns it said she'd watch 'em and gave me the direction to your house."

"Ah, that would be Meg --- sends me a few customers for the infirmary when the lads get too feisty and Dr. Pope is too busy. You picked a right one to trust your valises to," she said, then went on, "Now, as to your accommodations, though I have a number of unused bedrooms, as a woman alone it might be looked at askance if I brought you into the house, however, there are lovely rooms over the stable --- enough for a small family, and well appointed. My father's groom was a family man and the two lads lived there with their parents and helped with the chores. I have no need of many horses, now, being so close to the village and, not being a doctor, I have no patients to go to at all hours of the night. Father's groom is retired now, in any case, and his sons support him and his wife, for they are tradesmen now..... Are you certain *you* want to have a profession in which you will work day and night at all hours?"

In his innocence, he nodded his head, saying, "Oh, yes..... yes!"

I wonder, she thought...... Then, she took a key from a small drawer in the desk and, saying, "Come with me," walked out through the glass French doors of the study back into the garden again, around the side of the house, and down a drive toward a two-storey building which appeared to be the stable.

Hidden on the side he'd come along on his way from the village, the stable was down a slight slope and screened by a thicket of trees. When they came upon it, John saw that it was made of stone, comely, and well kept. The rooms were above a stable with stalls for at least four horses and plenty of room for two carriages, as well as, a large tack room and storage areas for hay and feed. Following her down the slope and then up an enclosed wide stone staircase, they came to the door of the upper rooms. Elisabeth unlocked it and ushered John inside.

He was startled. This was a lovely home. Here was an entry hall, sitting room, kitchen, three bedrooms, one of them large, and a dining room --- even a bathing room and a water closet. The doctor must have been a saint to have housed his servant so well.

Elisabeth showed him the rooms and asked, "Will this do?" knowing, of course, that it would --- and then some.

John Bishop asked, "And how many live here?" expecting this to be the quarters for a number of servants.

Elisabeth smiled and said, "Just you," watching his face turn to a look of incredulity. She smiled wider. Oh, how she liked to startle people! And, she had surprised this young man as he had never been surprised before..... Handing him the key, should he wish to use it, though she had only locked it against any vagrants, she continued, purposefully innocently, "Should you perhaps fetch your valises from the inn?"

"But what of your gardener and the lady servants?" he asked.

"Rose and Cook have rooms on the same level as the attic and Joe lives with his wife and grandson in the village, now," she replied.

Stunned, he followed her out the door and up the drive toward the road and the village to do as she had suggested, then, hearing her voice, turned back to hear her say, "Come to the house for dinner when you are ready and we'll discuss your allowance and salary. I don't dress formally, by the way....."

Elisabeth's house was on the outskirts of the village, Tring, near a hamlet called Little Tring, and, as he walked toward the inn, he marveled at his good fortune. Little did he know that she was marveling at her own good fortune, as well --- the perfect man to help her in the infirmary and with the many improvements she had planned, perhaps even capable of doing the accounts, and all in a body so intriguing, so virile, so arousing.....

A widow's life is a lonely life at night if she is to keep her reputation unsullied --- unless, of course, one takes a lover on the sly..... For a woman of some education, in a small village, this was not an ideal proposition..... Nor was she likely to find an educated man to suit her or offer her marriage.....

While John was retrieving his valises, she made good use of her time --- bathing and changing into one of her favorite dresses --- made of medium blue wool --- done in the artistic style rather than the more formal hoops she so hated, but sometimes tolerated. It set off her eyes and she knew it. She pulled her hair to the back in a chignon and set it with combs of pale beige tortoiseshell set with blue sapphires, a gift from her father.

When John returned, he washed himself and dressed in his best pants, shirt, and jacket. It was also his only jacket, but perhaps there would be an allowance for a new one for an infirmary assistant --- he reasoned, with hope.....

The maidservant showed him to the study when he arrived at the house and after twenty minutes, Elisabeth came into the room. He sat and stared at her, transfixed by her beauty in the simple styles, completely forgetting his manners and failing to rise. Then, somehow, he rallied, remembering the conventions, and rose to greet her, bowing. She came to him and sat, then asked him to sit as well, and soon they were engaged in pleasant conversation.

It was almost an hour, but seemed to have been minutes, when the maidservant announced that dinner was ready. Standing, John offered his arm to Elisabeth and took her in to dinner. She had asked that John's place be laid to her right --- that which she considered her 'best side', but also the side she favored when conversing.

The dinner was excellent --- good, fresh country food prepared by Elisabeth's cook, a lady who had served her father for the last few years of his life and now her. Neither of them were aware of what the talented woman had prepared, beyond the first course, though, for they were so deeply engrossed in conversation that it mattered not what they were eating…..

Elisabeth began by telling John of the cases he would encounter at the infirmary and the characters who lived in the village --- Meg, her staff, the shopkeepers and other tradesmen, their families, the blacksmith, and the country gentry and the farmers on their lands. There was little in the way of a constabulary and only one postmaster. He had two boys who could ride with incoming mail to the outlying estates, but some had their mail held and sent a servant to collect from time to time.

Soon, she had him laughing with her tales of life in a country village and, with each tale, their spirits lifted higher and higher. As he sat there listening --- and, in truth, laughing at the uproariously funny circumstances that she related --- he was quietly falling in love with Doctor Gray's comely daughter.

For her part, Elisabeth was not insensitive to his masculinity in the least --- and had felt tinglings in parts of her body that had long lain dormant. At times, during the evening, she felt as lightheaded as a maiden, while listening to his resonant voice and, at others, when his hand inadvertently touched hers in passing a dish, she felt the same shock as she had felt earlier. A place between her legs began to feel heavy with sensation, throbbing with feeling each time she heard his voice. She raised her eyes to his and saw there a reflection of her feelings. But they had just met! How could this be happening? And, so quickly! Calm down, she told herself. It only worked a little, but it was enough to get her through the meal.

Finally, when the last plate had been cleared, they retired to the study for their discussion. Elisabeth began by asking what clothes he had, aware that he had only the two valises. He gave her an inventory of his outer clothing and, knowing he would need more, she told him that, if he needed anything, he should make free use of her husband's or father's clothing, for they were both of a similar size to him, so there would be few alterations, if any. When measurements could be taken, he would be outfitted with clothing of his own, suitable for wearing to the infirmary, as well as for attending on the wealthy in their homes or any parties he would be invited to. She explained how important clothing was, for the patients saw this as part of the caregiver's persona and the ritual of healing --- their uniform, as it were, and it served as the robes of priests and shaman had for millennia in a venue of another type of healing. His lessons had begun.....

Then, she changed the subject to wages and allowances. His allowance was flexible and could be augmented to account for needs, such as special clothing needs or books, and she set it at one pound per month. His wage was set at ten pounds yearly, to be paid quarterly. John looked pleased, she thought, on hearing this.

She asked if he would like to walk in the garden on the terrace for a bit before retiring and he agreed, then placed a wrap from the hat stand by her desk around her bare shoulders and offered his arm.

The garden looked eerily beautiful in the pale moonlight --- it was not yet full, but still bright. It was late spring and there was still a distinct edge of chill in the air as they walked, arm in arm. She felt his strength and it made her weak in the knees, but it also made her heart sing.

John felt elated to be in her presence, wondering why fate had chosen to bring him here to her and hoping that there would be more than a stroll in the garden..... Someday.....

The sensation of her body leaning against him as they walked was almost more than he could bear and he thanked God that they were in the dark, for his member was rising up, becoming firmer and stiffer as his arm became alive with sensations where hers touched it. The softness of that skin..... The lightness of the touch..... All things were contributing to his arousal..... He knew it wasn't proper, but it was happening nonetheless. Perhaps if they stayed outside, it would abate, he hoped.

Elisabeth could feel his arm trembling slightly and wondered if he was as aroused by her as she was by him. Could it be? Would she find romance? .....and a man she could admire and work with? It seemed so impossible..... But, that telltale feeling in her heart, and lower, was talking to her.....

Somehow, she must manage to continue this evening without falling into his arms…..

Finally, when they returned to the house, the chilly air had brought their bodies better under their control. Had they lingered there in the study, perhaps they would have had a relapse, but John bid her good night and hurried off to his rooms, his sanctuary from the disobedience of his body.

Elisabeth made her way up the stairs, thinking about John and feeling more and more aroused again. As she readied herself for bed, it was as though each piece of clothing she removed was a removal of barriers to him. Finally, she lay under the down comforter, naked, and began to touch those parts which were throbbing. First, her breasts and nipples, squeezing and pinching to get the most sensation, then, the throbbing mount between her thighs and its wet opening….. Her fingers lightly pinched at the wet and slippery little button she found at the top of the mount. It seemed to feel better if she pushed on it with one finger and she began to do that. Her hips rose to meet her finger over and over, more firmly and energetically with each push, until finally it was so wet that her finger slid into the slit below it and found another place to play. She inserted one, then, two, and finally three of her slender fingers into that place, sliding them in and out, and feeling pleasured. Her back arched, involuntarily, and she strained against her hands, feeling the tension building in her inner recesses and the pace of her pleasuring increasing until, at last, she felt she could not bear it another minute. That was when the waves of pleasure began to roll across her body, satiating that hunger which had built up over the course of the day as she looked at John and spoke with him. Satiating that need which had been denied for so many years….. Once again, she was a woman! Once again she could feel! She slid her fingers in and out of herself again bringing herself to another, and stronger orgasm, for this was an orgasm of renewal.

She was exhausted and lay at rest, savoring her triumph in being able to feel again. When the last echoes of sensation faded and stilled, she still lay there thinking. Dared she have an affair with him? How could it be accomplished without discovery and censure? She didn't know, but only time would reveal all things….. The energies expended in her exertions finally took their toll and she slept --- deeply and refreshingly.

John lay in his bed holding himself and thinking of her. He remembered masturbating in the barn one day when he was not yet twelve, after seeing their stallion mount a filly. It felt good, then, and it felt good, now, to hold his stiffened member in his hand, stroking it and squeezing it, feeling the blood pulse through it, feeling the tautness of his skin and the firmness of his manhood. He stroked longer with that milking motion, feeling the arousal and beginning to breathe heavier and deeper, quicker and quicker, until he felt himself releasing ejaculate into the towel he had wrapped over it. Again and again his juices spurted into the towel as his hips rose upward, pumping toward the sky, releasing all of the feelings of need --- for the time being. Releasing them and satisfying them, allowing him to sleep --- and sleep he did, his member still held in his hand with the towel wrapped around it…..

❦Chapter 2 – Tuesday❧

The day dawned gray as old suet --- so often is the case in the spring --- as though winter cannot make up its mind whether to leave and spring has not yet decided whether to intrude on winter's sole possession of the land.

John Bishop was certainly no stranger to this sort of spring, having lived in Michigan. He got out of bed, and looked around his quarters, thinking what a comfortable lot had fallen to him --- and was a bit bemused by it all.

Usually an early riser, Elisabeth was already awake, dressed, and having her tea in the study when he came to receive his instructions. Little did he know that class would begin that day --- with instruction in property management.

Elisabeth took him first to the attic where chests and clothespresses filled with older or out-of-season clothing were stored. Finding her father's and her husband's, she asked him to sort through the presses and see if there were some pieces he could use to appear more business-like, while a tailor was preparing a selection of more contemporary articles.

Looking through the coats and jackets, trousers, shirts, gloves, and hats, he selected a number of them from both men's wardrobes and then found a pair of shoes in brown and one in black for dress, as well as boots for walking in the countryside. A pair of Wellingtons, a Macintosh, warm gloves, and a hat brought him up to snuff.

As she watched him selecting these items, Elisabeth took note of his practicality and knowledge of fashion --- as he overlooked the hopelessly outdated and selected from among the more au courant. All in all, he would present himself quite well, she thought.

As he tried the jackets on, she thought more, far more, but she tucked that into a hidden corner of her mind and went forward with the task at hand --- though, she could not help but notice that he was even easier on the eyes in the well-made clothing of the two men who needed it no longer.

Taking a small trunk from a shelf, they found it had very little in it and transferred that to a drawer in one of the chests, then used it to hold the items he had selected for transport to his rooms over the stables. Following her, he carried the trunk downstairs alone and left it by the kitchen door for the maidservant to air out the clothing at Elisabeth's instruction.

She asked him to follow her into a small dining nook where breakfast had been laid for them, each plate already filled with eggs, sausages, thick slices of toast and a plate of kippers on the side, should they desire them. He held her chair for her and then seated himself, looking at the breakfast with interest. It proved to be as good as it looked and, over it, they chatted animatedly as they slathered fresh butter and jam on their slices of toast. Neither ate the kippers for fear of offending the other, but the maidservant, Rose, brought four more rashers of sausages to the table at Elisabeth's request, then reported to Cook that the comely young man had a 'very good appetite' for his breakfast.

"Yeah, that ain't all's my wager!" came the reply and not quite completely under Cook's breath.

"What else," asked Rose, only to be told that the pans needed washing and that she should do them better than the last batch.

This time, Cook couldn't be heard above the pan washing when she muttered, "Some men be too 'andsome for a woman's good."

Meanwhile, in the breakfast nook, Elisabeth and John were finishing the last of the sausages and eating toast piled high with Cook's own berry preserves. John smiled when he saw the deep purple as they stained

Elisabeth's mouth and she wondered what he was smiling at, then smiled herself when she saw his purple lips and realised the answer.

Soon, they were ensconced in the study going over ledgers and drawings of her properties to see what improvements needed doing. She promised him that the very next day they would hitch up the one horse she had to her father's ageing buggy and ride out to the properties in the vicinity so as to see them first hand, but she wanted him to have a cursory knowledge of them beforehand.

She began to outline her plans for him. The schooling in the infirmary would begin the following week, barring any unforeseen farming accidents..... The infirmary was open two days a week for general complaints and every day and night for emergencies, which, thankfully, had been very few since her father died. This left plenty of time for John's studies as well as his duties as a property overseer trainee and laborer.

By lunchtime, his head was swimming with figures --- both accounting figures and the nearness of her body. He could smell something, a scent of flowers, when she moved, and it made him want to sweep her into his arms and carry her away --- to do what, he wasn't entirely certain..... He just knew that she had an effect on him.

Elisabeth called a halt to the lessons when she noticed that it was nearing the time for a midday meal and asked Rose to bring it into the breakfast nook where the light was good. Carrying a sheaf of papers, she adjourned their discussions to that corner of the house and, as they waited, she showed the papers she had carried to John. When he saw them, he let out an involuntary gasp. The drawings were beautifully executed --- birds and animals that seemed ready to spring from the pages, details of human organs --- the heart, the lungs, the eye --- and drawings of pathologies, such as he had never seen. "My father's work," she said, softly, with love and pride in her eyes and voice.

His heart was rent. Perhaps it was his relative youth, but he had fallen in love with her --- as deeply and soulfully as he knew how. To find a woman who could love so long and so completely that one could hear it in her voice --- this he wished for himself: that she might love him like this as well.

He looked at the drawings, devouring their essence, and, as she looked down at them, he watched her face with longing, as well as bodily urges (nonetheless soulful in their origin). He burned for her, that she might be his to hold, to touch, to care for..... His body ached for her, that they might be one in fleshly devotion, as well as in spirit.....

And, then, Rose arrived with luncheon and he must back off, hold off, bank the fires of his heart and his being, secreting them in abeyance to wait for a more timely airing if there was to be one at all.

Elisabeth, not entirely unaware of his predicament due to the tightening of his trousers perceived by her lowered eyes, rejoiced within herself --- this situation might come to fruition. But, for what? A tête-à-tête? An affair? More? An engagement? Marriage? She wondered, as she ate the cold meats, cheeses, and slices of over-wintered apples and pears from her plate. Her body was on fire for this man, but was it enough for the long term? Or, would it only be an affair, which would have the potential of ending badly, sadly, or worse --- openly?

Then, his hand met hers, as they both reached for the cream pitcher, and all doubts flew. She knew that she would have this man on any terms, at any time, and anywhere he desired --- as well as any way he desired.....

John, so moved by the contact with her hand, nearly threw up his lunch --- only managing to hold it down with the greatest effort he could muster. Ruefully, he thought: what a great lover I shall make --- spewing food all over my conquest! This dampened his ardor for the moment, and just in time, for they were both becoming more than a bit overwrought.

Or, as Rose put it to Cook, "Them's puttin' steam on th' windows in th' breakfast room!"

Nonplused, and protective of her mistress' reputation, Cook replied, "Aw, go on girl, that's me cookin' as done it. Ain't ya seen --- I'm doin' dumplin's!"

In the breakfast room there was indeed steam --- a lot of it --- and this steam was not from Cook's dumplings, but straight from the heart of an impending volcano, threatening to erupt at any moment.

After lunch, teacher and student retired to the study once again and spoke of the infirmary this time. Elisabeth asked, "What makes you think that you should study medicine, John Bishop? Have you any experience?"

Rising to the occasion, he answered, "Yes, ma'am, I do. Much of it was with animals, but I've also set bones and healed sores, both with salves and with the touch of my hand --- my uncle's wife is an Chickasaw Indian woman and she taught me many healing ways. Often, I've caused swellings to leave the body with just a touch."

"So, you are a faith healer?" she asked.

"I suppose I am, but not in the way you think, perhaps," he began, slowly, carefully, "I have faith that the universe's energy comes through me and passes into the person I touch or even think of and it has the power to heal them if they accept being healed as their path. Unfortunately, some people want to be sick, because it serves them in some way."

Oh, this man is profound, she thought, then said, "We must talk more on this sometime, but first I would like to make you familiar with the protocols of the infirmary and the staff that works with me," and thus she proceeded into a lecture on all phases of running an infirmary. Class was in session.....

At dinner, they again supped together, eating Cook's dumplings, as well as her roast capon and winter vegetables: two-year carrots as large around as potatoes and as sweet as honey.

This evening, as the last, they took a turn in the garden, Elisabeth's shoulders covered by a wrap and he, looking dapper in a smoking jacket which had been her father's. She shivered as they walked, not from a chill, rather from the state of arousal she was brought to simply by slipping her arm through his --- and they were both wearing long sleeves!

As they turned toward the house, her foot engaged a pebble and she leaned into John, almost falling. He caught her and, holding her in his arms and feeling their hearts pounding, he brought his lips down to hers and, parting his lips, kissed her passionately. Elisabeth returned kiss for kiss and passion for passion, pressing herself against him as firmly as he pulled her to him. Had there been a bed nearby, they would have made use of it, but only a stone garden bench availed itself..... Sitting there, they held each other, kissing and touching as much as they could reach. John lifted her skirt enough to run a hand up her leg and onto her thigh, then into the open crotch of her undergarment, designed to make necessities easier, but handy for lovers as well.....

Elisabeth gasped in her arousal, rocking her head back and forth, and feeling almost faint in the heat of that moment. Taking this for assent, John proceeded to explore with his fingers, the territory beneath that opening in her undergarment. It was very wet with a juice of some sort much like his of the night before and it made her body slippery. His hand probed further, finding a mound of fur, from which the juice seemed to be emanating. Yet, further, his long slender fingers encountered tissues not unlike lips and a crevice, into which he plunged his finger, then another, making Elisabeth gasp and moan. "Am I hurting you?" he asked.

"No....oooh," she moaned sensuously, "Please carry on," then placed her own hand on the mound grown in his groin, eliciting sounds of arousal from deep in his throat, as well.

He did carry on, running his fingers in and out of her and slipping them up to the risen button of flesh at the apex of her own furry mound, then finally, realizing that he could rub that with his thumb as his other fingers slid in and out of her, he experimented with her arousal. She reacted immediately with greater groaning, though he could see she was trying to hold it in, and finally, at the point that he thought he would faint away as more and more blood served his erection, she began to whimper and he felt the muscles of her interior parts convulsing on his fingers..... The tactile sensation was too much for him to bear, holding back, and his own orgasm rocked them both as it overtook him. He didn't have time to think more than a fleeting --- wish I could be free of my trousers --- and, suddenly, he was holding his fingers deep within Elisabeth and vibrating them to bring her to greater sensitivity and a more erotic orgasm.

Elisabeth held him more tightly than she had ever held anyone before, rocking with the force of the experience and kissing him deeply and with more passion than she knew she could feel or, for that matter, express. It seemed as though it would go on forever in the dark of that spring garden, scented by flowers and lit only by stars.

When they finally sat there holding each other, but no longer intimately, he ventured, "I'm afraid I must depart for my rooms, ma'am, for my trousers have become damp. May I see you to the door of your study?"

Still holding the bulge in his trousers, she gently squeezed --- and he first jerked as if shocked --- then, she squeezed again and he pushed forward into her hand, wanting to feel this contact with her again and again. Putting his lips to her ear, he whispered, "Tomorrow, dearest lady, tomorrow."

Then, he escorted her to the door of her study, embraced her, kissed her soundly, and turned on his heel and retreated to his rooms.

Once inside, all he could think of was his need for greater release and, stepping out of his trousers, he lay in his bed with his towel, now rinsed and dry, to ease his need. Stroking his manhood, he began to bring himself to completion again. Up and down his hand slid, milking that stiffened teat and hoping for a bumper crop of release. Squeezing it, from time to time, as well, he finally erupted into the towel again, spent and satiated for the time being. As his thoughts flew to Elisabeth, he could feel it stiffening again, though, and began a gentle massage to relax it, but succeeded only in arousing himself again, due to his thoughts of her, and this erection took much longer to put down. His right hand was sore and his arm, too, before juice had sputtered forth from his member for the third time that day..... What was this magic that she had --- to bring him to desire her so much --- he wondered, as he lay there nearly unable to move for the heaviness of his limbs.....

Left at the door, Elisabeth entered the study, crossed to the hall, then slowly ascended the stairway to her bedroom. She felt a languor, as though her limbs could not obey her and, undressing, she slid under the covers naked --- to touch herself and augment the actions John Bishop had performed. Finding the juicy slit between her thighs, she began to run her hands through the wetness and stimulated the sensory button he had so adroitly addressed with the mere touch of his thumb. It was very sensitive, very responsive, and she jerked with each touch to it, but she persisted and, eventually, she experienced yet another orgasm, this time arching her back and softly keening her pleasure. As she lay there afterward, she thought of him and let out a sigh, the sigh of a woman satisfied --- and well......

Thinking of what she had done with him shocked one part of her being --- the socialized, culture conscious part --- yet, it seemed so easy, so natural, a meeting of souls and minds joining in an extension of a cause of action, as well as, mutual pleasuring. She knew, in her heart, that this was truly not a wrong action or she would not have been able to do it, would not have found pleasure in it, and would have been shocked --- before the fact rather than afterward.

As she lay there musing, she wondered what he thought, what he felt --- beyond pleasure --- and where this would lead. She thought of her children and the brother-in-law who had attempted unsuccessfully to court her for a number of years after his brother's death. They would certainly be shocked and to cause them scandal would be an unkindness, a thing which she *would* feel great guilt over. In the warmth and security of her bed, she sought to discover how this relationship could work without hurting those who were dear to her, yet, without compromising her own needs and wishes. She knew in her heart that she dare not be so openly affectionate without incurring suspicion and must, therefore, bank her fires, as well as John's. She did not, however, intend to hold him off as she had her husband's brother! In pondering this conundrum, she ultimately fell asleep, still not entirely decided as to how to proceed.

ᎧChapter 3 – WednesdayᎧ

Elisabeth awoke with the first hint of light and lay there in her cosy nest thinking of all the things she had planned for the day: hitching Abernathy, the horse, up to her father's buggy and taking John out to the nearer properties, then, in the afternoon between three and five o'clock, working in the infirmary. They seldom had large amounts of patients, barring outbreaks of influenza, so a few hours should suffice. Usually, she was able to confine the time to less than two hours and typically opened on Wednesday and Friday. Generally, one of three girls from the hamlet helped her sort the patients out and all ran smoothly most of the time.

Deciding that there was no further purpose in laying abed, she arose and began to prepare herself for the day. By the time Rose brought her morning tea, she was already descending the stairway and asked that it be brought into the breakfast nook --- with an additional cup and saucer. It was fully a half hour before John Bishop showed his face, but he was certainly dressed correctly, she thought as she looked at him, for Rose had carried the aired-out clothing to his rooms before serving dinner the night before. He would do her proud as an agent!

Pouring him a cup of tea, she remarked, "That jacket becomes you, John Bishop. You will be very effective with my tenants, as well as the laborers."

"Thank you, ma'am," he replied, looking down at the front of the jacket he wore. "The clothing fits well, I'm convinced, and I hope that it will help me to be taken seriously, both as your agent and as your medical student."

Cocking her head to the left side, she observed, "Oh, yes, they will take you seriously. I take you seriously."

The hidden meaning was not lost on John and his heart felt light, as light as air for a moment, before it settled itself in his chest.

At that moment, Rose arrived with a tray and proceeded to unload its contents onto the table. This time there were no kippers, merely the sausages, egg and potato pie, and a bread so speckled with dried bits of fruit that no preserves were necessary and butter alone sufficed. They spent some time over this feast chatting and discussing the tenants and properties they would visit. It was not long before John had been caught up on everything of any importance, but he wasn't certain he would remember who belonged with which until he had been out to see it all and had a picture in his mind to tie it together.

By nine o'clock it was time for him to hitch the horse and buggy and fetch a suitable greatcoat from among his attic treasures, lest the day turn colder. Elisabeth showed him where the horse blankets were kept, as well as the lap robes for the buggy.

As he hitched the horse, she watched, appreciating his dexterity with the harnessing and his instant rapport with Abernathy. Yes, he had a way about him, she reminded herself. It wasn't long before he handed her up, passed her accounts brief to her, then walked around, swung himself up, and sat down beside her. She handed him the reins, saying, "You'll remember the way far better if you drive it yourself. I'll give you directions."

In a matter of moments, they were off down the lane in the direction she had pointed. Noting his agility with the reins, she directed him toward the high road and their first of eight stops. As they rode, she filled him in, saying, "A number of these properties were willed to my father by grateful patients --- or acquired by virtue of there being no heirs left or money to pay for his years of attendance on the deceased. A few were acquired by him in trade and one he bought outright when it was offered for a pittance by an heir with gambling debts. Had the man been of greater moral fiber, or married, he would have offered what it was worth, but, certain the man would merely gamble the money away, he paid only the asking price."

Eventually they came to a fork and she directed him to the right, the avenue leading to the high road, and they were away.

It was about a thirty minute ride to the farthest property reachable in a reasonable length of time and Elisabeth guided him there, because everything would go smoothly from that point. It was the one with the most work needing to be done and the tenants were a none-too-friendly old man, his manservant and the man's wife, who cooked and kept the place clean. She pointed out parts of the terrain which might interest John en route and told him the local folklore and legends. They were not so far into the wilderness that superstition was rampant, but pockets of it still survived. London was a good forty or more miles away, so he had come to a more elemental society; one which believed in things no longer given credibility in the cities.

As the journey passed, Elisabeth became increasingly aware of the pressure of John's thigh against hers and her body's awareness of it, as well. It made her feel weak in her legs, somehow, and gave her an intense awareness of that sensitive space between her thighs. It seemed as though her pulse beat there with such an intensity! Insistently, it demanded her awareness. She wondered what would happen if she touched his leg, but the Victorian in her reared its ugly head and she restrained herself. Little did she know that John had thought the same thing and abandoned the idea, for fear that, in the light of day, they might be seen and she would be censured. As they continued along the high road, they met few travelers to distract either from thoughts of the other.

The property, Close Farm, was not far from the high road and, soon enough, they found themselves pulling up in front of a large cottage after the design of a manor house. John lifted Elisabeth from the buggy, holding her waist a moment longer than necessary and slowly trailing his fingers away when he released her, an act so utterly sensual that she thought, for a moment, she would faint, then breathed deeply and gathered her composure.

The tingling between her thighs was undeniably there --- and stronger. She took the energy of it and focused on her tenant, Thomas Weatherford, when his manservant had brought her to him. "Hello, Mr. Weatherford," she said, more loudly than John had expected. "I've brought my agent and medical student, Mr. Bishop, to meet you. He will be assessing what improvements and repairs need doing to make the house more comfortable."

Surprised, and taken off guard, the old man, usually gruff, was almost, but not quite, cordial. He didn't offer them even a cup of tea, but he did say thank you and rose to his feet to hobble around showing them where he saw need. Elisabeth made copious notes and allowed John to take the lead, building a rapport with the old fellow, since he would be in charge of the doing of it --- or the contracting, at the very least. Finally, after about half an hour, it was time to once again take to the road.

After saying their goodbyes, John lifted Elisabeth into buggy once more and allowed his fingers to linger lightly, again, almost caressingly. In that moment she thought that, had he but known it, he could have had his way with her in front of the whole world. It was all she could do to keep her body under control.....

Then, he entered the buggy on the other side and his thigh slid along hers as he sat, positioning himself to take the reins. She jerked, involuntarily, as her body felt that connection, then breathed out suddenly. He looked at her questioningly and she took a deep breath, then said, "John Bishop, your body is very arousing to me and your limb is touching mine."

Thinking it a criticism, he moved away a bit, all that was possible in the small buggy, but she quickly said, "No, John, I am not unhappy, merely very, very affected."

In his somewhat younger brain, the light dawned and he smiled at her. "I am sorry," he said, "I didn't mean to do it. Truth is, just being near you makes me feel like that --- all unsettled."

By this time, they were already out into the lane and she made bold to put her hand on his thigh. He gasped and his body jerked, then he regained control. "Now, *that* is what I have been feeling," she said.

"Yes, ma'am, I understand now," he answered after a moment, then placed his larger hand over her hand on his thigh and squeezed it. Next, he lifted his hand and put it on her thigh for a moment, as if making a promise, before taking full charge of the reins once more.....

Elisabeth sat as if in a daze of bliss, every part of her body pulsing with some new kind of energy and with the private parts of her anatomy ablaze with a fire that she knew she would have to fight in public lest she be found out.

The chill of the day didn't effect her in the least. In fact, had she taken all of her clothing off, she doubted that she would have felt the slightest bit cold. Had he not been as warm as she, John would have felt the heat radiating off of her like a furnace.....

By the time they reached the next property, the intensity of their attraction had been brought with some effort to a more sedate level and Elisabeth was able to assume her business persona and introduce John to the Stillwell family --- husband, wife, and four young children. The property they rented was a modest home with only a smallish parcel of land for a county place --- enough for the children's exercise and lovely gardens for flowers and vegetables. Their manservant tended the garden and raised rabbits and hens on the side for eggs as well as the meat larder. Mr. Stillwell was a man of independent means, just not enough means to live any higher than he did without robbing his children's future. He was an excellent father and husband, earning him very high favor in Elisabeth's eyes.

After a mere quarter hour they were once again on their way and Elisabeth's notes were not nearly so copious, for the father and his manservant enjoyed puttering around the property and repairing that which needed mending.

Elisabeth kept her hands to herself, for she knew that the remaining properties would come up quickly enough that she dared not open that door of arousal and risk it being obvious enough to become the object of gossip.

In a matter of minutes they were pulling into a short drive and then she was stepping down from the buggy herself onto a raised platform with stairs, built especially for this purpose. This was a lovely home, the pride of her possessions, and she rented it to two older spinsters --- twin sisters, by the look of them, and so they represented themselves. She was the only one who had been taken into the confidence that Cora was three years Dora's elder, but looked the same age as her younger sister. Ah, vanity, thy name is often woman.....

They stayed longer than absolutely necessary, for the two spinsters flirted outrageously with John, plying him with tea and biscuits, chocolates, and even a glass of sherry. Smiling helplessly at Elisabeth, he saw that no help was coming from that quarter by the stifled giggles he sensed rising from deep within her. Finally, they managed to pry themselves away and with the smallest list, yet, though with invitations to dinner and a parish tea the Blakely sisters were hosting, they set out on their way.

When they were out of the drive, they looked at each other and could hold their amusement not one moment longer, bursting into a pleasant laughter, filled with the camaraderie they were feeling.

The next property was over a small rise and down a lane from the main road. It was not so pretty as the last, but it was a small farm and supplied Elisabeth with produce, eggs, milk, and meat as part of the rent. The farmer's wife came out to greet them saying that her man was down in the meadows with the cows. Elisabeth assured her that he need not be present as they were merely looking to determine which repairs needed doing. Mary Ellis, his wife, said that her man could do them if Elisabeth could just credit the supplies to the rent. She was happy to agree and they left with no list, having given it to Mary, with instructions for her man to keep track of his expenses in the projects.....

It was about fifteen minutes to the next property, and Elisabeth determined that this would be the last of the day, since it was getting close to clinic time at the infirmary.

As they came to a small house along the lane they were traveling, he saw that there was an elderly woman waving at them. "That's Kate,"

Elisabeth said. "She's alone with her grandson. The boy is strong, but slow in his thinking..... He looks after her and she looks after him. Fortunately, her son left her enough money to care for the boy, when he died in India. The mother died in childbirth and they're each all the other has. I think Kate will be needing a chair eventually and the boy can help build, but not plan, a ramp so that she can leave the house....."

John looked at his companion with new admiration, finding beauty in her compassion and insightfulness, qualities he valued highly. At this point, a young man came running out to the buggy, saying, "Lizza, Lizza, Lizza....." Elisabeth waved to him and he waved back. They stopped and Kate hobbled over to the buggy to talk to them. John got down and looked at the stoop to see how it would accommodate the planned revisions, then talked for a bit with Kate's grandson, who was delighted to discover that they shared the same first name.....

Elisabeth remained in the buggy, knowing that it was a matter of pride that Kate came out to the buggy. Holding on to it, she could stand fairly well and she wanted the younger woman, the nurse, to see her healthy, for she deeply feared that any hint of disability on her part would result in her grandson's removal to a home for the afflicted.

When John returned to the buggy with Kate's grandson at his side, Kate told the boy that he could help her and he fairly glowed. John put his arm over the boy's shoulders in a sideways hug, then stepped up into the buggy, as Elisabeth was explaining to Kate that John would be doing some revisions to her porch and that her grandson could help, which brought a smile to her own face. Waving good-bye, they headed for the village and home for lunch.

When they were on the road, Elisabeth asked, "You were doing some of your energy healing with young John, weren't you?"

"Yes, ma'am, I was. You see, sometimes these cases are from an injury, sometimes it runs in the family, others, it's due to a disease, but some appear to me to be a disruption in the flow of energy and I repair it if I can."

"John, if I promise to call you John, will you please call me Elisabeth, at least when we are alone?" she asked.

"Yes, ma'am, that is, yes, Elisabeth, ma'am," he said, reddening in his confusion.

The house was only a few minutes away at this point and soon they were alighting and, after Abernathy had been unhitched, Elisabeth led him to his stall..... John followed to get him some hay and oats to reward him for his good work and, once he had been seen to, they stood there looking at each other in the quiet of the stall. Then, suddenly, they were in each other's arms kissing passionately, deeply, as though there would be no tomorrow, then they were gasping for air, looking at each other again, and laughing at themselves.

It wasn't long before they remembered that the midday meal would be awaiting them and that patients would be waiting soon, as well. They walked up to the house with a gentle camaraderie, not touching there in the open, lest someone see, but each knowing that they were of one energy, one mind, one passion.

Once in the house, they went to the breakfast nook and Rose quickly brought their plates, aware that it was an infirmary day and that they should be on time. They made short work of the meat pasties that Cook had made, as well as the creamed spinach and asparagus spears. Dessert was cherry tarts and, like children, they each ate more than one, licking their fingers where the cherry juice dripped onto them.

Soon, it was half past two and Elizabeth and John began their walk to the village. It was only about a quarter of an hour away, but she never liked to be last minute. That might suit for the fashionable, but not for a nurse or doctor. So, it was, that they arrived at the infirmary at fifteen minutes before the hour.

Maggie, the girl who helped on Wednesdays was already at the infirmary, opening the office and preparing for the patients. Elisabeth went to a cupboard and got out a smock for herself and one for John. His was one of her father's old ones with a masculine cut to it. Hers accommodated the width of her skirt and tied in the back, not unlike a full apron, whereas his was more of a coat.

The first of their patients was the village busybody --- an elderly lady who wanted to see this new man that Dr. Gray's daughter was bringing into her father's surgery. Satisfied, after visiting with him for awhile, that he was no crackpot, she sailed out of the office, without a formulation for the chemist and heading for the first house where the occupants were certain to be at home.

Elisabeth smiled at John, and said, "That's one hurdle jumped without a fall….."

He winked at her and her insides felt as though they'd been scrambled --- why did she feel this way, she wondered. This was decidedly not how her husband had made her feel. As she remembered him, she felt somber. He wasn't really a bad or evil person, he just believed, as did so many men of the age, that women were property and, like children, must be obedient and subservient. He probably had no idea how that had challenged their marriage. Her father hadn't known, nor would she have told him, because it would have made him feel as though he had harmed her and it would have broken his gentle heart.

The saddest part of these relationships, she thought, was that women did not even have relief through the church, for the benighted clergy were men and subscribed to, no, ordained, the concept of male superiority --- to the detriment of women. How many times men had come into the infirmary with wives they'd beaten --- ah, but with a rod no wider than their thumb….. She was appalled by it, as had her father been. This was still an era of slavery and it extended into the fabric of the family in most households in the world --- even that part which considered itself civilized. And, the British, as a whole, were very good at considering themselves the most civilized of all people…..

Someday, she thought, someday there would be no slaves and no masters, women would be free to make their own choices, to marry or not, to bear children or not, and to work or not. It might be very far off, but it was coming --- she could feel it and the talk of 'redundant women' in London only underscored her feeling. When there are women who are deemed 'unnecessary' simply due to a lack of adequate men, something is dreadfully wrong with society. She had read that there were over eight thousand young women and boys prostituting themselves in London, because there was no work for them. This was not good government or good business.

While Elisabeth was considering her musings, Maggie explained to John how they triaged patients --- what was most serious down to least (though sometimes least appeared to be most, due to the volume of the crying).....

John, appreciating her humor, whether intentional or not, laughed, and the sound of it brought Elisabeth out of her reverie..... "Ah, you two are having far too much fun for an infirmary!" she stated, in mock seriousness. "There are patients to be attended to."

All three of them looked around the anteroom simultaneously and, then, looking at each other in realization of the absence of patients, burst out laughing again. Ah, this feels good, Elisabeth noted; this man is a ray of sunlight in my life.

Using the lull to their advantage, the ladies gave John a better idea of what triage was --- the aim and use of it. Yes, the screaming child with colic may be a nuisance to the serenity of the infirmary, but the adult with influenza needs to seen first to get them out of the infirmary proper and either into one of the two overnight rooms for isolation or sent home for recovery.

John was an avid learner, as well as, insightful and intuitive in his assimilation of the lessons. He extrapolated from the information he was given into other areas and amplified the expected end result many fold, surprising and pleasing Elisabeth in her assessment of him, both as a student and as a human being.

Only three other patients came to the infirmary that day, in spite of the gossip's efforts. Two were children: one which had been pecked on the hand, by a hen whose egg he had tried to collect, and the other with a broken arm who had discovered too late his mother's wisdom in telling him not to climb trees. The third was a farmer whose horse had kicked him on the thigh a few days earlier, resulting in a large, painfully swollen bruise. They came in separately, the broken arm being last, making for a smooth transition from patient to patient.

John watched Elisabeth work, noting and remembering every move and every result. He asked if he could put his hand over the wounds after she had treated and dressed them and she readily agreed, asking each patient if they were willing, before allowing this adjunct treatment.

She couldn't help but notice that they worked extremely well as a team and somehow knew that his duties as an agent would flow in the same manner.

It was a little after five when they closed the door to the infirmary and, after locking it, walked back to the house at a leisurely pace, discussing the activities of the day. Both felt a sense of accomplishment and an expanding sense of the camaraderie they already had experienced.

John offered his arm and Elisabeth slipped hers into the crook of it, feeling certain that this would be observed as proper for a gentleman to offer and a lady to make use of on an unpaved road. It did, however, begin to reignite the fires in their loins and thus, by necessity, they stood apart for a few moments before entering the house.

Leaving their wraps over a chair in the entry hall they made for the study, Elisabeth leading and John trailing in her wake, watching the undulation of her skirt as she moved and musing on what lay below. She was unaware of the train of his thoughts until she turned to sit and saw the look in his eyes, then smiled, nodded, and held up one finger, as though to say, "Be patient; in awhile; first things first."

He took it that way and sat down to see how things proceeded. Elisabeth talked first of the properties they had visited and gave him a ledger to write all of the information he had accrued regarding each property: location, tenant, work to be done, and supplies to be brought to them and/or purchased, as well as information on how and who might perform the work. She gave him the notes they had taken on their visits.

Then, she began to discuss the infirmary and her pleasure in his ability to learn, in addition to offering her prognosis for his becoming a physician, which was nothing but excellent. At this point, Rose announced that dinner was awaiting them in the dining room and they quickly truncated their discussion and migrated in that direction, lest their food become cold.

Cook had outdone herself, due to there being a man in the house, and they supped on roast leg of lamb, early peas with tiny onions in a cream sauce, and potatoes which had been roasted with the meat. When their plates were empty, Rose brought them warm slices of pie made with last season's dried apples from the garden's own trees and a wedge of Stilton cheese to cut slices from.

Each of the same mind, they didn't linger over the dessert, quickly enjoying it, then fetching their wraps and telling Rose that they would walk in the garden to settle the heavy meal.

Exiting through the study, she took his arm as they ambled in the dark to the far end of the garden, then sat on a bench facing away from the house where he put, first one, then the other arm around her. Tilting her head up to look at him in the dim light, her lips met his descending mouth eagerly, hungrily, as though there was no time to waste and he responded with equal or greater fervor.

As she leaned into his embrace, he could feel her firm breasts press against his coat and he opened it to enfold her within and bring her closer to the heat of his body. Taking her hand as he kissed her, he placed it on the bulging mound within his trousers and gasped mid-kiss as the sensation became almost too much for him to endure. Elisabeth held that bulging mound and gently squeezed it, rhythmically, feeling his passion arise and his kisses become more intense and insistent.

As the night before, he lifted her hem and found, this time, that she wore no undergarment --- that she was telling him that she wanted him to enter there with his hands, his fingers, and perhaps more. His heart rejoiced and he felt elation, an elation greatly enhanced by what her hand was doing to him. He began to reciprocate, his larger hand first cupping her mount and feeling the wetness where the tips of his fingers almost entered her. The slick feeling of her juices aroused him further and he wanted to do so much more, but reminded himself to be patient and wait for her to be ready for more, no matter how long it took. At that moment, Elisabeth opened her thighs a bit wider and pushed her hips toward him, offering her femininity to him as an opening flower courts the honeybee.

His dexterous fingers began to slide through the wetness, from the little button at the apex of her mount to the recess deep within her, riding on that slickness to pleasure her as he would like to pleasure her with what she was holding and more. Her hips began to move with his fingers --- surging forward to meet them, then back as they retreated, then forward again to envelope them within, almost sucking them into her opening --- and as passionately as their mouths were mating.

Taking her mouth away, she buried her face in his coat to stifle her soft cries as the sensations became so strong that she could not hold back vocalizing her ardor. He pressed his face into her hair, smelling the scent of her and feeling his ejaculation nearing. He went first, holding her tightly as his body tensed and jerked, but never stopping the dance his fingers were doing between her legs. As he began to be more himself, she stiffened, arching her back, and her soft sounds raised higher and higher in pitch, but not volume. Holding her tightly as she spent herself, he increased her pleasure in the orgasm --- and found her lips once again seeking his to maintain the contact and allow the experience to level off more slowly.

They sat there for awhile without moving, before they stood up and straightened their clothing, prior to returning to the house. By the time Rose came to the dining room to clear the dishes, they were back inside, discussing plans for the following day.

❧Chapter 4 – Thursday❧

Elisabeth lay in her bed, listening to the songbirds outside. It was their twittering which had awakened her and, being awake, she began to think of the previous evening. Had she lost her senses --- being so intimate with a man she wasn't married to --- she wondered? On the other hand, she rationalized, something that seemed so natural couldn't be wrong. Nevertheless, when she wasn't in his arms --- or even his presence --- she couldn't help but feel troubled to some extent over what others would say or think --- or do for that matter.

She knew that these things happened --- the 'on dits' in the papers were always about who was seen in the company of whom and the peccadilloes of the well known were sought out and often aired publicly, much to the shame and chagrin of their families and associates. A woman alone could not afford to have that sort of reputation and she chastised herself for not remembering that when she was in John's presence.

Ah, John. She lay there thinking of him and her betraying body began to relive the sensations of the previous night. No, she thought, I will restrain myself --- and for a few minutes she did. Then, his face came back into her memory, along with the feeling of his kisses, and her heartbeat became faster as the feelings of arousal filled her body. Her hands began to touch and dance over her skin, just as his had so recently, and soon they were sliding in her secretions as his had, as well. Her orgasm was long and hard, harder even than the last, and she turned her face into her pillow, lest her moans be heard.

John, oh John, what is happening to me, she thought. You stimulate me even when you are not present! You have enticed me to be alive ---

given me an oasis at the end of a desert trek --- and I am drinking deeply of that water of life. Please, please bide here with me, lest without you I wither again beyond retrieving!

As though communicating with her through some extra-sensory mystery of love, John lay in his bed, also, thinking of her, her face, her voice and her body. There were so many things he would like to do with her --- study, of course, and help with her properties, but also physical things. Frenchy, his father's hired man had told him of the pleasure that the mouth can induce in the body and how women beg for it when they've known it, but he had not been brave enough to try it, or anything else, with the women he knew and, in saving to pay his passage to England, he served a greater need than frequenting bawdy houses. Once again, the memory of that randy horse, his penis hanging nearly to the ground as he kicked the boards of his stall --- then mounting the filly he was led to and inserting its hugeness into her, came into his mind. He wanted to be that stallion, mounting this woman and mating with her in any way she would allow him. Feeling his member swelling, his hand took hold of that staff and, sliding it up and down the length, he slowly pleasured himself, thinking of Elisabeth the whole time, feeling her secret passage opening to his entry, and savoring each moment of imagining that blissful encounter as his hand moved back and forth faster and faster, then stopped, as his body jerked with the force of his ejaculation. He lay there for a few minutes, then milked the last of the semen from his now softer manhood into the towel.

It was perhaps an hour later that he came to the breakfast nook for the morning meal. Elisabeth was already there when he arrived, awaiting Cook's offerings and making notes in a small book. When she looked up from it and met his eyes, something in the connection, that day, melted his heart as though it were butter. Already showing every sign of being seriously smitten, this one moment would forever stand forth in his memory, encapsulated as the definitive moment of his life. Suddenly, he knew why Dr, Gray's book had come to him and why he had saved his money for passage. This woman could be, should be, must be his!

Elisabeth lowered her eyes as the blazing light of his being connected with her and made her body come alive. Not here, she told herself over and over again…..

Confused, at first, John felt dismay then, as Rose entered with their breakfast, he understood that this intensity was not for others to see --- at least, not yet --- and he seated himself at Elisabeth's right hand as before.

Once their breakfast was on the table, she set the small book aside and began a pleasant conversation over breakfast about their travels of the day before.

Falling into the mood of the moment, he chatted with her about the events of that day, excepting their evening encounter, and they made a plan of action for the properties they'd visited. With that off of their agenda, Elisabeth brought up the properties they had not had time for. She felt that they could be visited after breakfast and added that John might need to make a trip into Tring, soon, to order lumber and fittings. She would go with him the first time, she told him, since she knew the lay of it, to steer him to the right shops.

It was ten o'clock before they were on the road in the old buggy. John had lifted Elisabeth up into it and there, in the tree-screened privacy of the stable yard, had planted an unexpected kiss on her lips before he raised her up.

She sat there in the buggy torn between indignation and lust, not knowing which to express, so she merely sat there shaking her head with a slightly silly smile on her face.

John climbed up and settled himself next to her, saying, "Which way when we come to the road, love?"

Some part of her was singing as she realised that he had called her, 'love', but she managed to stifle it and say, "Left, John," with as much dignity as she could manage.

Smiling a secret smile, he did as she said, in the full knowledge that he had unsettled her with that errant kiss.

It was not far to the farm she directed him toward. She rented this property to a family, the Martins, with three sons and two young daughters. The boys were old enough to work with their father and rather than rent, she settled for a share of the profit, knowing that if the year was poor, they would have nothing for her anyway, but if the crop was good and prices were up, she stood to do well. This family could do their own repairs, but she wanted John to meet them and offer his opinions as her agent.

When they pulled up in the drive, Mrs. Martin was beating a rug while the girls were playing a game of tag. After greeting her and introducing John, Elisabeth asked, "Is Mr. Martin at home, Ellen?"

"Nay, he's in south field with the lads already, but I can send the girls for him if you want," his wife allowed.

"Oh, no, it won't be necessary, John, will drive me down there on the farm road," Elisabeth replied. "I want them to meet him."

The girls waved at them as they continued toward the fields, then resumed their game of tag, and she and John could hear the steady thwack –thwack of the carpet beater fading as they left it behind them.

The south field was not far and soon they saw four figures working among the plants, pulling out the weeds. John was surprised to see that the 'lads' were nearly grown when the girls were so young. Elisabeth saw the change in his face and said, "Ellen is his second wife --- the first died in childbed. The girls will be fortunate, should anything happen to their parents, to have three older brothers to care for them."

John agreed with her and saw that Mr. Martin, having spied them, was walking toward the buggy. When he came up to it, he said, "Hello to you, Mistress Hastings --- my missus must have sent you."

"Yes, she did, Martin. I've come to introduce my agent and medical student, John Bishop, to you and your sons. I would like to offer his assistance to you in any improvements to the property you undertake --- especially in the nature of procuring lumber or fittings."

Taken aback, the farmer paused, then said, "Why thank you, Mistress, I haven't planned anything that there isn't enough for, but, perhaps, you had something in mind?"

"No, nothing at the moment, but I hope that you will call on John to help should you think of something that would be necessary to keep the buildings or land in good repair."

"Yes, Mistress, of course," he answered, surprised and pleased by her generosity and willingness to keep up the property --- not the usual landlord at all....."

"Good day, then," she said, and indicated to John that he should go ahead to a wider space where he could turn the buggy around so that they could retrace their path. By the time they passed the spot where they had spoken with Mr. Martin, he was already working with his sons.

That evening, Martin said to his wife, "I feel there's somethin' afoot there --- mayhap he'll be the new master."

Meanwhile, Elisabeth and John continued onward to the next property, a very old stone house of imposing design. Coming up on it, John took a deep breath, then said, "This is imposing. Who lives in this one?"

"Shall we see?" she asked, waiting for him to help her alight, then proceeding to the door. Instead of knocking or ringing, she took out a key and, fitting it into the lock, unlocked, then opened the door with a creak.

Being closed up, there was a certain amount of mustiness, the smell of stale air. Coming up behind her, John asked, "Is this yours as well? And no one lives here?"

"Yes," she said, turning around to him, and waiting to see what he would do.

First, to tease her, he feigned a complete and total interest in the house, removing dust cloths and roaming about, but finally gave in and, taking her in his arms, kissed her deeply and so passionately that she nearly swooned.

When he felt that he could let go and they would both be able to stand up alone, he led her to a chaise longue he had uncovered and, sitting down, pulled her to his lap and began kissing her again. She responded with kisses as passionate as his own, allowing herself free rein in this private place, away from prying eyes, where they could do as they pleased.

Now, it was John who held back somewhat, not wanting to rush, or to hurry. He went slowly, savoring every moment, every touch, wanting to make the experience memorable for them both.

First, he undid her top, a fitted jacket of sorts, and allowed her breasts to spring forth from that binding, then squeezed them and pinched and suckled the large nipples until she was writhing with need. Then, standing her up, he began undoing the buttons of her skirt and, in removing it, he found her undergarments. The slip went first, then the pantalets, and, at last, the shoes and stockings.

Finally, she was naked before him and laying her back on the chaise, he began to address her naked body. Beginning with the breasts again, then lower, across her stomach, until he reached her furry mount. There, with Elisabeth initially protesting then ultimately submitting as her ardor rose, he began to do what Frenchy had described to him --- initially, by using his tongue on the little button he'd found at the top of the opening, then spreading those lower lips wider and sucking on the button very gently, then a little stronger, then gently again. Elisabeth was like a wild woman, for the sensations were so powerful, so moving, so erotic. Her body was outside of her control and she didn't care as long as he kept on doing what he was doing. At the last, her head was swimming and she felt as though she'd been transported to some other universe as spasm after spasm hit her body. She whimpered lowly in a rising pitch, "Too much, too much, too muuuuuch," as he relentlessly kept up the gentle sucking until, finally, she had to push his head away to give her body respite.

She lay there for many minutes, breathing deeply, as he licked her button from time to time, causing her body to jerk, but eventually she was able to function again, and knew that she was going to give this man a taste of his own medicine.

Standing up naked in front of him, as he reached for her breasts, she pulled off his clothing piece by piece, saving the trousers until last. Then she pushed him back on the chaise and straddled his hips. She began by kissing him full on the mouth as she pinched his nipples, rubbing her stomach on his and dragging her breasts across his torso. She could feel his imprisoned hips rising to greet her own sex, but without entry, for she was not done. Moving lower, she straddled his knees and bent forward to use her mouth on his rigid staff. It tasted salty to her and, for a brief moment, she wondered if hers had tasted the same to him. Then, she began to address her task and, taking it in her mouth, sucked that rigid member and licked it until John was bucking, his knees pushing against her own sex each time and arousing her further. By that time, juices were dripping out of her all over his knees and he was begging her to let him be inside of her. She could not have said no, had she wanted to --- they had gone too far to return to stasis.

She stood up and he followed her, then, in one swift motion, he had laid her on the chaise again and had his fingers inside of her, testing the entry, then, spreading her legs wide, he eased himself inside on the copious secretions she was producing. As she moaned her ecstasy at the invasion, he began to slide in and out rhythmically, pleasuring her while he pleasured himself, as lovers have done since the beginning of time. Somewhere, deep inside, he became the stallion mounting the mare and threw his head back as if he would whinny his triumph. She felt the thrill, the excitement inside him, as well as her own, wondering for a moment how it could be, then accepted it and rode that wave of passion to its meeting with the shore of its destiny.

It was many minutes before either of them could move. They had expended too much energy and needed to give their bodies rest. Supporting himself on his forearms, John had stayed inside of her, unwilling to leave the comfort of her body or the sensuousness of feeling her sex wrapped around his. Finally, he got up and gave her the pantalets to wipe herself with and hold between her legs as his ejaculate continued to flow out.

Then, they lay there together, on their sides and nested like spoons, Elisabeth in front and John behind. It was not long before they remembered that they must leave and visit one more property before they returned to the village. Dressing, they helped each other and kissed often between adding layers of clothing.

When they had replaced the dustcovers, they looked around to see if there was anything that might need repair, but all seemed in good order, so they went out to the drive and retrieved Abernathy from the patch of grass in the dappled shade of a tree he had wandered to with the buggy. When John lifted Elisabeth into the buggy this time, it was different. There was still some sexual tension, but there was also a feeling of comfort, of solidarity, of belonging to each other.

Each was lost in their own reverie, thinking of the other, and wondering, with amazement, how they had managed to go so far, so fast. This was far more true of Elisabeth, who had not known people who met and married the same day, then headed west with a wagon train. John was from a different world than she and his experiences had been far different. He was also a man who knew what he wanted and, being a man, would not be gainsaid by society when he reached for it.

They went on to the next property in a comfortable silence with their musings, save for Elisabeth's directions.

The last property for the day was a small house with little property near the road. When they drove up, an old lady, recognizing the rig, came out to greet them with a halloo.

"And a halloo to you, too, Miss Violet," answered Elisabeth. "How are you faring?"

"Oh, me, I'm in fine fettle. 'tis my Spotty as is ailing --- seems to be off his feed and doesn't want to drink, either."

"Better have a look, then," Elisabeth offered, beckoning for John to help her alight, then introducing him.

Miss Violet, no fool, and no gossip either, looked at the two of them and immediately knew that this man was not just an agent or a student.....
Leading them to where Spot, an old Clumber Spaniel, lay in his bed, in

the kitchen near the stove, she spoke about his ailment saying, "Seemed to come up fast and for no reason. He don't go outside much anymore and only eats what I give him. Baylor's shop boy brings me my supplies and it's always good, never past using."

Elisabeth looked at the languid dog, wagging his tail at her as he lay there in his comfortable box padded with a pillow filled with lambs wool. Gently taking his head, she lifted his jowls to get a better look at his teeth and gums and found the problem --- an infected tooth from a bone shard sticking into the gum. Showing it to his mistress, she said, "I'll have to lance this and clean it after I remove the bone bit. I carry antiseptic preparations in the buggy for just such occasions. Cleaned out, the tooth and gum may heal without incident, but keep giving him plenty of parsley water or his kidneys may fail from the infection. He is an old dog, after all." Then, seeing the tears gathering in her tenant's eyes, she said, "There, there, Miss Violet, he's strong and he'll try to stay here with you. Just love him and let him heal from that love you give."

John, watching all of this, knew that he could help the process along and, asking both ladies for permission to touch the dog, gingerly placed his hands under the old fellow's head. The ladies could feel the energy and heat that began to fill the room and watched his every movement. This was something new to them.

After about ten minutes, John removed his hands and Spot lifted his head and licked them. Miss Violet looked much comforted when she saw that. Then, Elisabeth retrieved her supplies from the buggy and went to work. With John's hands on him again, Spot was quiet, not even whimpering when she lanced the swollen gum to release the bone shard it had swollen around. Blood and pus drained onto the cloth they had placed under his head and Elisabeth applied her antiseptic (in this case, a spoon of Scotch whiskey), then gave the half-full bottle to Miss Violet to use if it became infected again.

Miss Violet asked if they would stay and eat lunch with her and they happily accepted, wanting to wait a bit to observe whether Spot felt better.

John stayed at Spot's side while the ladies prepared the meal. It was not lavish, but it was hearty: fresh bread, baked by their hostess the day before, a bit of country cheese, onions sautéed in butter to make a thick soup, and potatoes mashed and mounded on each plate to make a bowl for the dense soup. By the time the ladies had finished their efforts, Spot was already standing up and drinking from his bowl. Miss Violet was amazed and pleased. At first, when she saw his improvement, she didn't want to eat at all, but then, when Spot was willing to lick at some porridge John prepared, she agreed to eat, as well.

It was a very pleasant meal for them all. Their chatting and Spot showing his pleasure made for a lovely afternoon. It also convinced Miss Violet that these two were true loves and must stay together. She determined in her mind and heart that she would see to it if any tried to keep them from each other.

Elisabeth and John didn't take their leave of her until the sun's light began to wane into dusk. Abernathy, who had patiently waited, while nibbling at the grass along Miss Violet's verge, was summoned and, after giving Miss Violet hugs, the pair departed. It was a journey of only fifteen minutes or so before they were in Elisabeth's drive and headed toward the stable.

After releasing Abernathy from the shafts of the buggy and putting a blanket over him to absorb the sweat and keep him from a chill during the night, the pair walked up the drive to the house. They retired to the study to wait for dinner and went over the ledgers on the income from the properties Elisabeth owned. She wanted him to know everything about her finances if he was to be her agent and he diligently endeavored to absorb it all. It would take time --- the names, the rents, the repairs, the desired improvements, to say nothing of the infirmary and the things to learn there..... He felt a little overwhelmed, but hoped that this was the newness of it all.....

Then, suddenly, he had an epiphany as he sat there listening to Elisabeth. The reason he felt so calm was that he knew it wasn't a matter of 'if' anymore, but where and when --- and how..... He smiled to himself, thinking of the pleasure they had given each other and knew in his heart that he wanted this to continue for the rest of his life and hers..... Would she agree to that, he wondered --- she seemed to like her independence quite a lot.....

Looking at him, Elisabeth observed that he appeared to be deep in serious thought and she wondered what it was that took his mind away from what she was telling him about the properties.

Finally, Rose came and announced that dinner was served and they adjourned to the dining room. When they were seated, Elisabeth asked what he had been thinking of in the study. Looking into her eyes, he thought a moment, then said, with sincerity, "It was that I feel so happy about all of the things that this day has provided."

If she had not already been hopelessly in love with this man, she would have felt Cupid's arrow pierce her heart at this point --- as it was, she was in complete concordance with him.

They chatted over dinner, then took a turn in the garden, this time only sitting on the bench with John's arm around Elisabeth's shoulders. They both knew that there would be times when they could express their passion and they could bank their fires and wait for those moments as they came their way.

When they stood to go into the house, John enveloped her in his arms and kissed her with passion. Passion answered and they stood there for some time enjoying the flare of the fire, then they banked it again, to hold it in reserve for their next encounter.....

He saw her into the house and then ambled down the drive to his rooms over the stables. Stopping there, he thought of Abernathy and went in, put on a white coat to catch the dust and hair and removed the blanket, curried him, and then put a fresh one on him. Abernathy shuddered, then whinnied his approval.

As he lay in bed that night, John thought of Elisabeth in ways other than sexual --- he knew that he wanted her to be his wife as well as his teacher and mentor. What would she think of that, he wondered. He had nothing to offer her, but himself. Would her family even approve? How could they? And, surely, they could never be told of the depth of the relationship….. What if they told her not to marry him? Could he survive losing her?

Elisabeth was brushing her long, light brown hair and, as she brushed, she thought of John, wishing it was his hand holding the brush and running it through her hair. She could almost feel it when she pretended it was his hand doing the brushing and it was sensuous, making her body throb, making her pulse beat faster. Oh, surely, he would have to do this some time…..

She wanted John to be with her for the rest of her life and wondered what his thoughts were, whether he wanted to love only her for all time….. As she thought on this, she said, "Oh Lord, please let him want to be with me forever. My mother has gone to you, my father has gone to you and my husband has gone to you. Can this one please stay with me and love me?"

Both of them went to sleep thinking of the other, remembering their lovemaking in the vacant house, and feeling a calm descend on their desires within through the knowledge that they would repeat their trysts there, or somewhere else. They slept, each feeling the connection with the other throughout the night.

❧ Chapter 5 – Friday ❧

John awoke at the first light of dawn with a smile on his face. He had been dreaming of Elisabeth and could still feel her in his arms and smell the scent of her skin. It was a marvelous dream and the only reason he didn't mind waking up from it was that he knew she would be there at the breakfast table --- vibrantly real.....

Thinking about the day, as he washed himself, then dressed, he remembered that it was Friday and they would go to the infirmary in the afternoon. She hadn't said what they would do in the morning, though.

Elisabeth opened her eyes, then stretched and lay there in bed with her hand holding her furry mount, remembering the day before and John making love to her. It was so wonderful, so unlike what her husband's efforts had been, so daring, and so extremely pleasurable..... She closed her eyes and felt his body next to hers, as it had been on the chaise --- holding her with the feel of his softened staff against her buttocks and his pubic hair tickling her bare skin.

Remembering that she would see him at breakfast, she threw back the covers and went to the pitcher of water on her bureau to clean herself for the day. Soon, she was descending the stairs in a dress which would suit for the infirmary, as well as for the house, while thinking of the studies she would give him for the morning.

He was already seated in the breakfast nook when she arrived, but stood until she was seated. Then, waited to serve himself until she had served herself from Cook's bounty.

When they were eating, he asked what she had planned for the morning and she replied, "I think it would be best for you to study. I'll give you some things to read and we'll discuss them when you're done. This afternoon is infirmary day, you know."

"Ah, yes," he answered, with a smile, "I am looking forward to it."

As they spoke, their knees touched and each could feel the pressure of the other's body against theirs. It was erotic, yet did more to allow them to delay the sexual expression of their love than to further arouse them.

Finally, breakfast was over and she led him into the study and, as they sat there, she asked him what books he had read. She was surprised by the number and quality of the books he had read on the practice of medicine, as well as the ones he mentioned in other fields. When he had finished, she selected a book from the shelves and then brought it to him. "Please read the introductory four chapters of this one and we'll discuss it over lunch. Meanwhile, I'll be in the garden....."

Staring down at the first edition of King's American Dispensatory, he hefted it, felt the weight, and made a face which said, without words, 'That's a weighty tome.....'

She smiled at his antics, then turned about, opened the glass door and slipped through it out into the garden.

John looked at the tome in his hand then upward as though praying and, opening the book, began to read.

He found it fascinating and, totally engrossed, he lost all track of time. Four hours later, when Elisabeth came in from the garden, she had to call his name twice and, finally, clap her hands together, before he heard her and responded.

"Sorry, ma'am," he said, "I was so involved in the text....."

"I can understand that," she replied, "It is very engrossing, is it not?"

"Yes, indeed!" he agreed.

"I believe that Rose has something ready for us to eat in the breakfast room," she said. "Shall we discuss the book in there?"

"Of course, nothing like herbology over lunch!" he answered with a mischievous grin on his face.

Elisabeth smiled back at him and led the way into the breakfast nook where Rose had set their places and left platters of fruit and cheese, fresh bread baked that morning, and a tureen of strong beef soup with barley and mushrooms in it.

As she sat there, listening to him expound on what he had read, she realised that she had a very capable student indeed, far exceeding her high expectation of him. In medicine, he could go far --- further than her father had. She wondered if that would suit him --- if he understood the politics involved, and the potential disappointments..... Medicine, and the study of it, were largely underwritten by the wealthy --- and this was the bone that stuck in the craw of some who came to the study without funds.

During the course of the meal, John waxed very eloquent indeed, and she had to remind him more than once that his soup would soon be cold. Finally, she said, "Eat your soup, John, and save the talk for the fruit and cheese."

He chuckled, sheepishly, knowing that he had been going on a bit.....

Indeed, he did not forget her words and the fruit and cheese course brought them a very lively discussion. When they had eaten their fill, and his oration had somewhat come to a close, Elisabeth, eyeing the clock, said, "It is time we go to the infirmary now, John. Our patients will be waiting and wondering what has happened to us."

He smiled at her and said, "Yes, I know. Have I been a dreadful bore?"

"No, John, quite the contrary, I have been both fascinated and startled by your capability. You have hidden your light under a bushel ---even from me."

He was pleased at the compliment, and it showed on his face, but he quickly said, "I didn't mean to hide anything from you."

"I know that," she replied, as she walked to the coat rack in the foyer, "You are too kind and too genuine to do so. Come, now, we must leave."

Fortunately, the walk being a short one, they were soon at the infirmary, which had just been opened by the Friday girl, Emma. Elisabeth introduced the two of them as she hurried inside, wanting to be ready for the patients. The first five minutes were quiet, but then the waiting room quickly filled with villagers wanting to meet the new medical student. It was obvious that the Blakely sisters had got the word out that a handsome man was in town, by the number of spinsters in attendance….. Each had brought some little 'welcome' gift to the new student --- biscuits, tarts, tea cakes, all manner of sweets, and even a basket full of over-wintered pears.

Their afternoon was full --- and some patients were happy to leave at closing without even having been treated, for they had really only come in to satisfy their curiosity. Of such, is life in a small village…..

Walking home, Elisabeth and John discussed the day's events at the infirmary. He was amused that the women would think him handsome, but had been interested in the handful of legitimate patient's illnesses and had done his energetic healing with each of them.

Although they continued their discussion in the study at dinner, later, they were still animated. They had much to discuss about the patients and he still had things to say about King's, which he had not spoken of over lunch….. Cook had made a rabbit stew with hunter's gravy and her well-loved dumplings for them and, for dessert, there were prune tarts, with dollops of clotted cream atop them and cups of sweet tea with cream.

By the time they strolled in the garden, they were feeling full and very mellow. They sat for awhile on the bench, with his arm around her, kissing from time to time and touching also, but not so intimately as before, knowing that they had a place in which to be exquisitely intimate, from time to time, and without discovery.

Eventually, they came in from the evening's chill and John, taking the book with him, headed for his apartment over the stable.

He read long into the night by the oil lamp in the sitting room, assimilating information at breakneck speed. Finally, though, he knew he must stop or be too tired to do anything on the morrow. A bit later, laying under the covers, he thought of Elisabeth and stroked his manhood. No, he thought, I am too tired and I must rest.

Elisabeth walked up the stairs slowly to her bedroom after watching John depart. She felt as though she were floating, almost as though in a daze. After brushing her hair, she lay under the covers nude, touching her body where he had touched and wanting it to be his hands, not hers, touching it, stroking it, and bringing it to the full intensity of it's arousal. And, it was thus that she fell asleep --- one hand on her breast and the other holding her furry mount, but only for comfort.

೨Chapter 6 – Saturday❧

Saturday --- Elisabeth thought as she drifted out of sleep --- market day. The market in Little Tring was tiny, but the one in Tring was substantial, due to the large manor houses there. Perhaps they would take the buggy and go down there….. …..and she must remember to tell him that President George Washington's great-grandfather once lived in the mansion known as The Park at Tring. She lay in bed for a few moments, then, feeling a knot as she ran her fingers through her hair, she went to the mirror to see if she could remove it. She was chilly in the early dawn and. realizing that she was still naked, she first slipped into a nightgown. The knot came out without much trouble and she sat there, looking in the mirror at herself, thinking: who are you, Elisabeth Ellen Gray Hastings?

Thinking seemed to work better when she was laying down, so she lay back under her covers and stared up at the ceiling in the dim light of dawn, wondering if she was crazy. She had allowed herself to engage in sexual touching with a man she had known for only two days --- TWO DAYS! And then, had allowed him to make love to her on the fourth! At this point, her heart stepped in and reminded her that she felt as though she had know him for all eternity. Oh, yes, her mind said: I forgot…..

She wondered if a woman on some Pacific island would have these qualms. She found herself imagining how those cultures functioned and saw herself as a sultry tan island girl in a grass skirt making love with John, cast as a muscular native. The picture was too erotic for her to deny and she finally gave in to her hands as they touched, stroked, and aroused her further pleasuring her as she so enjoyed.

John woke when the sun was already up. He lay there for a few moments, then got his bearings and, realizing that breakfast would be over if he waited any longer, quickly performed his morning ablutions, dressed, and headed for the house. He slipped into his seat in the breakfast nook just as Elisabeth was pouring the coffee.

"Good morning, John," she said, with a smile. "Did you sleep well?"

"Oh, yes, very, that is..... when I finally left off the reading," he stammered.

"Oh, but this is marvelous," she replied. "You are indeed the perfect student."

John blushed, then said, "I wasn't thinking of that --- only, the book was so interesting that I could hardly put it down. I have never seen such plates!"

"Yes, they are special," she answered, remembering the first time she had read it two years earlier. "The man is a genius."

They ate for a few minutes in silence, savoring the thick slices of ham accompanying poached eggs on toasted bread. Then, she asked, "Would you like to ride down to Tring, to the market?"

"With you? Of course!" he bantered, with a smile and a wink.

It was the wink that made her giggle, as shyly as any schoolgirl, and she retorted, "No, with Abernathy! I have an aversion to pulling buggies."

John laughed out loud and said, "Now, that would be a sight!"

Soon, Abernathy was ready to be hitched and, in helping to bring him out of his stall, John managed to enfold Elisabeth in his arms and kiss her soundly, which elicited a smile and wide open eyes. They brought the horse out and, easing him between the shafts, John secured his harness. After lifting Elisabeth into the buggy, and getting in himself, they were on their way up the drive and off to town with a shopping list from Cook safely tucked into John's pocket. It was a very short drive --- only a mile and a half or so to the High Street and many of the town shops.

The market, in Tring, was a livestock market as well as a produce market and they found it interesting, though not what they were looking for and left the livestock area in favor of the produce and other wares. By the time they were done, Elisabeth had bought enough to fill the box behind the seat of the buggy to the brim --- all of it items that were not grown by a farm manned by one of her tenants or available in Little Tring's market. The large manors in Tring, which required a greater variety of produce for their house parties, brought the growers out to happily supply what was needed --- as well as the importers and tradesmen..... Looking at all the wares made for an interesting market day.....

They found a small public house on the High Street and enjoyed a meal of rissoles and grilled vegetables with custard tarts and a glass of dark beer on the side. Their knees met under the table and, occasionally, their hands, as well.

Finally, as the day wore on, they knew it was time to return to the house and put Abernathy in his stall with a manger of hay and a box of oats. It was a short trip home, but the sun was already waning by the time they arrived. Stopping at the house, John unloaded their purchases and carried them to the kitchen, then continued down the drive to the stable.

Abernathy was happy to see his stall and his dinner, as well. Donning the white overcoat, John curried him while Elisabeth held his head, then, they left him to his meal, and headed for the house.

Outside, in the garden, they washed up from the dust of Abernathy and the road in a barrel by a downspout, and carried a few stray bits of produce into the kitchen. As they passed through, Cook said, "Good thing ya washed --- dinner's on the hob."

The pair smiled at her dourness, then made their way to the dining room where Rose was setting the table. "Are we early?" Elisabeth asked.

"Oh, no, ma'am," Rose said. "Yer right on time. Cook asked me only a minute ago to lay the plates."

"Perfect," answered Elisabeth, winking at John, and then they took their places at table.

While they waited, and Rose was in the kitchen, he took the opportunity to hold her right knee with his left hand, it being the side she was sitting on. She found herself wiggling as the contact brought her body to life, then he removed it quickly when they heard Rose noisily coming down the hall toward the room.

Dinner was to be a roast of beef this night with asparagus spears on the side and little new potatoes cut into pieces and roasted with herbs. Later, Cook's masterpiece, raspberry trifle, reigned as dessert paired with mild coffee and cream.

As they ate, John's knee remained in contact with Elisabeth's and, from time to time, his left hand found its way under the table to stroke or squeeze her knee or thigh, giving her delicious sensations in her belly and hips, while she hoped that Rose would not come to see if they had everything they needed for dinner.....

Finally, after Rose had brought them the trifle, and moments before he took the initial bite, Elisabeth reached under the table with her hand and touched John's thigh, eliciting a swift intake of breath on his part as the trifle dropped off the spoon and back into his bowl with a plop. She smiled at him and said, "What's good for the goose is good for the gander."

He chuckled and smiled back at her, thinking of what he would do when they were outside..... She looked at his smile and suspected as much.....

Dinner over, they put on wraps and went to the garden --- ostensibly for a stroll. They found a bench at the far end, as far as they could get from the house, and sat there facing away from the house in the dark, lit only by the lamp's glow from the dining room and study windows. They embraced and kissed --- long, deep, kisses of passion..... He held her tightly to him, never wanting to let her go. She loved the feeling this gave her, this possessive passionate act, and she could already feel the juices flowing between her legs and waiting, no, begging for him to touch her there.

He made her wait, wanted her hotter --- so hot that she would flow all over them. Finally, he lifted her skirt and put his hand up into her pantalets through the opening and touched her mount. She jerked when he touched her button, that tender spot that she so loved to have his fingers rub. She arched her back, spreading her thighs apart a bit, and jerked again as he began to slide his fingers about in her juices, pleasuring her and himself in the process.

Then, her arms fell to her sides and a hand touched his knee to lightly slide up his thigh to the burgeoning mound at the top. He gasped at the feeling that went through him and shuddered as she squeezed his erection beneath his trousers. Her agile fingers easily undid the buttons and he was freed to expand further, moving his hips forward and back as his manhood rose, proudly freed from confinement and awaiting her touch. Touch it she did, and then he lifted her and sat her straddling his lap and facing away with her skirt raised, while he leaned against the back of the bench and, holding his staff slid it easily through the juices and into her innermost recess.

Now, it was her turn to gasp as even the slight weight of her body drove his shaft deep into her, bringing a moan of pleasure to her lips while, hands on her waist, he lifted her up and down on his manhood as he moved his hips forward and back. The pleasure mounting, he began to vocalize softly, deeply, and the sound of it, brought answering sounds from her throat as well --- soft whimpers of pleasure as her body responded to his lovemaking. Then, she began to hear the sound signaling his impending orgasm rising in his throat and it echoed in her own body, as they finished together, as though they were one being. He held her tightly as their bodies convulsed and for quite a time afterward. Finally, they began to move, beginning to unwind themselves.

"You'd better go straight to your apartment, John," she said, stating the obvious, "for this will surely show on your trousers in the light….." Then, she rose up off of his lap and, allowing his spent member to slide from her secret grotto, turned and took his face between her hands and kissed him passionately. She had wanted him to stay inside her forever, but smiled at the ridiculous picture they would make locked in that position for all time…..

They stayed there for a bit more, holding each other and kissing softly, then, he saw her to the door of the study and made his way around the house to the stable.

As he climbed the stairs he thought of her --- and how much he wanted to be together all night with her. How could it happen, he wondered...... One or the other of them would have to be secreted in the other's bedroom unless they left the area of Tring..... Impossible! Or was it?

Entering his apartment, he felt for the oil lamp on a table by the door, then lit it with a flint. Looking across the room, as he straightened, he spied King's American Dispensatory and carried the lamp to the table by the chair he had used the prior evening. After he had removed his trousers and cleaned them off as best he could, he put on a dressing gown of Dr. Gray's and returned to the sitting room, where he seated himself and began to read where he had left off the night before. He could have read the book in a few evenings, but he enjoyed the content so much that it would take longer as he read and reread passages and pored over the plates. When, at last, he went to bed it was very late, indeed.

Elisabeth went straight to bed. Satiated by their lovemaking, and tired from the outing, she fell asleep straight away, to dream of her lover and his ways with her body..... She felt his hands touching her and pleasuring her throughout, vividly dominating her dreams and sealing that oneness with her being.....

❧Chapter 7 – Sunday❧

Awakened by tapping on his door, John finally came to open it and stood face to face with his dream. It was, of course, Elisabeth, and in the morning light she looked like an angel to him. He embraced her, thinking that his wish of the prior evening had come true, and she responded, then said, "You must dress for church, John. We leave in half an hour for Tring. Joe and his family have already picked up Rose and Cook with their wagon and we have only a little time before we must leave in the buggy."

"Could we stay here until they return?" he asked.

"Of course not --- it would be remarked," she explained, patiently, then said, "I'll go and get Abernathy out while you dress and, then, if you'll get the buggy and hitch him....."

"Yes, yes, I'll hurry," he answered, wishing he had forgone the book the night before, but dressing and rushing nonetheless, as she went down to see to the horse.

In a matter of minutes he was descending the stairs, ready to bring out the buggy and hitch Abernathy between the shafts. He accomplished it in short order --- quite a feat for a man short on sleep --- and they were soon making for Tring and the church service.

They were not the only vehicle heading in the direction of Tring that morning --- a number of buggies and wagons made a long parade toward the town.....

When he had caught his breath, John remarked, "I didn't know you were so religious."

"Not so religious, but spiritual, and, of course, aware enough of what is considered proper that I often do it --- at least, if it suits me and isn't too much trouble," she commented, "And, besides, one is expected to set a good example to one's staff....."

At this, he grinned at her, and winked, causing her to blush a bright red and making her all the dearer to him.

They arrived before the church bells had rung for the last time and, leaving the horse to graze on the commons, along with the many others, Elisabeth hurried John into the chapel, where Rose and Cook were already ensconced in her pew.

The music was beautiful, the choir in full voice, the service well ordered, and the sermon..... .....passable.

After the service, Rose and Cook rode back in the wagon, with Joe and his family, and would take lunch with them and enjoy their half-day off. This left Elisabeth and John to their own devices and they chose to return to the house and forage through the kitchen, for the comestibles Cook said she had left them, before going for a buggy ride in the countryside.

Once there, they found the cooked mound of sausages she had left covered in a cast-iron pot on the hob and another pot there containing fried potatoes with green onions. They ate heartily of it, but quickly, knowing their ultimate destination.....

After they had filled their bellies, their buggy ride took them back to the unoccupied stone manse where they had made love previously. Screened from the road by thickets of trees and a winding drive, it was the perfect place for lovers who did not wish to be discovered.

This time, they walked Abernathy and the buggy into the stable and gave him hay in one of the feedboxes and water in an old enamel dishpan. Then, they adjourned to the manse.

Embracing, just inside the door, their hands went everywhere, touching body parts from head to hips. Finally, they broke apart in order to breathe and assess how and where they would make love. John led her up the staircase to the second storey and found the master bedroom. After disrobing the bed of its dustcovers, they disrobed each other, slowly and sensuously, one piece at a time, kissing each part revealed, sometimes superficially and sometimes intimately, and, after much of this foreplay, laying on the bed, they began to make love, beginning by kissing, then licking, tasting, pinching, squeezing, and ultimately pleasuring each other first with their mouths and hands.

When their ardor had reached its peak, they brought sword and scabbard together, she, crouched on all fours in the middle of the bed and he, on his knees, coming from behind and sliding into the slick, unresisting path to her secret grotto of bliss. She arched her back as he entered, pushing her hips back onto him and seating his sword to the hilt. One hand on each of her hips, he pulled her to him and then began the rhythmic sliding in and out that they so loved.

There, in the empty house, they enjoyed their orgasms as boldly as two savages in the wild --- free from intrusion and judgments, whole within and without, and not subject to anyone's censure. This was their love, their expression of it, and their freedom to do so. Outside, the world might look at them askance --- inside, they were in their own universe.

As they lay there afterward, John remarked, "Do you realise that we have only known each other one week?"

"Yes, I had thought of that," she answered.

"Don't you think it a bit strange?" he asked.

"I do, however, I also feel that it is destiny," came her reply.

"Destiny?" he asked.

"Yes, fate --- that reason for things that do not make sense to us. A week ago, I would never have believed that an American would come into my life and sweep me off my feet, bringing me to do that which I would never have done with any other. This is a very unusual situation, one which seems so out of the ordinary that it must have been fate. Fate that you read father's book, fate that you decided to find him, and fate that my husband is dead and I am free to love --- and be loved."

Those words brought him to hold her closer, enfold her in his arms, and feel the warmth of her naked body next to his, warming him as the sun warms a summer garden. Then, he asked, "And, do you love me, Elisabeth?"

Taken aback, that he would ask, she lay there for a moment, then said, "Yes. Yes, John, I believe I do. Had I not felt love for you from the start, I would never have allowed you to touch me beyond shaking my hand or helping me into the buggy. And you, John, what are your feelings?"

"I only know that I want to be with you all the time, to feel your hand upon me and to touch you, as well; to make love to you, and to never be away from you. My heart beats more insistently when I see you --- or even think of you --- and, each night when I go to sleep, I think of seeing you on the morrow. I don't know if what I feel is called love, for I have never felt this unnamed feeling before," he answered.

"I think I understand what you mean," she said. "I know something of love, for I love my father still --- even in death --- however, that is not the same feeling I have for you, for it lacks the intensity of our relationship. My husband was not by my choice, rather a bargain made between he and my father. I was dutiful to him, and gave him five children, but they were not conceived in love --- at least not mine --- yet, in spite of it, I love them. This feeling, love, is perplexing. I hope that what I feel for you is love, for I would like it to have that name and to last forever."

As the day waned and they touched each other again and again, both emotionally and physically, there came a point when they realised that, though they would sooner linger, they must return home for dinner or tongues would wag.

They tidied up the bedroom and dressed, then replaced the dust covers and returned to the stable for Abernathy and the buggy. Riding back to the village in it, they discussed John's readings in King's. Elisabeth was very impressed with his progress and his interest in the subject, as well as, his understanding of what he had read and she told him as much.

Not one to overestimate his prowess in anything, he took what she said with a grain of salt and chalked it up to prejudice in his favor. Little did he know how accurate her estimate was.

By the time they reached the house, the sun was nearly setting and, after brushing Abernathy, feeding him, and putting away the buggy, they walked slowly up the drive in the dusk, savoring the memory of their time together --- the few more moments of being alone together that they had eked out.

Once inside, they found that Cook had outdone herself and created a truly tasty dinner with a brace of ducks gifted by Joe's sons --- one for the mistress and her student --- the other for the kitchen staff.

Immediately, upon their arrival, Rose, followed by Cook, brought the platter to the dining room, held high as though it were the offering to a king, then placed it on the table for Elisabeth and John to admire --- blushing sweet-pickled crabapples accenting their duck, as well as, roasted new potatoes, carrots, and onions, with savory bread stuffing. Cook had come along with Rose to be the recipient of her own congratulations, rather than receiving them second hand and, hearing their exclamations of praise, she glowed with contentment, resolving to do the next meal up even better.

When Cook had made certain that they had been properly served, she and Rose retired to the kitchen to eat their own bird. In the lull after their departure, Elisabeth and John sighed, happy to be alone with each other --- and their meal......

They continued their discussion of King's, John expounding on what he had read, asking questions of Elisabeth and digging, always seeking, for interpretation and more knowledge. Why, he is like a foxhound, she thought, on the scent of his quarry and refusing to give up until he chases it to ground. Suddenly, it struck her that she might be his quarry as well, giving her pause for reflection. Then, she smiled a secret smile, which came with the thought that she was a quarry which wanted to be caught.

Their interest was so great in their discussion that, had Cook not given them a mandate to enjoy the fruit of her labors and, by hint, to report on how they found it, they could have been eating sawdust and not known it. As it was, they discussed the meal as well as King's, though the latter drew by far the greater percentage of their attention.

When Rose and Cook brought dessert and a bottle of brandy, for it was to be a flaming pudding, Elisabeth and John were effusive in their praises --- and indeed meant it, for the meal had been well prepared and the dessert was the piece d'résistances. Rose poured the brandy over the pudding and Cook lit it with the flame of a candle. As it glowed with a blue flame, they watched, with awe, until the alcohol had burned off and it snuffed itself out. Rose dished up portions for the pair and then she and Cook once again retired until John and Elisabeth went either to the study or for their stroll in the garden.

As they ate the pudding, tasting the caramelized bits of sugar, they agreed that Cook had outdone herself all around.

Finally, they withdrew, initially to the study, then for a walk in the garden, continuing to discuss the book --- and the man himself. Then, the conversation moved onward to the state of medicine in England vs. America --- and of research, as well. Elisabeth acquainted John with more of the ailments and foibles of her patients as they spoke and, even in the garden, they never stopped speaking long enough to kiss --- until they were at the study door and it was time for John to walk down the drive to the stable. Then, he took her in his arms and kissed her resoundingly, smiled a quixotic smile at her and, turning on his heel, walked around the house to the drive. She could hear his footsteps as he went and longed to run after him, take his hand, and rush up the stairs to his apartment over the stables with him, but that would not be proper and they were no longer alone, after all.....

Instead, she opened the door and went in, turned off the lamp, which had been left burning, and walked slowly up the stairs to her room by the light of a single candle in her hand. As she went into her bedroom, she felt that she should be with John so very strongly.

Her mind knew the code of behavior of society in this time, what with Queen Victoria on the throne, but her body knew another one --- one oriented to her needs rather than the needs of society. Had John been someone she knew, she could not have allowed herself to seek solace in his arms at all without marriage, for the local gentry and pseudo-gentry were hide-bound and narrow-minded, as well as gossip-mongers. In point of fact, she might have to ask her brother-in-law's permission even to remarry, a thought which troubled her immensely, for he had once tried to force her to agree to marry him by threatening to withdraw funding from his heir. He had not counted on her resistance there and had forgotten that she had her own means of support, but he had also not counted on her intelligence --- and she reminded him that as he sowed, so would he reap --- an heir worthy of his inheritance, or one who lived with little funding and resented his uncle for denying him his own father's money.

She crawled under the covers of her bed, then snuffed the candle and went to sleep, a troubled sleep for one so deeply in love.

John occupied a chair in the dining room of his apartment. It was pulled up to the table and King's was laying there, open to a page more than halfway through. John was intent on reading, but, every now and again, he stopped to think of Elisabeth --- and her face when she tried to hide a smile. Somehow, that smile had wrapped itself around his heart and just thinking of it made him feel an aching need for her. Each time, he returned to the text with renewed vigor, not to erase her from his mind, rather to study hard and meet her on her level, be the doctor that she, as a woman, found it difficult to be --- as a tribute to her knowledge and understanding of medicine and her talents as a teacher.

He read until he could stay awake no longer, then doused the oil lamp and went to his bed.

﹌Chapter 8 – A New Week﹏

Elisabeth stirred, awakened by the twittering of songbirds. She rolled over on her side to look at the window and saw that it was early --- very early. Thinking over the day before, she stretched and nearly purred, like a satisfied cat. It had been a lovely day, indeed, filled with pleasures of the body, mind, and soul.

She lay there thinking deep, deep thoughts as was her habit some mornings. No foolish Miss, this lady --- she had a very good head on her shoulders and used it well. On this particular morning she was remembering some of the points John had made when they spoke of King's work and those thoughts led to others regarding which books she would have him read next, then on to his position as her agent and the work she was planning to have done.

And, of course, the children --- none of them had written to her in over three weeks, but, then, they were growing up and had such an abundance of activity in their lives.....

Catherine and Caroline were surely busy with their Great Aunt Daphne, and her love of parties, while the boys had much to study at school. Besides, she thought, they moved in different circles than she had at their age. Sometimes, in spite of loving them such a great deal, she wondered how her life might have been different had she and her father not gone to a dance at the public rooms in Tring with her friend, Susan's, family. That was the day that her husband first saw her from across the room in her favorite celery green dress and immediately asked her father if he could call on him to ask for her hand. She remembered, when she saw Hastings, the sick feeling she had in the pit of her stomach. By the following day, her father had reasoned that this would be a good idea for her due to the condition of his health (something he had not shared with her at that point) and agreed to allow Hastings to press his suit. There was no real pressing --- she honored her father's wishes almost always and he seemed to be adamant in this matter.

Finally, her musings fading, she dressed and descended to the study, where she found an envelope on her desk. Opening it, she found it contained a note from her brother-in-law. He planned to visit her the following day in the afternoon. Odd, she thought….. Though, perhaps he wanted to discuss the further schooling of her sons…..

As she was wondering about this visit, John walked into the room and asked if he was too late for breakfast. "Oh, no," she answered, "Must be something special if it's this late of a morning."

And, special it turned out to be….. Apparently, Cook's success with the dinner had gone to her head and she had made a breakfast fit for the restaurant of a great hotel: a soufflé, light and fluffy, made of eggs and vegetables, which had been finely chopped and sautéed., a béarnaise sauce for the soufflé, strawberries in whipped cream, and fresh, buttery croissants. Elisabeth and John looked at each other and each read in the other's eyes, the wondering what to do to keep Cook from working so hard every day. They found it was decidedly the tastiest breakfast she'd prepared for them, but she was no lass in her youth to be slaving over the stove….. Elisabeth could tell by the look on Rose's face that she felt the same…..

With their stomachs filled, they returned to the study. Since it had once been her father's library, she went to a shelf of medical books and selected another volume for John to read --- this one slimmer by far than King's ….. It was a book of verse by her mother --- printed, apparently, not long before her death in Elisabeth's infancy.

She brought it to him and told him, "This was one of my father's favorites and I think that you will like it very much. He took it from her hand and held it, looking at the title, then opened it to the opening poem and read it aloud…..

Blackberry sweet, and dew on the meadows;
Summer is nigh and my heart longs to play.
Songs of the birds are heard in the treetops;
Paeans to nature on this, a bright day.

Past is the snow and harsh storm of winter;
Gone is the gloom and the lingering rain.
Now is the time of flowers' fulfillment;
Soon there'll be wheat fields heavy with grain.

"Beautiful," he said, "Simple and beautiful."

"I always loved to read her poems when I was a child --- somehow, it drew her nearer to me," she said. "My favorite was this one," and she recited from memory.

There is an angel in a garden made of stone.
I wonder why it sits there watching, all alone.
Must it remain transgression to atone;
Or, set to guard the graves and grass all freshly mown?

Someday I may stoke up my courage and inquire
Why it stands guard there over funeral pyre.
For, from this tedious sort of work I would retire;
To pursuit of many interests I'd aspire.

The small stone angel utters not a word;
In that still garden, meant for peace,. no sound is heard.

They sat there for a moment, each thinking their own thoughts, then he said, "It's beautiful, too. You miss her."

"In truth, I did not. I never really knew her --- I only had a vague feeling of someone's warmth and caring; perhaps an echo of her carried in my father's heart, though she was brought through to me by these poems. He read them to me even when I was quite small, so, you see, I know her heart, her innermost being, if I do not truly remember her face."

John looked pensive, then said to her, "I thank you for sharing this with me. I know that it is a tie to a very deep part of you and I feel that to know these depths is an honor."

Elisabeth sat there, simply nodding, in the grip of an emotion too great for words. With extreme effort, he resisted the impulse to enfold her in his arms and allowed her to regain her composure before taking her hand and stroking it, something far less worthy of comment, should one of the servants enter.

When she was more herself, he suggested that a drive into Tring might lift her spirits and she agreed, but decided that the longer drive into Aylesbury would give him a new experience and take them by way of a property she owned. Soon, they were off in the buggy, and saw Rose, who waved at them over the rug she was beating on a wooden frame between house and stable, as they passed her on the drive.

Elisabeth and John chatted amiably during the drive toward Aylesbury. She indicated points of interest to him and gave him the local history. In a number of places, medieval towns had been moved or abandoned, even incorporated into large estates or demolished..... She promised that someday they would take the time to explore one.

The drive took little over an hour even at Abernathy's moderate speed and they found a place to stop at a small inn at the outskirts of the town for refreshment --- for they, as well as Abernathy, needed something to wash away the dust of the road. They ordered tea and scones and debated the merits of a longer drive to include visiting the gravesite of Louis XVIII's wife, who died in Hartwell, a tiny village on the Oxford Road during his exile from 1810 to 1814. Ultimately, they decided against the additional miles in appreciation of Abernathy's efforts --- as well as the fact that they didn't want the death, even of a foreign queen, to mar their pleasant day.

When they drove into the town center, they found it interesting and bustling. Thanks to it being a branch of the Grand Union Canal, there were market goods in abundance and the trade was brisk. They found a place for Abernathy and the buggy, then set out afoot to explore the town. So many things to see! Elisabeth had been to London, but it had

been some time in the past and she had become used to country views ---
long vistas of fields and trees and tiny hamlets and villages. Tiny Tring
seemed large to her --- and here was a town much larger than Tring.....
It was exciting, stimulating, and it banished the sadness she had felt
earlier completely.

In their sight-seeing, they encountered many small shops and merchants.
At a stall in the market, Elisabeth found some lovely old handmade lace
for collars and cuffs and purchased a number of yards as well as collars
which were already made and ready to attach to a dress or blouse. They
found a new hat for John and bolts of fabric for Rose to sew into dresses
and nightgowns for herself and Cook, who couldn't thread a needle
anymore. Aylesbury was quite the place to visit!

With John carrying her purchases, Elisabeth led the way back to their
buggy and John stowed them in the box on the back, then seeing a tea
shop nearby, they entered, hoping for tea and sandwiches. To their
surprise, there was far more available. This shop was the outgrowth of a
soldier's travels and served curries and teas not usually seen in English
country towns. John had never tasted curry and relied upon Elisabeth to
order things that he might enjoy. When the food was served, it was far
better than he had anticipated, containing bits of candied fruits and fruit
rinds, and they ate every bit of the bright yellow curried lamb with rice
and vegetable pilaf. They took portions of the thick curry, as well as the
rice pilaf, home with them for Rose and Cook in glass jars wrapped in
brown paper and folded into oilskin to avoid sullying the fabrics they'd
purchased with grease.

By late afternoon, they knew that they must turn homeward or risk
loosing their way on the country roads as dusk fell. Thus it was that they
returned to the buggy, with no time left over to visit Elisabeth's property,
and pointed Abernathy in the direction of Little Tring.....

As they neared the end of their journey, Abernathy began to quicken his
pace, recognizing the lay of the land and knowing his stable was in the
vicinity. The buggy rolled into the drive before dusk had settled, but by
the time they had unhitched the horse, curried him, and pulled the buggy
into its shelter, the light was fading and they managed an embrace in the

stable before they stepped out and walked up the drive carrying their purchases.

They went to the back and entered through the kitchen, in order to pass the food and bolts of cloth to Rose and Cook. The ladies were very surprised and happy to see them back bearing gifts. Cook sniffed the curry suspiciously, but said they would give it a try, while Rose positively glowed over the fabrics.

Elisabeth and John continued on into the dining room chatting about their adventure and having smelled the lovely odors in the kitchen they were certain dinner was on the hob. Their noses were right on target, for within a quarter hour, Rose had appeared with a country dinner --- smoked eel, savory fried potatoes, and fresh peas from Saturday's trip to Tring market with green onions and a cream gravy. Their outing had given them quite an appetite and they did Cook proud. When Rose brought a cherry pie and coffee for dessert, she remarked, "Cook'll be happy to see those empty plates --- oh, and she's been heatin' the food you brought back and says it's good. We'll have dinner of it in a mite and I'll be back for the clean-up here when we're done."

John and Elisabeth smiled a knowing smile at each other when she wasn't looking. Then, with her on her way to the kitchen, they enjoyed their pie and coffee and, ultimately, migrated into the garden. Strolling to the end, they occupied their favorite bench and continued their conversation. It was then that Elisabeth mentioned her brother-in-law's impending visit the following day. John asked, "Does it concern you?"

"A little," she answered, "It may be about anything --- the boys' schooling or tuition, the girls' stay with his aunt, ...or he may be opening a new chapter in his assault on my widowhood now that the children are out of his way. I would appreciate your being in attendance when he is here."

"Of course! you will have it!" John quickly answered.

"Thank you, John," she said, putting her hand on his. He covered that hand with his free hand, sandwiching her smaller one between his, then raising her hand to kiss the back of it and turning it over to kiss the palm, an act of the utmost intimacy, which did lovely things to her body, sending little tingles to her most hidden parts and making her positively quiver with delight.

They restrained themselves, however, knowing that they would have other times for intimacy, and held hands or sat with his arm around her shoulders as they discussed medicine, the infirmary, their wonderful outing, and the schedule for the repairs she had planned. It was quite some time before they were ready to say goodnight; finally, though, he walked her to the door of the study, embraced her and kissed her, then left, that she might let herself in, alone.

She watched him disappear around the corner of the house, then went in through the French doors and, after closing the latch and drawing the drapes, she continued on into the hall and up the stairs to the comfort of her bed. It had been a long day, too long for fantasies and touching.

John read --- beginning with the slim volume of poetry, then more of King's American Dispensatory, and back to the poetry when he felt his eyelids were betraying him. The poetry of Elisabeth's mother was hauntingly beautiful at times..... Her thoughts seemed to reawaken his tired brain. Finally, though, he needed to sleep, lest he awaken too late on the morrow to be of any use to Elisabeth. Before he slept, however, he did something odd --- for him --- he asked her mother to awaken him at the correct time and to aide him in assisting her in whatever way she needed most at any given time. Oddly enough, he felt totally at peace once he had given voice to these thoughts, as though Elisabeth's mother had heard him, and sleep came to him easily.

❧Chapter 9 – Richard Hastings☙

After the lovely days of an impending summer, the morning dawned dreary, gray skies, gray light, gray feelings….. Elisabeth had hoped for sunshine to buoy her up in the coming meeting with her brother-in-law, Richard Hastings. In its absence, she hoped that John would buoy her up.

John awoke earlier than he had thought he would and, wondering why he was awake, remembered that he had asked Elisabeth's mother to awaken him in plenty of time…..

Thus, it was, that he appeared in the breakfast nook at such an early hour, freshly shaved and bathed --- and ready to eat.

Rose and Cook had heard of the impending visit and were up early, as well, knowing that they could nap a bit when afternoon came if need be. When John arrived, Rose had only just brought their sausages, toast, poached eggs and steaming coffee to the table. John poured their coffee and, after adding cream to cool it, sipped his. He could sense the distraction and unease in Elisabeth and wondered what he could do to help. By some sixth sense, she seemed to know that he was there for her and she said, "Don't worry, John. I am nervous about this morning's visitor, but I shall pull through --- besides, I have your arm to lean on."

He smiled and patted her hand, then said, "Last night, after I read more of the poems, I asked your mother to help me to help you. I believe that she is doing exactly that."

"Yes, I am certain that she is --- and father, as well," she agreed.

"Do you still wish me to stay with you during your brother-in-law's visit?" he asked.

"I plan to inform him that you are my property agent, as well as, my student and assistant in the infirmary. Thus, I feel it is necessary that you be with us when we meet. If he wishes to discuss the children, he will not ask me to dismiss you from the room. However, if he wishes to discuss something about his own estate or affairs, and most certainly if he is intent on acquiring me, he will either ask me to walk with him out-of-doors or ask that we may be private, expecting that I will send you on an errand to the study or some such," she answered.

"If he does, do you wish me to leave the room?" John asked.

"I am not certain. It will depend on how the conversation goes and, should he ask it, I would hope that you could find a reason to return. I simply have a feeling that he will open the issue of marriage with me again, due to your being here. It may be that he fancies me, but I have always thought it was more that, having no children, he wanted to make himself George's stepfather, so that he could say 'his son' was inheriting his estate. It seems rather pitiable, though I have compassion for him. However, I would not even marry him at his deathbed," she averred.

That matter settled, they adjourned to the study for her to assign readings to John. She pulled another of her father's volumes from the shelf: *Illustrations of the Atmospherical Origin of Epidemic Diseases, and of its Relation to their Predisponent Constitutional Causes, Exemplified by Historical Notices and Cases, and on the Twofold Means of Prevention, Mitigation, and Cure, and of the Powerful Influence of Change of Air, as a Principal Remedy* by T Forster, and handed it to John, saying, "You might find this one interesting. My father purchased it, but I purchased Gray's 1848 essay on the eye for my own edification," she said, handing him the essay as well.

That settled, he began to read, while she went to the garden to cut flowers. Through the French doors, he could see her speaking with Joe about the flowerbeds as she selected the stems she needed for her arrangements. Watching her was far more enjoyable than reading --- the graceful movements of her hands and body were mesmerizing ---

however, he pulled himself back to the reading, and just in time, for there came a knock at the door and Rose was soon admitting a man to the study to await Elisabeth while she went to fetch her from the garden.

John stood and, bowing, introduced himself to the man who, looking at him quizzically, introduced himself as well. At that point Elisabeth entered through the French doors, saying, "Oh, I see you've met. John is my medical student and infirmary assistant, as well as my property agent, Richard. He came all the way from America to work with my father, not knowing he had died. I've tested him and found him an intelligent and teachable young man, so I decided to put him to use and help him, at least, to reach his goals in medicine. Now, do sit down both of you and I'll ring for tea."

As she pulled the cord, Rose arrived at the study door with a tea tray, having anticipated her mistress. In a matter of moments, Elisabeth was pouring the gentlemen and herself cups and passing a plate of small tarts and biscuits, part of the previous Friday's bounty from John's admiring patients. She made a point of mentioning this as an aside to Richard, by way of letting him know that John was growing a following among the lady folk in the area. Richard nodded, saying, "Ah, yes, our spinsters and hopeful mothers..... I wish you well of them, sir --- many a wish to be bride there....." He then turned his attention to Elisabeth and spoke of the children for some time. He'd had word from Gerald and Justus' headmaster that they were doing well and Richard wanted to let her know that he had increased their allowances by way of a reward. Ah, she thought, ingratiating himself with me.....

Next, he confided that, although the girls had not written to her, apparently his aunt had written to him, saying that they were very popular at social gatherings and, furthermore, that she would not be surprised if they were spoken for by Christmas, due to their comeliness and vivacity. Elisabeth took this well, considering that his tone was almost one of triumph at being able to best her in the affections of her children --- or at least in the knowledge of what was transpiring in their lives. Little did he know that her serenity was based in part upon her knowledge that she must seem serene in order to keep him paying for their education and introduction to society --- but also due, in part, to the fact that she had her own special secret seated across from her with a book in his hand.....

John watched and listened with a feigned indifference, hoping to appear only a young student, intent upon his training. He succeeded, in his effort, and when Richard Hastings eventually went forth from Elisabeth's house that morning, he left believing that she had merely found herself another pup to nurture while her own children were away at school --- a colonial pup, at that.

When he had gone, Elisabeth let out a sigh of relief and went into the parlor to look out the window and watch his horse disappearing down the drive toward Tring. Now, she thought, they would have to be even more cautious, lest their true relationship become known.

John followed her into the parlor and saw her looking out the window. He knew why she was doing it and, moving to her side, he whispered, "Don't worry, Elisabeth, I will see you through. I may not have money, but I will be by your side as long as you want me there."

"I want you there forever, dearest love, but in order to achieve that, we will need to be very circumspect or my children could suffer for our pleasures. The girls are pretty enough they may marry well, even without a dowry, and that is nothing to be sneezed at. The boys are still at school and I couldn't afford to keep them there easily if Richard didn't pay their tuition, their upkeep, and give them an allowance. My eldest, George, may receive a scholarship next term, but what of the others? It all depends on their uncle."

John understood what she was saying, for he had seen it in America, as well, only not with the high-ranked and gentry so greatly, for there men were self-made more often than being inheritors of someone else's fortune and lands. He would be cautious along with her, watching for any pitfalls they might fall into and banking his fires for the time being, as he watched how her life --- and his --- unfolded.

He would be the diligent student, faithful assistant, and hard-working property agent to the best of his ability, bringing joy to her and praise for her ability as a teacher. She must never suffer loss due to his love --- or hers. His course was clear and he would attend to it.

She saw the play of emotions over his face and guessed what she didn't see in his eyes or through the 'knowing' of her intuition. Taking his hand, all she dared at the moment, she said, "Bear with me, my dearest love, and we may yet have a chance at having a lasting happiness." He squeezed her hand tightly, allowing every ounce of his emotions, his love for her to show in that clasping of her hand --- the only thing he dared touch in broad daylight and with servants in the house. From this point on, they would play roles for public consumption.

At that moment, Rose tapped on the door and they quickly let go of each other's hands before she entered, saying, "Luncheon, ma'am and sir, in the breakfast room." They followed her out of the parlor and down the hall to the room they called their breakfast nook, where she had already laid their places. As they seated themselves, she brought in the last of the luncheon platters and confided, "Cook didn't know if he (with a wave in the direction of the road) was to stay, so there's extra on the serving dishes."

Elisabeth smiled and reassured her that all was as it should be and that they would be happy to make short work of Cook's excellent viands.

When she had left, they began their meal and carried on two conversations, one in normal tones and the other sotto voce, for their ears only. The first was for others to hear and concerned the properties, the infirmary, John's training, and so forth, while the whispers concerned their feelings, their love, and how they would manage to continue without arousing Richard's suspicions until her children were better situated in life with their future paths more stable. This might be at any time, if his horse threw him as her husband's had done, but realistically, it would probably be a year or more. Ah, intrigue and opposition, two conditions almost guaranteed to increase ardor by leaps and bounds.

In a whisper, John asked, "Could we not marry? Then he would have no hold on you."

With a resigned look on her face, she raised her eyes to him, tilting her head to one side and said, "No hold on me, but what of the children? Do you think he is not capable of withdrawing his support on their behalf? Think of it! the girls might be settled by Christmas! If George gets his scholarship, that only leaves the other two. They're not poor scholars, only younger than George. They may find success outside of their uncle's support as well within a year or two....." Seeing the crestfallen look on John's face, she wanted to cry, but held back the tears, saying, "I am yours, John, now and always. If our love is real, we can do this. If we cannot, we do not truly love."

Nodding his head, he signaled his compliance --- he would go forward with their new pattern of life. Then, reaching underneath the table, with his left hand, he gently squeezed her right thigh, then patted it and grinned, as if to say, 'that's mine'.

Soon, Rose brought their dessert --- lemon custard tarts with clotted cream and cups of sweet spiced tea --- removing the dishes they'd used to the sideboard as she left.

Elisabeth and John lingered over dessert, savoring the tartness with the sweet. As they sat there, she said, "This is not easy for me, John. You are the only one who knows how warm my nature is, but I believe that we are able to do it, and that we will muddle through to the goal."

When they had finished, she returned to the garden and he to the study, where he buried himself in his assignment, then picked another book when he had finished as much as he felt he needed to know on that topic..... This time the subject was the technique of bone-setting, an art he'd seen practiced a number of times in the rural communities he'd been reared in.

It was growing dark when Elisabeth finally came into the house and found John on his third book. Amazed, she asked, "Have you already completed reading the one I gave you?"

"As much as I needed to read to surmise where it was going," he answered.

"And, what have you here?" she asked

"A volume on bone-setting," he replied, "And one on diseases of the circulatory system."

"My, you are a voracious student!" she exclaimed, with a smile. John knew that smile --- it usually meant that she was teasing him, but then she said, "No, I'm not making a joke --- you are quite advanced and certainly avid."

He picked up a bookmark and inserted it in the one he was reading, then placed it on the small table near his chair. In the growing darkness, he knew that they could not be seen and standing, he took her in his arms and kissed her gently on each eyelid, then on her mouth, then, taking her hand, he led her to the light of the dining room, where Rose was laying the plates. Coming up the hallway, they let go their hands and began talking about bone-setting. Rose left, with a grimace of disgust at the topic, to fetch Cook's offerings.

As she entered the kitchen, she said, "They're talkin' about settin' broken bones --- at dinner! Medical folk must be addled!"

Under her breath, Cook muttered, "Addled in love, mayhap....," then said, "Get a move on, girl, this joint is ready to carry in." Rose hurried to take the platter into the dining room and return for the next load.

Elisabeth watched John carve the joint of ham, thick slices falling to the platter, and envisioned him as the master of the house. It was a beautiful fantasy and it gladdened her heart.

When he had cut enough slices and served them both from the covered dishes, they began to eat and converse again --- speaking first of Cook's natural gift for the culinary arts, then moving on to the art of bone-setting. Having seen it done, John felt that it reminded him of joinery more than anything else --- that fitting of handmade dove-tailed joints by a cabinetmaker.

By the time coffee and dessert were brought in, they had moved on to the circulatory system, having dealt with bone-setting and joinery to the satisfaction of both.

Afterward, Elisabeth asked John to take her for a turn in the garden and when they sat in the dark at the far end of the garden, looking at the stars, John placed his arm around her back gently, thinking to avoid arousing her, but she said, "Dearest, if you touch me, it must be a firm touch if you are to avoid my arousal."

He immediately held her more firmly, rather than lightly touching her shoulders.

Finally, she remembered the book she had initially given him to read that morning, before Richard came, and asked, "What did you think of the book on the apparently airborne nature of some diseases, John?"

He thought for a moment, then replied, cryptically, "I am not one to ever mistrust the veracity of that which cannot be seen."

Looking at him in the darkness of the garden, she stated, "You refer, of course, to your energetic healing. Could that be something akin to the 'animal magnetism' Mesmer speaks of?"

"I don't know enough about him or his theories to say, Elisabeth, but, as a generality, it may be so," he answered.

Their conversation went along in this manner for some time longer, but they knew that they must, eventually, return to the house and then separate for the night. They also knew that to put it off too long might set tongues to wagging.

So, with regret, they made their way to the French doors and, parting, each went their way and into their aloneness to await their coming together again in the morning.....

❧Chapter 10 – The Waiting❧

They fell into a pattern for a period of time --- one of study, work projects on properties, working at the infirmary, and a tiny bit of time for themselves --- usually in the garden, at night. Their time alone was sometimes filled with quiet conversation and other times filled with things which had nothing to do with conversation and everything to do with communication --- of a sort.

Three weeks passed in this fashion --- three weeks without a trip to the vacant property in the country..... Three weeks with the tantalizing nearness of the object of their affections at arms reach --- or closer..... Three weeks of keeping themselves in check. The tension was growing day by day and, lest it come undone at an inopportune moment, Elisabeth brought up the subject on one of their garden walks in the evening, saying, "John, do you think we should allow ourselves to become so starved for each other? It seems unnatural and, though we must be cautious, wouldn't a bit of physical recreation be in order?"

Pretending to misunderstand her, he answered, "We could take a trip to the museums in London and perambulate the grounds....."

"London? But we have fine grounds right here in Tring!" she said, then realised he was having a laugh at her expense and continued, "Ah, you make light of me! You shall pay for this, you knave! You shall pleasure your contessa at her country house --- in any manner she deems fitting."

Entering the spirit of the love play, he said, "Oh, my contessa, this gentleman hardly deserves his sentence. He was merely suggesting a suitable outing....."

Continuing the repartee, she swore, "Nay, you varlet, your tone was mocking and your contessa will have her honor upheld. You shall serve at her pleasure, in many positions, before the morrow's sun has fled from the sky." Her smile was definitely one of excitement and, seeing this, he allowed fire to come into his eyes and his heart, as well.....

He took a deep breath and pledged, "Ah, the morrow will hold many pleasures for my lady contessa and I shall serve in any position required of me, for as long as needed my lady," then lifted her hand to his lips and pressed the back of it firmly against them. He turned it over, after a moment, and kissed the sensitive skin of her palm sensuously, lingering there and allowing the warmth to work its magic. Hearing her breathing become strained in her effort to contain herself, he felt remorse and released her hand, placing it back on her lap.

There, at the far end of the garden, on their bench, they held themselves physically restrained --- for the moment.....

When they departed for their respective sleeping quarters at a respectable hour, they squeezed each other's hands tightly, a commitment to the morrow and a revalidation of their love.....

Elisabeth entered the house through the French doors, as usual, and noticed an envelope on the hall table as she passed by. After a few steps, she turned back and, taking it into the study where a lamp still burned, she opened it and began to read it by the lamplight. After a few words, she sat down to think on what was written there.

The letter was from her husband's aunt, Daphne Merriweather, and she was pleased to announce that two young men, brothers, would be asking Richard Hastings for permission to marry the twins. To her mind, the girls were amenable to the matches and, the young men being brothers, they would be much together as they had always been. The young men were of good family with social standing and some not too distant ties to noble houses. There was wealth in the offing for them, with the elder inheriting the bulk of the estate and the younger a large manor and the income from a very generous trust. Neither girl would know want. Daphne went on extolling the virtues of the youths and their connections and, in reading of them, Elisabeth almost overlooked the last sentence. It mentioned that the young men would present themselves to Richard Hastings, first, on the following day and would then spend the balance of the day at his estate, making the journey to Little Tring with him on the day after to make known the particulars of the arrangements --- Daphne anticipated Richard's consent to the matches as the ostensible head of the family, for the men were indeed most desirable parties.

She sat there for a long time, thinking on this situation. She wanted happiness for her daughters, but worried so over protecting their ability to make their own choices. Unknown to all, she had drawn up a will with her solicitor and, at this time, it stipulated that her properties were to go to her daughters equally as their own property, leaving her sons with almost nothing. It seemed harsh, but this was a time when men had the ability to move freely in society and to make something of themselves more easily, while women were hampered in their ability to support themselves if they were without a husband. She had decided that she would rather have sons who married money without love, if need be, than daughters who sold themselves like a brood mare into the slavery of a loveless marriage or became kept women or even prostitutes in order to support themselves.

Finally, in a very serious mood, she went upstairs to her room and slept.

As she slept, John, who had been reading since he left her, finally began to yawn and, marking the page with a sheet of paper, went to his bed and lay there thinking of her. His ardor was aroused and his hand began to stroke his staff as the suppressed feelings for her came to the fore, bringing renewed energy into his body and a focus on their sexual relationship. The attraction was there in all aspects of her person, but, being young, his physical nature was in the forefront and it asserted itself strongly as he lay there touching himself in this way. Slowly, sensually, he moved his hand back and forth, allowing this magical member to grow in the sheath of his hand --- longer, harder, and more sensitive with each stroke.....

Groping on the table beside the bed with his other hand, he found what he was feeling for and readied himself for his goal with his faithful hand towel. Longer grew his strokes, and squeezing harder, he began to breathe deeply and moan slightly as he felt the orgasmic energy grow within him until, finally, his breathing became short, hard breaths and his hand moved faster and faster as his orgasm overtook him, spurting into the towel while his body jerked in spasms of release. He groaned his satisfaction deeply, again and again, his breath coming in staccato rhythms and his hips pumping back and forth as he imagined himself sending his erection and its juices into Elisabeth, the darling of his heart. It was many minutes before his legs stopped quivering and his hips spontaneously spasming with the force of his only ejaculation in three weeks. Laying there, his hand still wrapped around his softening member, he fell into a profoundly deep slumber, and dreamed of his love, his Elisabeth.

❧Chapter 11 – Renewal❧

Elisabeth stirred under her covers, rolled over, then, as she lay there, became aware that, by the light in the room, it was later than she had thought. She had slept the sleep of denial; that sleep we seek when life has challenges or issues too great for us to think of at the moment.

Suddenly, she remembered that she and John were to go to the country property and sat bolt upright in bed, then threw the covers off, stood up and went to wash herself with the water in the basin on her washstand. Soon, feeling cleaner and fresher, she dressed and went down to breakfast.

As she sat there, in the breakfast room, she heard the distant sound of John coming through the kitchen, so she closed her eyes and thought of him touching her, sending little shivers down her spine and making hard pebbles of her nipples as they drew erect. Putting her hands over her breasts, she could feel the stone-hard nipples against her palms. Oh, John would love this, she thought, loving the feel of it herself.

Entering at that moment, he saw her and, knowing that the two in the kitchen were occupied at the moment, he strode straight to Elisabeth and slid his hands under hers to feel the erect nipples and pinch them tenderly before he sat in his place. Those pinches had brought her to jerk with the sensation and the place between her thighs began to throb with desire that she had to quiet before breakfast could continue. John was quite moved, as well, with a bulge in the front of his trousers as testimony.

After a few minutes, she began to tell John of the letter she had received and the feelings she had experienced. He listened patiently and quietly, allowing her to finish and then asked her questions, guiding her into her acceptance of the situation and her realization that this would probably work out for the best. After all, the twins would always have each other to lean upon unlike her situation and, since both were provided for better than she had been in some ways, their lives had a better chance of having a fortunate outcome. For one thing, it sounded as though they had chosen the young men as much as the brothers had chosen them.

Perhaps, though, he advised, she should suggest to the elder boy that a trust be made for his wife to allow her to live reasonably well in the event of his death, if the estate was entailed, since it would then pass to his brother or son --- or perhaps another male relative should he beget only daughters and outlive his brother. He also suggested that a portion of the younger brother's trust be inherited by his wife even in the event that no heir was produced and that she be provided for should his estate go entirely to a son, as well.

She thought on these suggestions for a few moments and agreed that they seemed very reasonable requests of the young men..... If they truly loved her daughters, they would agree without question.

At that point, Rose made her entrance and they settled into the business of eating breakfast. It was a hearty one --- sausages, shirred eggs, thick toast with berry preserves and butter, sweet rolls, and strong coffee thick with heavy cream. They would need their energy.....

As they ate, they spoke of the children, citing that now she had only the boys to plan for. "Somehow," she said, "I know that circumstances will fall into place for their benefit. I do not yet know how, or what that benefit will be, but I feel that I must trust that all will come together."

He nodded, saying, "I feel that, as well, my dearest one."

She smiled at him, a blazing light of love flowing out with the smile, and his heart felt cupid's arrow, yet again --- his heart, and his anatomy.

In an unhurried manner, they prepared for their outing, lest anything be remarked. They remembered to wrap sausages in brown paper and oiled cloth to put into the box on the buggy, as well as a packet of dried fruit and a few sweet rolls. Ostensibly, they were going to visit the four reservoirs, and might do so, though their main destination was their place of assignation: the country cottage.

After he had hitched Abernathy to the buggy, he drove it to the house and, lifting Elisabeth into the buggy and making certain to squeeze her surreptitiously in all the most sensitive ways while so doing, he readied them for their journey. Then, seating himself next to her, he took the reins and they were off through the countryside.

It was not long before they pulled off the road and down the drive to the house, where they secreted Abernathy and the buggy in the shade and seclusion of the stable, once again, and, with their lunch in hand, they quickly made their way into the house.

Once inside, they left the packets on the kitchen counter and made their way to the bedroom they had used on the prior visit. Removing the dust covers, they bared the mattress and, taking sheets and pillows from the clothespress, they went about setting the bed to rights. In a few minutes, it was ready and, taking her hand, John drew Elisabeth to him, enfolding her in his arms and kissing her more soundly than he had in nigh unto a month, his hands caressing her back and her bottom firmly, then teasingly, and firmly again, with passion, pulling their hips together and feeling her need as she willingly pressed herself to him.

Finally, they had satisfied that need to be as close as possible and, separating for a moment, grinned at each other and began the ritual of disrobing one other. Elisabeth took off John's jacket and he reciprocated by removing her shirtwaist bodice and allowing her breasts to spring forth under the filmy layer of her silk camisole into his waiting hands. After squeezing them until she was nearly breathless, he lifted the bit of silk off over her head and she took the opportunity, when he put his hands on her now bare skin, to take hold the waistband of his trousers and begin the unbuttoning of his fly. For a moment, she hesitated, as he lightly pinched and squeezed her engorged nipples, bringing on waves of sensation in her groin and a throbbing between her thighs which was impossible to deny, then continued to divest him of his trousers as he once again squeezed and kneaded her breasts. His trousers a puddle on the floor, he stepped out of them and, removing his smallclothes, he bent to take a nipple into his mouth and work it lightly with the hardness of his teeth, then suckle it, causing her to throw her head back, leaning into the sensation as her back arched involuntarily. As her breathing became more intense, so had the low mews of her love sounds become more intense….. …..and urgent.

John, unfastened and removed her skirt, then her slip, and, finally her pantalets, leaving her naked, but for her stockings and shoes, as was he. Lifting her to the bed he leaned her back on the sheets and brought his attention to the space between her thighs, that juicy slit with the love button at its apex. Licking it and suckling on the button, he brought her to a frenzy, then stopped and began to take off her shoes, slowly, making her want more, as she wriggled her hips, with his feather-light touches at her ankles, then removed her stockings in the same manner.

Again, he stopped for a moment as he removed his own shoes and stockings, then returned to his task and brought her almost to a peak of bliss before entering her with his rigid member, causing her to gasp at the feeling as it slid on her juices into the deepest part of her hidden recess.

He took her on the edge of the bed, standing between her thighs and gaining purchase with his bare feet on the floor. He hesitated there, for but a moment, and then began to slide in and out, pushing forward into her as she thrust her hips toward him, begging for his entry, needing his member inside of her to satisfy her body's urge to be one with him.

Finally, as their bodies met and separated over and over again, she began that almost silent keening which signaled her impending orgasm and the coming release of her body's tension. He increased his pace and she met him thrust for thrust as they finished in concert with each other, then held themselves together as though unable to part their hips.

His legs felt weak standing there and he leaned over her, supporting himself on his forearms, until the last of his final round had fired into her and he could stand without feeling too wobbly. Then, he climbed up onto the bed with her and they lay spoon-like, John at her back with his arm around her. They slept that way for some time, then, realizing that they must drive around visiting a bit, before going home, in order to appear all innocence, they retrieved their clothing, ate their lunch and, retrieving the buggy, continued their outing in the direction of Miss Violet's house.

When she saw the buggy, Miss Violet came out to greet them, with Spot at her side and showing all the energy of a pup. They were amazed at his recovery, praising Miss Violet's nursing skills and stroking Spot's head, which he offered over and over again, being a very sociable dog and always on the lookout for treats --- when not ailing.

She invited them in for an early tea and they gladly accepted, enjoying her company and her earnestness. Elisabeth helped her with the preparations, while John and Spot became better acquainted. Spot remembered John, especially his hands, and nuzzled them often, asking to be touched with that special healing energy. John obliged, allowing it to flow freely through him and into the aging dog, bringing him relief from his aches and pains and stimulating his body's own healing qualities.....

In short order a lovely tea was laid for them in the garden, under a grape arbor, and a small bowl of half tea and half water was put in the kitchen for Spot, along with a bowl of lunch.

They visited as they ate the small sandwiches made with Miss Violet's own homemade bread and spread with cheese and fruit, as well as. other soft ingredients, and enjoyed the tea. She served a tisane this time --- a tasty blend of herbs and dried fruits steeped in boiling water and enhanced with wildflower honey, if the guests desired.

Their tea seemed never ending, but even happy visits must finally come to a closure and, as the afternoon wore on, they were reminded, by the lengthening shadows in the garden, that they must leave or risk losing their way home in the dark..... As they made their way to the buggy, their hostess pressed a packet of her tisane into Elisabeth's hand, saying, "For your Cook....." John took it from her and slipped it into his pocket for safekeeping.

Then, as she watched John lift Elisabeth into the buggy, after being hugged by each of them, Miss Violet's heart somehow knew that they

would marry --- not too far distant in time --- and hoped that she and
Spot would live to see it and dance at their wedding. With that thought,
came the reminder that Elisabeth had suggested that Catherine and
Caroline might be married soon and she began to think of an appropriate
gift as the buggy rolled out onto the road.....

She waved one last time at her guests, then called Spot who was, by this
time, investigating the rabbit burrows in the verge and turned toward the
house. Soon, she was sitting in her sewing chair, with Spot at her feet, as
she knitted a tiny sweater for the shop boy from Baylor's new baby
sister. She wanted to have it finished when he came two days hence to
bring her order.

As Abernathy proceeded toward home, John and Elisabeth basked in the
glow of a perfect day, not sitting so close that anyone seeing them might
remark it, but aware of each other, all the same. There was an air of bliss
about them that must certainly be due to more than eating Miss Violet's
sandwiches --- no matter how excellent they were --- and in their state of
contentment, they spoke little, each enjoying the nearness of the other
and knowing that, should they encounter anyone even on this lonely
road, they must appear to be merely friends.....

The buggy turned almost of its own accord as Abernathy, knowing his
own drive, pulled into it and headed for the stable, where he knew he
would have his dinner and a brush-off. Elisabeth fulfilled the former,
while John took care of the brushing, and they were soon on their way up
to the house and their own dinner.

As they entered the kitchen, after cleaning up in the rain barrel, the
aromas of Cook's savory meal greeted their nostrils and made their
mouths water. She looked up from the stove and. with a bob of her head,
said, "Better get t' th' table, dears --- Rose'll be bringin' this t'ya soon."

Obeying her edict, for a good cook is always queen of the kitchen, they
hurried to the dining room where Rose was laying the place settings.
Seeing them, she said, "Cook says dinner's any moment."

"Yes, we heard," they said simultaneously, then seated themselves.
Remembering it after a few moments, Elisabeth asked John for the tisane

packet Miss Violet had given her for Cook and he pulled it out of the pocket he'd put it in for safekeeping, then handed it to Rose, while Elisabeth asked her to take it to Cook from their erstwhile hostess.

"Oh, she'll be that pleased, ma'am," Rose said, with a smile, then hurried off to the kitchen to deliver the tea and return with dinner.

Dinner was magnificent --- another of Cook's triumphs. Creamed wild mushroom soup, an enormous roasting hen with savory stuffing, the famous dumplings to soak up the drippings, and steamed small vegetables with butter laced with savory herbs, rounded out with a dessert of fresh strawberries from Richard's orangerie over cake slices, topped with whipped heavy cream and coffee.

As they ate, they spoke of the pleasant day they had spent with Miss Violet and Spot, making certain that Rose heard them, to insure the secret of their assignation and, then, after the meal, they retired to the study and much discussion over the progress of John's reading and his work in the infirmary. Elisabeth was very pleased with him as a student as well as a lover!

The following day was a Wednesday and she asked him to man the infirmary alone, with only Maggie to steer him right, in case Richard and the young men chose to arrive in the afternoon. His confidence was less than she had expected at this request, but she knew that he could do it, barring any truly serious situations arising, and she knew that she could trust Maggie to tell him when he was out of his depth after her years of helping out.

They continued on the topic of the infirmary for awhile and then moved on to the properties and the renovations. Preparations for these had been moving along slowly, for he found that it took time to assess each job accurately in these old buildings and calculate the amount of materials and supplies needed to complete the tasks. Why, some of them had been standing before a house in the colonies had been built! He asked whether she had preferences as to which jobs he should complete soonest and she answered, "Just so long as you do anything for Miss Violet and Kate first of all."

He smiled and nodded, approving of her answer. It was his own thought, as well, but he had wanted to hear it from her own lips. Elisabeth sensed that he had been thinking along the same lines and loved him all the more for his compassionate nature.

They sat there chatting comfortably until the hour became late and John reminded her of her appointment with Richard the following day as Rose was entering to ask if they wished a cup of cocoa, for Cook was making it just now. Elisabeth answered, "Thank you, no, Rose, none for me or I'll be awake all night. John may, though….."

"Yes, Rose, I would like one if I may carry it to my rooms….." he said.

"Oh yes, sir, of course you may --- that is, if Mistress is in agreement," Rose stammered.

"Of course, Rose, we wouldn't want my student to go without cocoa," Elisabeth said with a smile, putting Rose at ease.

Rose returned in a few minutes with a steaming pitcher of the brew and a cup, announcing, "Cook gave him your portion, as well, since you didn't want it. ma'am," and bringing a smile to both of her listeners, before she hurried back to her own cup of cocoa.

Knowing she would not be back, John embraced Elisabeth before leaving for his rooms and carried his cocoa gingerly --- for it was, indeed, hot.

Elisabeth lingered for a bit after he left, tidying up her paperwork and selecting some reading for him to do in the next few days. Then, she too, left the study and sought out her bedroom.

She found it difficult to sleep though, even without the cocoa, for she would be meeting two men who would likely be her son-in-laws on the morrow and she was not certain that she was entirely comfortable with that, seeing her daughters were even younger than she had been when she married…..

Finally, her fretting abated and she slept, though fitfully.

❧Chapter 12 – The Suitors❧

Elisabeth and John had finished their breakfast and she had gone out to nurture the garden, while he read a book on diseases of the digestive tract in the study, when Richard and the hopeful suitors arrived. Rose answered the knock and ushered the gentlemen into the parlor, then went to the garden and recalled Elisabeth to the house. Fortunately, she had not been exerting herself too much and with a pat to her hair, after removing her sun bonnet, she sailed into the parlor, leaving the door slightly ajar, so that John might hear most of what was said from his place in the quiet of the study.

Her guests stood when she came into the room and waited until she had seated herself to return to their places. Ah, one point in their favor, she thought.

Richard, introduced the two young men, Quentin and Justin Balfour, to her --- adding that Quentin was interested in seeking Catherine's hand and Justin in winning Caroline's. She looked at the two of them with her head tilted a bit to one side and asked them each, in turn, to tell her what they liked most about the girl of their choice. Quentin answered that it was Catherine's positive nature and confidence and Justin spoke of Caroline's gentleness and sweetness touching his heart. Another point in their favor, she thought, for they had assessed the differing characters of her daughters perfectly.

Then, she asked how they planned to support her daughters and, when Richard began to answer for them, held her hand up for him to remain silent and looked at the young men expectantly. Quickly understanding, he acquiesced gracefully.

Quentin spoke first, saying, "I am the eldest, Mistress Hastings, and I will inherit the estate, lands, cash, and investments, other than Justin's trust and house and a few bequests. I believe that I can provide every luxury to Catherine, now and in the future for, until I inherit, I have a very generous mandatory allowance and a manor of my own in the country, as well as a townhouse in London."

"That seems very good, Quentin," she said, "But, what provision will you make for her, should you, as my husband did, die before your time?"

"I.... That is..... I had not considered that eventuality, ma'am," he stammered, blushing.

"It is a very real consideration, Quentin," she replied, "As I well know. We are, none of us, above illness or accident and must make provision for our unplanned departure from this mortal coil. A man's family must be protected in whole, not only his heir, for how many times have we seen a second or even third son inherit? Our Queen is an example, herself, of inheritances moving about." With this point, she saw a light dawn in their eyes.

Looking at Justin, she asked, "And you, Justin, do you have a living as well?"

"Yes, ma'am, I do," he offered. "I have a trust which my father made for me which would keep my family comfortably, but I am also my aunt's heir, for her husband left her everything and she is past the age of bearing children. She felt that Quentin, since he was the first, didn't need it and I might. She is a lovely person and I hope to have a large family to share with her. I understand your concerns about your daughters being provided for, should either my brother or I die precipitously, and I would, of course make provision for my wife and any children even before our marriage regarding such a turn of events."

"Well said," she answered, chalking up a number of points on his behalf --- one for caring, another for being forward thinking and responsible, and yet another for being articulate.....

"Now, gentlemen," she said, "We have come to an important question ---

do my daughters love you?"

This time, both of them blushed and stammered, almost in perfect unison, "I….. I believe….. that is, she said she did," then looked at each other with an expression that was utterly comedic as they realised that they had spoken the same words.

Elisabeth smiled and said, "I believe you both and I find myself fond of you already for your oneness of purpose --- and your affection for my daughters. I give my blessing to your intentions and if my daughters will have you, I will welcome you into my heart as deeply as my own sons." At this pronouncement, both young men looked intensely relieved and began to speak to her at the same time. Rose entered at that perfect moment with a tray of refreshments and all sound ceased as she carried it to a low table and invited all to partake of lemonade in tall glasses, ginger biscuits, and fruit tarts fresh from Cook's oven and sprinkled with confectioner's sugar.

As the gentlemen partook of Cook's offerings, the conversation began in stops and starts as they ate and drank. What a lovely thing refreshments are, Elisabeth mused --- they give conversation an ebb and flow, allowing all to partake between bites and sips with no one person monopolizing the conversation, lest they forfeit their portion of the sweeties --- or choke on them.

Richard hardly had a word to say and ushered them out of the door at one o'clock, for his own cook was expecting the three of them at two o'clock for luncheon. Letting them out of the door first, he asked her, "Where is your student?"

"Ah, he is in the library with a tome I gave him to read on bowel disorders and such," she answered, "Would you like me to call him?"

"No, I was wondering if he was still hanging about," Richard replied.

"Why wouldn't he be? He is, after all, my student and has a long course of lessons before he will be capable of going onward to London or Europe for further study. I have great hope for his future as a physician, for he learns quickly and easily. He helped me with Miss Violet's dog when it had a bone shard imbedded in the tissues of its mouth and the dog was totally docile with him."

"A dog doctor!" Richard nearly spat the words out with a harsh laugh.

"Richard, a number of the leading physicians began as students of animal diseases, even my own father" she admonished.

Realising that he'd made a serious faux pas with her, he apologized graciously in outward appearance, but failed to note that she had known him too long and could see through his every failure to be genuine.

Taking his leave of her, he asked her to call on him if she had need of anything and she politely thanked him for that and for all he had done for her, knowing in her heart that, although she did feel gratitude, she was being almost as false as he, but honoring social convention, nonetheless.

She stood in the doorway, waving to them as they mounted their horses, which had grazed the verge of the drive during their visit, then rode down its curve to the road and turned in the direction of the Hastings family estate northeast of Berkhamsted.

When she could see them no more, she closed the door and leaned against it for its strength, feeling as though a weight had been lifted from her shoulders and, yet, strangely, she still felt weighted down.

John, hearing the door close and lock, came into the hallway and led her into the study, then poured her a small glass of sherry, which she sipped until she felt more herself. After a bit, she began to tell him what had transpired. He had heard most of it, but knew that she needed to tell someone about it so that she could let go of it --- and he listened.

In about an hour, Rose announced that luncheon was served. It was a light lunch --- Cook knew that she usually did not like to eat very much when she would be going to the infirmary and John had fallen into her habit, as well. So, they had a collation of a variety of small sandwiches, fresh strawberries, and a fluffy rice custard.

At half past two, they set out for the infirmary and, walking a bit slower than usual, they arrived in about twenty minutes.

Maggie was already there and soon there might be patients, as well. Elisabeth and John put on their smocks and prepared themselves for the task at hand.

The afternoon went well --- there were few patients, four to be exact, two of them being minor cuts, the third, a return visit for removal of a plaster cast, and the last of the day, a man whose wife had thrown a dinner plate of cold food at him the night before, when he came in late from a trip to Aylesbury --- drunk. He had a good-sized 'mouse' on his eye and a scab in the middle of his left eyebrow, where the plate had made contact, but no damage to the eye itself. Elisabeth tilted her head and, looking at him with an amused smile and a chuckle, said, "Martin, your wife has a good arm --- do you think, perhaps, you had best belay the drink?"

Hanging his head, he mumbled, "I was only out w' the lads for 'while after I hauled me vegetables to the wharf and I di'n't spend me money --- I won the darts, so they bought. I ask you, can a man refuse free drink?"

Sighing, she said, "I would not judge you, Martin. I am merely telling you how to stay on her good side….. Perhaps some new silk flowers for her hat would mend her mood? Walk home with us and I'll give you some from my collection."

And, so the infirmary hours ended --- with John, Elisabeth, and Martin walking the road to Elisabeth's house, chatting about darts, pubs, the wholesale price of produce, and how to stay on the good side of a woman….. Martin waxed quite philosophical, surprising and delighting his companions.

When he had left Elisabeth's house with a small bouquet of the flowers --- enough for his wife to decorate her hat for seasons to come --- John pulled Elisabeth to him and, holding her in his arms, looked her in the eyes and said, "I'd like to buy you silk flowers for the rest of your natural life."

Tilting her head to one side, she looked back at him and asked, "Is that a proposal, John Bishop?"

"Yes, ma'am, it is. Question is: do you accept?" he replied, with a serious tone.

"I will not play the coy and fluttery maiden with you, John. Yes, I accept. I have met no other man in my life that I would say this to of my own volition. You are the only man I have ever loved as a woman loves a man."

Hearing Rose make her way down the hall to lay the places for dinner, they stepped apart and were, ostensibly, chatting over a book, when she came in to announce the meal.

Dinner was a lovely meal --- Cook, as usual, having spent her greater effort on the evening of an infirmary day, convinced that one should eat heartily after tending the sick to ward off illness. They dined on breast slices of the roast chicken they'd enjoyed the night before, this time with a thickened version of the mushroom soup ladled over the meat, with its accompanying dumplings as a gravy, and sweet winter carrots from the preceding year, boiled and mashed, then topped with raisins and a drizzle of honey. Dessert was light --- an aspic containing slices of strawberries and bits of candied citrus rind and ginger. A weak coffee was served afterward with ginger biscuits, lest it interact with the zesty citrus rind to produce stomach irritation. Cook was truly an artiste in her field and they strove to make her aware of their appreciation.

As full as a pair of ticks, they adjourned to the study after their meal. It had been a long and stressful day and the food had gone a long way toward diverting their bodies from dwelling on the stress. Digestion has a way of leaving less energy for the brain to waste on fretting.

After much discussion on John's current reading --- diseases of the digestive tract (and some of it involving their own recent meal) --- they made for the far end of the garden and their favorite bench. Too full to consider making love, they sat there, his arm propped up by the back of the bench and laying around her shoulders. There was a mellow feel to their energy that evening --- even more so than usual. They both sensed it and commented on that aspect of their relationship. She thought it was due to the food, but John felt it was the calmness they felt over the settling on their future path --- a path they would walk together and, in the words of the old hymn, 'What E'er Betide'.

As the hour grew late, they returned to the house through the French doors and, after finding a few more books to delve into, John kissed Elisabeth gently, then, with the books in hand, he slipped outside to make his way to the rooms over the stable.

She sat in the study for a long while, thinking. Rose came and asked if there was something the matter, wanting to go to bed, but not wanting to leave her alone there in the study.

"No, no, Rose, nothing is amiss. I merely have much to ponder these days. It appears that the girls will be married soon and there is much to consider even before one begins to think of the wedding arrangements."

Instantly empathetic, Rose offered, "If I may help you in any way, ma'am, I will be that pleased to do it."

Smiling at her earnest face, Elisabeth said, "Ah, Rose, thank you for your unfailing kindness, and you will most assuredly help with many things involving the weddings, for you are a part of our family circle and we would never fail to include you."

This brought tears to Rose's eyes and, seeing them, Elisabeth continued, with a sigh, "I do have other matters, weighty matters, to consider, as well. The boys' education, their positions in life, the properties, the infirmary, my student, and the unwelcome attention of my brother-in-law. Will he somehow cause difficulties for my children, I wonder, if I refuse him outright? It is a fine dance I must do to sail this frail barque to the harbor of contentment. I hold no resentment, though I sometimes wish that my father could see the difficulties he has engineered through his good intention."

Compassionate to a fault, Rose, with tears streaming down her face, said, on impulse, "You can always count on me and Cook, ma'am. We will always strive to help you in any way you need --- always," then wiped away the tears with her apron.

Taking her hands, Elisabeth answered, "I know that, dearest Rose. You have helped us in so many ways for so long and I know that your kind heart will continue to do so. You are very much appreciated, here."

These words brought another round of tears from the overwrought Rose and Elisabeth found herself putting her arm around her shoulders and comforting her. How people could remain entirely aloof from their servants, as though they had no feelings, was something she simply could not understand or condone. Perhaps it was her medical training, bringing her to know that all are the same under the flesh, but she laid it to her father's training her in his egalitarian beliefs as he fought the concept of slavery, whether emotional or physical, in every venue in which he discovered it.

Few of those with stature in the community would have bared their own crosses to a servant, but Elisabeth did not consider herself above others and her life would have been far lonelier if she had held herself aloof from these two women who had been such an integral part of her family's life.

Finally, Rose calmed herself and was able to go back to the kitchen and report to Cook that the Mistress would be studying for awhile longer and they might go to bed, if they pleased. Seeing the light still burning late into the night, they made their way upstairs to their rooms and quickly fell asleep, for they had been up early in preparation for the morning's guests.

It was quite some time before Elisabeth ascended the stair with her oil lamp and went to her bedroom. She had pondered for so long that she was weary at last --- quickly finding solace in the arms of the gods of sleep when she had slipped beneath the coverlet.

John had left off reading and retired to his bed only shortly before her. His staff in hand, he thought of her, then found that he was too tired to complete the act and drifted into slumber, her face before his eyes and his heart yearning for the day when they could be together all the long night.

⧼Chapter 13 – Three Youths and More⧽

Weeks passed and Elisabeth and John waited patiently, most of the time, for the aspects of her life, which were up in the air, to play themselves out and level off, while occasionally visiting the vacant cottage and stopping in at Miss Violet's before or afterward.

It was decided that her daughters would wed in mid-September on the same day --- and in one ceremony --- making it a month of double celebrations for the rest of their lives. Their prospective husbands, and their parents, were delighted at the decision, for it would reduce the costs of the celebration by nearly half --- a thing to be desired even by the wealthy. And, of course, as the years passed, their anniversaries and birthdays would likely be celebrated in conjunction --- an excellent excuse for a summer fete.

The twins' brothers had indicated that they would attend and, also that they would be coming home to Elisabeth at varying times during the summer months. At this news, Rose was set to dusting and washing windows in their rooms, airing the bedding, and making certain that everything was tidy for them, a chore she dearly loved, for she doted on the boys, not unlike a maiden aunt.

The first to arrive was Justus. He came, bringing the news that his scholastic work had been deemed so excellent that he was being offered placement in the Medical Sciences Division at the University of Oxford a year before he was to receive his certificate of completion. He was very pleased with his announcement, as was his mother….. Her youngest son having success at such an early age! Her father would have been so pleased…..

He employed himself in reading every book in the study that he not yet found and was thrilled with King's American Dispensatory, which had only recently been published. So, temporarily, Elisabeth had two students' education to contend with. Justus and John got along well and began a camaraderie over their studies. She gave them instruction in the mornings, three days a week, and both helped in the infirmary, which became quite the place to congregate with two handsome young men in attendance. She found, with some amusement, that for each patient, there were two who were 'simply visiting'.

Then, Gerald appeared. Not one for medicine for the most part, but with quite a head for figures, he had excelled in all areas of mathematics from arithmetic to trigonometry and was planning to enter Oxford also --- with a stipend for mentoring the students of wealthy families in mathematics.

He brought his own books along, but also searched through the shelves in the study for volumes to peruse and visited with John and Justus as they studied, adding himself to their group and enjoying the camaraderie, as well.

They continued in this manner, enjoying the mild English summer, Cook's tasty offerings, and Rose's hovering. The two brothers attended social events in the district --- in particular, dances at the same public rooms where their father had first seen their mother. Both were in demand to partner ladies at the dances and received many invitations to picnics, garden parties and musical evenings in the country homes of the lesser gentry and influential men of business. One, in particular, a member of a wealthy and influential banking family, showed an interest in Gerald's skills and, after conferring with him one day at a garden party, offered to sponsor the balance of his college career, if he would agree to work for the bank for an equal amount of time after his matriculation. It was a very tempting offer and Gerald considered it the entire summer.

The only person who looked at the offer in a different fashion, was John. He pointed out to Gerald that his interest was in all facets of mathematics and that there were many professions which mathematics was a large part of: architecture, astronomy, chemistry, clothing design and production, mining, and engineering of every sort. Finance might be a field in which he could grow rich, but, in the long run, he would be better served to define what would serve his heart best.

Then, one evening, George arrived and the house was full to the rafters with men.

The news he brought of his scholarship achievements was very good, only not quite as good as Justus', which put his nose out of joint for a bit, being the eldest, but then he remembered that he was his uncle's heir and would likely never have to work for a living, in any case, and, reflecting on that fact, his state of mind improved immensely and any resentment of his beloved younger sibling evaporated.

He joined his brothers in their pursuit of pleasure in the company of the fair sex and many young ladies of the district were smitten by the charm and grace of the handsome Hastings youths who were invited to virtually every event of any consequence within at least a fifteen-mile radius.

Elisabeth was very pleased with their successes and, though they were too young for marriage, particularly with their careers still pending, she fostered hopes of seeing them successful in that venue as well --- not so much in the acquisition of a wife of social standing as one they could love --- and have a relationship in which they could find their most tender feelings reciprocated.

She enjoyed having her sons at home, though it put a bit of a crimp in her ability to be private with John, who took the change in their time together quite well, all things considered. John knew, of course, that her sons would eventually return to school and he and Elisabeth would be alone again. He could wait --- it made the coming together again that much more meaningful.....

John enjoyed the boys, as well, and they became good friends, though at times he wondered how they would take it when he and Elisabeth married. Marriage --- it was not something he had ever thought of or considered a potential part of his life, but he had never met a woman in any way like her before. She engaged his mind, his body, and the very depths of his soul.

The summer passed in this pleasant manner, one day at a time, but all seeming to blend into the flow of time. Few days retained a distinctness, a clarity which set them apart from the others, but one such was the day her daughters visited with their great-aunt Daphne.

The weddings were only six weeks in the offing and the girls had come to the country to spend a few nights in the homes of their family members. The garden was at its height in the sunlight of summer when they arrived at their mother's house and Elisabeth was occupied with cutting flowers for her vases. Seeing her there, the girls went out to her, leaving great-aunt Daphne behind in the gentler light of the study.

"Oh, mama," Caroline said, "So many things are happening. We're to be married to brothers and they are so wonderful."

Then, Catherine chimed in with, "Yes, mother, it's true --- three months after our birthday. Can you imagine it? There are still so many things to be planned and we've already been at it for months. Great-aunt Daphne is funding most of it and sparing no expense. She and the Balfours are sending us to the continent for our wedding trip --- all four of us, with servants. Quentin said it had to be all 'four' of us for we would all be Balfours. He is so witty!"

Elisabeth, feeling a bit overwhelmed by the two of them chattering away, said, "Shall we go inside and have some refreshment?"

They helped her carry her flowers indoors and took them off to the kitchen for Rose to arrange, then returned and announced in almost perfect unison, "Cook said that she'll have Rose bring something right in after she sets the flowers in a bucket of water." With that bit of information given, they sat down and began to talk with their mother and great-aunt about the wedding arrangements --- the topic foremost on their minds.

In a matter of minutes, Rose arrived with a tray holding four tall glasses and a pitcher of cold lemonade from the spring house, plates of ginger biscuits, Cook's famous fruit tarts, and slices of lemon cake with a bowl of clabbered cream to spoon on it.

The girls were enchanted and began playing hostess, pouring and passing out the lemonade and bakery to Elisabeth and Daphne. Watching them, Elisabeth was reminded of all the tea parties in which the two of them had played hostess when they were little girls, with their dolls and stuffed toys as the guests. Their older brothers had not the patience to sit and pretend that the building blocks from their toy box were slices of cake and the girls were left to make do with the dolls and such, while the boys played outside in the huge garden of the Dower House on the Hastings estate.

As the thoughts slipped through her mind, she found herself remembering those days and feeling the greater happiness she knew here, in this home of her childhood. It was too bad that the girls and Daphne would be staying with Richard Hastings, she thought, but at least she had them for the day and, perhaps, they would come again if they weren't caught up in the excitement of buying things for the weddings. It was difficult for her, a country doctor's daughter, to compete with Daphne's money, position, and panache, but she liked her enough that her compassion for this woman's childless state left her no room for rancor.

In the midst of her musings, she heard the girls addressing her and when she finally let the words filter in, she heard Caroline ask if they might go to the attic and see if there was anything left of their grandmother's wedding attire. Elisabeth led the way upstairs, leaving Daphne in the study with the tray of biscuits and her weak knees.

There were many trunks and ancient armoires in the attic and the gabled windows brought in adequate light for them to look through everything. Elisabeth knew which ones would be unlikely to hold anything they would be looking for and steered them to what she thought was her mother's trunk. To her surprise, it held not only belongings of her mother, but also of her grandmother. The girls were delighted to have handkerchiefs from both of them, then Caroline found two embroidered silk camisoles and asked her mother to which they had belonged. She looked at them and decided, by the style, that one was from each and the girls decided, on the spot, that they would wear them under their wedding dresses.

Then, carrying their trophies, they descended to the study, once more. "Look, Aunt Daffy," Caroline said, "We've found our grandmother and great-grandmother's camisoles and handkerchiefs! They're to be in our weddings!" Daphne, to her credit, was truly excited and happy for them.

They went on the rest of the afternoon in this vein over a tea tray filled with fancy sandwiches, fruit, biscuits and toast with lemon curd, more of the fruit tarts and, of course, tea.

Stirring the cream into her tea, Elisabeth asked if they were staying the night and had mixed feelings when they answered that they were staying at the Hastings estate. With the boys, she already had a houseful and, though the girls' bedroom was available to them, she had nowhere to put up Daphne unless she gave up her bed to her husband's aunt and slept in a room over the stable. Hmmm, she thought, for a moment, wouldn't that be lovely..... Though, perhaps that would be the answer --- one of the boys could sleep there..... Thus, she offered it as a possibility, but their luggage was at Richard's and, since they'd been there two days already, they felt obliged to stay with him rather than hopping about.

And, so it was settled. The polite niceties had been observed and she didn't need to have more guests after all..... Perking up at the thought, she selected another fruit tart and began to converse in earnest, having no more worry over whether she had been quite correct in her duties as a hostess.

By five o'clock, Daphne and the girls were on their way out the door to Daphne's carriage, which had been pulled under a tree along the verge of the drive. Poking her cane up at the coachman, dozing on his perch, she managed to rouse him and, startled, he climbed down in the awareness that he had slept the afternoon away, saying, "Oh dear, oh dear, it's gone evening already."

He fetched the stepstool and helped each of the ladies up, though the twins were quite capable and agile. Then, when all were comfortably settled, he took the reins and off they went toward the road and the Hastings' estate.

Elisabeth watched it all from the drive, smiling first at the sleepy old coachman, then, at the thought that her two lovely daughters had fallen into such a fortunate set of circumstances --- a great-aunt to fund them and enjoy their company, two suitors who had every indication of being head over heels in love with them, and the suitors were brothers and gentlemen!

When she returned to the house, John stuck his head out of the parlor and asked, "Have they gone?"

"Yes, dearest love, you need not see them until the weddings," she replied.

"Oh, I did not mean that I was avoiding them, I merely stayed out from underfoot to leave the conversation to the ladies," he said, with a grin.

Elisabeth smiled back, knowing that grin. This man had more than conversation on his mind….. Pushing the door open and entering the room, she closed it behind her and stood there, waiting, but not for long….. He enveloped her in his arms and kissed her long and hard, lifting her skirt with one hand, and finding the opening in her pantalets waiting for his hand to enter and touch her more intimately. When the kiss finally ended, both of them broke away, breathless, their bodies reacting to the sensuality of the contact.

She found her voice first and said, "The boys will go to a dinner party and musical evening tonight and should be coming home to change into dinner attire any moment, but they will surely be late coming back after the affair --- and we shall have the garden entirely to ourselves."

The boys returned, then went --- all three of them --- to an affair over an hour's ride away, even before dinner was served to Elisabeth and John, who were waiting, almost with bated breath, to be alone. Though the dinner was of Cook's usual high standard, it might as well have been sawdust for all the notice they gave it, preferring to look into each other's eyes, deeply, and allow their fingers to brush up against each other from time to time, or touch knees under the table…..

By the time dinner had ended and they walked into the darkness of the evening garden, they were of one mind and, unfortunately, it wasn't going to happen easily in the garden..... They strolled to the garden's end and, selecting a bench which faced away from the house, giving them the most possible privacy outside of a bedroom, they sat down with John's arm around Elisabeth's shoulders. Looking up at his face, only dimly visible in the fading dusk, she said, "It's all right, John. We're alone, now."

He bent his head to kiss her and his other arm came around to hold her closer, then, he lifted her onto his lap and the kiss became more passionate --- deeper, and insistent.

Her hands found the back of his neck and she ran her fingers up into his hair, as her body became more and more aroused, needing to move, to touch, and to feel him --- all of him.

John's hands were busy, as well --- his exploring fingers having once more discovered the opening in her pantalets and the wetness of the slit concealed therein. They delved into the mysterious depths of her body, touching and feeling, sliding through the slippery wetness and bringing with them a friction which heightened all of their individual sensualities. His fingers, dipping into her, felt as though they were on fire with sensation, feelings that John wanted to experience again with his saber, to slide it into her sheath to the hilt, that point when mound touches mound and their juices blend into unison.

Elisabeth, aroused to the point of small orgasms shaking her body, one after the other, wanted to feel him within her, his manhood, that saber of union, deep with its scabbard and bucking her like an untamed horse until its energy was spent between her thighs and both of them could feel release and contentment.

It was then, that John remembered a hip-high stone retaining wall he sometimes sat on a few feet away and, carrying her to it, sat her there and then, lifting her skirt, ran his hands up and down her thighs a few times, then bared his rigid shaft and, spreading her knees wide in the dark garden, entered her.

She gasped at the feeling, the sudden fullness, as he began to move back and forth, entering and retreating, time and again; the friction building and her passion following suit; her small whimpers stimulating him and bringing the rhythm to a faster pace. A low rumble began in John's throat, almost inaudible, except to her. The muscles in her buttocks began to thrust her pelvis forward, as that sound from his depths signaled his oncoming orgasm, and they finished in a hushed symphony of pleasure. Her body continued reflexively pumping his, long after he had spent the last of his ejaculate, and she had felt the tightening spasms of her own completion.

He stood there, leaning into her for a long time, his arms tightly wrapped around her. Her arms encircled his waist and held him close to her, as well, for that space in time unwilling to allow separation into two individual beings. And, in truth, they were not, for, at that moment, they were temporarily conjoined at the hip.

Finally, she sighed and he followed suit. Sliding out of her, he stopped the flow of his ejaculate from her with a handkerchief from his pocket and returned her dress to its normal position, then lifted her from the wall and stood her on the ground. He brushed off the back of her skirt where it had touched the dry soil to make certain there were no marks left and they returned to the bench.

They sat there in the dark for another hour, talking and planning, reviewing their hopes and dreams as lovers do, knowing that they must be patient, yet reaching for that star when the opportunity arose to experience intimacy with each other. Had she been a virgin girl, she would not have dared, but, as a widow, there was no physical barrier to the consummation of their intense attraction.

In time, when they felt that their fires had been adequately banked, they returned to the study and, hearing a sound in the hall Elisabeth called out to Rose and asked for cocoa, citing the chill of the night air. Rose was startled, and asked, "Are you some kind of a medium, ma'am? Cook just asked me to come and see if you want some."

"No, Rose," she answered, with an indulgent smile, "Just a lady who feels a chill in the weather as well as Cook."

John took it all in and, when Rose had left, he asked Elisabeth, "Have you heard of the Fox sisters? I read about them and saw them before I left for England."

"Oh, yes, and Daniel Home, and others," she answered, "But, I believe that everyone has intuition, an ability to know what is unknown. How many times has a mother dropped what she was doing to suddenly go to where her child was and rescue them from danger?"

"I would like to speak with you about this at a later time, when we are not tired and ready for our cocoa," he said, with a grin.

"Of course! I await your pleasure, my love," she retorted, matching his grin.

Then, taking a volume from the bookcase, for she heard Rose's footsteps, she said, "I believe that this should be the next medical treatise you read, John. We could discuss it tomorrow."

At this point, Rose entered with the cocoa --- large steaming cups with froth and a shaker of ground spices, should they care to add flavoring.

"Thank you, Rose, it looks delightful," Elisabeth purred.

"Oh, and it's that good, ma'am. Cook makes it better than anyone!" Rose avowed.

As they waited for their cocoa to cool they chatted --- mainly about Elisabeth's children. She felt great joy in the positive prospects for their futures and John shared in her happiness for many reasons, the first being that she would be more inclined to marry him once their prospects seemed secure and the second being that if they married, he would become their step-father and would have good reason to wish for their success in life.

Finally, it had cooled to the point of 'bearable' and they began to take tiny sips. Then, when she took a larger one and had a cocoa foam moustache, he licked it from her face and, fortunately, heard Rose coming in time to move away.

"We've a bit left over for refills if you like," Rose said, pitcher in her hand.

"Have you and Cook had refills, yet?" Elisabeth asked, and when Rose said they hadn't, she urged her to take it to the kitchen and share it with Cook --- on which advice, Rose left the room smiling like a child at Christmas.

Looking at John, she said, "With these enormous cups, we certainly cannot want more."

He smiled, noting her endearing kindness, knowing that she would have done the same if their cups were small, and his commitment to her rose higher still.

They talked for a little longer, but the hour grew late and soon it was time they must say goodnight. He took her hands and, looking deeply into her eyes, said, "Dearest One, I love you deeply, but what is more important --- I like you, as well. You are everything a man might hope to find --- in the gentleness of your being."

Elisabeth's heart swelled with the love she felt from him, as well as, her own love for him. Their hands brought the energy of that commitment together --- and their eyes. He was for her and she was for him --- that was how it would stay through this lifetime and beyond. Both sensed the truth of it and knew it was right.

As he left through the French doors, he turned back to her, as she followed to lock it behind him, and placed a chaste kiss upon her lips, just one, saying, "Sleep well, my love, sleep well," and then he was gone into the darkness of the night.

She stood there, by the door, looking into the darkness, seeing a bit of her reflection in the glass, and wondering how long it might be before they could be married and show their love openly. Certainly, it would not be before October --- she would not upstage the girls in their happiness. Perhaps, at Christmas, when they could all be together.....

Finally, turning the lantern down until it sputtered and went out, she took a smaller one from the hall table and made her way up the stairs to her bedroom, where, under the covers of her bed, she floated on a sea of bliss, until sleep claimed her.

❧Chapter 14 – Preparations❧

For the balance of that summer the days fairly flew by. With the boys coming and going from outings and parties, then to stay with friends from school, the house in the country was awash with activity. Elisabeth and John lived their quiet lives amidst the confusion, reserving time for themselves --- both there and in the vacant house where they were able to express their love openly. Then, as August waned, the boys were invited to a fortnight of hunting and fishing at the estate of a schoolmate of George's and, finally, Elisabeth and John were as before --- lovers, alone.

The preparations for the girls' wedding(s) were going ahead without so much as a finger being lifted by Elisabeth. Between great-aunt Daphne and Mrs. Balfour, the boys' mother, all was coming to fruition. Elisabeth was just as happy, perhaps happier, not being consulted --- and, since she was not the one paying for the festivities, she felt those who paid should have their say and design the event as they wished it to be. For her, the happiness of her daughters was all she asked, remembering her own marriage to an older man who had little idea of the needs or thoughts of a female half his age --- a child bride he thought of as a pretty doll for him to show off, and who would bear him an heir, at least, or perhaps more children --- a notion which came to fruition much like the queen who was exactly one year younger to the day and had produced nine children.

The girls were being married from the Hastings estate, a perfect venue, with its quaint old chapel and the large dower house for additional guests. John had agreed to escort Elisabeth and the boys would be available, since they didn't begin classes until October, though, as undergraduates, they must arrive the Thursday before Michaelmas at the latest. The girls wanted a Saturday, so as to not inconvenience the pastor and to give the guests time to recover from any excesses at the reception before returning to work. Thus, they had chosen September 17, 1854, a day almost three months after their sixteenth birthday on June 28th, which was, by coincidence, also the sixteenth anniversary of Queen Victoria's coronation.

It was during this time that Miss Violet became their confidant. Sensing how much they loved each other, she asked Elisabeth one day, while John was taking some water to Abernathy, "Do you ever plan to marry him?"

Elisabeth was startled, then looked keenly at her and, seeing no malice, she answered, "Knowing that you are no gossip, I feel that I may tell you we are secretly engaged. It would be a gross unkindness to steal a march on my own daughters by marrying before them and we are old enough to wait until after they have had their special day and have found their wedded happiness."

Miss Violet began to cry softly and Elisabeth put her arms around her in alarm, but Miss Violet said, "You are so kind and thoughtful of everyone. I am proud and blessed to call you friend --- would that I had married and had a daughter such as you. My young man went to fight Napoleon and never returned and, with the dearth of men, I never found another, though I suppose that I never truly looked."

Elisabeth replied, "You shall be my special guest at the weddings, for the girls have always loved you, and you have ever treated them kindly."

Miss Violet could hardly believe what she had heard and her eyes began to sparkle like street lamps in a city on new fallen snow. She would have a new dress made and a hat..... Then, she thought to ask whether it was a garden wedding or a church wedding and what Elisabeth thought appropriate to wear. Elisabeth became a part of her excitement and suddenly realised that she had not thought of having a dress made, herself. What had she been thinking of?

Together, they went to Miss Violet's bedroom to look through her wardrobe. She had many beautiful dresses, albeit of a former style, but one which was in the early artistic mode struck Elisabeth's eye and she pointed out that it could be made very contemporary with little refurbishing, and thus, would be much less expense than a new gown. Miss Violet grew more and more excited about the prospect and, finally, Elisabeth had to quiet her, saying, "We have plenty of time," lest her pulse become unsteady.

Next, they discussed a hat and, though she had many which would suit, she remained adamant on that issue --- a lady must have a new hat from time to time and always for special occasions. There was a milliner in Tring who made them for the gentry and Elisabeth suggested that they visit the woman's shop together, for she would want a new hat, as well..... With that settled, they returned to the parlor where John was awaiting them, as he read a book from Miss Violet's small library, *Mesmerism or the system of inter-relations. Theory and applications of animal magnetism, a translation from the original German.*

"What have you found?" Liz asked, seeing a book in his hand.

"A book by Mesmer," John answered.

"If you treat her nicely, perhaps Miss Violet will loan it you," she retorted.

"Oh, but of course I would," their friend chimed in.

"Now, now, Miss Violet, you must be careful of your things --- I might be a robber, after all," John said, with a smile and a twinkle in his eyes.

"Oh, you tease!" exclaimed Miss Violet.....

By that time, all three of them were laughing and Miss Violet remembered that she had not offered them tea, which error she promptly corrected.

Helping her carry in the tea, Elisabeth said, "Miss Violet and I are planning to shop in Tring, for wedding hats, tomorrow. Would you mind riding atop the box to accompany us?"

"No, but if you drive very slowly, I could as easily walk ....," he answered.

"You have a good point," she conceded, smiling at him, then returned to pouring the tea.

Thus it was that, the following day, John collected Miss Violet early and brought her to Elisabeth's house, whence the trio set out for Tring to look for hats.

Abernathy was pleased to plod the mile or so into Tring for a change and, holding the pace, John conversed with the ladies as they went along at that slower pace.

In less than half an hour, they had arrived and stopped first at a small inn for an early luncheon and rest. Afterward, they headed straight for the milliner's shop where Elisabeth and Miss Violet found styles and colors to suit them. The shopkeeper had designed them in such a fashion as to accommodate different color schemes easily and she quickly altered the models to conform to their desires.

With a large hatbox in each hand, lightweight of course, John accompanied them back to the buggy and waited there, with Abernathy, for the ladies to return from a store showing beautiful silk shawls in the window. After half an hour they returned with two more packages, which would fit into the box, and told him that they had finished their shopping. All seemed of the opinion that it was time to return to Little Tring and environs.....

Retracing their steps, the caravan set out --- with John carrying the two hatboxes. The return trip took a little more effort, for it was nearing the dinner hour and the shadows were becoming longer. On the way, Miss Violet invited them to sup with her, but they declined, asking her pardon, for Rose had told them Cook was roasting something special --- a haunch of venison..... Then, Elisabeth said, "You could stop there and eat with us..... John could take you home in the buggy, after, and surely be back before dark."

Miss Violet was pleased to eat with them --- and enjoy venison!

John smiled at the two ladies, for both were dear to him. The one, as a lover and future wife, and the other as though she were a maiden aunt.

Abernathy was set to graze at the verge of the driveway while John carried the hatboxes and packages from the box indoors and left them in the study. Rose informed them that dinner would be ready momentarily and was pleased to see Miss Violet. She hurried to the kitchen to tell Cook that there would be one more cover for dinner and another mouth to sample the result of her excellent culinary skills. Rose always knew how to say things in a manner that brought out the best in Cook.....

Soon, the three were seated and sampling Cook's recipe. When Elisabeth summoned her --- and told her how much they had enjoyed it --- she fairly glowed. With hair askew from the humidity of the kitchen and sweat beads forming on her forehead, though she had wiped it on her apron before coming to the dining room, she thanked them over and over again, when Elisabeth said, with a smile in Miss Violet's direction, that she was certain that the lady could not resist telling Baylor's shop boy about Cook's ways with venison when next he delivered to her.

In the kitchen, Cook told Rose, "A reputation, that's what it is. Before those weddings, every soul in Tring and beyond will know that I'm the best. Now, Rose, take those fruit tarts and trifle to them --- and then the coffee. The heavy cream, mind you, girl."

With a smile, Rose obediently played the corporal for her general and the aforementioned items quickly made their way into the dining room.

Seeing the sun nearing its time of setting, Elisabeth hurried their dessert a bit, not wanting John to drive the country lanes in the dark, lest he lose his way. And, as he and Miss Violet set out, she cautioned him to spend the night there, should darkness overtake them, for Abernathy was growing old and depended on light to see him home.

John urged the horse to a good clip and they had deposited Miss Violet, her new hat and shawl, as well as a small paper bag of fruit tarts, on her doorstep, then turned around and made it back to the stable in under half an hour. Abernathy, none the worse for wear, nuzzled John's hand when he offered him oats and ate every bite, then began on the hay, eating the oats in his feedbox alternately. John curried him as he ate, then removed the duster and went up to the house where he knew Elisabeth awaited him.

He washed up in the rain barrel in the garden, before entering the study through the French doors, and stood there admiring her, poring over her ledgers, through the glass panes before he ever touched the handle.

When he stepped into the study, she was startled, at first, then, seeing it was John, she calmed herself. He crossed to the desk and, listening for Rose's footsteps, bent to kiss her neck where the nape showed above the collar of her dress. She sighed a sigh which ended in a near groan and bent her head forward to expose more of her neck to his mouth. He obliged by raining kisses on it --- and her ears, as well..... Then, she bent her head back and looked up at him, inviting a kiss on her mouth, which he also obliged, with pleasure.

"Let us adjourn to the garden," she whispered, her voice husky with emotion.....

Had they not exercised restraint, they would have flown out the door to their bench, but instead, they spoke of inconsequential matters until they were over halfway to the bench, then continued in a leisurely fashion toward it, with his arm around her waist as they walked.

Elisabeth was finding it difficult to walk with his fingers lightly stroking her side where his arm encircled her, for the light touches aroused her to a fever pitch. The thought ran through her mind that, had her husband had a tenth of the skills and sheer physical magnetism John had, she might have had fifteen children before he died. Oh, this man, she thought, how much I love him --- and how easily he can bring me to want to be ravished by him more than anything else.....

When they reached the bench, they embraced and his hand slid up her waist to the underside of her breast and cupped, then squeezed it. She arched her back over his arm, glanced skyward, and he turned toward her slightly, then, brought his lips down to her waiting mouth and finally both of his hands around front to her lust-swollen breasts. They cupped those promontories much like limpets suctioned onto a seawall as he kissed her mouth deeply and, at last, she put her arms around his waist and rubbed her hands up and down his back before lowering them to the swell of his buttocks beneath his trousers. She could feel the mount between her legs aching with desire for the sensation of his member sliding into the recess there and the pulsing rhythm flowing through it was akin to some primitive fertility rite in a far away tropical island paradise. The drum within her beat time to her heart and her hips began to move forward and back as they urged him to do it, as well. But for their clothing, they could already be copulating, judging by their movements.

Suddenly, he sat on the bench, unbuttoned his trousers, and, turning her around, lifted her skirt over her back, and, through the opening in her pantalets, settled her on his rigid member. After a moment's shock, she noted that she could put a leg on either side of his lap as he leaned back on the bench and, holding onto his knees under her skirt in front of her, she could lift herself up and down on the staff she was impaled upon so sensuously.

Oh, she thought, this is good, this is very good, as she went up and down, enveloping his manhood each time she sat back on it. Under her skirt, John had his right arm around her hips and was gently squeezing and rubbing her juice-covered little button with the fingers of his right hand, while, above the dress, he was squeezing her left breast and nipple with the other, meanwhile, thrusting his pelvis toward her every time she sat back on him.

The recess within her slit grasped his manhood with all the force of a calf suckling its mother's teats and encouraged him to rise higher, to breath deeper, to pump against her until he found his release inside of her, spurting his juices in the forceful manner that she, a woman, could not do with her own and bringing her to her orgasm with his rigid staff and his talented, loving hands.

They stayed in that position for a long time, her body bent forward at the waist, until, finally, she leaned back onto his chest and he cupped both of her breasts with his hands, feeling the large, swollen nipples through the cloth of her dress. It was extremely erotic and he found himself being aroused in spite of having spent himself so recently.

Surprised, but pleased, she could feel him growing hard again within her, energy or no, and she moved up and down on his manhood as she had before. Then, she stood up, turned around, and, kneeling in front of him, she sucked his member into her mouth as far as it would go and began to press it firmly against the roof of her mouth with her tongue. He began to moan softly, more like a groan, an uuuhhh, uuuhhhhhuhhuhh, sound, as the sensation moved to a new level. He had not done this before, so soon, and had not known that he could. Her mouth continued suckling at his groin, her fingertips pinching his nipples lightly, then, her hands finding and squeezing his buttocks, and, all the time, with her mouth, that talented, insistent mouth, sucking and nibbling, licking and sucking on him again.

He tried to relax into the orgasm when it came, but it was too big, too hard, to minimize. It hit him with all the force of an avalanche and it was nearly a quarter of an hour before he could talk. Elisabeth kept licking him like a mother cat cleans her kittens, light licks, so that he didn't spasm each time her tongue touched the sensitive head of his staff. He sat there, immobile, his brain saying it had never suspected that feeling like this was possible.

She sat next to him, eventually, then snuggled close. He didn't even have the energy to lift an arm or straighten his posture, much less embrace her. His mind was willing --- and wanting --- he simply could not make his body obey......

An hour later, he was able to move, to stand, to embrace Elisabeth, then kiss her, escort her to the French door --- and slowly walk to his rooms over the stable.

❧Chapter 15 – Countdown❧

Elisabeth lay there in her bed looking at the patterns of morning sunlight on the bedroom walls. Time was passing quickly --- unusual, for it often seems to slow down when an event is anticipated. She had decided that she would see the dressmaker and order a new dress for the wedding --- she had good dresses, but, after much thought, felt that it was incumbent upon the mother of the brides to wear something new and elegant. She decided on a dark royal blue, John's favorite color, and one which would complement her fair skin and light hair exceptionally well --- to say nothing of her new hat.

This was the day they would go into Aylesbury to have the measurements taken and she planned to carry a dress with her which was of a style she favored to inspire the dressmaker…..

When she had dressed, she descended to the breakfast room and found John there, waiting. Rose had brought him a cup of coffee, but he asked her to wait breakfast until Elisabeth was at the table.

As they ate Cook's excellent sausages, poached eggs, and toast, they went over their plans for the day --- the shops they must visit to buy cooking supplies for Cook's larder, not available in Tring, the dressmaker, of course, and the haberdasher to look at some things for John, as well as, the bookseller she ordered from, for she had more ideas for additions to John's reading.

When they had finished, they set out in the buggy, enjoying the beautiful summer morning. In an hour and a half, they had made their way to the shops of Aylesbury and found the one Elisabeth sought. Leaving Abernathy outside in the shade of the building, they stepped into the coolness of the shop and were greeted by the dressmaker, herself.

She was English, not French --- Mistress Caldwell --- nor even one who pretended to be French in order to gull her customers. Her training had been in the convent schools and her stitchery was perfection itself. She could design, make patterns, and sew with the best of the French seamstresses, but her preference was in the simple and elegant lines of the artistic mode and she had no patience with the hoops and falderals that made women look like fools, to her mind, taking commissions for those garments only from her very favorite customers who could not be convinced otherwise and, with annoyance, those who paid an obscene price --- in advance.

She liked Elisabeth and had been known to show up at her small infirmary from time to time in spite of there being one in Aylesbury. She also liked Elisabeth's taste in clothing --- simple lines and understated elegance. When Elisabeth told her their mission, she congratulated her enthusiastically on the girls' matches and asked if the purpose of her visit was to fashion a mother-of-the-brides dress. Finding she had guessed correctly, she pulled out color swatches she knew that Elisabeth would like and began drawing the design of a potential ensemble in an artist's sketchbook.

Elisabeth asked John to fetch the dress she had brought with her --- and her hat from the buggy. In a trice, he was back with them --- as well as a book to while away the time with.

Finding a comfortable chair placed in a quiet corner, he surmised that he was not the first male to wait there while the ladies discussed fashion and seated himself with his volume. Meanwhile, the artisan worked diligently with Elisabeth on the design for her dress.

After nearly an hour, Elisabeth called to him, saying, "Oh, John, I think she has it! Come, tell me what you think of this."

Putting his thumb between the pages to hold his place, he carried the book to the other side of the shop where he was to be shown what had made her exclaim with such delight, then, upon seeing the drawing, he nodded in agreement, and said, "I do believe you're correct. It's more than lovely. You will not outshine your daughters with their bows and lace, but you will be elegant, very elegant. That shade of blue will be especially attractive on you, in my opinion."

Good man, she thought --- he is always remembering to maintain the distance of propriety in public. Then, in her mind, she agreed: the deep royal blue silk, better for late summer than the velvet of the dress she had brought as an example, would indeed be elegant and portray her in her best light.

The dressmaker took her current measurements and noted them on the design --- already looking at the drawing and tilting her head as though thinking of the cut. She spoke up, telling Elisabeth that it should be two weeks and they agreed on an appointment for fitting only a little longer than two weeks later.

As she and John were leaving, Elisabeth remembered to ask for a fringed shawl of the same fabric, lest the evening air chill her on the way back to Little Tring after the wedding. Then, as an afterthought, she sent John back inside to ask that a matching small bag with beading be made for her to carry a few things.

Having completed their adventure in ladies fashion, they decided that a meal was in order and selected a small restaurant near the canal --- and its trade. Food might be fresher here, they reasoned, and they wanted to watch the boats traveling up and down; loading and unloading cargo.

They found a little public house, which served the shoppers looking to find a bargain fresh from the boats; very cosy. It had not so many patrons as the Kings Head Inn, but they enjoyed the quiet as they ate the simple meal of bangers and mash and discussed the girls' wedding.

"Do you approve of the dress?" Elisabeth asked.

"Certainly," he replied, attempting to appear aloof to anyone watching.

"The fabric feels so rich and has a wonderful hand," she continued, wondering why he had become so taciturn.

"I fear I am no connoisseur of female garments," he answered.

Taken aback, she wondered if he was teasing her or annoyed at having waited so long in the shop, but after a moment of silence realised that he was trying to be inconspicuous. It occurred to her that she was seated against the wall and could see the entire room, but, seated across from her, he could see nothing but her and the trophy plaques on the wall behind her, so he didn't know that the only other patrons were two pensioners seated at the bar deep in conversation with the tap man.

"We are not being watched, John," she whispered.

Startled, he was silent for a moment and then smiled that smile which twisted her heart into little knots of emotion. So beautiful it was, that she wanted to cry and laugh at the same time, grab him and dance in circles, run naked through sunlit meadows, and lie with him in a leafy bower somewhere deep in a forest grotto. Unable to speak for fear of her voice cracking, she extended her shaking hand and touched his.

It was as though an electric shock ran through them at that moment, for each jerked slightly, but the contact remained. He moved his hand to cover hers and looked deeply into her eyes as though he were reading her soul. She knew in that moment that she would follow this man to the ends of the earth, no matter what hardship or privation they might encounter, no matter what censure or trials would be their lot. Their lot --- there, she had thought it. It was no longer John or Elisabeth, it was we, and us.....

Customers came and went as the day passed, but still the two of them sat and chatted. Finally, they could delay no longer or they would be driving the country lanes in darkness, so they left the inn and returned to the buggy where Abernathy had so patiently waited, all the while eating oats out of a bag hanging from his halter.

The journey home was serene; with their bodies side by side, thighs touching, they were in their own cocoon of emotion and it seemed that nothing could intrude on that moment.

When they arrived home and drove down the drive to put Abernathy in his stall, they teased and touched each other, but it was as though they were floating on a cloud of love --- they were other than themselves and somehow detached from their humanness. They dined and walked in the garden as well --- all the time sailing on that cloud and never touching in to port.

In parting for the night, they kissed deeply and thoroughly, each promising the other that their day would come soon and their sleep that night was filled with dreams of happy days in each other's company.

ⰷChapter 16 – Waitingⰸ

Elisabeth awoke the following morning still feeling as though she was floating. She admonished herself for the frivolity of being unable to control oneself, but it served no purpose --- she couldn't seem to feel that her feet were on the ground. With the preparations for the wedding proceeding at a rapid pace and little left up to her, it seemed as though nothing was waiting for her to think it through. She lay there under the coverlet, looking at the bed curtains --- and beyond them the early sunlight filtering through the windows --- and thought to herself: why must time seem to be going so slow for John and I while it seems to be going so fast for the girls?

When she had pondered the question for some time with little enlightenment, she saw that the light was becoming brighter and remembered that she had a day filled with tasks ahead of her. Putting her musings aside, she pulled back the coverlet and made for the clock on her bureau to assess the time: half past eight! She gasped, and slipped out of her nightgown, quickly folded and tucked it under the pillow, then washed herself and dressed for the day.

John looked up from his book as she entered the alcove of the breakfast nook, smiled and said, "Hello, sleepyhead."

A smile quickly came to her face, illuminating her being further, and she said, "Oh, dear, I resemble that remark!"

John chuckled and replied, as he stood to help her with her chair, "Me, too --- I arrived only a few moments ago."

At this admission, she positively glowed. Her husband would never have admitted to being late for anything. Oh, she thought, I love this man --- as John pushed her chair toward the table.

Lifting a cover, she found that Cook had been very busy. Steaming hot sausages and fresh shirred eggs were under one. Meanwhile John exposed the contents hiding under the other cover, finding it harbored thick slices of buttered toast, hot rolls and fresh fruit tarts. An 'aaaah' escaped from Elisabeth's throat as she savored the delicious scents and John echoed her sentiments, breathing deeply to absorb the delectable aromas escaping from the serving dishes.

They grinned at each other, then they filled their plates, and Elisabeth poured the steaming coffee as John spread jam over a slice of the thick toast. Finishing the cups off with a generous bit of cream, she asked if he cared for sugar or honey in his and as he considered it and finished chewing his bite of toast, she turned to her own breakfast and began to eat.

"I believe I'll have sugar today," he said, with such a comedic countenance that she was sent into peals of laughter, then began coughing.

When she had regained her composure, she looked at him sternly, saying, "Mr. Bishop, there will be no more of that at the breakfast table, lest you cause your mentor an injury," then looked at him with a quixotic lifting of the corners of her mouth which told him quite clearly that she was flirting with him.

"Ah, my dearest instructor," he retorted, "There are things I would like to cause you, but never would I wish to cause you an injury." At this pronouncement, he slipped his hand under the table and squeezed her knee.

She gratified him with a somewhat muffled squeak, then said, "Mr. Bishop, I do believe that we need to visit some of the tenants today."

John chuckled low in his throat, then answered, lest Rose was coming to see if they needed more food, "Yes, Mistress Hastings, I would be pleased to see how the Martin's repairs are progressing." Then, with a wink to her, he said much lower, "And, how fare the dust covers at the vacant cottage."

Elisabeth blushed, then smiled. Her glow had increased with his wink and anticipation was in the air.

Amid more bantering, they finished their breakfast and made preparations for the trip to the Martin farm. Hearing of their destination, Cook sent Rose to them with a basket containing small jars of jam, hot rolls, and a small pot of beef stew for Miss Violet, for she surmised that they would be stopping there, as well. Seeing the kindness Cook was bestowing on her behalf, Elisabeth said, "Rose, please tell Cook that I thank her for her thoughtfulness and be certain to tell her that Miss Violet will much appreciate a respite from her own cooking." Then, moving the contents a bit, she noticed the raw marrow bone for Spot and shared a smile with Rose --- the dog would be happy with his good fortune.

By mid-morning, the buggy was swaying along the country lane at a modest clip toward Miss Violet's, the pair having decided to stop there first with the basket, then drive onward to the Martin farm and backtrack to the empty house before returning home. In short order they were rapping at Miss Violet's door, behind which Spot was voicing his excitement with yips and whines. Miss Violet was hard put to open the door while he pushed up against it, but finally, and as sternly as she could muster, she said, "NO! Go to your bed, Spotty!" and suddenly the door was pulled open as the dog gave way.

In the sunlight her beaming face was barely eclipsed, so happy was she to see them. Then, spying the basket, she clapped her hands and fairly chortled, "A basket for me?"

Spot mistook the clapping for a signal to leave his bed and come to welcome the guests, so all was betwixt and between for a few minutes as they sorted out dog from people and basket, but finally they were seated at Miss Violet's table, water for tea was heating on the hob, the basket was on the counter, and Spot was ensconced upon John's feet under the table.

John and Spot listened to the ladies chatting about the news since their last meeting. Elisabeth recounted the previous day's adventures in Aylesbury, down to the last detail of the new dress on order, including the fringed shawl and the bag for her extra hairpins, a few mints, and a handkerchief. Miss Violet was the perfect friend, listening to the very end and making all of the correct ahs and ohs in the right places. John watched them conversing and thought how like a dance it was. There was something lulling about it and he almost fell asleep, when suddenly Elisabeth startled him with, "Isn't that so, John?"

"If you say it is, it must be," he answered, "For you would never fabricate an untruth."

Elisabeth nodded, then noted that, while he had agreed with her, he had no notion of what she had asked him to verify. Tilting her head and looking at him quixotically, she asked, "Have you been sleeping, John?"

Unable to prevaricate, he grinned and answered, "Just dozing to the dulcet tones of women's voices....."

The ladies laughed and Elisabeth countered, "Flattery will get you nowhere, my dear, we weren't born last Monday! Perhaps you should rest before we continue our errands."

John quickly denied needing more sleep and Miss Violet took up his cause, saying, "Ah, the poor man is undoubtedly reading too many of those books in your father's library into the wee hours!"

John smiled shamefacedly, for such had been the case.

Elisabeth grinned at the pair and then laughed. Soon they were all laughing again and Spot came out from under the table to see what was going on, then began yipping along with them. This engendered a new round of laughter which lasted until the kettle began to whistle.....

John jumped up to take it off the hob and Elisabeth got out of her chair before Miss Violet could raise herself, saying, "We're the servants today, dearest --- just sit back and enjoy the service."

Feeling a bit strange at first, the sweet lady relaxed into her friends' tea party, thinking how wonderful it was to have such a kind landlord and friend.

John carried the tea tray to the table and Elizabeth served. It was no high society affair, but they sat there in the kitchen enjoying the tea, biscuits, and fruit tarts baked by Miss Violet herself, just the same.

All too soon the time came for Elisabeth and John to leave. They had had their few hours and after hugs, good-byes, and promises to return soon, they turned Abernathy's head toward the road again and in the direction of the Martin farm, waving to Miss Violet and her faithful companion.

As they proceeded along the road, conversation turned to their next destination and what repairs they might see. "What do you think of Martin?" Elisabeth asked John.

He answered, "A stalwart fellow."

"Yes, and you're a man of few words," she retorted, smiling at him.

"Yes, I suppose so, however, that leaves more time for the ladies to have their say," he said, with a grin and a twinkle in his eyes which spoke louder than words of what she could expect later.

A little tingle rushed through her body and it was as though the place where their thighs touched, as the buggy made its way down the lane, was on fire. With both hands occupied holding the reins, John could not touch her and the tension of anticipation mounted. Shortly, they arrived at the Martin farm.

On hearing the buggy, Martin's wife came to the door and asked them in, saying, "Himself will be up from the field shortly. May I offer y' refreshment?"

Elisabeth told her that they had only just come from Miss Violet's and had enjoyed a tea there.

On hearing that, Mrs. Martin said, "Ah, then, y've had better than I can offer, for Miss Violet's fruit tarts are the finest here'bouts. Himself goes over to help her betimes and she always sends a packet home wi' him."

Elisabeth smiled and nodded her agreement, then, seeing her tenant framed in the doorway, said, "Here he is."

Martin, proud of the repairs he had made, showed them everything: the patches to the dormer roofs, the new door on the barn, the new windowpanes which had replaced cracked ones, and the new hen house, which was his pride and joy. "We'll have no foxes making off with any of *these* hens!" he exclaimed as he showed them the workmanship and design innovations.

Elisabeth smiled at this and praised him for his hard work and craftsmanship. At this point, John weighed in with a few thoughts of his own. "Martin, this is well done. If you have any time available, perhaps you can earn some cash by working on other properties." John looked at Elisabeth and, seeing her nod, continued, "Mrs. Hastings has other properties occupied by ladies which need some repair, as well and I'm certain she would prefer to put the work out to a local man."

Mr. Martin, rubbing his chin with thumb and forefinger, thought for a moment then said, "I can do it. You mean the Blakelys, Miss Kate and Miss Violet, of a certainty. They're good women and good cooks," he said looking upward as though remembering the dishes he'd tasted at some past social event. "I would do my Christian duty and help them without pay, but s'truth the money would be handy." He nodded his head toward the kitchen where Mrs. Martin was busy cooking, saying, "The love of me life wants to visit her family and since I have the farm to attend to, it must needs be the train for her when we have a little set back and even with that I'll lose a half day's work for my trouble."

John began to discuss the repairs at the properties he had mentioned with Martin and Elisabeth, seeing that the men were fully engrossed, wandered inside to visit with Mrs. Martin for a space. Finding the lady deep in preparation for baking, Elisabeth sat down to keep her company. " Does your family live nearby?" she asked.

"Oh, no, me sister married above herself and he has properties. She took our parents and brothers to live w' her; a place near Birmingham --- in the countryside there'bout," came the swift reply.

"All of them?" Elisabeth asked.

"Every last man jack of them!" Mrs. Martin retorted with a hint of latent annoyance in her voice at the inconsiderate act of decampment, all the more so due to it being her sister's new affluence at the root of it.

"When did you see them last?" Elisabeth questioned, to maintain the flow of conversation.

"Gone six years now or more," Mrs. Martin allowed, then murmured, "I miss 'em."

"Have they visited you?" Elisabeth gently prodded.

"Not a one!" came the succinct reply, "And they ain't even seen the girls nor have I clapped eyes on their children."

Elisabeth thought for a moment and concluded that this was partly a case of hurt feelings and partly of genuine longing for family. That was the moment in which she had an idea.

She began hesitantly with, "Would you visit them if you were able?"

Mrs. Martin stopped her stirring for a moment as if mesmerized. Then, with her head cocked at an angle and looking somewhat upward as if for divine guidance, she said, "Yes, I would, if only to say how put out I am w' the lot of 'em." She stood there silently for a moment, then continued, "But I do love 'em, 'tis true, and I would be that happy to see 'em again."

With this affirmation of her suspicions, Elisabeth took the bull by the horns and asked if she would like to visit them before winter set in.

"Oh, yes!" Mrs. Martin said, with vigor, "But we haven't enough set aside for a trip and, besides, I'm needed here to cook and wash."

Elisabeth, meanwhile, was contriving a plan. She would send Mrs.

Martin and the girls to visit and she could ask Miss Violet to prepare the evening meal for Mr. Martin and the boys. One could go and fetch it every day since they were close by. After all, Mr. Martin had said that she was a good cook….. Then, she became aware that the girls were not anywhere in sight and asked after them, since they seemed too young for school…..

"Oh, they're in the attic playing among the trunks left there by someone; old gowns and such. I hope it ain't wrong of 'em," Mrs. Martin replied, "I don't let 'em do it unless they've bathed."

Elisabeth laughed her delightful, tinkling, infectious laugh and Mrs. Martin began to laugh with her. Hearing that, the girls came hurrying down from the attic in antique hats and wraps to see who was there and soon all were laughing as gaily as children.

Once the girls had migrated outdoors, sans their finery, to say hello to John, Elisabeth broached the subject of her idea to their mother, cautiously beginning again with, "Mrs. Martin, if you had the money would you visit your family?"

The lady stared at her, not comprehending at first, then, answered, "Of course I would, but I haven't enough money --- farming takes it all at times."

With this, Elisabeth mustered her strength and said, "What if I helped?"

Mrs. Martin looked at her blankly for a few moments, then told her flatly that Mr. Martin would never stand for it.

Elisabeth knew that men were often prideful and understood the predicament she had encountered, but she was not one to give in easily and resolved to approach the matter in another way, asking Mrs. Martin if the girls had been christened, yet.

"No, Mistress, they haven't," Mrs. Martin said with some trepidation evident on her face (was the landlady very devout, she wondered).

"Well, there you have it!" Elisabeth exclaimed, "It shall be my christening gift to them, that you should take them to your family to be christened!"

Mrs. Martin's face showed her exceeding admiration for the utter brilliance of Elisabeth's idea: Mr. Martin couldn't refuse a christening gift, neither could he refuse to allow the girls to be sent to family for that ceremony. Both women sat there so impressed with the inspiration that the baking was set aside and forgotten completely.....

When the men entered, Elisabeth greeted the girls' father with, "Mr. Martin, do I understand that your daughters have never been christened?"

"Why, why no they haven't, Mistress," the poor man stammered, clearly out of his depth.

"Do you object to the practice?" she asked with a look of incredulity.

"Oh, no!" he uttered emphatically, for fear she would think him a heathen.

"Then, it's settled," she declared imperiously, "As my christening gift, I am sending them and their mother to her family for the deed to be done next week. You and the boys may go if you wish but, with harvest in the offing, I suspect that you'd do best to stay here. I'll ask Miss Violet to prepare the evening meal for you and the boys while Mrs. Martin and the girls are away if that would be to your liking."

Mr. Martin, trumped on all scores and with no way in which he could refuse a Christian offering, agreed to all she had said --- relieved that she hadn't remembered to ask if the boys had been christened.....

There was not much more to be said so, settling on a day, Elisabeth and John got into the buggy and, waving at the girls playing tag in the drive, headed Abernathy toward the lane.

Once away, they both laughed at her imperiousness, John shaking his head in amazement at her bravado and saying, "One would have thought you were The Queen, herself."

Elisabeth smiled a tiny secret smile as she pretended to look out over the fields behind the hedgerows, thinking to herself that her father hadn't raised any timid Miss.

It was not long before the buggy was driving up to the stable of their private retreat and, once inside, Abernathy was happy to quietly chew on the oats they had brought with them.

Elisabeth unlocked the door of the house and she and John stepped inside and into the vaulted foyer. Once the door was closed, he scooped her into his arms and rained kisses upon her face, then her neck and what he could reach of her bosom. Throwing her head back, she managed in a husky voice, "Oh, John, …..my John, …..yes, oh yes….."

Lifting her off her feet, he carried her to the bedroom they had used before and, with one hand, pulled back the dust cover to expose the sheets they had left on it the last time they were there, then lay her on the bed as tenderly as though she were made of the most fragile glass.

She looked up at him with love in her wide open eyes; there for him to see in all its glory. Looking at her this way, he felt very tender toward her; a tenderness beyond what he'd experienced in their other couplings. This was different: he had seen a new depth to her character and the beauty of her spirit and was touched, himself.

He removed their clothes, then lay beside her and held her for a long while before he began to stroke her body --- reverently at the beginning, then with more abandon as the passion rose in each of them --- and, finally, they began their lovemaking in earnest.

He ran his hands down the length of her body and brought them to her nipples to pinch them lightly, then more insistently as she began to run her hands along his chest and upper arms. He kissed her deeply and she responded with all of the passion she knew, opening her mouth to his wantonly. She needed to have him deep within her and her hips were beginning to dance back and forth, then from side to side in her excitement, but he wanted her to be even more aroused before he entered.

He lay her on her back in the middle of the bed and, kneeling between her legs, he began to suckle her nipples first, then trailing his mouth down her torso to her belly, he found the furry mound at the top of her thighs. His mouth was ravenous and he suckled there and licked until she experienced an orgasm so strong that she bit the sheet to stifle a scream. As it subsided, he licked her furry mound and its hidden button and recesses gently, ever so gently, just enough to send shocks through her body without being too much for her to bear, for the orgasm had made her very sensitive.

Then, he went back to her nipples and began to suckle at them again, but this time he had other plans. His manhood had asserted itself and, though he had managed to avoid ejaculating up to that point, he knew he must soon be inside of her and, rubbing the tip of it along the furrow between her thighs, he sank it slowly and gently into her furry mound. She moaned a long oooooohhhhhh as she felt its length penetrate her, filling her to the core while her muscles contracted, pulling it deeper.

John began a rhythmic entering and retreating, the ritual practiced by all of humankind, since the dawn of time. As he sank into her, the sounds she made deep in her throat were a stimulant to his ardor, the sharp intake of breath as he entered her and the 'ooooohhh' as he slipped himself down into that cleft deeper and deeper. Finally, he could hold back no longer and, as he convulsed above her, spending his seed within her, he, too, vocalized his completion --- a-ah-a-a-aah---hah.....

He lay there atop her for some time --- the weight of his upper body supported on his forearms, not wanting to remove himself from that warmth and softness. Her breasts were squeezed between them, forming a cushion of sorts for his chest and the feel of her thighs wrapped around him was what he wanted to feel for the rest of his life.

They were both experiencing the limbo of satiation, for Elisabeth, too, had felt the deeper sense of belonging and the greater arousal of this coming together. John had brought her to an orgasm of monumental proportions and she was contemplating the wonder of a lifetime with this man; of sleeping in his arms, of feeling him inside of her at any time she wanted, and of all the wonderful things they might do. It was as though, for a moment in time, her body didn't exist and she was pure thought.

Was this what happened, she wondered, when the body was so thoroughly satiated?

Much like an observer on the sidelines of a horse race, she was seeing a review of all that they had done and was experiencing it intellectually this time. The satisfaction was different in the thought process but it was satisfying nonetheless, for it was a completion of 'the act' and, in the analysis, it was as beautiful, as perfect, as it had been in the flesh.

John stirred, and Elisabeth, aroused from her reverie, asked, "What now?"

Casting an eye to the window, he said, "I do believe that supper might be in order and as we brought none with us, I suspect that we must turn homeward."

Sadly, or perhaps it was poignantly, she agreed with his observation and, before leaving the bed, they rolled onto their sides still locked in each other's arms and kissing deeply and arousingly. With that kiss, nature had her way and John's youthful staff was quickly firm and ready to pleasure his lady love once more.

This time, he lay on his back and she sat astride, impaled on his member. This was a good position --- he had access to her breasts and could even use his thumbs on the delights hidden in her furry mound as she lifted herself up and down upon him. He might not go again, but he could pleasure her right enough.

His hands cupped her breasts with his thumb and forefinger of each hand pinching a nipple in a milking motion as she began the rhythm of rising and falling upon his member, keening with delight. It was not long before he placed his hands on her upper thighs with his thumbs on either side of the button hidden in her furry mound. Feeling this, she pushed against them as he pressed his thumbs toward her and the sensation was enhanced a hundred fold. This caused her to buck like a wild horse, unbroken to the saddle and wanting to be free. Elisabeth, however, wanted only to feel the force of her orgasm come upon her and John's shaft buried inside her --- and up to the hilt. Even the thought of pleasing John had eluded her in the height of her passion --- she was at the point of no return, the point of the ultimate satiation, a mindless being intent on one thing --- finishing what they had begun..... She could not stop, though her thighs began to ache, and she rode the stallion beneath her --- for John had begun to buck, as well --- to the end of their journey; one which left them barely able to move for many minutes.

Then, John raised his arm and pointed to the window, saying, "We must go very soon or Cook will think we've eaten somewhere else."

This pronouncement had the desired effect and Elisabeth was off the bed and dressing in a trice --- with John only moments behind her.

Setting all to rights, then locking the door and retrieving Abernathy and the buggy from the stable, they hurried onto the road and home. Abernathy was pleased to receive another ration of oats --- they had forgotten he had already had one --- and they quickly walked up the lane to the house and Cook's supper awaiting them.

As usual, Cook had outdone herself. It was as though, suspecting that they might have eaten something tasty in another house, she always made certain to give them a good meal when they'd been out, just to help them remember that she was the best.

They lingered over the sumptuous meal, touching toes and ankles under the table as lovers are wont to do, each small touch a reminder of their passion. Finally, they finished and asked Rose to convey the message to Cook that the steak and kidney pie had been especially tasty and her crust quite flakey --- statements certain to please.

Carrying their coffee out of doors into the air of summer along with a plate of small jam tarts, they found their bench at the garden's end and sat there chatting, sipping coffee. and eating their fill of the sweets.

It was such a mellow time that they didn't want it to end, but as they began to stifle yawns, they knew they must go to their bedrooms and sleep, secure in the knowledge that a day would come in the not too distant future when they would retire to the same room, where pleasures unimagined awaited them.

John walked her to the door, held it open and saw her into the house, cups and saucers and the tart plate safely in her hands and on their way back to Cook's kitchen, before he turned and walked around the corner and down the drive to the stable and his quarters.

They lay there, each in their own bedroom and each thinking of the other until late in the night. For once, John didn't read.

∽Chapter 17 – Dresses, Dresses↩

The time passed quickly, with something new happening each day and soon a week had been and gone and it was time for Mrs. Martin to go to her relatives. Meanwhile, Elisabeth had sent them a letter advising them of the impending visit and noting that they would also be seeing their nieces christened, so a cleric would be needed. She had enjoyed composing it, remembering her own children and their christenings. Their reply affirmed that they were in residence and they were pleased that they would be hosting a family celebration.

Before the day of their departure, Elisabeth had found dresses for the girls from among those packed away in the attic that the twins had worn in childhood; beautiful dresses of soft creamy white velvet, not usually the fare for farm girls, but since they were calling on relatives of higher status she felt it was in order. She also brought them luggage for their journey, a few other articles of clothing the twins had worn in their youth and a dress of green watered silk for Mrs. Martin to wear if she cared to. She gave her an envelope holding spending money and John smiled at this when he saw her hand it to Mrs. Martin and winked at her. Elisabeth smiled back and nodded.

Finally, when Elisabeth and John came to see them off on the day they left, Mr. Martin seemed to be at sixes and sevens with his wife going away for a week, but he managed to hitch the wagon and stow the luggage in due time. They would be leaving from Aylesbury Station and it would take Martin the best part of the morning going and returning. In due time Martin, his wife, and the girls, had found their seats and the girls waved goodbye to Elisabeth and John from the back of the wagon, as it began the journey to the station, holding their hands high in the air until long after they had rounded a bend and could no longer see their benefactors.

Elisabeth sighed audibly and John looked at her quickly, tilting his head a bit to ask, soundlessly, if there was a problem.

She understood and said, with an air of wistfulness "No, there's nothing wrong --- it's just that I was thinking of the twins and their christening day. They seemed so precious --- just as these two....."

Days passed and soon it would be time for Mr. Martin to retrieve the women of his household from the station but, in the meantime, he stopped early one morning, on his way to the Tring market, to bring eggs, a brace of rabbits, and produce and to tell Elisabeth that her plan had been a good one, admitting that Miss Violet had prepared meals to brag on for the four men left behind --- though, of course, nothing was like having one's wife at home.....

Elisabeth smiled and told him that he was bound to have a new woman in his house --- one who had been refreshed by a taste of the wellspring of family and renewed by being a guest rather than a hostess. He listened and began to understand, remembering how tired his wife had begun to look before this trip was planned. He shook Elisabeth's hand and thanked her before he turned the wagon 'round toward the road and onward to the market day.

His benefactress stood there for a time in the drive, watching him and then simply thinking. Did all men undervalue women until it was pointed out to them, she wondered, then, thinking of John, knew the answer: some men valued women without having to be told to do so. This was why she had been so drawn to him: for his appreciation of women and their ability to do things so often considered the sole domain of men. Finally, she remembered the flowers in a basket by the door, for she had been cutting them when Mr. Martin drove up, and took them in for Rose to arrange in vases, then sat in the breakfast nook sipping tea and reading as she waited for John to arrive.

It was not long before he entered, looking as though he had not slept well or long and, furrowing her brow, she asked, "The books again?"

With a lopsided sheepish grin, he murmured, "I couldn't put it down."

She smiled back, but said, reminding him of their appointment, "Today we make for Aylesbury and a final fitting, for the dress is nearly finished and I hope that your driving skills are up to the task.'

"Of course!" he answered, with bravado, "I can manage Abernathy at any time!"

"Well, perhaps, you can take a nap on a chaise while I am fitted....." Her voice trailed off as she began writing down everything she wanted to accomplish in Aylesbury that day, then she added, "Take a book, John....."

They were underway before much time had elapsed, she with her list and he with the reins, chatting animatedly --- a ruse on her part to keep him awake --- but also simply because they each enjoyed the other's company.

With a destination in mind, and anticipation hanging heavy, the ride seemed to take longer than the day the dress was planned, but they arrived before the noon hour and found the same spot, with its dappled shade, for Abernathy to await their return.

Mistress Caldwell greeted them as soon as they opened the door and stepped inside, for she had seen them drive by and leave the buggy in the shade. Noting the look of a tired man, she directed John to a smaller room where there was, indeed, a chaise in which he could take a nap and took Elisabeth to a fitting room across the hallway from it.

When Elisabeth stepped into the room, she gasped, for the dressmaker had already dressed a mannequin in her exquisite creation so that Elisabeth could have an objective view of how she would present when she wore it before beginning the fitting. Seeing a chair, Elisabeth sat down suddenly, as though her knees were too weak to support her.

Concerned, Mistress Caldwell poured her a cup of tea from a tray on the table nearby and held it out to her. Elisabeth waved it away and just sat there, staring.

Finally, she roused herself from that reverie and whispered, as though afraid to break the reverent silence, "*You* are an artiste."

Smiling at the compliment, the dressmaker asked if she wished to proceed with the fitting, but Elisabeth didn't answer immediately. After a few moments, she stood and said, "Yes, I am ready."

When she had removed her clothing and been helped into the dress, she looked at herself in the mirrored walls of the fitting room with utter awe. Could this be her --- this exquisitely dressed young woman? Yes, she thought --- young --- in this dress, at least. Who was this person and where had Elisabeth gone, she wondered?

"Would you like a male opinion?" she heard the dressmaker ask and nodded.

In a few minutes, John entered, rubbing his eyes and then running his fingers through his hair. When he perceived her, the effect was comedic: he stopped in his tracks, his jaw dropped, and he was very suddenly wide awake. As beautiful as Elisabeth was, he had no idea she could be this ravishing, this elegant, or this exquisite. Blue was definitely her color and this dress the product of sheer genius.

His heart was beating frantically, but not precisely with arousal --- more akin to awe. At first he just stood there staring, then began to walk toward her. When he reached her side he said, taking her hand, "You are the most beautiful woman I have ever seen and I want you to be mine forever."

She smiled that enigmatic smile that mystified him so, and answered, "John, I have been yours and only yours since the day we met."

Tactfully, the dressmaker had closed the door for the two to be alone, sensing that there was a relationship, and seeing that they were alone, John took his love in his arms, holding her in her beautiful dress tenderly, as gently as if she were a fragile flower, and thinking to himself, she is mine..... mine.....

When the dressmaker knocked on the door, then discretely waited before entering, they had time to step apart and appear to be assessing the gown. She could easily see that her artistry had worked its magic and there would never be a backing away from this match. After noting that, she asked if there were any improvements to be made.

Both John and Elisabeth were quick to reply that the dress was perfection itself. Mistress Caldwell smiled and said, "Ah, but there is more." She opened a shawl draped over the back of a chair and showed her how to use it in many different ways, attached to tiny buttons concealed at the waist and the shoulder seams of the gown. It could become a flounce, a train, or a capelet, depending on how it was attached, or serve in its original purpose: as a shawl.

Then, she picked up a box which she handed to Elisabeth, saying, "Open this."

Elisabeth lifted the lid and drew out the beautiful bag from its recess. She was at a loss for words, but her face expressed her feelings more clearly than mere words could have done. This bag was simply exquisite --- the royal blue silk set off with crystal beading in flower designs.

Mistress Caldwell nodded and smiled when Elisabeth looked at her, glowing as she held it in her hands.

John watched the interplay with interest, for he had seldom seen his beloved in this state of being 'speechless'. It intrigued him.

The few alterations to the dress were so minimal that they could be accomplished in a few hours and its creator suggested that they lunch and enjoy the city, then return for the finished product in the late afternoon.

After removing the dress and emerging from the fitting room in her street clothing, Elisabeth, knowing the hardship of being a woman in business, promptly settled her account with Mistress Caldwell, but the dressmaker refused to accept payment for the bag which had so pleased her client. Elisabeth was one of her favorites, to be certain, but she gave it, rather, as a gift for being the model for this new creation of hers, for no other could have looked so radiant or youthful in it and many women would come to her shop after the wedding, hoping to look as beautiful in her creations as Elisabeth --- and garner as much appreciative male attention. Advertisement brings custom…..

Elisabeth and John chose to walk to the public house they had found on their last visit, hoping to enjoy bangers and mash again and perhaps a bowl of rich soup and some of the pastries displayed in a glass case near the taps. As they passed the stores and buildings, they looked into windows filled with wares, chatting pleasantly and surmising that the canal had certainly increased trade in the district. Occasionally, they stopped to admire a display or to enter and purchase items that caught Elisabeth's eye, but for the most part they were window-shoppers until they came to the booksellers.

Here, they both turned in and browsed. The shopkeeper knew Elisabeth well and had been holding a few books in reserve for her --- the latest treatises on medicine --- as well as a few new periodicals.

When they finally reached the public house, they found it was busier than the last visit, it being after the noon hour and boatmen as well as shoppers had stopped in for a pint and a bit of food. There were still a few tables available, though, so John placed their order and brought back a pint of ale for himself and a pot of tea for Elisabeth. They spoke of the dress, the weddings, Mrs. Martin, and even of the potential of their own marriage at Christmastide --- the latter, of course, being foremost on their minds, though less pressing. In due time, their meal arrived and they continued to discuss the holidays as they ate.

Elisabeth felt that the best day for their marriage would be Christmas Day, since then their anniversary would be part of a family celebration. John, on the other hand felt that New Year's Day would be better, for their marriage would be a new beginning for both of them and their vows would be resolutions as well….. However, after much discussion, no conclusion was reached other than the food was still excellent and they had no room left for pastries.

They lingered there after most of the other patrons had eaten and left for their work or to complete errands, conversing in low tones and laughing the way lovers do, though seated across from each other and to all intents and purposes, merely friends. All good things must come to an end, though, and as the afternoon waned they knew that the dress would be awaiting their arrival. And so it was.

Elisabeth spoke with Mistress Caldwell for a few minutes and asked for a few of her cards, while John strapped the dress, in a valise they had brought along for it, securely atop the box behind the buggy's seat; protecting the smaller purchases inside the box from flying out into the lane.

Having bid their farewells to the dressmaker, John turned Abernathy toward home and soon the buggy was out of the town onto the road. Abernathy had enjoyed his rest in the shade and had grazed a bit on some grass he noticed, but he knew that there would be a ration of oats and fresh hay for him in the stable at home and he pulled the buggy along eagerly --- or at least as eagerly as an older horse could manage.

Elisabeth and John were content, being full of sausage and potatoes, to enjoy the serenity of the countryside and the beauty of a summer afternoon turning to evening.

It was not yet dark when Abernathy turned into the drive of his own accord and pulled the buggy down to the stable, rather a twilight, in which all seemed somewhat hazy and mystical, much like something from Shakespeare's ethereal Midsummer Night's Dream.

When the buggy stopped at the stable door the sky had not yet gone dark. John stepped down and went around to help Elisabeth find her footing, but took the opportunity to hold her in his arms for a long overdue kiss. They stood there enjoying the serenity of that moment, locked in each other's embrace and returning to the kiss over and over again. Elisabeth could feel John's firm saber pressing against her abdomen through the layers of her clothing and felt as though her body was vibrating. She knew that there must certainly be a day at their retreat soon, but, for the moment, kissed him with wild abandon in this private moment.

Abernathy's whinny brought them back to the moment and John asked him, "Hungry, boy?" The body movements and his obvious excitement indicated he had answered in the affirmative, so John unhitched him and led him to his stall where he filled his hay rack with fresh hay and gave him a handful of oats. Elisabeth brought in a few small crabapples from a tree across the drive and fed them to him, as well. John put on the coat he wore when currying the horse and gave Abernathy a cursory going over before joining Elisabeth at the back of the buggy.

Then, John removed the packages and set them momentarily on the steps leading up to his lodgings, while he took the time to push the vehicle into another section of the stable. In short order, he was carrying their packages up the drive to the house with Elisabeth at his side.

Going around the house and entering through the kitchen, they found Rose and Cook in the midst of preparing supper and both ladies, being of the gentle sex, were curious about the packages, so Elisabeth opened the valise first to show them the folded dress. Even folded, its beauty had the expected response: they were struck dumb, experienced a sharp intake of breath, then couldn't find enough words to describe it adequately. It is an effect that truly beautiful things have on women.....

Before asking John to carry her purchases upstairs, she showed them the multi-purpose shawl, the beaded bag, and the contents of some of her other packages and then asked them to delay supper a bit, for she and John were still full of their noonday meal, but encouraged them to eat their own supper whenever they were hungry.

After carrying most of Elisabeth's packages up to her room, John came to the library, where he found his intended. She had a book in hand and asked if he had read it yet. He walked over to her and, taking her hand, held it up so that he could see the title, *The Contagiousness of Puerperal Fever*, then answered, "Yes, I have."

"Oh, that's good. I would like to discuss it with you," she said, "For I have delivered more than one mother of her child."

John asked, "Will I be doing this as well?"

"Of course, John," she replied, "A good doctor must know at least something of all aspects of medicine."

'That seems reasonable," he answered, furrowing his brow, then added, "I've delivered foals and helped with calves."

"Yes," she said, "It is much the same except for the position and, as we now are certain, it is important that the doctor's hands and instruments be sanitary. You may have read of poor Dr. Semmelweis in Vienna, who cannot bring the doctors there to wash their hands between touching corpses and delivering babies. He will have grief of those arrogant fools, yet! I do not envy him his predicament. Why, Dr. Alexander Gordon wrote a treatise on Puerperal Fever sixty years ago!'"

"Are there many babies born here?" John queried, pensively.

"Not very many --- at least not many in the infirmary. Most use the midwives unless there is a problem," she elaborated, "However, it is for that reason that we must familiarize you with the process. We will see the ones that are not commonplace, for a good midwife usually knows when she is out of her depth long before the birth and will send them along to a doctor or, in this case, a doctor's daughter."

Elisabeth continued, "I know of no tenants of mine with child at the moment, but they are only a small fraction of the people hereabouts, so we should address this tomorrow when we're in the infirmary. I'll show you the instruments and techniques that are used --- it's Maggie's day and she can help if we are not too busy."

At that moment Rose appeared to enquire whether supper could be served and class was summarily adjourned for the evening.

Inspired by the brace of rabbits brought to her by Mr. Martin that morning when he delivered eggs, milk and produce, she had made them a rabbit pie with a crust as thin as layered parchment and as flaky as a croissant, while side dishes were made from the fresh produce. For dessert she served them Stilton cheese and a hot fruit compote with sugared biscuits to nibble with their tea. They ate the feast in relative silence after their conversation in the library, enjoying the serenity of a meal together and the nearness of their beloved. Mere words seemed only an intrusion on the peaceful atmosphere.....

After the sumptuous dessert, and happy that they had foregone the pastries at lunch, they carried their tea and biscuits out into the garden and their favorite bench. Too full to be amorous, they sat and discussed the twins' wedding; mere weeks away. The girls and their soon-to-be mother-in-law were totally occupied with the arrangements, leaving Elisabeth to her own devices --- a circumstance entirely acceptable to her, though a bit unusual. Certainly, though, with both of her daughters marrying into a family of such wealth and consequence at the same time, it made good sense.

As they spoke of her new dress, she suddenly realised that she had neglected to see to new clothing for John and said as much to him. He smiled his gentle smile and said, "Ah, dear Elisabeth, you need not worry. Surely there will be something in the attic that will fit me. I have no need of finery, my love --- a dark coat will do the job, for styles have not changed so greatly for medical students." At this she brightened, for there were many coats and trousers in the attic from both her husband and her father, though many more from the former. She even remembered a dark hat or two, though her husband had favored a light gray for his ensembles and smiled at the thought that all was solved in such an easy manner.

Resolving to visit the attic the following morning, they returned to speaking of the twins and ultimately to the book on childbed fever and their plans for the following afternoon at the infirmary.

At last, the biscuits and tea were gone and they migrated back to the house via the French doors. As often, John embraced Elisabeth at the doors and kissed her deeply, then headed for the side of the house and the path toward the stables and his lofty lodgings, this time softly whistling the wedding march.

Ah, you are the one, Elisabeth thought, as she watched him disappear around the corner of the house and closed the doors against the damp of the night.

Chapter 18 – Outfitting and Planning

After breakfast the following morning, Elisabeth led the way up the stairs and showed John, once again, to the attic. Nothing had changed and, throwing open the shutters over the dormers, they quickly found satisfactory clothing for him --- an ensemble in navy blue and two others of different cuts in medium shades of grey. All enhanced his rugged good looks and Elisabeth found herself aroused when he tried on the coats.

While he posed to show her the fit, she walked around him as though assessing his finery, then standing behind, put her arms around him and let her hands slide down to the bulge in his trousers and hold it. Almost immediately, it became rigid rather than merely a bulge and she held it and squeezed it as he fought with his passion --- to keep from making any sound. Finally, unable to bear the sensation any further without entering her, he turned and gathered her into his arms, lifting her onto an old linen press which was a comfortable height. Then, standing in front of her seated there, he lifted the skirt of her dress and, finding the opening in her pantalets, he opened his fly as well and pulled her hips forward to meet his and to accept the saber she had so easily aroused to action. Alone in the attic, where none could enter without making enough noise to announce themselves well in advance, he had his way with her --- and entirely with her consent.

She clung to his shoulders as they made love, his strong hands pulling her hips forward, then pushing them back, his staff entering and leaving rhythmically, again and again. Stifling her urge to cry out with ecstasy, she whimpered her excitement and her passion as she rode that stallion of a man until fireworks went off in her head.

John continued pumping himself toward her and pulling her to him until, moments later, he was seized by a forceful ejaculation and held her tightly as his body jerked forward time and time again, then finally, and slowly, very slowly, he began to relax, though his manhood, not yet flaccid, remained embedded within his love. They remained that way for some time --- not moving and holding each other --- kissing as the spirit moved them, but never moving apart from that connection which so satisfied and gratified them.

As they finally drew apart, John said, "That was very much needed, my love, perhaps we could visit the attic more often......"

Elisabeth grinned at him and said, "It was my thought, as well --- at least until we are wed....." Then, after closing the shutters to protect the attic contents against the light, they filled their arms with clothing and descended the stairs.

Rose met them in the hallway of the main floor and, seeing the clothing, said, "Oh, ma'am, as soon as I've cleared the breakfast away, I'll begin freshening those jackets. The pressing room is ready."

With that bit of news, Elisabeth turned in the direction of the kitchen and soon she was laying her armful on a sideboard in a sunny room off of the hall --- the place where both clothing and linens were ironed and mended. She remembered that the sideboard held a drawer filled with skeins of thread of the most commonly used colors, packets of needles of every size, scissors and darning eggs. Another held pillows of various sizes to use in pressing collars and such. And a third held various cleaning solutions, packets of starch and bluing. Elisabeth had always liked this room with its many-paned windows that brought in bright light on even a dreary day and, standing there, remembered how it brought her joy as a child to watch their maid, Daisy, press the clothes with irons hot from the stove in the corner.

After a moment, John asked if all was well with her and she laughed her tinkling laugh and said, "Only happy old memories of childhood. Now, do set those down on the chair in the corner." Relieved of their burdens, they began to think in terms of the infirmary visit that afternoon and retired to the library for discussion.

Elisabeth sat in her favorite chair and John in a large wing-back which had been a favorite of her father. Broaching the subject of midwifery once more, she began, "Perhaps we will have someone coming in to the infirmary soon --- after all, the Martin brothers are old enough to marry..... Some of the others nearby have children old enough as well. Why, even I am not too old."

At the look of alarm on his face, she quickly said, "No, no --- at least, not yet. However, we could potentially have children....."

Somehow, John hadn't thought of that facet of their physical relationship and now all of the 'what ifs' were going round and round in his head. To think that he had exposed her to the possibility of that without regard to her position and her reputation made him feel as though he had a pit in his stomach. The consideration had simply escaped him before this moment --- perhaps since she was older than he and her children were grown, she seemed beyond the age of child-bearing or perhaps he was simply too smitten to let reality sink in. In either case, he was aware now.

Elisabeth, sensing that something had shifted, tilted her head to one side and asked, "John, what are you thinking?"

Ingenuously, he answered her with complete truth and sincerity, apologizing for not thinking of that aspect of what they were doing and berating himself for lack of consideration. Artlessly, he told her how much he loved her and that he would never purposely hurt her or wish harm of any kind upon her and then professed his desire to marry her. At that thought, a frown furrowed his brow and he said, "Am I good enough for you? That is, will your family allow me to marry you when I have so little and you ... so much?"

She disabused him of that notion immediately, for she was her own woman and did not need her family's permission to wed. At worst, her brother-in-law could stop helping the children, but the girls were already well on the road to successful marriages and the boys were establishing themselves as winners of scholastic prizes and assistance. A pregnancy would certainly be inconvenient before they married, but not the end of the world..... Then, she let him know that she loved him, as well, and was just as avid for their tete-a tetes as he.....

John sat there amazed at the strength of purpose that this beautiful woman possessed --- HIS woman, by her own declaration, and he felt elation and a sense of connection beyond even what they had already shared in the past few months.....

Elisabeth felt her own power and wished it could be so for all women, but knew that as long as there could be such a thing as 'redundant' women, they would never have power. Why, she thought, why didn't the ones who wanted a man of their own emigrate to the colonies, where there was a dearth of women? Why did they stay in England and become prostitutes? For that matter, why didn't the government offer them free passage?

Owning one's power seemed to be partly having resources, but also there was a component of having been nurtured to be independent by a parent --- preferably male --- and perhaps trained in a profession. She would ponder that thought the rest of the afternoon and long into the night.....

Rose interrupted their conversation at that moment to say that luncheon was laid and they'd best hurry for it was infirmary day.

Spurred into action, they made for the breakfast nook and tucked into Cook's croquettes and parsley potatoes; not too heavy and good for a work day. They bantered back and forth over the meal and then hurried off to the infirmary.

It was a day of few clients --- too many harvesting and no time to take care of any but the most serious of injuries. Once the harvests were in, they would bring their aches and pains as well as the swollen finger or infected injury..... This lighter load gave them time to speak further on the topic of childbed fever. There had never been a case of it among the patrons of the infirmary as her father (and she) had always been particular about sanitation --- washing their hands continuously. Even the area midwives had experienced few cases and only where there was extreme lack of sanitation in a farm cottage. Filth --- filth and crowding, that was the guilty combination…..

Maggie brought out the charts on those patients who had delivered at the infirmary and they discussed each case --- how the baby presented and how the birth was handled, and further care for the baby and mother, as well as any anomalies in the baby's condition or development.

The afternoon would have passed slowly but for those charts and their continuing conversation. In point of fact, they overstayed the infirmary's hours by thirty minutes before they started for home, talking along the way --- and without the usual banter. Infection was a very serious matter.

When they went in to supper that night, the topic quickly changed to the upcoming weddings. Elisabeth had received a letter at the infirmary from the twins and she waited to open it over dessert and read bits of it to John:

"We are all to stay at the Dower House, Mama, and have our own rooms, as before, though the bedrooms not used might be pressed into service for others. The Hastings family, other than our group, are to be housed at Uncle Richard's since he has his twenty-odd bedrooms, although Great-aunt Daphne may prefer the Dower House in order to be near us.

You must have Rose accompany you, Mama, for there will be parties and a ball and you will require a lady's maid to care for your wardrobe. We have been assigned our own by the Balfours. It makes us feel so very grand.

Quentin and Justin will be staying with their parents at an estate they own not three miles away and they plan to accommodate and entertain their relatives there. I believe that the Balfours will be there beyond the wedding, though --- perhaps even the whole time we are on the continent. We leave two days after we are wed, but we will bide with you at the Dower House until then, I believe. Our mother-in-law asked that we decamp to their estate after the wedding reception, but we stood firm and said that our husbands must come to our family since it will be the last time we share our old quarters with you. She will have us for the rest of our lives, after all is said and done.

I know that you are partial to country dress, Mama, but do please bring some pretty things, for there will be two dinner parties, a lawn fete and a ball. Not a ball as in London, of course, for we will be mainly en famile with friends and neighbors, however we must still dress."

Elisabeth looked at John and smiled. Things were so simple between the two of them and life was so calm in the vicinity of Little Tring. Understanding, he placed his hand over hers and let her feel the warmth and protection of it.

So, there were to be parties and a ball before the actual wedding. All told, it appeared that Elisabeth, John and Rose would be away from home the better part of a week, if not longer. This was to be a major disruption of their peace. Why, even the infirmary would be left to the staff! Hopefully, only cuts and scrapes would appear at the door, she thought. Perhaps the man training with the doctor in Aylesbury could come down one of the infirmary days.

Actually, it wasn't so terribly far and she and John could drive it each day, but by the time they arrived back in the small buggy, their clothing would be wrinkled and the dust of the road would be upon them, whereas people like the Balfours, with their enclosed carriages, could travel in comfort.

They discussed the transportation with Rose and decided that either John must make two trips or they would speak to Martin about letting one of his boys bring a wagon over. The latter seemed a better arrangement, for there was the baggage to consider, after all…..

Finally, they adjourned to the garden, where the light had faded and carried tea and biscuits to the far end and a bench that held many memories….. They sat together looking up at the stars and sipping their tea, Elisabeth leaning into the curve of the arm John had placed around her shoulders, and both feeling deeply at peace. It was as though they were married and had been thus for a lifetime already.

❧Chapter 19 – A Season for Weddings (Sept. 1854)❧

Elisabeth awoke in darkness. It felt like early morning, but there was no light streaming in the windows so she lay there wondering why it was so. As the minutes passed, she remembered that this was the Dower House with its heavy draperies blocking all light. The shutters were actually open, she later discovered, but the heavy velvet and thick lining did their job well. It was not long before there was a tap at her door and Rose entered, carrying a tea tray.

"Sorry to wake you, ma'am," she said, trying with all her being to be a lady's maid and a credit to her employer.

Elisabeth laughed and the tinkling sound brought a quick smile to the woman's face. Rose said, "Oh, ma'am, I'm at sixes and sevens trying to be a lady's maid. Hearing your pleasant laughter brings me right back home!"

Elisabeth held out her hand to Rose and Rose took it thinking to help her from the bed, but Elisabeth took it and squeezed, saying. "This, too, shall pass, dearest Rose, and we shall once again be at peace in Little Tring."

Now, it was Rose's turn to smile and, when she did, she glowed.

This was their second day in residence and, though some of the estate's farm wives had been pressed into service in the kitchen and to keep things clean in the big house, freeing up a few of the resident staff for the Dower House, guests always taxed the servants.

Elisabeth sat and enjoyed her tea while Rose prepared the clothing she would wear that day; a morning dress, then another for afternoon tea and yet another for the dinner party in the evening. Fortunately, she thought as she watched Rose shaking out the folds, they had brought adequate clothes for her to appear well before the bridegrooms' parents.

It was Wednesday already, she mused, and the Ball would be the next evening with a day of leisure at the afternoon Fete in the gardens on Friday before the second dinner party. Then, the couples would take their vows on Saturday afternoon with a reception lasting into the evening and church on Sunday morning. Perhaps she and John could leave on Sunday afternoon, but she suspected that it might be Monday before they escaped the excitement. Ah, well, she reminded herself, it was all in a good cause and now it was time to go down to breakfast.

When she came in to breakfast, John was already there with her sons, who had returned at the last moment from their hunting and fishing, enjoying the bountiful repast provided by their host. The sideboard was filled with covered platters of meats, shirred eggs, fried tomatoes, Kedgeree, a tureen of porridge, and a variety of breads, toast, and pastries as well as fresh fruit. While it was probably not as varied as the fare in the main house, it certainly met their needs well enough.

She acknowledged them all before serving herself from the sideboard, then sat between John and George and listened to the young men bantering as they ate. Some of the guests were known to them, being related, even if distantly, and the neighbors were also familiar if only by name or reputation, but some few guests had been invited as 'wild cards' to pique their interest and then, of course, there were the Balfour's relatives who were soon to be their by-marriage relations.

John had asked the boys about their hunting and fishing, but once she arrived, the talk turned to who might be coming to the Ball, for it would be a far larger affair than the dinner parties and it was interesting for her, a woman, to hear the manly side of courtship --- the surmising which girl had set her cap for them or which was the belle of the ball.

Loyalty demanded that they deem their sisters the fairest of the fair, but the two of them were indeed so pretty and so vivaciously outgoing in the confidence of being of like mind that the brothers needed not champion them, for they were a pair of bright stars on the horizon of local femininity as well as further a-field.

Listening to them, she had no need of making conversation and enjoyed her hearty breakfast immensely, as she sat there next to John, their ankles touching under the table, content in the contact of that small portion of their anatomy. John, nearing the end of his meal, contributed a bit to the conversation and she quite enjoyed being witness to the camaraderie of the four of them. Such a wealth of contentment, she thought to herself, basking in the warmth of it all.

John finished what was on his plate and went for a cup of rich coffee and sweets, bringing Elisabeth some of the same, perfectly sweetened and creamed to her taste. This sensitivity was not lost on Justus, though the others were oblivious. He smiled knowingly to himself, approving his mother's choice of companion, then entered the conversation once again.

None of the three youths were fixated on any one girl, though they easily could have been. Each, however, had a certain maturity born of their dedication to scholastics and knew that they needed to remain focused if they were to be successful in their quest for a degree so necessary to their careers. In all truth, George didn't have need of a career in the long run, but he loved learning --- stretching his mind and acquiring knowledge, a love his mother and grandfather had instilled in him. Fortunately for him, he would have the means to do that for the rest of his life should he choose to do so. His uncle obviously was holding out for his mother so, unless she refused him, the title was certainly George's.

George thought about this, wondering if his uncle would prevail or his mother would retain her independence, but his brothers seemed to be oblivious to the undercurrents in their family. He wondered if the girls had any inkling, but dismissed this thought summarily, assured that their only thoughts were for their husbands-to-be and the details of their impending marriages. Their beaux' mother had surely coached them in all of the proper etiquette for society marriages --- he had happened upon the twins' letter to Elisabeth on the desk in the study one day and smiled at the memory of it. His dear little sisters telling their mama how to dress! She, who had the good taste to keep it simple!

Elisabeth wondered fleetingly why George was so quiet, but her own thoughts began to rumble within her head and her heart. It was wonderful sitting here with John en famile with the boys. It was a shame that she had not been able to love their father as she loved John --- a shame, also, that he died before they had grown. Mentally, she expunged that last thought, for somehow she sensed that, had he lived, their sons would have been influenced by him rather than following in the footsteps of her father on the path of higher education. Unfortunately, her husband had not believed in moderation in drink or in spending. He had, for a certainty, lived within his means, but his means were exceedingly ample and she felt it important that their sons learn prudence with capital and good husbandry of their resources. They were achieving all of her dreams for them --- and her father's --- already. How could she be any more proud of them, she thought, unaware of the honors which would find them in their futures.

Her heart swelled with joy of them as they were at that moment and her daughters, as well, in their happiness. Could she feel anything more, she wondered, then thought of her own wedding and smiled a secret smile, then rubbed her ankle against John's.

Before long, the brides ambled in looking for all the world like a Gainsborough painting in their gauzy summer frocks and filled their plates, then, found their seats. The conversation became more spirited with their arrival and soon they had the gathering smiling and laughing. Watching, Elisabeth thought to herself, no wonder the brothers were so enchanted with them that they whisked them off to a country wedding, lest some other gentlemen come a-courting.

After a bit, she and John left the young people in the breakfast room and found their way to the garden through a pair of French doors in the morning parlor far wider than hers. The garden was as she remembered it --- impeccably trimmed and tidy. It had no sense of wildness about it as hers had and that saddened her somewhat in spite of the huge blossoms and heavy scents of late summer. She and John strolled for quite some time as it was a very large garden, being connected with the estate. Even the kitchen garden was as orderly as soldiers on parade, though more understandably so, what with the rows and all.

When they came to the small pet cemetery at the furthest point of the gardens, they sat on the bench and looked at the tiny headstones. John smiled gently at the poignancy of such a scene, obviously the resting places of the children's pets, and squeezed his love's hand.

Elisabeth returned the gesture and began to talk, "They so loved their little animals when they were children. It seems as if it were a hundred years ago and, yet, it seems only moments as well. Sometimes I wonder, does time really exist or do we only imagine that it does? Our eyes tell us of the passage of the days, but perhaps they are faulty organs."

John smiled. He had heard this thought before from others and he admired her all the more for having had it. He decided to change the topic, however, and asked about the pets.

There were twenty-two headstones by his count and she verified the amount, then began, "We only buried the smaller ones here, not the pony. He has a place of honor in the gardens behind The Hall. Few notice it, but the small hillock in the background was erected over him with a plaque at the base and I have no doubt that he has nourished the stately garden above him." She smiled at John, then, looking lovingly at the headstones, she continued, "The smaller animals are seven cats, four dogs, three birds, a turtle, a squirrel, and six rabbits." She knew the list by heart and could have given him the names as well had he but asked --- what her children loved, she loved also. "The rabbits were English Lops, a breed you may not be familiar with. They are large rabbits, and comedic with their long ears dragging on the floor, but so gentle and loving with children. One can hold them in their arms like a baby."

John smiled at the thought of a rabbit dragging its ears everywhere and stifled a chuckle. Guessing what he found funny, Elisabeth looked sideways at him and echoed it. Soon they were both laughing, but suddenly she stopped and said, "You see, they are still doing it."

"Doing it," he repeated.

"Yes! They are still making us laugh, bringing us joy, and soothing our sorrows with the memory of their essence. They are timeless," she averred, "Utterly timeless."

"I believe that they are," he added, pausing a moment, then repeated himself, "I do believe that they are."

They passed the balance of the morning walking the grounds of The Hall and admiring the gardens and park-like layout. Elisabeth acted as tour guide, having lived in both houses on the property for a number of years. They ambled along until she remembered that luncheon at the Dower House was to begin at one o'clock. Hurrying then, they arrived back at the Dower House with a few minutes to spare for a freshening from their exertion.

To Elisabeth's surprise, she found that they were the only adults in attendance with her children, the Balfour children, and assorted children of other wedding guests --- all ranging in age from approximately twelve to twenty years and already seated in the large formal dining room. With John and Elisabeth, they made a party of eighteen. Surprised by their duties as host and hostess, she and John rose nonetheless to the occasion and made certain that all enjoyed their meal and participated in the conversation.

So this was how Mrs. Balfour treated the future mother-in-law of her sons --- much like a glorified governess, Elisabeth mused. It would take some thinking and some reasoning to find a way to be at peace in her heart with this treatment and she suspected that this lady was used to having her own way always and managing people as if all were servants in her employ. By all that's holy, Elisabeth thought, the woman had best not treat the girls wrongly or she would have a termagant on her hands, in the form of their mother, to champion them!

In actuality, the luncheon was excellent and the younger children well-behaved --- most likely due to the older ones giving them their attention and treating them as equals. The viands were excellent, of course, though nothing so elaborate as those being served in The Hall, but she hoped that the dinner party would make up for it. Once luncheon was over, however, she went to her room for a nap so that she would be fresh for the evening and, after visiting with the young men for a space, John did the same. The young people sought out their own age group and either played on the lawns or visited in the parlor or on the terrace over card games. At a table in the shade of a tree situated on a level bit of ground between the houses, a groom from The Hall was serving fruit juices and refreshments for those who preferred to play or stroll the grounds. The scene was the epitome of a day in the late summer at an estate of some consequence.

After a few hours of refreshing sleep, Elisabeth woke and realised that she should be setting about her preparations for dressing. She rang for Rose and in a few minutes was giving her directions for helping with her hair and pressing any errant wrinkles out of the dress she planned to wear. Dinner was for seven o'clock and it was already gone half past five. They would be all right, but just.

She knew that the girls would be in their rooms and she went to ask if they knew about the arrangements for childcare during dinner and found that the children over fourteen would be included in this dinner at The Hall, while the younger ones would be the domain of the few nannies in attendance. Whew, she thought, at least that's settled, then returned to her room and Rose, who was waiting with the dress already pressed and the curling irons.

John, her sons, and the grooms were waiting when she descended the stairs with the girls and, after the gentlemen had complimented each of the ladies on their ensembles, they formed a rather festive party walking across the well-kept lawns toward The Hall rather than going by the road. She and John hung to the back, walking arm in arm, and listened to the banter of the young people, smiling at their witticisms and laughing out loud when called for.

She became aware that this was a once in a lifetime event. Both daughters were being married and, though her sons might marry, being the mother of the bride is entirely different than the mother of the groom. She felt a wistfulness come over her and she savored the moment, storing up the feelings for review at another time, perhaps when she missed her daughters.

Holding onto John's arm, she felt so safe, so encompassed in love and support, that she knew she could face anything, even the future absence of these daughters she bore and raised. John, feeling that something was not quite the same with her, held her all the more tightly and put his other hand over her arm where it linked with his.

Soon they had achieved the circular drive at the entry to The Hall and were admitted just minutes before seven. Once there, the ladies were relieved of their wraps and all proceeded in to dinner with the group gathered in the parlor when the dinner announcement was made.

Elisabeth found herself seated next to her brother-in-law, whose place was at the head of the table, rather than John, when they found her card. Can I bear it, she wondered, then put on a happy face and dealt with it as she had done everything else so far. Watching him look for his card, she observed that John had been seated far down the table between two of the younger ladies and George was seated at the far end, as his uncle's ostensible heir.

Glancing up and down the table she saw that the brides and grooms were the only ones in attendance seated next to their partners across from each other midway down the table --- an honoring of their affianced status, she supposed. Richard's attentions fairly made her flesh crawl throughout the meal, but she managed to persist, and in truth the dinner was splendid, taking two hours to serve and consume. Fortunately, there was another gentleman on her other side and she was able to enjoy her conversation with him very much, for though he was apparently a close relation of the Balfours, he was a man of medicine and had much to say.

This man might be a possible connection for her boys and John, so she tucked his name away in her memory. He seemed to find her interest in medicine fascinating and had read some of her father's works. He earned high honors in her mind when he mentioned the need for colleges for women desiring to enter the medical profession and she found the conversation so intriguing that she almost forgot Richard was seated next to her. He spoke eloquently of the lectures of James Paget and mentioned that at one in 1850, during her enrollment at Saint Bartholomew's Hospital in London, he had actually met Elizabeth Blackwell, the first woman in the United States to graduate in medicine, and his dinner companion found herself thinking: there is hope for the women of our kingdom if more men can be as accepting of us as this one.

During the course of the meal, it seemed natural that there were many toasts to the beauty of her daughters and the good fortune of their affianced beaus. She smiled, basking in the glow of their happiness, and blushed with delight when the toasters vowed they had received their looks from their mother. Down the table, she could see John holding his glass highest and smiled at him. Fortunately, Richard thought she was smiling at her daughters, seated only a few chairs away.

Finally, the desserts had been served and eaten and dinner came to a close. The men adjourned to the billiard room or the terrace for cigars and the women and young people visited or played cards or board games in the parlor. In an adjoining room, one enterprising young man found a pianoforte and began playing some of the popular songs of the day, gathering a few listeners who knew the lyrics.

It was a pleasant scene, Elisabeth thought, as she sat there contentedly contemplating the fact that someday this house would most likely belong to her son. It was how it should have been when his father died.

She met many more relatives of the Balfours that evening, the mother of the grooms being one of them. Watching her, Elisabeth felt that her assessment of the woman had been spot on, then dismissed all thoughts of her for the balance of the party.

John, not being an aficionado of cigars had stayed with the young people and was intently engaged in a game of chess with a prodigy about twelve years of age. From time to time his eyes met Elisabeth's and they smiled, then looked away lest it be noted by one of the dowagers.

Looking across the room at her daughters, she felt that they were as happy as ever she could have wished them and thought of her own marriage and how different it had been. Perhaps they would be no more happy than she had been in the final tally, but at least the decision to marry these particular young men had been their own and not contracted by anyone else --- not even someone with good intentions. They were the masters of their own lives and were creating their future with their own ideas, as they would have it be. If that independence was all she had given them she could be happy, she thought to herself.

Eventually, the men, smelling of cigar smoke and expensive brandy, returned to the group and began to sort out their families, admonishing the young ones to make tracks for their bedrooms and taking possession of their wives. The party from the Dower House found each other as well and, after the gentlemen had placed the ladies' wraps on their shoulders and said their goodnights with lanterns held high, they took the safer route along the lane, lest the ladies dress hems become soiled with the dew which had already fallen. A light mist had come up during the party and, though it was thin enough to see through, it gave a decidedly eerie chill to the air and they agreed that summer was definitely fading into autumn --- giggling and hurrying for the warmth of the cosy fires surely lit in their bedrooms.

Elisabeth and John brought up the rear as before, but he was able to sneak more than one quick kiss in the dark before they had to press onward toward the lantern light as the younger members of the party hurried along ahead of them.

ᔥ Chapter 20 – The Fate of the Fete ᔥ

Tap, tap came the insistent noise rousing her from sleep. Tap, tap, tap. Suddenly, she sat up in bed, in the awareness that someone was at her bedroom door and it was too early for a tea tray. Putting on her robe, she quickly opened the offending portal a crack in the dim room and saw Caroline standing there illuminated by the frail morning light filtering through a window at the end of the hallway. She opened the door wider, inviting her in, while wondering why she was there at this early hour when all the family members were sleeping.

After the door was closed, her daughter began to cry and wordlessly sought the comfort of her mother's arms.

"Why whatever is the matter?" Elisabeth asked.

"Oh, mama," her daughter began timorously, "I shall miss you so very much and my life shall be so different…… I wonder if I am truly ready for marriage."

Elisabeth held her, then led her to the settee where they had enjoyed many chats when she was a child. Sitting there, it seemed as though time had reversed itself and here was her little girl needing her again. Holding Caroline's hand she waited patiently and finally her daughter resumed. "It's nothing wrong with Justin. I love him very much, but I don't know if I'm ready to have my own house and deal with servants in the way his mother does. She is so overbearing, mama. Catherine seems to take it better, but Mrs. Balfour makes my stomach ache so. I cannot imagine calling her 'mother' as she would have me do. You are my mother, not her and you are kind and loving. How can I even call her mother?"

Elisabeth began, as mothers have begun for millennia when their daughters experienced wedding jitters, saying, "Oh, Carrie, my little Carrie, all mothers probably seem a little intimidating to children who are not their own. Will you be living with her --- or Justin? Surely, with your own home, you will be mistress of your house and she will respect that."

Through the sniffles her daughter managed, "Perhaps, mama, but just being near her makes me feel unsettled. Do you think Justin would fear that I could not truly love him if I asked him to wait? I do so love and cherish him."

Elisabeth felt certain that he would, youth being prone to leap to conclusions, but said, "Carrie, I believe that you need to discuss this with him. Surely he knows his mother and how overbearing she is. He has learned how to deal with her and may give you some ideas --- after all, he and Quentin have had to learn to deal with her from their first breath....."

The thought of her affianced facing off his mother while still in nappies made Caroline giggle a bit, in spite of the tears which were rapidly fading. As she giggled, she stole a look at her mother, who saw it, and suddenly they both were laughing and holding their hands over their mouths to keep the sound from escaping the room and waking everyone else. Ah, Caroline, Elisabeth thought as she laughed, you always were the more easily cajoled, then hugged her daughter closer to her for a moment.

Now that the tears were gone, Caroline understood that her mother was most definitely in her corner and that Mrs. Balfour would have more than a schoolroom miss to deal with there. She had watched her mother set limbs while grown men screamed in pain and knew that Elisabeth was anything but meek. With that remembrance, she suddenly understood that her mother had been banking her fires on behalf of serenity with her soon-to-be family and stepped back a bit in her mind to the previous day's luncheon with a knowing that her mother had been displeased at the high-handedness of Mrs. Balfour. Looking at her mother's face carefully, she asked, "Mama, why were you displeased about the luncheon? Did you not enjoy sharing the table with the children?" To her discerning eyes, all was revealed as the emotions passed across Elisabeth's face: anger, concern for her daughters, anger again, then self control.

Her mother, composure regained, said, "Your father's parents were both already gone when we married, so I suppose I was fortunate in not having to deal with a mother-in-law, good or bad, but not all women are so fortunate; even the farmer's wives have their crosses to bear in that all men have a mother. Some are treasures and others, many others, are self-righteous, demanding, and pure harridans to be near." She waited a few moments after that emotional pronouncement, then continued, "I have found in life that there is one thing contrary behavior cannot overcome and it is a truly loving heart so filled with joy and light that no mean or ugly thought can assail it." She paused, for effect, then went on to say, "You have that sort of love, Carrie. You have it for Justin and must extend it to all of his family. Remember that there are two of you --- you and Catherine --- and added to your husbands, you are four. Four Balfours, against whom she shall not prevail no matter how long she attempts to do so."

Caroline sat there wide-eyed and dumbfounded, listening to her mother's words, but growing as she heard them. She had not thought of the four of them as a team; a team for the conversion of Mrs. Balfour. Then, she jumped up, pulling her mother with her and said, "Mother you are a genius! That is exactly how it is --- we shall overcome her! She shall not prevail. Oh mother, I feel so powerful and so capable. You always help me to find my way. How will I find it when I am married and fighting the battles of life?"

Filing away the thought that she might well be doing exactly that, Elisabeth hugged her and replied, "You have plenty of courage within you, Carrie --- sometimes you just need to be reminded which drawer you have tucked it into."

Caroline laughed, delighted at the thought of herself tucking parts of her into a chest within her, then said, "I can marry Justin now without a moment's hesitation. Thank you mama for helping me to see things more clearly!" With that, she left and hurried very quietly back to her room, mindful of the early hour, and left her mother to try to go back to sleep.

Elisabeth took off the robe she had pulled around herself before opening the door and slid between the covers once again, savoring the lingering warmth. How am I to sleep now, she thought, as her mind reviewed the encounter with Caroline and thought of the great distance soon to come between her and her children. Her body overcame her brain, however, and soon enough she was drifting back into the arms of Morpheus and deepest slumber.

Hours later, Rose arrived with her tea and the day began in earnest. Not long after, her daughters, following on Rose's heels, carried their tea trays into her room and climbed onto the bed to share the morning with her. Caroline had, of course, already shared the gist of their conversation from the night before and Catherine, not to be left out, was avid for more..... Ah, thought Elisabeth with a smile, Mrs. Balfour hasn't a chance with my girls --- they will stick close to each other just as they did when they were little!

When the three of them finally descended to take breakfast, the young men, who had opted for an early morning ride in the surrounding countryside, were just coming to the table as well. Fresh from the saddle and commenting on the absolute perfection of the sunny day, they were excited from the invigorating exercise and her daughters, in a quieter way, were also energized --- from their precious time spent with Elisabeth.

Conversation centered on the Fete and the Ball, once the excitement of the ride had been calmed by the breakfast feast on the sideboard. Catherine, who had made most of the plans, explained the order of the day to them. First, a short concert at noon featuring the premiere students of the music teachers of Aylesbury, then luncheon. Afterward, active games for the young and cards or a leisurely walk for the adults then, in the mid-afternoon, a rendering of A Midsummer's Night Dream by a group of Shakespearian theatre aficionados brought in from Oxford. Dinner was to be en famile for those who desired it, but most would forego further refreshment until the Ball began with its extravagant menu, chosen by Mrs. Balfour and Richard. This day was to be quite a full one, but the evening would extend it even further, for dances often began as late as nine o'clock and didn't end until the cock's crowing dragged the sun from its slumber.

Elisabeth felt tired just thinking of the activities of the day, but she knew that the girls' excitement would carry her through it. Watching them was one of her great joys --- there is something about twins that is special and for her it elevated her energy rather than depleting her. She knew that Aunt Daphne found it the same and that this was part of the reason that she had taken them to live with her when it came time that they could begin attending social gatherings and balls. Her thoughts turned to ones of gratitude for Daphne's help in securing suitable husbands for them, men whose social standing and income would insure their futures --- but her greatest gratitude was in her relief that they had both found love matches!

Now, Elisabeth, enough of this nattering about in the brain, she thought --- it is time for action and she did just that, saying, "I do believe that it is time we were out for a walk to settle this meal and view the preparations for the Fete." She found no disagreement and soon they had formed a party walking the grounds. The girls took the lead, each on a brother's arm, with Catherine taking the George and pointing out the preparations, then came Elisabeth with John and Justus ambling along at her other side. It felt like a family outing to Elisabeth and then, quite suddenly, she realised that soon it would be, for John would become their step-father, and she relaxed against his arm a bit more, feeling the joy of their secret flowing through her body and mind. He put his free hand over hers where it lay on his arm and patted it. She smiled in response and he nodded.

Catherine was in her meter here, talking non-stop, much like a tour guide, and giving them the entire story of how each part of the Fete had been arranged: booths with various refreshments situated about the grounds providing relief from the summer sun as well as a sampling of the capabilities of Richard's kitchens, a puppet show booth to enchant both young and old, while jugglers, clowns, and other entertainers strolled about the grounds --- almost more like a child's birthday party. She had even planned races for the boys and games for children of all ages.

Catherine was ever the one for fun and frivolity..... However, she had a serious side as well and had included a number of booths for fund-raising for the church in Tring --- one where tatted, knitted and crocheted articles of all sorts were displayed for sale, another offering carved items --- animal figures, knife handles, pipes for smoking and ones for playing, as well as, spoons, ladles, and other kitchenware --- while a third booth offered a staple of the reservoir region: artificial fishing lures. She told them that she anticipated the last bringing in a fair amount for the church's widows and orphans fund and was gratified to see her brothers eyes light up at the mention of fishing lures as well as John's.

By the time they had perambulated the grounds, and sampled a few of the refreshments, it was nearly time for the concert and she looked forward to the musical offerings of these talented students. Perhaps this would open doors for some of them or inspire some of the wealthy to sponsor students further in their studies, she mused. At that, the thought struck her that it was unfortunate for medical students that they couldn't showcase their gifts in such a venue.

Slowly, the group found their way to the concert seating --- an area under the trees, where a low platform with a piano had been erected that all might see the performers and, stopping to chat with those already seated, they gradually found their places at the front. As it would be in church, the distaff side was seated on the left and the groom's family on the right; however, Catherine and Caroline had been placed next to each other with their respective grooms at their open side to the relief of both couples. Elisabeth felt their joy from a distance as she sat there, surrounded by her men-folk and remembered how alone she had felt at her own wedding parties at this very estate --- even with her father in attendance. From so many years in the past, it still touched her heart with a snippet of pain; that feeling of having no mother and no siblings nor grandparents. She must thank her husband for this one thing --- her sons and daughters and their love for each other. Had he lived longer, the boys might have followed his example of high living, drinking and betting on sporting events, but their living situation and their closeness to her after the shock of his death had brought out the best in them --- scholars to the core every one. Their uncle was more conservative, a person after her own way of thinking, so they had seen examples of well-ordered living on both sides.

At this point in her musings, one of the music teachers came to the platform and spoke for a few moments about the concert, describing the students in glowing terms and speaking well, also, of their teachers, his colleagues, and their hopes that someday there would be a music conservatory in Aylesbury, then asked the first performer to come forward.

The performances were surprising in their competence --- these students were indeed well advanced. She hoped that they would do well and saw that the enjoyment of the listeners was evident, for all conversation came to a halt with the opening few notes. What a delightful idea Catherine had conceived!

As the last chord faded away on the light summer breeze under the trees, there was a pause and then the guests rose first one by one, then all together, and applauded. All of the musicians took this as a call to the platform and stood there in a row, bowing their heads toward their audience. When the applause ceased, the teacher who had spoken at the beginning came forward to thank both the students and the listeners, then released the guests to their luncheon. The adults, he directed to The Hall with its formal dining room and terrace, while the young people and children were to picnic al fresco on the lawns and receive their meal from the well-laden tables set up there.....

John escorted Elisabeth to the indoor meal, but her sons had encountered friends from the balls and parties they had been attending that summer to take lunch with in the open air. She knew that youth fares better in an outdoor setting when the energy of summer is flowing in their veins and happily let John partner her in the dining hall.

The luncheon was set up against one entire wall of the dining hall and guests were able to help themselves to that which suited them, then eat inside or adjourn to the terrace and the fresh air. This time Richard was too busy playing host to seat her near himself and it happened that the selfsame doctor from the prior evening sat next to her with John at her other side and bringing her fresh viands from time to time to tantalize her palate. Little accustomed to the traditional pattern of speaking to the person first on one side, then the other, he listened to the medical conversation going forward next to him, between trips to the buffet, and tendered comments and questions across Elisabeth when he could not contain himself any longer. Between his interjections, Elisabeth introduced John to Dr. Milton Walford as her pupil and their behavior was all that is proper other than John's leaning forward to talk across to the doctor, who enjoyed the questions and repartee, but was clearly interested in hearing more from the mother of the brides, who looked nearly as young as her daughters.

All things eventually have a conclusion and the luncheon was no exception, though it remained in place for hours longer to serve those stragglers and slow eaters as was necessary.

Moving outdoors to the Fete, the doctor stuck like a briar to Elisabeth as did John, perceiving his interest, and the three of them sampled the wares of the booths, from Punch and Judy to the artificial fishing lures, laughing and chatting the entire time. The men bought a number of lures, comparing their technique and had the grace to wait on Elisabeth, as she had waited on them, while she compared lace collars and crocheted slippers before making her purchases.

At three o'clock, the refreshment booths began serving a light tea and they sat in the shade and partook of the beverage, as they watched the rendition of A Midsummer's Night Dream from afar, but little about the sandwiches or desserts tempted them after the luncheon., so they exercised restraint, knowing that there would be more at dinner and again at the Ball….. When five o'clock neared, Elisabeth stood up and made to excuse herself from the gentlemen's company in order to take a nap at the Dower House, only a short walk away. Both men began to rise, but John was up before Dr. Walford and offered his arm, saying, "I believe that some rest would suit me as well. This has been a long day already."

Dr. Walford looked dejected and Elisabeth, ever compassionate, put her hand on his arm saying, "We will see you again at the Ball, I believe, Doctor."

He nodded, lifted her hand from his arm and pressed his lips to the back of it, not noting John's displeasure at the act, then answered, "Of course, dear lady, of course."

The pair made their way to the Dower House, stopping from time to time to say hello to friends or family, but finally reached the entry hall and mounted the staircase. Once in the upstairs hallway, John, seeing no one at all, enveloped her in his arms and kissed her soundly. She relaxed into his arms and answered his passion with her own ardor, but when voices could be heard below, they separated and quickly walked to their separate rooms.

Elisabeth lay on her bed and slept after only a few minutes, having been awakened early and knowing she dare not let her mind be active or she would rue it halfway through the Ball.....

Behind a locked door, John lay on his bed with his arms folded behind his head, looking up and thinking of Elizabeth, the swell of her bosom, the sweetness of her lips, and the warmth of her lovemaking. As his body became aroused, he got up, took off his clothes, and lay down again to ease his discomfort. His hand went to his groin and he began stroking his rigid member as he had done often before in the dark of his bedroom above the stables. As the pleasure built, he held the cloth he had found by the water pitcher over the head of his manhood with his left hand while his right made long strokes, each one bringing him nearer to his release, each one heightening the sensations, each stroke an imitation of what he really wanted: the steamy warmth of her femininity wrapped around his member, pulsing, squeezing, sliding by as he entered her again and again until he had spent his seed within her body and held her in his arms.

It was no long time before he fell asleep after this --- his body's need temporarily sated and his mind cleared of its focus. His dreams were of Elisabeth --- her body, her mind, her being --- and his love of all three.

An hour or more later he awoke feeling rested and wondering why he had a cloth covering his groin, then remembered and lay there for a few moments savoring the beautiful memory of his interlude before he began to dress for the Ball.

๑ Chapter 21 – A Ball to Remember ๑

Elisabeth woke slowly at first, then, memory of where she was and what day it was flooded back into her mind and she quickly glanced at the clock on the mantle. Nigh unto seven, she said to herself, surprised that Rose had not already roused her. Best be about dressing! With that thought, she threw back the coverlet she had pulled over her when she lay down and stepped onto the floor just in time to hear Rose's tap at her door. "Come, Rose," she called out and Rose let herself in, carrying freshly pressed clothing,

"Oh, ma'am, 'tis that busy below!!" Rose said, with high excitement in her voice. She and the other maids were to be allowed to watch the dancers from one of the musician's galleries, balconies situated above the ballroom, for this was a wedding ball and all must rejoice with the happy couples as their stations permitted. And, of course, being close at hand should they be needed had crossed Mrs. Balfour's mind......

Elisabeth helped Rose unburden herself of the clothing she had pressed, then waited for her to help her into her undergarments, for even the artistic style required that one wear them. With all but her ball gown in place, she went to the dressing table so that her hair could be pinned up into a style befitting the mother of the brides. Rose had a gift for this task and created an upswept style certain to complement her ensemble.

Turning her head this way and that in front of the mirror to view Rose's work, Elisabeth noted, with pleasure, that her appearance was extremely elegant and youthful. John would be pleased, she thought, then took the pale beige tortoiseshell and sapphire comb her father had given her from its resting place in her jewel case and asked Rose to place it in her coiffure, for the color would be perfect with her cream-colored gown.

Then, she pulled her mother's cameo wedding pendant from the case and Rose, placing it around her neck, fastened the clasp. Now she was ready.....

John and her sons were waiting in the library when she descended with the twins. They had missed the ladies' descent, however, neither the staircase of the Dower House nor the foyer were large enough to make a truly grand entry, so little was lost --- at least from the male point of view.

Though it was still twilight when they left for The Hall, they walked the short distance along the lane to avoid staining their clothing with grass or food dropped by children during the Fete. The road would have its own hazards once the horses had come through, but they had been instructed by Mrs. Balfour to arrive early for the immediate families of the betrothed couples would join them and be part of the receiving line, welcoming their guests. With the Ball, their numbers would swell at The Hall, for some would arrive from London or further and stay through the weekend. They had been warned in advance that the additional bedrooms in the Dower House might be put to use.

Chatting as they walked, they fetched up at The Hall half an hour before the guests were to begin arriving and socialized with those few of the wedding party who were present: the grooms, eager to see their future wives in their newest finery.

One by one, the rest of those who would make up the receiving line descended or arrived in their carriages and by the required hour, all were present greeting those who cared not that they were out of fashion with their punctuality and waiting for the fashionably late ones. When most of the anticipated guests had arrived, the receiving line began to thin out and its ranks had dwindled to only a few souls by ten o'clock, who then joined the gathering in their revelry.

Elisabeth danced with many, even John, though she took care to avoid seeming exclusive with him. Dr. Walford claimed her for more than one foray to the floor and she caught a scowl on John's face as they sailed past him partnering someone in the waltz.

Rather than a formal dinner, the dining room had a sumptuous buffet laid on the long sideboard and ample beverages for the dancing couples to partake of often during the evening..... .....and the morning, as well, for the Ball would continue well into the early hours of the following day.

After three hours of dancing relieved by two sojourns in the dining room --- one with Dr, Walford and the other with a serious young man by the name of Evan Poole --- Elisabeth was ready for the night to end, but knew with an ominous sense of dread that it was far from over.

In the ballroom she introduced young Mr. Poole to her son, George, and left him safely engrossed in conversation, then flowed up the grand staircase in the entry hall with other ladies seeking to rest, primp, or relieve themselves.

Once there, she asked if she might join the occupant of a settee elegantly upholstered in a sulfur-colored satin brocade. Seeing the woman's nod, she eased herself down next to the dowager in whale-boned black satin with a black jet necklace and earrings already in possession of the settee. She saw that even the woman's evening bag was trimmed in black jet. Elisabeth smiled, then decided to engage her in conversation, for she was curious as to her choice of clothing, wondering if perhaps she was a widow.

She began with, "I am Elisabeth Hastings, the mother of the brides," as she had done in the receiving line with those she did not know and she was unprepared to hear the frail voice rasping somewhat like brown autumn leaves scudding across a dry pavement when the woman answered.

"I arrived after the receiving line had dispersed, my dear, for of late I must have a long nap before these social events. I am Lydia Balfour's great-aunt, Emmaline Roberge. My husband, Charles, was born in the colonies --- some even said his mother was a red Indian --- but it didn't stop his French father from becoming a wealthy man, nor did it stop him from multiplying his share of that wealth as a financier. I am always invited to these family affairs, for they hope to curry favor with my fortune. My husband died, you see, and I was the only heir." She paused for a moment for a sip of sherry from a glass Elisabeth had not noticed on the table beside the settee, then continued, "We were not blessed with children, though his lineage was usually quite prolific. He was uncle to many, but they are Catholic and he had left the church, so he felt that his fortune was best served by staying in my hands to be dispersed where it would not enrich the clergy."

Elisabeth listened quietly to Emma's tale, but she was surprised when the widow confided that she was nearly eighty for, though her clothing was quite severe and ageing and her voice was not strong, she looked twenty years younger in spite of it. Perhaps, thought Elisabeth, freedom from the trials of childbearing and rearing had extended her youth.

Sensing that Emmaline had said as much as she would for the moment, Elisabeth began by telling her that she was a widow as well and confided, "How wonderful that yours was a love match, or am I assuming too much?" then continued when she saw Emmaline's smile, "My father was a well-loved and comfortably situated country doctor and when George Hastings asked for his permission, to all intents and purposes he chose my husband for me. Oh, he allowed me the latitude to refuse, but made certain that I knew he wished me to be safe and thought that this was the way to do it. How could I disagree? My husband was no ogre and I thought I might begin to love him, but that was an error. He gave me five wonderful children, but failed to change his will to give us equitable treatment. I see it as no small miracle that our children, with the exception of our eldest son, have made successful lives for themselves."

Emmaline interrupted at this point, interjecting shamelessly in the manner of the very elderly who need to get the words out while they are still able, "Ah, my dear, you had the engineering of that! Those apples have not fallen far from your tree. I remember George Hastings and, while not a bad sort, he drank to excess and gambled some, though not enough to lose the fortune or his holdings. Pity he got on that horse after drinking, though, but at least it was quick."

Surprised that Emmaline knew such a great deal about her family, Elisabeth was stunned into momentary silence and sat there for a few minutes remembering the day the servants brought her husband back to The Hall on a gate. His neck had been broken with the fall, or perhaps it happened when he had not ducked low enough to dodge a branch as his horse galloped through the thicket. Either way he had ended on the ground --- dead. She remembered the burden of consoling the children, who had, at least, seldom been exposed to his over-indulgence, not that he was rowdy or abusive, simply incoherent. In her heart, she was rejoicing on some levels for her freedom and found it difficult to feel the sadness that they were feeling. In this moment, she wondered if they had known or suspected it.

The two widows sat there quietly for a time, each engrossed in her own thoughts. Then, Emmaline began again, "You are not aware of it, but I am a careful warden of my husband's fortune. Having no children, we took it upon ourselves to find young people whose lives would be measurably enriched by small, sometimes subtle things that we could provide; a word in the right ear; a scholarship; an opportunity offered or created; an introduction; an invitation; and more....." Then, looking deeply into Elisabeth's eyes, she said, "Your children are beautiful and talented. They have had a good education and will be stable members of society, contributing to the good of all and enriching this kingdom as we would wish, my Charles and I. They have been helped."

Shocked into silence, Elisabeth sat there with her mouth open for a moment, then realised that she should close it, though she continued to digest what she had just been told.

"Do you mean that you have supported my sons?" she found the courage to ask.

"No, not with money, but with opportunities," Emmaline answered. "They have had the foresight and intelligence to make success of those doors, your sons. However, they do not know that they were helped and I trust that you will not tell them --- or any other person. This is my secret and it is with a very great trust that I share it with you. You have triumphed in raising your family and you are as intelligent as they. These children of yours will do more than you can imagine. Your protégé will, as well. He is intelligent and you are a fine teacher. If women were accepted in the medical colleges in this country, you would be teaching them. However, in the United States, this is different. I attended the lectures of James Paget in London, for he was one we helped, my husband and I, and I noted that Elizabeth Blackwell was there also. Someday our men will change, both in this kingdom and elsewhere, only not as soon as we would have it. We shall have the vote and more. Many will pay dearly for that enfranchisement and your work and your children will help to bring it about, for they have seen a mother both intelligent and competent in all that she does." Emmaline stopped to sip at her sherry again, allowing Elisabeth a space in which to speak.

Elisabeth began with awe, "You helped James Paget and you met Elizabeth Blackwell? Are you a part of the movement for female education?" Then, taking a breath, she asked, "And you have made the way smooth for my sons?" Then, as she saw the nod of Emmaline's head, she made bold to take her gloved hand and say, "If that is so, then bless you dear lady, for they were in sore need of a clear path and a champion and my many prayers seemed to fall on deaf ears at times."

Emmaline smiled at this and answered, "Remember, child, that the answer to a prayer is not always 'yes'. Sometimes the best answer is 'wait 'or 'be strong and carry on' for the need may be for helping oneself more --- that confidence may grow. This is the reason that my work is seldom overt. The recipient must retain their belief in self and in prayer as well as their confidence in their ability to carry on and go forward. I merely assist the process." As she spoke, it seemed as though she grew younger still and her voice became stronger as she remembered her own confidence, remembered how her husband's love had assisted her process of growth and development into who she was at this time.

"Elisabeth, I wish to be your friend," she said, placing the sherry glass on the little table again, "And, I hope to enlist you in my cause. I feel that we are of the same mind and I believe that you will carry my mission forward as I desire when I have made the transition to the other side." Seeing the surprise in her listener's face fading to confusion, she added, "Yes, dear one, I mean to make you my confidant and follower and you will manage my work when I have gone. It may be many years before that time and I hope that is the case, but I am giving you advance notice that it is my plan to name you as my successor in this work and it will be you who point the attention of those in power toward the direction of those who will best serve the kingdom and society's future. I suspect that your protégé will soon be your husband by the annoyance in his eyes when he looks at your dance partners thinking no one sees and I approve. He is honorable, intelligent and committed to service. I trust that he will be successful, for the spirit medium, Miss Britten, has told me as much."

Elisabeth did not know what to say and was confounded by her lack of words. She moved her hands as if to speak, then said nothing. She looked up as though seeking guidance, but found none. She drew in a breath as though preparing a statement, yet no sound issued forth. Ultimately, she sat quietly with her hands in her lap wondering how to proceed when a woman, who had been a complete stranger until half an hour earlier, overwhelmed her with a future planned out for her.

Emmaline watched this with an uptilting of the corners of her mouth indicating her gentle amusement. Yes, she thought, Elisabeth has been enlisted --- she has no good reason for declining, rather many good ones for accepting the task and in her the future of my work has been secured.

Finally, Elisabeth drew in a another deeper breath and let it out quickly in a gesture of resignation to the future Emmaline had planned for her.

Sensing capitulation, her companion asked, "May I visit you from time to time? It would help you to have information I can share with you while I am still alive."

Her gentle, loving manner being unchanged by this new task for the future, Elisabeth answered, "Of course you may, Emmaline. It is only that I thought we would have time to be together before I had more responsibilities, you see. I could still have more children, though this time I would make greater use of nursemaids." She smiled shyly at her companion with this revelation.

"Goodness, surely you are not….." exclaimed Emmaline.

"Oh, no! However, I am but thirty-six and many have had children far later in life."

"Yes, that is true," Emmaline answered, then smiled and said, "However you need not worry, my dear, I plan to live a great deal longer."

At this point Elisabeth remembered that she had come upstairs to use the facilities and asked Emmaline to wait for her, but her new friend answered, smiling, "I will call on you in the very near future and you may be certain that I will advise you of my visit well in advance," then, with a conspiratorial wink, she sallied forth leaving Elisabeth to her necessities.

When Elisabeth had relieved herself, powdered her nose, and dabbed a bit of scent behind her ears and between her bosoms, lest the exertion of dancing give her a musky odor of sweat, she returned to the bedroom cum ladies' lounge, and seeing only a few young girls deep in conversation, she descended to rejoin the milling guests.

John spotted her at once from a vantage point across from the grand staircase and came quickly to her side, asking, "Is there a problem? You've been up there for some time."

She smiled and was quick to allay his fears with, "No, John, I was visiting with a dear friend I met."

He breathed a sigh of relief and led her to the dance floor, taking her in his arms with all circumspection and waltzing as elegantly as any of the fine gentlemen. Only she could feel the greater than normal pressure of his fingers on her back with one tracing little circles from time to time.

Glancing up, she saw Rose's face in the musician's gallery raptly watching the dancers whirling about the floor as though she were enchanted. She smiled and commented to John, "I believe that our Rose is living her dreams tonight and I know that she will have a month of stories to relate to Cook." He followed her eyes and, catching sight of Rose, gave her a nod.

Then, smiling down at the woman in his arms he said, "So, Madam, have you had enough of dancing, yet?"

"Oh yes, John, I have" she answered, "But we must stay later for we are family. I doubt we can continue until dawn, but we must surely remain until two o'clock even though I am not the hostess."

He countered with, "We could return to the Dower House and I could make love to you."

"Yes, and be caught out when the girls return!" she retorted.

"You could ask that George and I see you safely home," John mused, "For he will surely return to dance with the young lady he fancies." With that, he nodded in the direction of George, who was smiling down at a lovely girl in white organdy and very pale pink lace as he danced with her.

"Hmmm," she said, "It might work."

"Then it's a plan," he answered, leading her to the dining room once again.

She ate sparingly, for she had partaken earlier, but it was pleasant to sit and converse with those who were enjoying the refreshments. Richard had spared no expense and the offerings were plentiful, of the highest quality and well prepared. She especially enjoyed the smoked salmon, though many women avoided it for fear of offending their dance partners. Her remedy was mint oil --- a drop on the tongue to dispel any lingering odors.

She danced with many others and, indeed, by two o'clock she was more than ready to adjourn to the Dower House --- even without John's companionship. At a quarter past the hour, she sought out George and asked him to find John so they could walk her back together for she was very weary after the long day and wanted two strong arms to lean on.

When George returned, bringing John with him, Rose, having seen them preparing from the gallery, came and asked if she was needed, but her mistress shooed her back to her vantage point to see the Ball through until its end, for who knew if she would ever attend another..... Thus, Rose watched from the gallery as the trio departed, with George promising his friends that he would return soon. Elisabeth had wondered why they brought no lantern, then saw the coaches lined on both sides of the drive with lanterns lit so none would cross wheels with them.

After the relatively short walk to the Dower House, the young men watched as Elisabeth ascended the stairs to her room, then stopped in the study for a sip of brandy before returning to The Hall. John noticed a book on diseases of the lungs which Justus had left on a chair earlier that afternoon and began reading it as he sipped his drink. George however, eager to return, asked if he was ready, but could see that John seemed engrossed in the book and pressed him no further, bidding him good night as he left to resume dancing.

John waited for five minutes, then, pretending to yawn on the off chance that a servant might enter, he carried the book as he ascended the stairs and made for his room, where he quickly changed into his nightshirt and robe and made for Elisabeth's room a few doors away. He tapped lightly and, on receiving no answer, he turned the knob and entered only to find Elisabeth soundly sleeping in her bed, with her hairpins still in place. He looked down at her, so peaceful and so weary, and decided against disturbing her, then leaned over and kissed her first on the mouth and then on the forehead, as gently as a butterfly's alighting. Elisabeth stirred only slightly then, reaching her arms to his head, she pulled his mouth to hers and kissed him once again, rolled over and fell back into a deep sleep.

John, gazed down at her lovingly for a few more moments, and his lady love smiled in her sleep. He hesitated a few moments, thinking she might awaken, but she did not and he cautiously departed for his own bed; quietly turning the knob and peering into the hallway before entering it, then slipping soundlessly back into his room. He was tired, as well, though anticipation had brought him hope of the romantic interlude they had planned. All in due time, he thought to himself.

He sat for a moment, then his own bed beckoned and he accepted the invitation sans book, falling into the arms of slumber as easily as Elisabeth had done.

Meanwhile, the music continued at The Hall and the youth of many great houses danced into the sunrise. Some of their elders bided, reliving their own youthful energy and others discussed politics or the latest in science, world trade or medicine, but the adults had, for the most part, decamped --- at least those who had participated in the afternoon's Fete. The carriages awaiting their owners on both verges of the drive almost to the Dower House had dwindled to less than half their original number and even the servants in the musician's gallery had begun to leave, either with their employer or to their beds on the estate, that they might be awake the following day, which would bring a dinner party and final preparations for the wedding and reception, as well as the family luncheon.

Though the sun had not yet made its journey into the sky, it was indeed already Friday and all was as it should be on the eve of a wedding.

✨Chapter 22 – After the Dance✨

Rose dreamed of couples waltzing and then, suddenly, she was awake and staring at the ceiling of the small servant's room with its narrow bed and armoire. She turned her head and saw the stand with it's washbowl and pitcher and sighed, closed her eyes and saw the dancers again, then opened them, knowing by the light coming through the window, where she had forgotten to draw the drapes to hold the warmth, that it was late morning and Elisabeth would be expecting her tea.

She closed her eyes once more for just one moment's glimpse of the dancers looking something like birds in flight, captured the feeling of their ecstasy, and bending her mind to the day's work, she threw back the covers and steeled herself for the cold water she knew resided in that pitcher.

Half an hour later, she was tapping at Elisabeth's door with a tea tray, but received no call to enter. Lightly, she tapped again and this time heard her mistress' voice.

Elisabeth was already awake and at the window reading. She had not heard the first tapping, but the second had aroused her from her book and she called out to the person to enter. She had donned a morning gown of pale green lawn with a figure of small flowers and Rose was surprised to see her sitting there completely dressed and awaiting her tea.

She moved her book so that Rose could place the tray on the table between her chair and one on the other side, then asked, "Did you enjoy yourself last night, Rose?"

Flustered by virtue of being so late with the tea, Rose murmured, " Yes, ma'am."

Elisabeth smiled and continued, "What did you like the best?"

Blushing, Rose answered, "Oh, ma'am, 'twas all so beautiful..... I do believe that the ladies looked like flowers in their gowns and all --- and the gentlemen so handsome like. Did you know that the servants from The Hall even brought us as were in the galleries some refreshments? Lemon-waters and something they called 'ordy-ervies'. 'Twas really little toasts with pieces of smoked salmon and creamy farmer's cheese, but they said to take as many as we wanted so I filled me plate. There were other things brought as well and the pastries! I have never in me life eaten that much food and only stopped for fear I would be sick and cause you problems."

Elisabeth smiled widely in amusement at Rose's ingenuousness and the smile encouraged Rose to tell her more, which she promptly did, saying, "And the girls was that beautiful! They glowed so bright with happiness that they could have lit the room if the lanterns died. And those Balfour boys --- such tall and handsome ones, ain't they now?" That last bit, and the method of delivery (Rose had winked broadly, tilted her head and nodded), sent Elisabeth into peals of laughter.

Rose, delighted that she had amused her mistress, continued with, "Never in all me born days have I seen such elegance and style, nor may I again. Cook will be that amazed when I tell her all!" There she ended, for she had thought of Cook and knew that she would have loved to come as well, so she made a mental note to tell her story in a way as not to offend her over not having been invited.

Elisabeth drank her tea as Rose tidied the room, her thoughts of Cook having ended her confidences, and finding Elisabeth's dress from the evening before draped over a blanket holder she carried it into the dressing room to be packed for the journey home on Monday.

The tea was reviving and soon Elisabeth was asking after her children and John, to which Rose replied, "'Tis truth, I've only been awake this last hour meself, ma'am, and the dancing went until morning I'm told, though I left earlier. The dining room was empty when I passed, but the dishes was on the sideboard, so I'm thinkin' there's nobody gone down yet."

Elisabeth thanked her for the information, finished her tea, and leaving Rose to sort out the bed she left for the dining room and breakfast, though it was already eleven o'clock and the luncheon was to begin in a few hours. Perhaps something light, she thought, descending the staircase into the entry hall.....

It was there she met John coming in from the lane. He appeared to have been walking and quickly confided that he had taken a morning constitutional to help him revive after the festivities of the prior evening, for he was not accustomed to such. Elisabeth smiled and asked if he had eaten. He made a dour face and said he had not, which elicited a smile from her and the invitation to accompany her to the dining room.

Without a moment's hesitation, he had taken her hand, by way of leading her to the table and seated her, saying, "Your every wish is my command, ma'am. Now, what would you have?"

Falling into his comedic mood, she answered, "Oh, curds and whey, of course."

He laughed, then countered, "Now, really!"

"A spoon of the shirred eggs and one of the fried vegetables, two rashers of bacon, one toast with butter and jam, and a currant bun, please. You may bring me coffee afterward: plenty of cream and two spoons of sugar if the cups are the large ones," she answered, to his surprise.

John complied and she waited for him to seat himself with his own full plate as well, before she began to eat. As they ate, John said, "It seems as though we are the first, for the serving dishes were untouched."

Elisabeth was not surprised. She had heard tales about these high toned balls and the revelers sleeping nearly the entire day afterward, then partying again the next night. She ventured, "I doubt it will be wasted, though --- the staff will probably have it for their midday meal or the cook will incorporate it into another dish," then added, "However, it leaves me to wonder whether the young folk have slept at all."

As she gazed at him, she saw first one and then another of her sons appear in the mirror behind him and turned to look at them. With eyes still sleepy, but dressed and able to walk, each of the three said their good mornings as they entered the room and began to serve themselves from the sideboard. Elisabeth looked at them in amusement and observed, "Bit of a late one last night, eh?"

As if it had been rehearsed, they turned to her in perfect unison, and began with, "Yes, mother...." Then, however, each began on a different tack and cacophony reigned.

They looked bemusedly at each other when they noticed it and began to laugh heartily, a jolly sound to Elisabeth's ears: one she had always loved hearing when they were children. How she missed them, she realised. Was this what grandchildren were for --- to ease the pain of having your children grow up and leave the shelter of your house, taking their laughter with them? How much she loved these children she had borne, she thought to herself. How very much!

John laughed along with them, enjoying the energy of it all. To think that these young men would be his stepsons --- and the eldest only ten years his junior! What a lively family they would be! He patted Elisabeth's hand for a moment and nodded, while they were still occupied in selecting their food from the sideboard and she smiled at him, knowing that he was the perfect choice for her and her family.

By the time the young men had seated themselves, Elisabeth and John were discussing the prior evening and soon they were all engrossed in the conversation but, when a maidservant came to add a platter of freshly baked pastries, Elisabeth asked after her daughters.

"Oh, ma'am, they are both in one room with breakfast trays having a coze over the ball this last hour and more," she answered. "Their maid told Cook they be the happiest girls she ever served." A decidedly besotted parent look came across Elisabeth's face on hearing this and the maidservant, reading it correctly, added, "Prettiest around, too, by my way of thinkin'."

She was rewarded with a glowing smile from Elisabeth and reflected it back at her, dipped her head shyly, then hurried away in the direction of the kitchen.

Elisabeth returned to the conversation to hear more about the male perspective of the Ball just in time to hear Justus say, "I enjoyed it, but the time would have been better spent in the library," and to see his brothers look at each other and shrug their shoulders as though he was a hopeless case.

A chuckle arose in her throat and she looked at John, who was smiling as well, then turned to Justus as he defended his statement with, "Oh, I enjoy social interaction, but that library has many rare volumes, you know….." and everyone giggled --- not at him, but in appreciation of his youthful innocence.

George offered seriously, "'Tis well and good, Justus. We love you even though you are a bookworm and when I inherit you may come and live here and read to your heart's content."

He was rewarded with a chuckle from Justus, who said, "I will take you up on that, brother, and I hope that you will keep this cook in your employ, for her tarts are even better than those at Mum's!" At this pronouncement, the entire table dissolved into laughter.

Elisabeth laughed with them, but part of her laughter was joy at having sons who loved each other so well that they could take a ribbing and rise to the occasion. It was as though she was sitting back in her mind and evaluating her family and their strengths and weaknesses, their love and what they had assimilated from her teaching and that of others. Perhaps it was the late night which had shifted her a bit, bringing on this assessment, perhaps the impending wedding, but she had a feeling that it had more to do with meeting Emmaline Roberge, hearing her vision for Elisabeth's future, and knowing that she was a force of change for the betterment of all. In retrospect, it was as though she had met God --- or at least one of His agents --- and somewhere inside she had become very serious and contemplative.

George broke into her reverie, saying, "Mother, are you free to stroll the grounds with us?"

"Of course, my dear," she answered, "In which direction would we be going?"

"I thought, perhaps, the gardens around The Hall, for Uncle Richard has installed some lovely new rose varieties there as well as some topiary that you may not have seen, then down to the stables where we will admire his new jumpers and you can visit Abernathy and tell him you are well." He laughed at this last bit, a tease from his youth, for he knew how much his grandfather had doted on the horse, now grown old in their care.

Elisabeth liked the plan --- all of it, even Abernathy, for he was a dear old boy --- and soon they were off.

Richard had done wonders with the formal gardens and it was the only time she had seen them since she left the Dower House for her childhood home; the other outdoor festivities having been offered on the spacious lawns at the sides and front of The Hall, lest his precious roses be trampled by children and dogs. She understood his concern, for he was obviously breeding them, hoping for a true purple, though she doubted he had the focus to be the first to succeed. The scent of the gardens was magnificent, redolent of the heavy, intoxicating perfumes of the roses of the Middle East, so succulent and cloying that they seemed to be one of the rich desserts of the region.

The topiary was exquisite --- a menagerie of exotic animals and a few common ones..... Elephants trumpeted, swans were in flight, giraffes stood tall and gazelles leapt. A pair of lions guarded the entrance and a village of topiary shops and houses bordered the whole. She had never seen any so imaginative, nor so well trimmed and kept. This was a side of Richard she did not know and it surprised her a bit. She had been so busy holding him at arm's length that she had failed to appreciate his good qualities.

After they had seen and discussed the merits of the gardens, they wandered toward the stables where John and the brothers were eager to see the quality of Richard's horses. The jumpers, of course, were foremost in their minds, but he had fine horseflesh of many sorts and, as they reached the stables, one of them had been saddled was being led to the drive at the front of The Hall. The groom, seeing the party, asked if any of them planned to ride. Looking at each other questioningly, all shook their heads from side to side in the universal sign of negation and he continued on without further conversation.

Another groom, seeing them, asked if they wanted to see the jumpers and this one was rewarded with a hearty chorus of 'yes, please'.

"We won't take them down to the green pastures today, due to the quantity of people on the grounds, but they are taking turns in the out of doors in the large paddock behind the stable. Do you care to follow me?" he asked, by way of conversation.

Without words, they made a line, with Elisabeth and John bringing up the tail, for she needed help in keeping her dress from dragging the ground and being muddied or worse. The groom entered the paddock and closed the gate behind him, then waved his hand to indicate they should continue up to the fence. From that vantage point, they were able to watch him parade each horse by them on a halter, pointing out their best traits and citing their lineage. They were all impressed, though Elisabeth less so than the menfolk even though she was country raised. It was a jumper her husband had been riding when he died and she had no real affinity for them since then, though the horse had not been at fault --- the event had simply changed her life too greatly for her to forget quickly, though her future surely looked brighter these days.

Their last stop was to see Abernathy, who was enjoying his sojourn with companions of his own kind, but came to the gate of his stall to greet them and nuzzle their hands for a treat. Seeing this, the groom cut an apple in slices and passed them to Abernathy's visitors so that they could feed him.

Abernathy was delighted with his handout and whickered his appreciation as they stroked his head and shoulders after he had eaten the tasty bits. Finally, they had to leave for the luncheon and the groom passed Elisabeth a small apple to give to Abernathy as consolation for their departure. The old horse took it gently from between her fingers and ate it happily as his visitors left.

They returned to the Dower House to freshen up before the meal, washing the scent of horse off of their hands and changing into clean stockings and shoes, lest any mud or odor offend others at table. Shortly, and augmented by the twins, they were on their way to The Hall.

The meal was held al fresco on the terrace in the waning summer weather. It was comfortable being in the open air and visiting with family; children playing tag on the lawn and a few of the older folk dozing in their chairs with their meals half eaten, for weddings are a celebration of family, though shared with friends and community, and this was one of the private moments in the double joining of two great houses; a memory all of them would remember chronicle in their own journals and enter in their family bibles.

As the afternoon passed, the guests departed for naps or other activities and so it was with the Dower House party. The dinner party would begin in a few hours and it would be the girls' last dinner as unmarried women.

The small group returned to their temporary abode and spent some time napping or relaxing over a book, each wrapped in their own private thoughts about the momentous occasion of the morrow: Elisabeth, joyous for her daughters, but reminded of her own wedding in the chapel; the girls excited, but apprehensive at they knew not what; Justus, mindful of the scant year between himself and his sisters, felt awe at their audacity; Gerald wondering if he would ever be able to support a wife; George resolving that he would see to it that his family was always able to marry where they found love; John holding the tender secret that he and Elisabeth would be the next to marry.

It was almost seven o'clock when Rose came to wake Elisabeth and found she was already washing herself. "I think the violet dress, Rose," she said, "And the pearl brooch that was my mother's --- only a few amethyst clips for my hair, though."

Rose sought the dress in the rosewood armoire and pulled the required pin and clips from the case in which Elisabeth kept her jewelry. "Did you want the amethyst brooch as well?" she asked.

"No, Rose, it would be lost in competition with the violet of my gown. The pin will be better and in that way my mother can be at her granddaughters' wedding eve party."

Rose was touched by the thought of Elisabeth bringing her mother to the dinner party and wiped an errant tear away with her sleeve. Elisabeth saw it and touched her hand, saying, "'Tis all right, Rose, I cannot say I remember her, for I was too young and my father worked hard to be all that was wonderful for me, but I feel that she would have wanted to be here for her granddaughters --- and, to that end, her brooch can represent her for them. After all, it was her wedding gift from my father and he pinned it on her at their wedding eve party." At this confidence, Rose's tears began in earnest and her tender heart fair' broke at the beauty of the sentiment. Then, in the midst of it all, she envisioned herself telling the tale to Cook, when they returned, and reaping great wracking sobs from the dear lady with her heartfelt rendition, for Rose had a flair for amateur theatrics.

It did not take Rose long to pin up Elisabeth's locks into a couture style, both elegant and flattering, though she little needed augmentation and wore no maquillage --- not even a beauty mark. "There, that's done it," said the mother of the brides, "You are the best in a hundred leagues, Rose!"

Rose blushed at the blatant flattery, but she knew she had a way with hair. What she had no idea of was that had she been more than a demure country-bred girl, her gifts could have taken her into sophisticated homes. Elisabeth kept that information from her for, in her innocence, Rose could easily be taken advantage of and suffer greatly in those venues through the turpitude of mankind.

It was nearly eight o'clock, lacking but a quarter hour, when the Dower House party began the short walk to The Hall behind George and Gerald with a pair of lanterns. The brides were arrayed in purest white, a lovely foil for their mother's violet. Their brothers and John had complimented the ladies on their beauty and elegance, a sentiment sincerely echoed by others only minutes later at The Hall. Soon came the call to dinner and the ladies were all led in and seated.

Richard, at the head of the table, raised his first glass of wine in toast to the bridal couples seated, as always, halfway down the table and opposite each other. All those present raised theirs high as well. His toast was short and sweet. "To you all: bounty, healthy children, long life and great happiness." Moved by the words, the betrothed repeated it in chorus to all present.

Richard had seated Elisabeth by his side as before and Justus at her other side, hoping to forestall her attention being diverted from himself but, the dinner party being what it was, the family interacted haphazardly all around the table rather than in the formal manner of conversing from side to side in sequence, in order to allow equal time for each participant. His plan thwarted, he was left to chat with his Aunt Daphne seated on his other side, while Elisabeth held sway with a couple seated across from her and down one, a cousin of Daphne's, Albert Waverly. who had made the excellent decision to invest in mining ventures and then, in 1850, in the newly established American Express Company, a merger of express companies held by Henry Wells, William G. Fargo, and John Warren Butterfield. His wife, Alice, seated beside him, was as vocal as he on the subject of investment and Elisabeth was an apt student.

It appeared, from their glowing reports, that this company would be a successful financial venture, bringing them greater wealth and financial security on into their dotage and securing their children's futures as well. She had read of the Butterfield Stage Company once, in a London tabloid, but had little real appreciation of the magnitude of business being conducted in the Kingdom's former colony. John, seated within earshot of the conversation, but too far away to partake in it politely, made a mental note to question the couple on the security of their investment for future reference.

Conversing in this manner, without regard to the stilted conventional style, was a breath of fresh air and imparted a truly family feeling to the gathering --- as in truth it was! It continued this way throughout the courses, until during the dessert, when Justin and Quentin stood and asked for everyone's attention. Each made a beautiful and heartfelt speech to his intended and, since the ladies were twins, placed identical teardrop pearls set in gold and threaded on a finely worked gold chain about the neck of their betrothed as a wedding gift to be worn on the morrow. Seeing that the presentation concluded the ceremony, the entire company clapped and cheered, then returned to their sweets and the fruity dessert wines Richard had selected, each eating more than they had planned, but unable to stop at just one dessert when so many delectable choices were presented. Elisabeth had the raspberry trifle laced with brandy, then a ladle of melted dark chocolate poured over it. It seemed so very decadent by comparison with the fruit tarts Cook made, but she enjoyed every mouthful nonetheless and the sweet wines served alongside, especially one wine made from raisins.

By eleven o'clock the evening was nearly over --- the men had retired to the billiard room or the terrace and smoked their cigars and the ladies had visited to their heart's content, bragged on their grandchildren, and speculated on the future of the colonies as well as the on dits from London. Fortunately, Elisabeth had been visiting with Alice Waverly on the subject of mining in the United States and had been oblivious to the small talk. It was at this juncture that the men appeared and her sons and John asked if she was ready to return to the Dower House. Knowing that the morning would be an early one, she was grateful for their intrusion and before long all of them, even the girls, were walking along the drive with George and Gerald's lanterns leading.

Falling a bit behind the group, Elisabeth and John leaned closer to each other than necessary and enjoyed the comfort of that closeness, knowing that with everyone accompanying them there would be no chance for other contact back at the Dower House --- outside of the common rooms.

When they arrived, George ushered them all in, then closed the door with a flourish and stated, "I'm for a snifter of brandy --- anyone care to have one with me?" All agreed and they had a private family toast in the study to the girls' forthcoming wedding, with John participating as well, for he felt like family to them, though more like an elder brother than the role he would, unbeknownst to them, be taking.

The ladies left for their beauty sleep after a bit of conversation, but the men stayed in the study for some time discussing a variety of subjects in great depth, for during the past few days they had gleaned a large amount of information on finance, investment, politics and world markets, as well as their favorite topics: medicine, science, and engineering.....

It was late when they adjourned and set out for their beds. John groaned when, upon reaching his room, he remembered he had promised to fetch Miss Violet to the wedding in the morning, then went down to the kitchen with a note to the cook asking to be awakened at seven o'clock if he was not already on his way.

ᔥChapter 23 – Something Old, Something New᙮

Elisabeth lay in the dark room, certain that it was very early morning, but savoring the warmth of her bed and sorting out her feelings about her daughters becoming wives in a few hours. They seemed so young and, yet, they were so deeply in love. She came back to that thought every time --- so much in love. It gladdened her heart that they would have what she had not experienced until this year, for her time of being in love was a wonder-filled addition to her life. Her thoughts flew to John and the feelings they shared, as well as their experiences. He was so perfect for her, so aligned with her being….. Mulling over their relationship, she drifted back to sleep and dreamt of him sleeping next to her, feeling great comfort in that.

A few hours later, Rose's tapping awakened her and she sat up in bed to drink her tea, watching Rose preparing her clothing for the wedding. The girls came in, but had already had theirs and laughed gaily as they told her that their maid had said they must bathe as a symbol of leaving their old life behind. She smiled and hugged them both, then sent them to their baptism of soapy water. Yes, she thought as she sipped her tea, things they are a-changing…..

It was not long before she went down in a morning frock for breakfast and enjoyed Justus' company, for the older boys had gone for a ride and John had left with the buggy for Miss Violet's cottage. Judging by the time he left, Elisabeth surmised that he should be back an hour prior to the service and he and Miss Violet would have time for a bite to eat if they were hungry.

Justus had found a book on diseases of the bowel and was consuming the volume along with his breakfast, but she made him lay it aside and visit with her about his plans for the future. She was well satisfied in all she heard --- he had clear vision and a consuming interest in knowledge, particularly in the field of medicine, but in the other sciences as well. Knowing what she did of Emmaline, she knew for a certainty that his dreams would be realised and he would find both fame and fortune, but it pleased her that he did all that he did in spite of having no idea that his future was being assisted.

It was after half past nine when John arrived with Miss Violet and they found Elisabeth in the dining room nibbling at her breakfast still. As she suspected, Miss Violet had forgotten to eat and John had not bothered, so they both sat with her and tucked into a light breakfast, knowing that the reception was only a few hours in the offing..... She suggested that Miss Violet slip a few biscuits in her handbag against any hunger pains and, with a grin, her friend did just that.

Elisabeth invited her to come up to her room and visit while she dressed for the wedding and John asked, facetiously, "May I come?" knowing full well the answer. He would not have asked in front of anyone else but, after all, she was their confidant.

Elisabeth looked at him with a lopsided smile and said, "No, John, you too must dress. That suit is not the one you planned to wear."

"Well, saints above! I had forgotten," he answered, with a wink in Miss Violet's direction, causing both ladies to begin laughing.

At that moment, George and Gerald strolled in, dressed for the wedding and asked what was so funny. John told them as the ladies escaped for the second floor and soon they were laughing as well.

Upstairs, Rose had readied everything for her mistress. The girls were still using the bathtub, so Elisabeth would wash in the basin with the warm water Rose had brought.

With Miss Violet seated in one of the chairs near the window, Rose moved a screen between the ladies for privacy while Elisabeth washed, but they conversed quite well in spite of it --- only, not about John, of course.

Her friend was curious about the Ball and Elisabeth, as well as Rose, delighted her with their recounting of the evening from two perspectives while Rose helped Elisabeth dress. The screen had disappeared once her undergarments were in place and Elisabeth so enjoyed this more face to face part of the visit with her friend. When Miss Violet complimented her on the elegant new dress, she returned the favor, saying that the pastel violet fabric Miss Violet had chosen for her new dress gave her blue eyes a tinge of the same hue as her name, and it brought a smile to her face. The ladies exchanged compliments on their choice of hats and smiled, for each knew that they had chosen them together.

When the two ladies descended the stairs, the gentlemen were awaiting them in the entry hall and gave them a round of applause, before they all departed for the chapel near The Hall. The seating being less than one hundred, the many arched glass doors along its sides had been opened and chairs placed for those of lesser stature or connection under the grape arbors abutting its stone walls. These chairs would give most a view of the nuptials and a portion, at least, of the brides' entry and departure for the reception, which was to be held on the terrace and grounds and inside The Hall as the Fete had been.

❧Chapter 24 – Vows and a Surprise for Miss Violet❧

Miss Violet sat with the brides' family in the front row and when Richard, as acknowledged head of the family, had picked the brides up in his carriage and delivered them the short distance, he then walked with them, one on each arm, up the aisle to their prospective husbands and handed them over to them when the minister asked 'Who gives these women in marriage?' saying, "I do and their mother does, nodding in her direction."

The girls looked exquisite in matching dresses of rich, white French lace, both heavy and expensive, and made in the artistic style their mother so favored, free of excessive ornamentation, bustles, and artifice. Their hair had been pinned up with their curls falling from a center tiara and their veils were of the sheerest gauze. The doubling of their beauty left the guests speechless and their husbands could not take their eyes off of them. Great Aunt Daphne had been very astute in presenting them as a pair, for the sight of two such comely girls was indeed a treat for the eyes and that they were identical made the sight all the more appealing.

As always, the wedding itself proceeds quickly unless the participants ask a number of friends to sing, and that was not the case in this family. Within half an hour it was over and done with, the girls' names had been changed to Balfour and they were standing in the receiving line outside of the chapel to be wished well by their guests --- and to direct them toward the reception areas.

The immediate families were also expected to be in the receiving line with Richard and the Balfours and Elisabeth and her sons shook the hands of many they knew and many they had only just met, while John walked Miss Violet past the carriages lining the drive to the terrace.

The reception went on all afternoon with food, musicians tucked here and there playing ballads, and people visiting and even playing cards. As Elisabeth introduced Miss Violet to some of the guests, they came to one she recognized: Alice Waverly. Both were stunned, for their mothers were first cousins, but they had not seen each other in decades. Soon, they were chatting as though the many years had never passed, catching up on old stories and discovering who had married, been born, or buried. They continued in this manner until Miss Violet asked John to take her home a short time after five o'clock, for she knew that Spot would be looking for her --- and his dinner --- and she wanted John and Abernathy to be on the road only during the daylight hours. She and Alice exchanged their directions and promised to visit each other soon. Elisabeth saw a light in Alice's eyes which to her indicated sincerity and hoped that someday in the future Miss Violet could live with her and be less lonely.

Elisabeth hugged her friend, promising to visit soon, then John helped her into the buggy, which a groom had brought around to the drive in front of The Hall. Elisabeth and Alice stood there, watching them until they went around a curve and disappeared from sight, then returned to the terrace and the guests.

A number had already left, but those staying at The Hall were still there, as well as the Balfours. Justin and Quentin would be spending the night with their wives in a suite of rooms at The Hall, due to the greater privacy and size of the rooms as well as symbolizing a transfer of the girls to their husbands. The girls would see to the packing of their trunks after church the following morning in preparation for their departure on Monday and Elisabeth, John and Rose would leave for home after church in a carriage offered by the Balfours, that all might be managed in one trip. A groom would drive the buggy along behind and he would ride back with the coachman.

Elisabeth went into the dining room to fetch a plate of tidbits for an elderly cousin of Richard's who used a walking stick and heard a voice known to her as she was spooning a bit of thick, rich custard onto his plate next to a slice of camembert and soft buttered toast. Turning, she saw Dr. Walford and said, "Were you at the wedding? I must have overlooked you."

"Ah, no, I had an emergent case in the direction of London yesterday and could not return in time to see the nuptials," he replied.

"A friend or a patient?" she asked politely.

"Both, in point of fact," he answered, "A relative of Her Majesty --- a patient one may never turn away from the door."

She smiled at his name-dropping, misjudging him, for he had not done it to impress, rather to complain. "Are you often called away from your other pursuits to attend this patient?" she asked.

"No, fortunately, though if the man would but cease his drinking, he would live a far more comfortable life --- and a longer one!"

At that point she was rescued by none other than Richard, who asked if she had finished with the plate for his cousin and sent her scurrying out to him with it in hand, then turned to visit with the doctor --- mainly to determine if he could be a potential rival.

Elisabeth brought the plate to its intended destination and, after visiting for a few moments to assure herself that the ageing gentleman was satisfied with her choices, she left him to his dinner companion and went on to another table to visit with a Hastings cousin she remembered. Caroline Adams had married away from the Hastings name, but she was still an integral part of the family and, though Elisabeth's daughter was not named for her, they were both named for a Hastings ancestor. The lady was happy to see the twins married, having enjoyed them as small children, before her husband had been posted to India with the diplomatic mission. His health had suffered there and he was back in London for treatment and possible retirement, so she had been quite happy to hear of the twin engagements and said, "They were so very close as children, Elisabeth. It is a blessing that they will sustain that as grown women and, having married brothers, their children will have, in effect, four parents. I remember reading of a family in which twins had married twins, but I disremember whether they had all had children."

Elisabeth's interest was piqued. In her medical studies she had noted that the children of those closely related had a greater risk of inheriting problems and filed Caroline's story in the back of her mind for future study, then asked, "And how are your husband's treatments progressing?"

"You know what the colonies can be, Beth, little sanitation, insects and debris on every hand, to say nothing of the abject poverty….." I call it a miracle that we survived!

Elisabeth smiled, for she had not been called Beth by anyone other than her father, and hearing the name brought back memories that left her in an even more tender place within herself than usual. It was a moment before she continued, holding up her end of the conversation with, "Yes, you may well be right. Poverty means little to eat and even that of low quality….." She trailed off, thinking of the poor of London, as well…..

Caroline began again, saying, "It was interesting being there, for we were invited to the homes of the wealthy, not the poor, of course, though the streets were filled with throngs. However it was the insects that were the most insidious."

"Yes, they are that," answered Elisabeth.

At that moment another Hastings cousin came to claim Caroline, asking after her husband, and Elisabeth moved onward to the Bride's Table to share a meal with her daughters one last time before they entered their lives as married women. This table was large, with the couples at either end and space for four on either side, thus accommodating a total of twelve. Initially, she sat next to Caroline and pointed out to her their cousin of the same name, sitting at a table nearby. After a bit of conversation, she went to Catherine's side and told her the same, reminding her of the porcelain dolls this cousin had given them as children. Catherine's was her favorite toy and she still propped the beautiful doll in the middle of her bed.

Seeing that others wished to visit with the newlyweds, she made her sojourn at their table shorter than she would have liked, but went on to a table of children, who were becoming unseemingly boisterous, thinking how easily an excess of sugar and high spirits brought children's voices to be intrusive. She spoke to them quietly and suggested that if they wished to be noisy they should move to the lawns, where others were having a game of badminton. At first, they wanted to stay where they were, but finally capitulated and moved to the lawn to have a race.

Immediately, their table was annexed by the adults present and, since seating was at a premium on the terrace, the children had nowhere to go but inside, the last place they wanted to be --- or on the lawn.

It was a little after seven when John returned from seeing Miss Violet home. Elisabeth could see that the brisk pace of his journey had reddened his cheeks from the wind whipping by and somehow it excited her as the wedding itself had done. He came and visited with those he knew or had met during the course of the week and, from time to time, managed to brush her hand or bump against her in moving from one group to another. Each time, it was as though a shock had gone through her which she felt in every part of her being.

By this time, supper dishes had replaced the luncheon and reception offerings on the sideboard along one dining room wall: pheasant, rabbit, huge roasts of beef, fish, timbales, pates, dressings, vegetable dishes, exotic fruits, and pastries and breads of every description. Along the entire wall opposite, tables had been placed for the gifts received and they were laden to the groaning point with the bounty of the wedding guests.

Elisabeth went in to bring food out to the ageing, and even brought a few of them in with her to sit at the indoor table. Meeting John in queue, she asked if he would help her with some of the plates and he answered, "Only if you'll eat here with me afterward."

"Ah, John, would that I could, but I've more plates to fill," she demurred.

"In that case, you have enlisted me as your trusty servant," he countered.

"Done!: she retorted, handing him another plate with a grin.

They took out four plates the first trip, four more the second, and three on the third, then returned to the dining room to eat indoors, sitting across from each other to be less conspicuous. Their shoes, however, touched under the table, hidden by the long cloth covering it. It was delicious, that knowing that they were one --- at least in that small contact.

Their conversation centered on the banalities that people utter on such occasions, so as to not appear to be lovers --- and talk of medicine and what they had gleaned from those present. Finally, there was no one seated close by and John said, quietly, "The girls are to be in The Hall tonight and the boys are talking of a trip into Tring for a bit of ale with some of the young men later. Perhaps we will be alone in the Dower House."

She looked up in surprise and said in a near whisper, "Really? Perhaps you could come to my room --- for they would never enter like the girls do and they are certain to be late in returning and merry, as well."

By way of answer, he smiled a smile which made her want to throw her arms around his neck in the most wanton manner. It also made her tingle --- and not only where their toes met under the table.

With their proposed assignation arranged, they parted company to socialize once more and Elisabeth soon found herself engrossed in conversation once again with Dr. Walford. She could see Richard staring at her from the other side of the now lantern-lit terrace and presumed that he was thinking the good doctor was a rival. Good, she thought, it will divert him from such thoughts of John. Meanwhile Dr. Walford was discussing the problem of wayward women and the Magdalene Sisters solution in a light not at all flattering to the sisters, for he had been called to one a few months earlier where a woman was giving breech birth to a child, yet she had been incarcerated in the asylum for over a year. The sisters dismissed it with, "All in God's time," contending that she had already been with child when she arrived, but he had a feeling that either a priest or one of the men who delivered the goods the women laundered had a hand in it.

Elisabeth was fascinated with what he had to say, knowing of the plight of so many women in the larger cities --- especially London --- and they went on to discuss the dearth of men from war and the women who had no hope of marriage or children to succor them in their old age. Then, however the talk turned to the cholera epidemic currently plaguing the city and the doctor estimated that ten thousand or more would die before it was controlled. He had read of and seen these epidemics before and they worked their havoc quickly and brutally.

George saw her there on the terrace and came, as though seeking her out, to tell her that he, Gerald and Justus were going with a few of their cousins to enjoy a pint of ale in Tring. As mothers always do, she said, "Remember, George, it is best to be moderate in all things," with a nod of her head that indicated she was giving him a gentle hint.

He smiled, as did Dr. Walford, and said, "Yes, Mum," for he truly loved and respected her and had no feelings of being over-parented, then quickly strode away to join the group, but turned after a few feet and said, "We may go back home for the night --- don't fancy church in the morning and Little Tring is closer, especially after a few pints....." His mother smiled and stifled a chuckle.

The remnants of the revelers who had come only for the day were leaving and John came to ask if she was ready to be walked to the Dower House for he was going in that direction and she quickly agreed since the lanterns of the last coaches lining the drive would soon be gone.

Elisabeth took her leave of Dr. Walford and, taking John's arm with a circumspect distance between them, they forayed onto the drive, moving from side to side to accommodate some of the departing carriages, and made their way back to the house now devoid of anyone but the few servants.

John told her that he would wait in the study while she changed her clothes for a nightgown, but she answered, "No, I am back early enough that Rose will undoubtedly come to help me. You may go to your room and wait so that she will be unaware you returned and may think you have gone to Tring with the boys."

"Ah, you are a sly puss," he answered, stroking her cheek now that they were out of sight of any coaches.

With that, they came to the door and he showed her in, immediately ascending to the second floor as quietly as he could while she called for Rose, who came in with her hands full of flour. Elisabeth smiled and asked, "Are you showing your new friends how to make Cook's fruit tarts?"

The answer in the affirmative was visibly obvious and Elisabeth said, "Well, get along and be about teaching them a thing or two. Oh, and I will be going straightaway to bed for I am very weary tonight and we still have church in the morning. The young men have gone to Tring for a bit of ale and then will sleep at home --- for it is closer."

Rose stood there, hands in the air, attempting to keep bits of flour from falling to the carpet, and her face showed that she had no idea how to proceed without being rude and asking if she could leave. Elisabeth smiled a conspiratorial smile and winked at her, then shooed her off to the kitchen by waving both hands in a 'shoo, away with you' movement.

Grinning back, Rose made for the kitchen post haste and Elisabeth sailed up the stairs to her bedroom.

Moments later, she was admitting John, who had heard her door open and close, and locking her door once he was inside. She turned and they looked into each others eyes for a moment, then flew into each other's arms and kissed over and over again, deeply and passionately. John whispered, lest someone be in the hallway, "Let me undress you," and she nodded and went to stand on the rug in front of the fireplace which they had no need of, yet, at this time of year.

He followed her and began to remove her clothing, piece by piece. First, he opened the beautiful dress with its tiny pearl buttons from the nape of her neck down the length of her back, then proceeding forward, he whispered, "Now, raise your arms," and lifted it off without even mussing her hair, then laid the beautiful garment reverently across the chair.

Seeing her in her chemise, he took her into his arms for the kiss he could not resist, then stepped back to behold her beauty again and, loosening the ties, he removed her chemise as well. Feeling a sudden chill at the nakedness above her pantalets, she covered her bosoms with her arms and he whispered sibilantly, "Show yourself to me, Elisabeth. Hold your breasts in your hands and offer them to me," to which she immediately acceded, cupping her breasts and pushing herself forward as though inviting him to take them.

And take them, he did. He held them and massaged them, then began lightly pinching the nipples as he knew she so liked --- and as did he, also. She began to moan and he whispered, "Quietly, my love, quietly….." Her voice became softer and her hips began to undulate as the pinching began to awaken her nether regions to fuller passion. Leaving her left breast, his right hand found the opening in her pantalets and, entering there, his fingers found her soft furry mound and the firming bump of the button within. He began to stroke it gently, ever so gently, and she shuddered with the sensation he was arousing. He continued sliding his finger back and forth over it and soon there was a slipperiness to the motion as her body responded to his ministrations. He could feel that her legs were beginning to shake and knew it was not from a chill, so he backed her to the bed and opened his trousers to take her leaning over the side, then undid the tie holding her pantalets in place and they dropped to the floor leaving her completely and utterly naked.

His staff was at the ready and he turned her in one motion, then, spreading her legs with his knee, eased himself into her warm, juicy recess. Elisabeth arched her back as she felt him enter and sucked in a deep breath, held it for a moment, then let it loose, and John began to move in and out of her slowly, tantalizingly slowly, making her want more and faster. His slow pace was more erotic than it would have been had he entered and taken her quickly and he knew this. He would make her body respond to him over and over before they slept that night!

As he slid into her, he leaned forward and pinched her nipples, smiling as he felt the response of her muscles contracting around his manhood, then pinched them again and again, bringing waves of sensation to himself as well. Slow down, he thought to himself, we want this to last a long time and he moved even slower, but she pushed herself back onto his staff and squeezed her muscles down tight, letting him know she must have him and have him now. He obliged and picked up the pace, and her body responded with copious lubrication for his continued entry.

He groaned as quietly as he could and her moan became higher pitched as she felt completion coming to her soon --- then, suddenly, it was upon both of them. It was as though neither was aware of anything outside of their body and yet was fully aware of the orgasm of the other, almost as if they had somehow become one body, one flesh, and had no other way of being.

Slowly they stopped as John's own juices began to spurt into Elisabeth and he held himself inside of her as deeply as he could reach, standing there, his hands on her buttocks, squeezing them tightly in his excitement --- and now it was his turn to arch his head back as his body spasmed in its completion.

They stayed there locked in the culmination of their lovemaking for longer than usual, until he withdrew and reached for a handkerchief on the bedside table to stem the resulting tide of long withheld passion.

Elisabeth waited until he had stopped the font and then turned to him and, putting her arms around his waist, nestled into him feeling the fabric of his jacket against her nipples arousing her again. This would be a night of much love-making, she felt, and hugged him tighter, then turned her lips upward to him to be kissed, then kissed again and more slowly and thoroughly.....

✣Chapter 25 – Church, Then Home At Last✣

Elisabeth woke with a start. Where was he? She looked around the room and, seeing his clothing gone, surmised that he had left earlier to avoid detection. She lay back on the pillow, basking in the glow of their night of love-making and took a deep breath, then let it out as she assessed her satisfaction factor and found it had been utterly and totally gratified --- over and over.

It was not long before Rose knocked with her tea and, hearing Elisabeth bid her enter, she brought it in and placed it on the small table near the window.

"How did your tarts fare?" Elisabeth queried.

"Oh, Ma'am, they are top o' th' trees! You have some on your tray," she said, pointing to the tea tray, then continued, "This morning is church and afterward I 'spect we'll be traveling back to Little Tring."

Wondering why she mentioned it, Elisabeth said, "Yes, Rose, that's correct. I suppose that we will dine after church, but I doubt that we will tarry very long, for home awaits us. The Balfours have offered one of their carriages to us so that all can be accomplished in one journey. I suppose that one of their grooms will bring Abernathy and the buggy with us and then ride back here with the coachman."

"Yes Ma'am, I heard, and I had hoped I might ride in the buggy with the groom if they choose the one I like," then she blushed as pink as any flower, lowering her head to hide it, then peeking up shyly at her mistress to see if there were any repercussions to her admission.

The light dawned on Elisabeth --- she was not the only one with a beau!

Now the reason for baking tarts became clear and she smiled at Rose and said, "Of course you may ride with your beau, Rose, I am no dragon!"

At this, Rose lit up as bright as a sunny day and with a smile and a quick, "Thank you, ma'am," she hurried from the room to tell her news to the ladies in the kitchen.

Elisabeth enjoyed her tea in quiet, thoughts of the day ahead mingling with memories of the night before, and soon was descending the stairs to breakfast.

She walked into the dining room and, seeing only John, remembered that all of her children had decamped the day before. He had been watching the open doorway and as soon as she entered their eyes locked. She felt as though she were floating through the morning from that point onward, moving as in a dream and waiting for the afternoon, when they would be riding toward Little Tring --- and home.

John rose and embraced her, then accompanied her to the sideboard, where they both filled plates from the offerings, and then sat at a corner of the table so as to have more intimate conversation while they ate. Their feet touched, as did her right knee and his left, and the sparkle of the night before was still abundantly running through their bodies and flowing through that contact. They ate, enveloped in their own energetic aura of love, thinking not of the world outside it, but of their now and their future.

"It will be good to return to Little Tring today for I so love the cottage," Elisabeth mused.

"Yes, it will be good. I missed our clinic day and meeting the neighbors," John added.

Elisabeth smiled and said, "Yes, we have a good life, my love, and I look forward to more of it with the greatest of anticipation." She was gratified to see his face break into a grin and his eyes light up.

"Anticipation, is it? Oh, I'll anticipate you all you want!" he whispered to her grinning still.

She chuckled deep within her throat, then answered, "Oh, dearest, you may anticipate me from dawn until dawn without a murmur of complaint!"

"Ah, but will you anticipate me?"

"With the greatest pleasure," she answered, pretending to appear aloof, but stifling a smile. Their breakfast passed in this manner, jocularity ruling the table.

As they were finishing their meal, Rose entered to tell Elisabeth that her daughters were in a coach at the door asking that they ride into Tring with them for the church service, to which Elisabeth said, "Of course! Tell them we will be with them momentarily." Then, Rose, who would follow later with the staff, fetched a short cape, hat, and gloves for her and soon they were ensconced in the coach with the girls and their husbands, chatting gaily about their impending tour of the continent.

Elisabeth always enjoyed the aspect of the church when they arrived: the tower appearing to be a fortress and reminding her of the old hymn, 'A Mighty Fortress Is Our God'. Had she not been aware that the church predated the hymn, she might have assumed it had been built to echo the words of the forceful and inspiring song. In any case, the massive stone structure always lifted her spirit and gave her comfort.

Alighting from the coach, they discovered that the young men of the Hastings family were already in attendance, Cook having dislodged them from their beds early with a rousing rendition of her favorite hymn and the words, "Breakfast is being served, me loves!"

Later, Joe and his family had picked her up and the boys had ridden their mounts ahead. She confided to Rose, when she saw her, "I left dishes in the sink, else I've naught to do 'til they return this evening."

On this Sunday, the sermon was better than passing, the topic being love and commitment. The minister did it up well and it appeared the service was quite enjoyed by all.

Afterward, the day being balmy, the congregation milled about on the grounds, visiting and enjoying light refreshments and juice from the removable tables the elder Mrs. Balfour had commissioned her staff to set up on the grounds. It was a pleasant time of fellowship and an introducing of the grooms and their family to the community at large.

The minister had never seen such excellent attendance in his tenure at the church and moved from group to group smiling for all he was worth and shaking every hand in sight. The poor in this district were a heavy burden to the church and he hoped to bring more funds into its ever-lessening accounts in order to forestall the abandonment of farms by those too poor to hold themselves together, much less the land.

After the fellowship of a few hours, the visitors decamped, led by the bridal party (including Elisabeth and John) and Mrs. Balfour's servants began to clear the tables and disassemble them for transport by the arriving wagons. To his delight, much of the food was donated to the minister and his family to distribute to the poor, which left his wife and children scrambling for containers.

The journey back to The Hall was comfortable in the coach and the obvious happiness of Elisabeth's sons-in-law with their choice of wives was a joy to her. She knew they would treat her daughters well and she need never worry on that point.

She asked if this was the coach she had been offered for her removal to her home and Quentin assured her that it was, then suggested that Rose ride in the buggy and the boys' luggage be transferred in the coach.

Ah, she thought, if you only knew, then answered, "That would suit admirably," and watched him glow at her approval, making her wonder how much or how little approval he received from his mother.

They stopped at the Dower House for Elisabeth to speak to Rose and she reminded her that their belongings must all be packed by half past three, for the coach would return to carry them to Little Tring. Rose, still excited by her outing to church, nodded and hurried upstairs as the coach moved onward to The Hall, where the occupants would share the noonday meal.

Luncheon was largely a family affair, for a number of the guests had left after church, hoping to reach their homes by nightfall, and the long dining table was not completely filled. As always, the sideboard was well stocked and the conversation interesting. Richard had neglected to arrange the seating and Elisabeth found a seat with her daughters and their husbands, as well as her sons, John, and the Balfours. Richard, at the head of the table, appeared more than a little out of sorts with Aunt Daphne on one side and another dowager who was hard of hearing on his other.

Now that her sons were married, Mrs. Balfour seemed somewhat less overbearing and Elisabeth conversed with her for a time without feeling annoyed --- and, sensing that her daughters' mother-in-law would mellow, she forgave her for sending all the children along that first day.

When the luncheon was over, Catherine and Caroline, as well as their husbands, walked with her and John to the Dower House to bid her farewell. The coach had already been loaded with everyone's belongings, for the boys had left the luncheon earlier to pack, and it was awaiting them on the verge with Abernathy and the buggy behind it. Elisabeth stole a look at the groom driving the buggy and thought to herself that Rose had picked a handsome one if this was her beau.

It was not long before the adieus were said, the hugs bestowed, the tears released, and the hands waved. The distance between mother and now-married daughters was widening and inside the coach she sank into John's arms for comfort. Sensing that it was not his body she wanted at this moment, John gave her what she sought --- his nurturance.

The girls --- who were now married women --- stood and waved from the security of their husbands' embraces until the coach and buggy were out of sight, then, each dabbing her eyes with a petite square of embroidered lawn edged with lace, they turned toward The Hall, knowing that they would leave on the following day and be the ones riding away to their destiny. Seeing their sadness, their brothers decided to stay another night and see them off when they left The Hall the following morning for their ship and the crossing to the continent. They had decided to bypass London due to the dreadful reports of the full blown cholera epidemic and the many lives it had claimed, though it had been their earlier plan to break the journey there. The Balfours senior, who had decided to bypass their home in London as well, urged for the party to make for Southampton or Portsmouth instead of Brighton, for they had friends along the way in Newbury and Winchester and could break the journey south and back as necessary there.

"Perhaps, if it would be faster, you could take the train to London, then transfer to a train to Southampton," George interjected when he understood their predicament.

"Oh, George dearest," answered Catherine, "We want to avoid London for the moment due to the epidemic. Dr. Walford told us that some doctor named Snow believes it starts with contaminated food or water, which would mean we would have to carry everything with us and we already have so much!"

"I see," he said, "Bit of a conundrum."

Caroline spoke up, saying, "I believe that we need to go to bed early, make certain all is packed, and leave at the earliest possible hour. We will need two coaches: one for the servants and one for the rest of us and the baggage can ride in the boot and on top of both."

"Excellent, my dear," said her husband, "You are a wonderful planner. Since mother and father have brought one, we must needs beg one of your uncle."

"I doubt that will be a problem," answered George, "I will ask him."

"Shall we send someone to let mother know we'll overnight here?" asked Justus.

"Good idea," answered George and headed for the stable to ask a groom to carry the message.

In his absence, Richard entered the drawing room and became part of the conversation. As soon as he heard their plans, he offered one of his coaches to the enterprise and said he would have liked to be one of the party, but had many things to do in the next few days which he had already pushed ahead due to the wedding festivities. His nieces went to him and hugged him unabashedly for his offer and he pretended gruffly that it was nothing.

Meanwhile, Elisabeth and John were still en route to her cottage, though growing nearer, the country roads never being so suited for travel as the highroad. They were alone, for Rose was in the buggy with her beau, and they were locked in an embrace, savoring the moment and the luxurious surroundings.

Rose, for her part was being entertained by her groom, Seth, in the buggy --- with memories of his childhood and anecdotes on his upbringing. His father was an ostler and he had many tales to tell of the fine horses he worked with and the fine folk he saw. On horseback, the groom caught up to them mid-tale and relayed his message, then turned and made his way back.

When the coach and buggy finally arrived at their destination, the shadows were lengthening and it was late afternoon. The coachman and groom saw to the baggage and soon the entry hall was filled with valises and containers of many shapes and descriptions --- even Elisabeth's hatbox. Looking at the mound, the coachman sighed and said, "Best ye be telling us the rooms to take these to, ma'am, fer yer maid shouldn't carry it all."

John pitched in and in short order the three men had deposited all of them in their proper rooms with only John's own bags awaiting removal to the rooms above the stable. Then, Rose said she would show the groom the way to the stable and he, being a kind man, put the bags into the buggy and led Abernathy down to give him a short brush down and an extra ration of oats, for he had become attached to the old fellow in his days at The Hall. It was a half hour gone when they returned and Rose was blushing. Elisabeth saw the groom wink and Rose's color grow deeper. She smiled at that --- Rose was very much in need of a beau.

Finally, the coach set off for The Hall and the loading of the newlyweds' luggage --- for the morning would surely be an early one if they were to make Southampton by nightfall.

Cook had come to the front of the house to see the cause of all the commotion when they arrived, then scuttled back to the kitchen to prepare a meal for them, lest they find her derelict in her duties, and within an hour had an excellent dinner prepared for them. She had even baked that day, thinking to see them on the morrow, so there was fresh bread and her special tarts. Elisabeth and John thanked her from the bottom of their hearts and presented her with a slice of each bride's wedding cake, rich and preserved with rum. A few tears fell, but she quickly made use of a corner of her apron and whisked them away, saying, "Thank you ma'am, thank you," and holding them close like treasures.

Then, leaving them to the eating of it, she and Rose went to the kitchen for the preliminaries to a long coze at the servant's table. Rose began chronologically by telling her of the luncheon at which, she was sure, Mrs. Balfour had slighted Elisabeth.

Meanwhile, Elisabeth and John ate and then adjourned to the study and waited for Rose to peek her head in so that they could make a pretense of being tired so that they could journey solo to their separate bedrooms. In due time, she unknowingly obliged them and Elisabeth made her way up the stairway after telling Rose she could go and visit with Cook to relate her adventures, while John pretended to doze over a medical volume. He waited for a bit then, stepping lightly, he quickly went to Elisabeth's room and, locking the door behind himself, he turned to her and said, "Now then, what shall we do tonight?"

She looked at him with mock innocence and answered demurely, "Oh, sir, whatever do you mean?"

John grinned broadly, loving every moment of their interchanges, then replied, "Why, I mean to ravish you, to tantalize and tease you to a frenzy and then withhold what you are longing for until you can bear it no longer and demand that I give you what you desire immediately."

Smiling back at him and now working hard to maintain the character of the demure innocent, she laughed softly and winked, saying, "Why sir, I have no idea of your meaning."

Looking at her sidelong, he paused, then answered, "Shall I give you a sample?"

The sidelong look had its effect on her sense of humor and she could not keep herself from laughing, so she turned it into a throat-clearing.

John seated himself in one of the chairs and beckoned to her, saying, "Come sit on my lap."

With sudden inspiration she asked, "And shall we play doctor?"

"Oh, yes," he answered eagerly, "And as it happens, I am studying to be one. Would you care to enhance my training?"

"By all means," she said and flew to his lap.

With his arms around her, holding her snugly there, he asked, "By all means?" and seeing her nod he kissed her, savoring the moment and feeling the beating of her heart as his energy surrounded and intermingled with hers. Their interplay had sharpened the edge, titillated them and stimulated their bodies as it honed their minds. Now, their kiss was more gratifying, less ordinary, and filled with their passion for each other.

As they kissed, his hands began a light, tantalizing massage of her back and whatever else he could reach, but ultimately, voice ragged with need, he said, with seriousness "I believe that we must adjourn to another location."

Lightly, she sprang from his lap and, going to the bed, pulled the coverlet back, saying, "Would this do?"

John was directly behind her when she turned and she startled, then laughed and began to remove his jacket. "No," he said, "Yours first."

Understanding his meaning, she began to remove her own clothing stopping occasionally, and seemingly unaware, to pose seductively for him as she proceeded. Finally, clad in no more than her pantalets, stockings, and shoes, with one hand on the bed for balance, she bent over to languidly remove a shoe and, seeing her in that purposefully erotic pose, he could longer be patient. His trousers bulging, he quickly lifted her to the bed and intently watched her wriggling there while he pulled his clothing from his body in a fury of need.

Watching him thus, Elisabeth became more and more excited herself, feeling the energy of his arousal and she began to rock from side to side to relieve the energy of her excitement. When he finally released his stiffened member from its prison and it sprang forward at her as though searching, she drew her breath in sharply, involuntarily feeling a contracting of her inner recess and shuddered. Oh, this is going to be fun, she thought to herself, then lost the thought as he came to her and, with one swift move, pulled her to the edge of the bed still on her back with legs dangling and entered the steaming hot center of her femininity with his rigid staff. He stood there holding himself within, then, as he felt her muscles contracting around him in encouragement and tiny shudders rocking her body, he began to move in and out, only not quite out completely, and to pleasure her as well as himself.

At some point, he lifted her legs to his shoulders and, holding her hips, he pulled her onto the rigidity of his manhood over and over until his body began to shake so he could hardly maintain his footing. As he spent himself, he fell forward onto Elisabeth and holding onto him, she used that leverage to squeeze her hips forward and upward to feel every bit of the fullness of his possession of her as her body finished its jolting spasms of completion.

They lay there for many minutes unable to move or perhaps not wanting to break the energy, the connection they had experienced.

At last, he righted himself, but did not step back and she mentally thanked him for that continuing of the contact. Then, with gentleness, he removed himself and she stood up.

"I dare not keep you here tonight, John," she said, "For the boys may yet arrive."

"I know, and I will depart quietly," came the whispered reply --- and, after a few more embraces, he did exactly that and none were the wiser.

✋Chapter 26 – Rose and Cook✌

Cook sat with her elbows on the table, raptly taking in every word that Rose uttered.

Rose was in her glory --- she had a story to tell and she told it with a native genius for timing and effect.

Cook, on the other hand, had never been near to a dance of any type, much less a ball. A country woman, born and bred, she had her own genius --- for cooking --- however, the kitchen is many steps from the ballroom and so they sat there, with Rose recounting every detail of her six days at The Hall --- and, toward the last, even of her own beau. Travel, she had found, not only broadens, it gives one something more to discuss.

"Would you have another cup, Rose?" Cook asked, then smiling, said, "I made more'n enough for four --- bad luck for them they were sleepy….."

"Oh, yes," Rose answered quickly, pushing her cup toward the pot, "I love it dearly and yours is far better than anyone's. Me mum never made cocoa --- we had no money for it, of course, with so many of us."

Cook poured the rich, steaming liquid into the earthenware cup and some into her own as well, then prodded Rose to continue her story.

Taking a sip of the cocoa, Rose recounted, "The house was so full of people --- that bein' the Dower House --- that we were cooking and serving and cleaning up forever --- morning and afternoon. And, can you believe that that mother-in-law of our girls sent all the older children from The Hall to luncheon unbeknownst to the mistress the first day she was there?" This last she delivered with all the indignation one would have expected of Elisabeth and Cook was properly impressed with her annoyance.

"How many was they?" she asked.

"Eighteen, with her and John the only two grown, though five were her own children," Rose answered.

Cook snorted and said, "Eighteen! Too many children by far!" then asked, "What were they fed?"

"Oh, it was all fancy fare and Mr. Richard spared no expense, which was only right, him coming into the estate accidental like," Rose commented.

"But for children?" Cook asked, looking up and rolling her eyes as though expecting Heaven to open and the Lord to declare shame on wasting fancy food on children.

Rose chuckled at her friend's theatrics, but continued, "Mrs. Hastings was that annoyed, I tell you. I could feel her all prickly when I helped her dress for dinner, but she came back all right. It weren't the children she minded, it were the slight."

"And, what of the staff," Cook asked, and Rose allowed herself to digress into telling her what she had learned of the servants, who had been sent over from The Hall, for the Dower House was seldom used.

Then, picking up the thread of her story, once again, Rose told her of the Fete, explaining that it was a garden party of sorts. "I was told to serve refreshments at one of the tables on the grounds for the guests walking about. It was not far from the Dower House, but I enjoyed it ever so much. The ladies wore the most beautiful dresses you can imagine!"

Cook asked, "And, what did they serve?"

Rose patiently told her every detail and satisfied her friend's heart to the core, then returned to her story, with, "The ball was that evening and some took a nap, but others just walked about until time to dress. We didn't prepare dinner at the Dower House that night, for they had an informal sort of serve yourself affair at the ball. The cooks at The Hall did that one up. I went through the kitchen on my way back and they gave me a big plate to take with me --- pate, cheeses, desserts --- I was already too full and saved it for the next day."

"What desserts?" Cook asked, ever the culinary critic.

"Mmm….. Tarts, but more flavors than you make, only the pastry was not as good as yours." Cook smiled at the compliment, then Rose continued, "Then there was strawberry trifle and lemon teacakes and others I couldn't name."

"The trifle, was it good?" asked Cook.

"Yes, but they had too many berries and not enough cream for me," answered Rose, and was gratified to see Cook's smile for she was very proud of her vanilla cream. "The lemon teacakes were good, a little dry, but they didn't serve them with lemon curd like yours, only a hard, brittle lemon icing."

At this last, Cook spoke up, with, "I don't know why people are afraid to use enough vanilla! And teacakes without lemon curd is absurd!"

When she had calmed a bit, Rose began to tell her about the ball --- as seen from her vantage point. She began talking about the lighting, the décor, and the music, but then, beginning with Catherine and Caroline, she set the scene by giving a detailed description of every dress, hairdo, jewel, and dandy. Once her enchanted audience of one was listening with rapt attention, she began to tell her who had danced with whom and how often, how many times they went to the dining room (and somehow she managed to steer clear of more questions on this point), and at what time each person departed up until the time she, herself, made haste for her bed.

Finally, Cook was like a vessel so filled that it overflows and can hold no more, so she asked Rose to save some for the next day, that she might continue hearing the saga of the ball. Rose obliged for, though she loved being center stage, her mouth was a bit dry and they did have many days ahead in which to chat.

They sat there quietly for a long time, these friends and co-workers, each thinking her own thoughts and sipping the cocoa, curious about the doings of the upper classes and wondering and imagining how they would feel in that position.

Rose, savoring her memories of the ball, closed her eyes to see the dancers, smell their perfumes, and project herself into the dance. It made her feel so light, so happy, so in love with life --- and her young man.

Cook looked lovingly at the shelf behind Rose, where she kept her copy of William Hall's 1836 translation of *l'Art de la cuisine française; Le Pâtissier royal; Le Cuisinier parisienne* written by the great French chef, Marie-Antoine Carême, thinking of all the wonderful dishes the gentry had eaten at the ball.

Then, Rose began to tell Cook about her groom.....

℘Chapter 27 – A Letter from Abroad℘

John awoke in his bedroom over the stable and lay there only half ready to allow wakefulness to take over his being. He closed his eyes on the intrusion of light stealing through the window and tried to regain sleep, but to no avail. As he lay there, his mind began to wander to many thoughts: the past week, his love for Elisabeth, his feeling of camaraderie and belonging with her family, his love of learning, and even his childhood and youth. It was as though his brain was taking inventory of his life to that moment and as he lay there he began to come into the greater awareness of the lessons he was learning in this place and it was not only about medicine.

That does it, he thought to himself, I can't sleep another wink, and with that he threw back the covers and having left no banked fire at the hearth, he found himself very chilly when he went to the basin on the bureau to wash up before breakfast.

He dressed quickly and descended to give Abernathy a cup of oats and fresh pails of water, then made his way to the cottage to return the books he had finished to the study and wait for Elisabeth in the breakfast room. To his amazement, when he arrived, she was already seated and reading a letter, while a little pile of unread ones and other literature lay on the desk.

"A lovely letter from an aunt of my mother who is too old to travel. She sends her best wishes to the girls and a large bank draft to them as their personal funds….." she said, without looking up, then continued, "Oh, and there is one for you, as well."

Thinking she meant that the aunt had sent him a letter, he set the books down and looked for it, wondering why she would do so, and found the letter addressed to him. It was from a legal firm in the United States and his hands trembled a bit as he opened the thick vellum envelope.

Once opened, he read it through twice, then sat there silently, not knowing what to think. After a few minutes, he read it through once again, attempting to fit this new information into his life.

Elisabeth, having come to the end of her great-aunt's epistle, looked up, assessed the situation and, becoming alarmed, asked, "What is it, John?" with concern.

He looked down at her oddly, as though words failed him, so she took the letter from his hands and read it herself then, realisation dawning on her, said, "It seems as though you have inherited quite a fortune, John. Do find a chair and be seated."

He shook his head, as though to clear cobwebs, then pulled a chair close to the desk, not wanting to be even a room's length away from her as his mind grasped the possibilities of this new information. He needed the rock of her being to stabilise his emotions. He had believed his aunt was in good health and now wondered if she had met with an accident and those thoughts were all mixed together with the realisation that she was no longer there to talk to. He felt bereft and at the same time blessed that she had made him her heir and these feelings and the ones they engendered were swirling around within him like a whirlwind, leaving him unable to express the emotions, for he was not one to release the energy as sound and fury.

Elisabeth took his hand and held it, feeling the energy pass out of him and through her, grounding into the earth and dissipating. She read amazement on his face as it happened and thought to herself: he has acquired a new medical tool. When he had become calm, she said, "You may find it difficult to speak for a few minutes, John. Relax now and begin to organise your thoughts without emotion." Then, she continued to hold his hand and only released it when she was certain that he was able to verbalise the situation calmly.

"My aunt," John began, "Was always good to me. I never knew that she had much to will anyone, save her house and the land it stands on. I don't believe that any of my family knew she had been married when she was young or that she and her husband owned a gold mine. It looks like she held her cards real close."

Elisabeth looked at him with head tilted and an enquiring look at this last and he explained, "It means that she didn't let anyone know what she was holding. She was like that --- didn't give away much information," then continued, "It seems she had a lot of secrets and I won't know all of them until I contact her attorney. Did you read the part about not inheriting until I marry?"

"Yes, I did, John," she affirmed, then added, "Does this mean we should marry before Christmas? That is, if you still wish to marry me now that you will be rich."

"Don't talk nonsense!" he growled at her --- the first time he had ever been surly --- then said, "I love you Elisabeth and whether I have money or you have money makes no difference to my heart."

Surprised by his surliness, yet gratified by his sentiments, she replied, "Are you feeling well? You seem a bit out of sorts."

"You are my only passion, my love. I don't crave gold or property, only you," he declared, then smiling he added, "And knowledge….."

Elisabeth smiled back broadly and there was a decided twinkle in her eyes when she said, "Ah yes, knowledge, my rival!" then laughed the delightful, tinkling laugh he so loved, which drove him mad with desire. Seeing his discomfit, she chuckled deep in her throat and said, "Not now, my love, there are people about."

"Soon, dearest Elisabeth, soon," he affirmed.

At that moment, Rose came to remind them that breakfast was ready and they happily adjourned to their nook, where their knees could touch and they could steal a kiss from time to time as they breakfasted. For a while the boys would return and breakfasts would be served in the dining room, but with class term beginning they would go their separate ways and John and Elisabeth would resume their solitude. Meanwhile their knees spoke for them as they ate their breakfast in that cosy and intimate room.

There was a light rain beginning, so typical of the island country and, thankfully, but for morning mist virtually absent during the days of the wedding festivities. Elisabeth knew that the boys would stay over at their uncle's an additional day if necessary and almost hoped for an inundation.

When Rose came to clear the table, they adjourned to the study for more conversation and some reading. Elisabeth asked for coffee to be brought in when Rose was done and before long she arrived with a tray holding a pot of the fragrant beverage, cream, sugar, and two cups. Seeing it, Elisabeth said, "Thank you Rose, we will help ourselves when we are ready," and returned to her discussion with John.

After Rose left, they pored over the letter together and, feeling that it had no time limit, decided to leave their wedding for December. Then, Elisabeth had an idea. Perhaps they could consult a solicitor in Aylesbury when the rain stopped. John concurred, but since it showed no sign of relenting, they chatted and drank their coffee, then read for some time and finally began a game of cards to while away the hour until lunch was served.

Midway through, the rain stopped and the sun peeked from behind the clouds, but they deferred the trip to Aylesbury for the next day, since it was past noon and it might begin again.

At one, Rose called them to the midday meal and Cook had outdone herself, hoping to erase the memory of fine dining at The Hall. Elisabeth smiled conspiratorially at John and winked. Once Rose had left, she told him that they must praise Cook to the heavens when she returned to ask if they needed anything, for Cook was very sensitive about her people eating the delicacies of anyone else. John nodded his understanding and when Rose popped her head in, they sang Cook's praises en duet very competently.

In the kitchen, Rose regaled Cook with their compliments of the coq au vin, the pâté, the vegetable soufflé and the croissants, buttery and flakey as thin parchment. Cook glowed as brightly as a new bride and served up the same for Rose and herself, which pleased her friend immensely.

Meanwhile Elisabeth and John were still discussing the inheritance over their meal and she suggested that they could always be married by the magistrate soon and have the church wedding later, if they needed one at all. John looked a bit Friday-faced at that and when she asked him about it, he said, "I don't need it, but I want you to have the respect of your friends and relatives and I don't want them to think that I persuaded you to forego a church wedding." Understanding his predicament, she conceded the point and agreed to a church wedding.

All was serene when Rose came to clear away the meal and they returned to the study. About an hour later, though, the boys arrived at the cottage wearing the same clothing they had worn the day before and, after telling Elisabeth that their sisters had left at the break of dawn, they went to the kitchen to beg Cook for lunch before stabling their horses in the empty stalls next to Abernathy. Laughing at their teasing, she cut them generous slabs of beef, spreading them with creamy horseradish, and placed them between thick slices of her own fresh bread. She pulled tarts fresh from the oven as an encore and the boys ate heartily right there in her kitchen, praising her with every mouthful, and Rose, listening to the banter, knew Cook would have pleasant dreams that night --- and perhaps the boys, as well, for her beef roast had a reputation for excellence.

As soon as they were done, she shooed them off to the stables and reminded them to bathe and change their clothes for dinner.

John surmised that there would be no opportunity for lovemaking until the boys had left and resigned himself to celibacy for the time being.

ॐ Chapter 28 – Flies in the Ointment ॐ

As she was coming down to breakfast the next morning, Elisabeth heard a knock at the door and opening it saw, to her utter astonishment, Dr. Walford. Hesitating for but a moment, she asked, "Will you come inside?"

"Thank you, thank you," the jovial doctor said and looking at her questioning eyes added, "Your sons happened upon me as I was exploring the old Roman Road yesterday afternoon and invited me to breakfast this fine morning, but I'd wager they neglected to inform their mother."

Elisabeth, hoping they had informed Cook, chuckled and said, "It is the fate of motherhood that children forget to tell us things, but you are more than welcome, Doctor, for our Cook prepares prodigious amounts of food when the boys are in residence."

Showing him into the dining room, they found, on the sideboard, covers concealing mounds of food on the platters beneath them. Moments later, John entered with the boys, who had encountered him while returning their horses to the stable after a morning ride. They greeted the doctor with the high energy of those who have exercised and asked what he had discovered on the road, but waited to hear his answer until all had filled their plates with Cook's edible offerings and found their places.

The doctor asked if they offered a prayer before the meal and they waited while he said one, then began to eat and talk. Finally, Justus remembered to ask what the doctor had discovered on the Roman Road if anything.

"Not much, young man, though it is still beautifully intact. They may have had their faults, but engineering was certainly one of their strengths --- at least the engineering of roads and aqueducts," he said, with a smile, adding, "To be sure, even exquisite tile work has sometimes been uncovered when farmers plowing their fields happen upon the site of what was once a Roman household." His comments brought up the topic of archaeology and soon the table was buzzing with conversations on local historical sites, but including the more recent engineering of the canals and the railroad cuts, some being nearly forty feet deep. Breakfast was a long affair that morning and it had gone eleven before Rose was able to clear away the dishes.

When they adjourned to the parlor to continue the conversation, they lost Justus and Gerald to their studies, but George found the adult company stimulating, as well as the talk of engineering and ruins. Finally, he left with John for the stables to help him muck them out while the horses grazed along the verge of the lane.

Alone with Elisabeth, Dr. Walford seized his opportunity, saying, "Mistress Hastings, I never hoped, when my wife died many years ago, to encounter a woman with a mind as facile as hers --- or as knowledgeable, but you are her equal and more and that is an accomplishment, indeed. It is likely improper to ask so directly whether you had thought of marrying again, but I am daring to ask it, for I wish to marry you if you are so inclined."

Elisabeth was unable to speak for a few moments as she marshaled her thoughts, for she had not had any inkling of his interest in this direction and had not prepared herself for it. Finally, she smiled a gentle smile and began, "Dr. Walford, I respect you very greatly and I am honored that you would ask that I share your life, but I must ask that you remain my dear friend and not consider me a possible wife."

A crestfallen Dr. Walford asked, "Is it my age? I am quite healthy, you know."

"No," she answered, "You are a wonderful man and ten years is not such a great deal older. It is that my affections are engaged elsewhere and I hope that will come to fruition."

The doctor, mistaking her completely, assumed that Richard was the object of her affection and nodded his understanding, seeing the logic in her marrying the children's uncle and securing the estate for George. He patted her hand, saying, "I understand, my dear, one must do what one can for family." Elisabeth did not understand this last, but let it go supposing he meant seeing the children into adulthood before thinking of herself.

They chatted for awhile and she showed him her father's study and his collection of books and treatises by all of the well-known men of medicine, as well as those who were paid little heed, for he had known that they often spoke more accurately than those who pleased the hierarchical minds of scientific pursuit. As they looked through the titles, she noticed a small book of poetry and took it down. It was a recent publication, *Voices of Freedom and Lyrics of Love,* by one Gerald Massey. Opening it, she saw the inscription, 'For Dr. Gray with thanks for mending my arm that I might write. Gerald' and wondered which patient this had been and how the volume so recently published had come to reside on the shelf. I shall check on it tomorrow, she thought, during clinic hours, and thrust the slim volume of verse into a packet of papers on the desk which she planned to take with her.

Meanwhile, Dr. Walford had found her copy of Gray's 1848 essay entitled "The Origin, Connexions and Distribution of nerves to the human eye and its appendages, illustrated by comparative dissections of the eye in other vertebrate animals", and was completely engrossed. Another Justus here, she thought. Then, an idea came to her, why not begin a medical training school here in the country? Perhaps it could be one in which women trained, she mused, only to be interrupted in her thoughts by Rose asking whether the gentlemen would be taking lunch. Pensive for a moment, she answered in the affirmative for all of them and Rose hurried to the kitchen to warn Cook that luncheon need be a hearty one.

Cook smiled broadly when she heard the news --- cooking for men with large appetites was her greatest love, for most women ate too little to gratify her need to nourish the world. Rose helped her as much as she knew how, but Cook was the only culinary artiste in the house. Lunch was served promptly at two o'clock, an hour later than usual, but the group had dallied so long at breakfast that Cook felt it was best.

George and John had cleaned up from mucking the stalls and laying fresh hay and when luncheon was announced all was well with them. Justus and Gerald had abandonned their studies and even Dr. Walford set his reading aside.

As always, Cook had outdone herself with what she had at hand: three large rabbits. Her rabbit in pepper gravy was well known in the local area through church bazaars and she served it to them with braised vegetables and dumplings, a casserole of rice made with green peas, bits of ham, and cheeses, a soup of chicken broth filled with sliced vegetables and, for dessert, hot berry or apple tarts with thick slices of Stilton cheese and a small snifter of brandy.

Talk at the table was brisk, for they all had much to say --- if it wasn't about medicine or science, it was about the exquisite meal. While they ate, Dr. Walford declared that he had never tasted a piece of rabbit so sublime. And, in truth, Elisabeth thought, it was excellent and she asked Rose, after she had served the dessert, to summon Cook, that they might compliment her. Minutes later, having changed to a clean apron and with her mobcap barely containing her curls, Cook appeared before them, her eyes shining when they began to applaude. Blushing, she began a curtsy, but decided to bow her head instead. Dr. Walford was quite eloquent in his praise of her skills with rabbit, as well as fruit tarts and she blushed even redder for, appreciated as she was by the Hastings, none had been quite so skilled with words as he.

She and Rose left the company to their dessert and, back in the kitchen, she glowed like the sun. Usually luncheon was a lesser affair and she would have saved the rabbits for dinner, but something told her to cook them while the doctor was there and he had been so appreciative..... Rose could have her groom, but she would dream of the doctor, thank you very much.

At the table, the conversation wound down a bit with the delectable tarts and Stilton and, of course, with the soothing effect of the brandy. Elisabeth was happy that Cook had made it special rather than serving something light like sandwiches and such. It had pleased them all and it was a joy to see her face beaming when she was complimented. She suspected that Cook had few of them when she was young.

It was half past two when they were finished eating and Dr. Walford announced that he must surely depart or lose his way should darkness or rain overtake him. George offered to accompany him to The Hall, for he planned on meeting some of his cousins at an alehouse in Tring for dinner, and his offer was quickly accepted. The two set out before half past three and Justus and Gerald having returned to their studies, only John and Elisabeth were left in the parlor. John took her hand and helped her up --- right into his arms for a kiss before going to the study to talk.

They sat at the desk, one on either side and when John saw the book among the papers, he asked why it was there. Elisabeth replied, "'Tis a strange thing, an anomaly. This man is gifting my father, with a book he wrote a few years ago, for saving his arm, but I do not remember him and I wonder why he sends it now, when my father is dead so long."

"Perhaps, like me, he didn't know that your father had passed," John answered.

"That is possible, but how did the book arrive in my father's library?"

"I see your point, but could it simply have been put there by one of your children or servants?" he asked.

"I suppose so," she replied.

"What is the title, then?" John asked.

"It is a book of poetry, *Voices of Freedom and Lyrics of Love,* by Gerald Massey," she answered.

John blanched, then said, "I believe that is a boy your father wrote of in his book, Elisabeth. He worked in the silk mill in Tring and was hurt. They thought he might even bleed out or lose his arm, but your father saved it and his life and wrote of the treatment in his book."

Now it was Elisabeth's turn to go pale. "Do you think he still lives in the vicinity? I have never heard of him."

"We can ask after him --- perhaps write to his publisher," John offered.

"Yes, yes, I believe that would serve," she said, "And I will ask after him in Tring, for perhaps he still lives there, though I cannot say I remember hearing of him in all my years here."

"A splendid idea!" said John, "We could go and return before dinner."

"Yes, John, let us do it," she answered eagerly and in a matter of minutes they were walking to the stable to hitch up Abernathy and ask after Gerald Massey in Tring.

The drive into Tring was short, but pleasant. They could have walked it in a matter of twenty or thirty minutes, but then would have had to carry anything they might purchase with them rather than putting it in the box behind the seat.

They stopped at the bookseller's shop and found that he had known Massey as a youth hanging about and reading, perhaps ten years earlier or more. He remembered reading some of the lad's writings in The Spirit of Freedom newspaper a few years later and mentioned that the material was well written and people seemed to like it. When they asked if he had a copy of the paper, he told them that it appeared to have closed in 1849 or 1850 and the last he heard of him was that he lived in London with his wife and was writing books --- mostly poetry and treatises on the workers, he thought, for the man was a chartist.

Elisabeth asked if he lived in Tring and the man answered, "Oh, not since childhood, madam, but he lectured in Aylesbury on Mesmerism and Clairevoyance early last year. I saw the notice in The Bucks Advertiser and Aylesbury News."

She stopped and looked at him for a moment, then asked, "In Aylesbury?"

"Oh, yes, madam, the man's a spiritualist and his wife, Rosina, is a medium and can read anything with her eyes completely covered," the shopkeeper replied, "Our Dr. Pope, who came after your father died, gave him a thrashing in the periodicals, saying he was a fraud, but few of us paid it much heed."

"Now that, I must see," she said and, turning to John, asked, "Shall we find them and ask his wife about your aunt as well?"

"It might be interesting," John agreed.

Elisabeth thanked the bookseller and they left and turned Abernathy toward home, where they began to make their plans in the study once he was released from the buggy. They would go to Aylesbury on Thursday and contact the paper to find Massey's direction in London so as to make enquiries by post rather than risking exposure to the cholera raging there.

About half an hour after they arrived, one of Richard's grooms brought an envelope for Elisabeth and waited for her response. The note inside stated that Richard would be visiting her at ten o'clock in the morning if she was available and he apologized for planning his arrival so early, but knew that Wednesday was her infirmary day. Quickly, she penned a note to let him know that he might share breakfast with them if he cared to and, giving it to the groom, she told him to go around to the kitchen for refreshment before he returned to The Hall. Rose, who had answered the rap at the door, hurried to let Cook know that he was coming.

In short order, Rose wrote a brief note for the groom to deliver to her beau, then finished bringing the evening meal to the dining room and went to inform Elisabeth and John that all was ready. Elisabeth sent John up the stairs to pry Justus and Gerald away from their studies and Rose hurried back to the kitchen to eat her own dinner before they were ready for the desserts to be served.

The two scholars entered shortly after John and began lifting covers to see what dinner had to offer them. Warmed over casserole, fried tomatoes, boiled potatoes with butter and parsley and thick slices of ham in abundance were under the covers and fresh bakery as well: both country bread and fluffy rolls. The boys filled their plates to the groaning point and John carried one to Elisabeth along with his own.

Justus and Gerald spoke of their lessons and the impending departure for their schools. They had been reading ahead on their studies in order to excel and prove themselves worthy of their training. Hearing this, Elisabeth was touched with pride in their dedication and knew that her father, and her husband as well, would have been proud of them.

John was surprised at their singleness of purpose, for he had seldom seen such scholastic prowess in the circles he had frequented in the United States, and he commended them for it.

Justus said, "Well said, John, but you have proven yourself one of us, for you read until the late hours, too. Confess now, for from my window, I have seen your lantern still alight when I snuffed mine."

John laughed and answered. "Yes, Justus, you've caught me out. The books are so fascinating that I cannot put them down."

Elisabeth sat there smiling at them, for they were all her students; she loved them dearly, each and every one.

When Rose came with the dessert, she was surprised to hear so much laughter, but it soon abated as the youths began filling their plates with berry cobbler and rich custard --- two textures and flavors which were their favorites --- and when the meal finally ended, they both filled a bowl with a second serving of each for later in the evening, when they were burning the midnight oil and reading every book they could lay their hands on. Making a brief stop in the study to seek out more, they adjourned to their rooms.

John and Elisabeth were left alone, but the nights were becoming cool for walking (or sitting) in the garden, so they followed the boys into the study and remained there talking about the future and their plan to contact Gerald Massey. It seemed so frivolous compared to some of the other issues they were juggling, but sometimes it is those seemingly small things which turn out to have great import.

Finally, they said good night and John left, with two more books in hand, for his rooms. Daring to kiss her since the boys were upstairs and Rose had just collected their cocoa cups and headed for the kitchen, John whispered, "Our day will come soon," and squeezed her tightly.

Elisabeth, her arms around his neck, sighed and leaned into his arms more deeply, then said, "Yes, but for now we must be circumspect, my love," and eased away to hold his hands and see him out the door.

She watched him walking down the lane with his lantern for a moment before closing the door against the chill and ascending the stairs.

ᔑChapter 29 –Infirmary Day and More Proposalsᔐ

Rose's tapping awakened Elisabeth to her tea and the maid reminded her of Richard's visit for breakfast. Ah, yes, as though I could forget, Elisabeth thought, remembering the hours she had lain awake wondering what he wanted. Was he going to ask for reimbursement of his costs on behalf of the weddings? So many questions…..

As she drank her tea, she felt calmer --- tea had that effect on her, especially the lovely Jasmine tea that her father had loved. Drinking it always reminded her of him. Remembering him, she thought of Dr. Pope in Tring, a relative newcomer to the village who was very opinionated and outspoken. He was the reason she kept the infirmary open --- many of the country folk didn't want to avail themselves of his services.

Finally, she knew she must rise, wash, and dress for the morning. She chose a skirt and blouse of pearl grey with a thin figured stripe of a slightly darker grey, for she didn't want to look too fetching to Richard. No scent either, she thought to herself, and set the bottle back on the mirrored dressing table. Holding Richard at bay seemed to be the occupation she was to follow for the moment.

She descended and went to the study where she could see by the clock it was a quarter to ten. Richard would be arriving shortly, she thought, little realising that he was already in front of the house and waiting politely for the appointed time before dismounting and knocking at the door. She sat and waited with one of her father's favorite books in hand to dispel her anxiousness. In a few minutes, all of her sons came down the stairs, greeted her, then went to the dining room. George must have come in sometime during the night, she reasoned, then was startled by a knock at the door just as John came in through the French doors from the garden.

He sat down with a book and they waited for Rose to answer the door and show Richard in. He asked if his groom could have a bit of breakfast and coffee in the kitchen, for the horses would be fine with her thick verge to nibble on and Rose went to tell him as soon as she had shown Richard into the study. Happy she was to see which groom had accompanied Richard.....

John and Elisabeth took Richard into the dining room and soon all were engaged in converation --- mainly centering on the boys' return to school. Richard said that he had heard many good things about their skills, but also that they attended well to their studies, never slacking or carousing in preference to applying themselves to the work at hand. They all beamed under the compliment and thanked him for apprising them of what had been said. It was then that he told them how proud he was to be their uncle, for they brought honor to the family name. It was the nicest thing he had ever said to them and the last thing they had expected of him, having thought him very judgemental and stern. It brought the conversation to a temporary halt as they processed the information and the change in their perception of him, but then, boys being boys, they began to talk again, including him more readily in the camaraderie. He seemed pleased.

John and Elisabeth exchanged a glance, then looked away quickly. Elisabeth said, "I am happy that my sons can bring honor to the name of Hastings, for it is an old and worthy family."

"Yes, it is," added Richard, "And so they have."

"I take it that the Balfours' made their way south without mishap," she prompted.

"Oh, yes, I had a telegram to let me know that all was well and they are on their way. It came after I dispatched the groom yesterday. The Balfours may break their return journey at The Hall, but they were not certain."

"I am so happy that all went well," she answered.

"Yes, but the news is not good from London, for many thousands have fallen to the cholera now. Some doctor has proven that at least some of the cases --- perhaps all --- are the result of a contaminated well or pump, I disremember which. Perhaps if they boil all the drinking water....." Richard said, trailing off into his thought.

"Yes, boiling seems to help in many infectious situations," she concurred.

"I have instructed my staff to boil all water intended for food preparation and internal use, in any case," he said. "I want no deaths on my head due to lack of sanitation."

"To be sure," she replied.

The boys and John began a discussion on contagious diseases at that point and she sat there thinking, only in the home of a physician would this be a topic over a meal.....

When all had finished, they moved to the parlor, but it was not long before the boys went for a ride before they began reading again and John went to the study for a book, leaving Elisabeth and Richard in the parlor. Richard stepped to the door and closed it, saying he would like to speak to her privately. He hemmed and hawed a bit, but then finally began with, "Elisabeth, I have waited a long time, but must now make my feelings known to you. I care deeply for my neices and nephews --- as though they were my own children --- and I would like to make them that. I care for all of you and I am asking that you consent to marry me. You know that I can provide all that you need. Please say you will."

Elisabeth took a deep breath and braced herself for what she must say and say tactfully, then said, "Richard, you have been and are a wonderful uncle --- no child could ask for better, nor could your brother. You are the fatherly person they remember most and will remember all of their lives. The twins know no other. However, I cannot marry you, for I will not marry again without love --- true love. I hold you, and will always hold you in the highest regard, for you are a good man and a responsible man --- far more so than your brother. We must thank God for that for, without you, your brother's sons might have followed in his path. In his death, he gave you a gift, the gift of raising his sons into professions and of feeling the joy in your right action."

Never had a man been refused so eloquently or with such praise and, in losing the possibility of being her husband, he gained the honor of being his brother's stand-in and the affirmation that he was a good man doing a holy deed.

Soon, she saw him to the door for, his mission concluded, he did not tarry and seeing his groom had already breakfasted and collected the horses, he took her hand and bent over it. When he stood up, she gave him a quick hug and said, "I am happy that you are my brother-in-law, Richard and I believe that your brother is happy, too."

At a loss for words, he turned and went to his horse, then mounted and, with a nod of his head to Elisabeth, they took to the road. She stood there until they were out of sight, then went to the study to speak with John, where she came upon him engrossed in a text on diseases of the foot.

"Is he gone?" John asked.

"Yes, poor man," she answered.

"Poor man?" he queried.

"Yes, he thinks he loves me, but I believe he loves the idea of being a father without having to hear them crying," she postulated.

"Cynic!" he shot back at her.

"No, just a realist. If he truly had loved me, he would have been chasing me and courting me when they were small," she asnwered, "And he never would have been so self-centered."

"Hmmm....." mused John, "I do believe you have his measure."

"Of course," she said, going to her chair at the desk, "I am a mother ---

we know these things." Then she chuckled, low in her throat, the sound he loved to hear, for it was so similar to the sounds she made when they lay between the sheets together.

John inserted a bookmark into the book he had been studying and, laying it aside, went to her and pulled her up from her chair and into his arms, then kissed her lips sensuously. "And do you know these things, as well?" he asked.

"Hmmm....." she said, "I believe I need another sample in order to make a clearer determination," then smiled up at him coquetishly.

Hearing Rose coming from the kitchen, he quickly stepped away to pick up his book and said, "Yes, Elisabeth, I have already read the book on dysentery and have just begun the one detailing diseases of the foot.."

Rose came to the door just in time to hear this last, then pardonned herself for interupting their conversation and asked when they might be having lunch. Elisabeth answered, "Oh, Rose, I suspect it should be soon --- at least for us --- for today is infirmary day. I forgot that Justus asked to go with us so we will be three or perhaps four; best go up and ask Gerald and George if they prefer to eat later. If we are only to be three at table, the breakfast room would be better, I think." With this, Rose hurried off up the stairs to the boys' rooms.

Elisabeth and John had a few more moments to visit before Rose came back to tell them that only Justus would be with them and that George and Gerald had asked for trays in their rooms. "Would half an hour be enough time for Cook," she asked, and Elisabeth nodded.

After a moment and before Rose had left the room, Elisabeth added, "Dinner should probably be at half past six and perhaps a very light tea when we return from the infirmary."

"Yes, ma'am, I'll tell Cook right off," Rose answered, hurrying toward the kitchen.

Elisabeth snuggled directly back into John's embrace as Rose disappeared down the hallway, but she lingered not long for footsteps were heard upon the stairs and Justus soon appeared in the study with a book he had already finished reading.

"Hello Mum; John. I hear that we three will be lunching soon, then off to the infirmary," he said pleasantly.

"Yes, Justus," she said.

"Are you done with the diseases of the foot, yet, John?" he asked.

"Not yet, Justus," John answered. "However, I am finding it very interesting. Would you like to read it next."

"Of a certainty!" Justus replied, "I am hoping to read as much as I can before classes begin again."

John smiled at his youthful ingenuousness and said, "I'll read quickly."

Elisabeth enjoyed their easy exchange and the camaraderie pleased her more than they knew. If they were to be father and son, soon, she knew that this would be necessary to her children's acceptance of John in that role.

It continued throughout lunch and the entire afternoon at the infirmary. When they arrived, Elisabeth set about telling Maggie what she was looking for as regards the poet and Maggie looked through everything she could find, while Elisabeth supervised the patient visits. Finally, Maggie came upon something --- a note in Dr. Gray's clinic records for 1936 showed that he treated a boy from the silk mill in Tring for an injury to his arm from a broken piece of glass he had fallen upon. He had lost such a quantity of blood before the manager was able to bring him to Dr. Gray that it was feared he would die, but he was a hardy one, that lad, and it had been noted that he survived his injuries. When she showed the entry, with no name, to Elisabeth, there was no doubt on Elisabeth's part that this was Massey and at least a part of the mystery was resolved and she breathed a sigh of relief on that score and knew that she and John had work to do in Tring on the morrow. Elisabeth smiled, praised Maggie for her help, and was rewarded with a happy smile in return.

As the three walked home after clinic hours, Elisabeth talked about the notation in her father's journal, using it as a teaching tool to remind her students that all must be documented so that others might continue from that point should the doctor or nurse become incapacitated and, also, to keep a record of all treatment to a patient. To do less, she told them, was sloppy medicine, and as she said it, she could hear her father's voice saying it to her.

They arrived home at about a quarter past five and Rose brought them tea and small cucumber sandwiches in the study to hold them until dinner after they had washed their hands in the ironing room off the kitchen. They had not seen anyone contagious that day, but Elisabeth was a stickler for cleanliness.

They enjoyed their tea and the sandwiches, as well as the ginger biscuits Rose had added to the tray, and continued chatting about the afternoon's work and Maggie's find in the records until George and Gerald came down and joined them. Then, they were asked to recount the progress of their afternoon all over again. Soon, though, Rose called them to dinner and the discussion was transferred to the dining room.

While the boys spoke of their reading continuously, they also began on this evening to make suggestions as to their departure days. Since they had no need of their horses at their schools, nor a place to stable them, they told her that they would leave them with Richard as they had always done and that he would send a groom to fetch them before they left. Justus and Gerald had made arrangements with Richard to use one of his coaches to take them all to Aylesbury Station the following Monday after lunch to see George on his way and the coachman would bide the night in one of the bedrooms in John's quarters and take Justus and Gerald to Oxford early the morning after. A groom, would ride over with him and take the horses to The Hall. Richard had made arrangements through his agent for their rooms in Oxford and they were anticipating their studies there with growing excitement. All of this showed in their voices and Elisabeth enjoyed listening to their banter as well as their conjectures as to what the fall and winter would bring. Their anticipation was palpable.

Finally, their dinner was done, though they lingered long over it --- and

Cook's wonderful desserts, for she was baking them continuously before the boys left and the appetites of those she was left to nurture were less ravenous.

It had been an active day and Elisabeth and John knew that the morning would bring them an early trip to Aylesbury, so they said their goodnights without lingering and, for once, John did not take a book with him to bed.

Rose came up to help Elisabeth get ready for bed and asked, "Ma'am, may I speak to you of something?"

"Of course you may, Rose," Elisabeth answered.

"It's only that it was, well, the groom this morning," she began, then continued, "That is," and finally blurted out, "He wants to marry me!" and sighed with relief once she had discharged the words.

"Oh, Rose, how lovely!" Elisabeth exclaimed, then asked, "What is his name and when do you hope to wed?

"His name is James Robinson and we have set no date, nor even posted the banns, yet, for we didn't know if it would be allowed, us being in service and all. He must ask Richard, as well, and you must be willing for me to wed."

"Yes, there are many things to consider for we do live at a distance," Elisabeth mused, then asked, "Would you both continue working or would you go to live with him?"

"We haven't spoken of it, but we know that we want to be together."

"I understand that very well, Rose, believe me," Elisabeth said, "We will see how things go and hopefully your beau will ask Richard soon and postulate some idea of his plans for your life together. Does he like being a groom or had he ever thought of farming?"

"I don't know, ma'am. We didn't talk about that, only mostly how taken we were with each other."

Liz chuckled and then smiled, saying, "We will work it out somehow, Rose. Now, seek your bed early and have pleasant dreams of your love."

Rose glowed with the knowledge that she had a confidente --- one who believed in romance and who would help her --- she was certain of it.

As Elisabeth lay in her bed, she thought of all the lovers: her daughters and their husbands, she and John, Rose and her beau, and the two men who had proposed to her in the last few days. Life was fascinating, she decided, then rolled over and fell asleep.

❧Chapter 30 – A Trip to Aylesbury❧

Breakfast was an early affair for Elisabeth and John the next morning and by half past nine Abernathy had been hitched to the buggy and they were beginning the journey to Aylesbury. She enjoyed sitting in the buggy with him with the breeze blowing across them and sun beginning to warm the land. Anticipation was high, for they expected to discover an address at which they could contact Mr. Massey.

Abernathy sensed their urgency and carried them faster than was his usual pace. The trees were still green, though the color was dulling and beginning to presage the change into the dress of fall and there was also a feeling of crispness to the air, a warning of the season and its cousin, winter, in the offing.

They snuggled into the lap robe over their knees, leaning toward one another, each feeling the energy and body heat of their companion as Abernathy carried them along toward their destination. This was a day of sun, though the trees, still heavy with the leaves of late summer and they only beginning to dry, screened it, and they were glad of the light, for an overcast day would have forced them to hurry along even faster to be certain that they finished their research and arrived at home before dark overtook them.

They reached the outskirts of Aylesbury by eleven o'clock and, stopping to ask Mistress Caldwell for the newspaper's direction and to tell her of her creation's great success, they found the office was not far from her establishment and walked the rest of the way, leaving Abernathy in the shade of his favorite tree with the dappled sun warming his old bones.

Introducing herself, Elisabeth asked for the editor or the owner when a typesetter came to greet her at a counter over which business was transacted. When he left to ask if she might see someone higher than himself, she said to John as an aside, "Always ask for the top person in an establishment --- the worst you can hope for is to be relegated to someone higher than the one you have sent on this errand."

John smiled and chuckled, then noted, "You are quite a philosopher, Mistress Hastings. I must explore this quality in you."

Grimacing at his formal address of her, she observed, "My dearest, you are a tease," and then, seeing that the typesetter was returning, she became all that is prim and proper as she waited on his findings.

"Mr. Robert will see you and your companion, Mistress Hastings and he said to tell you that his family remembers your father. Will you follow me?" he asked.

Robert Gibbs stood up and greeted his visitors cordially, saying, "I remember Dr. Gray, madam. He was a fine man and an excellent physician --- saw my son, John, who has now passed over, through a bad patch, once," he paused for a minute or so, reflecting, then continued, "Now, how may I be of service?"

Elisabeth came quickly to the point of their visit and apprised him of the signed volume from Massey, telling him she had no idea how it came to be in her father's study and wanted to write to the man to thank him and let him know that her father had passed over not many years after Massey had been healed from the accident at the silk factory.

"Yes, I have his direction in London here. I would not give it to most inquirers, but I know that you have the integrity of your father, for I have heard of your work in the infirmary, my dear," he said, then copied the particulars onto a small card and handed it to her, saying, "Please share the tale with me if it is an interesting one when you have discovered how the book came to your home --- perhaps it will be newsworthy." Then he smiled and came around the desk to walk his visitors to the street and asked, "I've heard that this fellow is your student and your youngest son betimes as well. Are you hoping to begin a school of medicine? That would be an item to write!"

Elisabeth thought for a moment, then answered, "Perhaps one day, but would there be many pupils willing to learn from a woman and would men of power tolerate it?"

"Yes, my dear, I see the predicament clearly. Perhaps things will change," he said without great conviction, then shook their hands and returned to his office.

By this time, it was past the noon hour and Elisabeth and John walked on to the pub by the canal before tracing their path back to Abernathy. Meat pasties seemed an excellent lunch and with fresh apple slices for dessert and rice pudding to dip them in they found their meal complete and, on this visit, they felt no need to linger, for both were anxious to begin composing a letter to the poet. Though, with the cholera still raging, they had no intention of visiting at this juncture --- but, when it subsided.....

John asked her about the card Gibbs had given her and she showed it to him; the direction being neatly printed thereon: *Mr. Gerald Massey, 28 Henrietta St., Brunswick Sq., London.* He looked at it for a minute, then said, "At least that is falling into place."

"So it is," he answered, then added, "Time for us to leave, my dear."

They found Abernathy happily standing in the shade where they had left him, finding a bit of grass here and there and watching the activity of the town, both pedestrian and mounted. Being the inhabitant of a one-horse stable, he seemed lonely at times, with only a few barn cats for company and the occasional visitor's steed. The boys' sojourn had been a happy time for him with the stable full and the sounds and smells of others of his kind surrounding him. First, he saw John and then Elisabeth coming behind him and whinnied softly to let them know he had seen them. John had saved some of the apple slices and fed the delectable treats to him while Elisabeth walked to the shop to bid Mistress Caldwell good-bye and tell her of their success. In a few minutes, she had finished and emerged again, ready to begin the journey back and John helped her up into buggy, then turned Abernathy toward home and his stable.

It was two o'clock by this time and they took to the road in a leisurely fashion, not pressing the horse and allowing him to pick his own gait.

For him, it was a fast walk and it was two hours before they saw the house again. The time had been well spent in discussion and kissing in the concealing shade of the buggy's bonnet. Both were in a very mellow frame of mind when they reached the drive leading to the stable. As they drove toward it, George left the deep shade between its open doors to unhitch Abernathy and said, "I've been grooming the horses --- sometimes I need to have a bit of physical activity to get my brain going again. Might as well finish up with this old boy," then led the tired horse to his stall, a curry comb and a double handful of oats while his mother and John walked up the incline to the house.

In the study, they composed a letter to Gerald Massey thanking him for remembering Dr. Gray, while advising him of her father's death fifteen years earlier and inquiring when and how his book might have come to be in her home. They planned an excursion into Tring the following morning to post it and then walked in the garden until the air became too chill for Elisabeth's shawl. Back in the study, they discussed their journey into Aylesbury and the thought which seemed to be cropping up: a school for female doctors. It would require at least one doctor to teach it and there might be a few who would feel it was of interest, but the largest hurdle was not finding teachers, but finding enough patients. This need for the sick drove the medical schools to the large cities, which were packed full of humanity, for who in their right mind would confer a degree on, much less consult a doctor who had seen few patients as a student.

The folk of the district were by and large a healthy lot by comparison with the smoky cities --- having fresh air and food available. One was more likely to find farm accidents in the area, which could be quite serious as well, but not contagious, and accidents in the small factories as well, such as the one Gerald Massey had experienced.

Eventually, the shadows lengthened until darkness fell and Rose came in to announce that dinner was ready. George had returned to the house some time earlier and with the advent of dinner Rose went to summon all three of the boys.

John stood and, crooking his arm for Elisabeth to take, led her in to the evening meal where they were soon joined by her sons, who were ready to eat an ox by their telling of it. However, with none in sight, they settled for prodigious portions of steak and kidney pie with a host of vegetable dishes, freshly baked bread with butter and, of course, one of Cook's excellent desserts --- this time baked pears topped with honey and sugared ginger root.

They lingered long after they had finished the meal, drinking coffee with thick cream and nibbling digestive biscuits, while enjoying their mother's company. They knew that they would not see her for a few months and were basking in her nurturance before facing the austerity of school once again.

John watched the scene and felt a very protective, fatherly emotion, which seemed somewhat odd to him, considering he was of an age which could easily have been their older brother had their father married younger.

Elisabeth glowed. She loved her children very much and her sons were becoming men of accomplishment and consequence. This pleased her and she knew it would have pleased their grandfather.

John saw this, too, and loved her all the more for it.

It was past nine before they adjourned to the study and, after half an hour, Elisabeth found herself sleepy from the outing and the rich food and, saying her goodnights, excused herself and went to her room. When Rose brought a pot of cocoa in and learned that her mistress had already gone up, she left the pot and quickly went up. When she knocked, Elisabeth was fussing with her buttons and called for her to enter. Once inside, Rose made short work of getting her out of clothes, into her nightgown and under the covers and before Rose tiptoed out the door after hanging Elisabeth's dress, her mistress was soundly sleeping.

John and the boys, however, enjoyed each other's company for the better part of another hour, discussing nearly everything under the sun and solving all of the ills of mankind: physical, political and moral, before seeking out their beds and the oblivion of sleep.

John lay in his bed and thought of Elisabeth and the light he had seen her in that evening. It appeared that with each new day she showed him a new facet of her being and evolved into something more than he had seen originally. As he lay there musing, he became aware that with each subsequent revelation of her inner self he loved her more deeply than before. Involuntarily, he chuckled at his own innocence in thinking that love would be static and that physical attraction was the major component of it, while realising that this love, this awareness of her inner beauty and her depth, was the one he treasured more than life itself. Finally, he rolled to his side, the feather bed beneath him and the quilts above, and fell into the arms of the dream time easily and completely.

ᔥChapter 31 – Back to Schoolᔥ

Rose rapped at George's bedroom door lightly, then again, louder, and heard him stirring. She waited a few minutes before the door opened and, in his nightshirt, he said, "Is it already time?"

"Yes, Master George, it is time," she answered solemnly, settling the tea tray on his bureau and adding by way of conversation, "Gone half past seven on Monday morning and time you bathed and dressed. The coach has already arrived and the coachman is in the kitchen breakfasting with Cook. He came early to bring the groom, for the fellow is needed back at The Hall later, and he is already saddling one of the horses. The coachman said it was good to come early so that he could taste Cook's victuals."

In his somewhat befuddled state, George only heard bits and pieces of her conversation and thought it odd that a groom was bathing and dressing over breakfast with Cook. When she had left, he tried to make sense of it, then let the thought fly into the ethers and tended to his morning rituals until, clean and in his dressing gown, he began to pack the clothing and other items he would take with him in a trunk and two sturdy valises --- one of them for schoolbooks.

By nine o'clock he had packed, put on his traveling clothes and was descending the stairs at the same moment Justus had chosen. The rest were already seated in the dining room when they entered --- and enjoying Cook's genius with a frying pan. In the kitchen, a very sated coachman could also attest to her prowess.

They lingered over breakfast until nearly ten, when Rose came to tell them that the baggage was already loaded and those who wished to accompany George to Aylesbury Station for good-byes had best secure a wrap for the wind was picking up.

In less time than it had taken Abernathy, the coach horses had delivered the group to the station --- and that with having stopped to pick up meat pasties for George to enjoy on his journey --- however, it was still nearly an hour before departure. Elisabeth sat and visited with Justus in the coach while John and the other two boys checked George's baggage for transport and then walked up and down the road to help burn off the energy of their excitement until the train arrived. The time passed quickly as other passengers, some with friends or family, began arriving and provided an interesting tableau which stimulated conversation.

Soon enough the train arrived and a few passengers stepped down, but more embarked before it made its way out of the station for points north. Dutifully, George's family waved at the train until long after his face in the window had passed by, feeling that they sent their love and protection with him by this act.

The coachman suggested that they stop for lunch in Aylesbury before turning homeward and so it was that they dined at the public house near the canal, all five of them sharing a table and eating the same meat pasties that George would enjoy when his appetite reminded him that they were wrapped in heavy paper in the smaller valise, which had not been sent to the baggage car with his trunk. Theirs, however, were served with fried potatoes and dessert --- fruit tarts with a dollop of heavy cream for good measure. …..and a mite of ale for the men.

The coachman was a talker and had many stories to recount to them. In truth, it was a bit difficult to eat when he had them laughing with such abandon, but they managed to be ready for the journey home in only an hour --- and, after stopping to post the letter to Gerald Massey, they were on the road shortly after half past one.

Elisabeth and John were dropped at the infirmary on the way. They were late, but Maggie who was filling in had been advised of their errand and, fortunately, there were no patients as yet. In fact, they discussed office practices for some time before a patient appeared, asking that he be allowed to see John about a personal matter. John took him into one of the examining rooms and waited for him to elaborate. He hemmed and hawed for a bit, but finally came to the point and told John that he had a rash on his "willy" and didn't feel comfortable talking to a woman about it. He had heard that Dr. Pope was not in Tring, but felt it couldn't wait due to the itching and burning.

John asked him to present the offending member and he shyly brought it forth. Seeing the rash, John felt it was yeast or fungus stimulated to over growth due to sugary urine, for he could smell the sweetness on the man's pants.

"Do you have the urge to relieve yourself often," he asked.

"Yes, yes, I do," came the anticipated answer.

"If you will give me a moment with my teacher, I will be able to advise you further," John said, leaving the man in the examining room.

Since only the three of them were present, he gave Elisabeth his findings and tentative diagnosis and she concurred completely: diabetes mellitus. He suggested restriction of sweets and starchy foods, as well as eating some meat with each meal for a greater measure of control, while using a rinse of vinegar and water for the rash. Elisabeth agreed with this regimen and John returned to his first patient under her tutelage and gave him instructions on how to care for the rash and keep it from recurring. Then, when the man had left, John made notes in his file and put it away in the drawer as he had been taught.

Elisabeth felt proud of his attention to details as she watched him --- her only medical student, but for Justus, who didn't count for he was related.

Five o'clock came without the door opening again and Maggie said, "I'm off --- time to prepare dinner for my father."

"We will go first and you may lock the door," said Elisabeth. Then, taking John's arm, she headed toward the road and home.

They walked slowly, each savoring the physical contact with the other.

Elisabeth loved her sons, but her mind kept saying 'one more night, one more night and we will be alone'.

John's mind was not speaking to him, but his body was aching with longing for her in very intimate ways and she could feel her arm linked with his as though it was a burning branch. No woman had incited his body to feel this intensity before. Only Elisabeth.....

It was after half past five when they arrived and skirted around the house to sit on the far bench of the garden to talk. With it being light, yet, and twilight not fallen, they must remain circumspect to all who might see them --- a bit like being in a fishbowl.

At six, Rose came out to tell them that dinner was served and they washed their hands in the rain barrel, as they had the day they met, and went into the house through the kitchen and down the hallway to the dining room.

Justus and Gerald were already there. When Elisabeth and John had taken their places, they told their mother that they had packed their clothing and books while she and John had spent time at the infirmary. The coachman had told them he would be up very early and could load their trunks and bags before breakfast if they left them in the entry hall and they said that they had obliged him gladly. Meanwhile there was food to be eaten and Cook had outdone herself. The roast beef was tender and rare, with creamed horseradish and pan juices to drizzle over the top. Cook had prepared escalloped potatoes and steamed broccoli with Cheddar cheese and seasoned bread crumbs as well as other vegetable dishes. She had prepared soup as well, for the weather was beginning to have a chill in the air and she was strong in her belief that soup warded off the ailments of winter. This evening's offering was her strong beef tea with freshly made noodles.

The boys said they were hoping to seek their beds early, but Elisabeth doubted they would be able to keep their resolve if a book beckoned, so she added a bit to their conversation, saying, "Oh, what a good idea, for surely you will need to unpack and settle in when you arrive and that should take you until dinner. I know that you would not want to sleep through that." They laughed, but the point was well taken and, indeed, they went to sleep early.

Elisabeth and John sat in the study with a warm fire to take the chill off of the fall evening, talking and each feeling the other's energy without touching. In actuality, they found it was erotic --- this closeness without touching. At some point Rose brought them cocoa, but they were so engrossed that they scarcely noticed and she smiled at their intensity, thinking, ah, these medical folk.....

In time, the hour grew late and they knew they should be awake to see the boys away, so they let the conversation trail off and, first touching each other's fingers and feeling the energy vibrating in their loins, they then embraced and it seemed as though their hearts beat as one and they were one flesh. They enjoyed this for a few minutes, as long as they dared and, then, after one long deep kiss, John let himself out the front door, saying, "Soon, love, soon..." and Elisabeth walked slowly up the stairs to her bedroom, savoring the feelings she was experiencing.

Morning found both of them in the dining room eating a hurried breakfast with the boys while the coachman ate heartily of Cook's victuals and then, with three hampers of food, one for himself and one for each of the scholars, he went around to the coach waiting in front of the house on the drive. He had already taken the trunks and valises to the coach and stowed them for the journey, so he placed two of the hampers in the coach and one under his own seat outside.

Meanwhile, Rose had gone to the dining room when he left the kitchen and it was not long before Elisabeth, Justus, Gerald and John, emerged from the house. The boys told them they would be home on December 12th or a few days later, then hugged their mother, shook John's hand and climbed into the coach where, seeing the hampers, they opened a window to say, in unison, "Mother, tell Cook thank you and we love her!"

Rose, standing in the doorway, heard them and smiled. Cook would be in her glory tonight, she thought.

Elisabeth promised them she would pass the message and, with that, the coachman cracked his whip and the horses began to move forward, pulling with them the coach and easing it toward the road. In minutes, they were heading toward their future and she and John waved until they were out of sight, then turned and retreated to the house and the study. They sat there quietly for a bit, for it was still early morning, and their second early rising in as many days. Finally, rather than fighting to stay awake, Elisabeth said with a tired smile, "John, I suggest that we each take a nap, have a late lunch and then visit Miss Violet."

John's ears perked up at this, for he knew that this was their code for a visit to their vacant house and he was very ready for a visit. He paused for a moment, then asked, "Are you certain?"

"Of course, my love, but I am too sleepy just now," she answered, then added coyly, "Surely you would want me awake to enjoy the visit."

"Oh, yes, Elisabeth, my sweet," he affirmed and they both rose and went into the entry hall, where they parted ways and went each to their respective bedroom and fell quickly into a deep sleep with thoughts of their beloved running through their head.

At one o'clock, Rose came to awaken her mistress for lunch. It wasn't to be served for another half hour, which would give her time to dress and freshen herself and she set about doing it.

John had awakened a little earlier in his rooms over the stable and readied himself as well, taking care to wash and shave afresh since they were planning to be intimate, then dressed and went up the drive to the house. He entered via the kitchen and snagged a small tart from the table as he passed and heard Cook's fading admonition not to spoil his meal by eating the sweeties first as he headed for their breakfast nook.

Elisabeth was already there and she teased him about sleeping so long, but then admitted that she had only just arrived. He seated himself with his knee touching hers as he tucked it under the table and sent an electric shock through her body, which tightened every muscle in her groin. She drew in a sharp breath at the sensation, then slowly released it and said, "Oh, it is definitely time for us to visit Miss Violet."

They ate heartily --- far more than they had at the early breakfast. As they ate they conversed, conjecturing that the coach had already arrived at its destination in Oxford and the boys would be moving into their lodgings by now and, in arriving a week early, would have time to explore the town and be ready for their tutorials. They had told Elisabeth and John that Uncle Richard had done his best for them --- securing large, furnished rooms in the home of a widow who was reputed to employ an excellent cook. The pair imagined them moving into their rooms and putting their clothing and books away, then settling down to a wonderful lunch with the widow and strolling through town afterward, perhaps with their landlady pointing out the sights. John thought about that one for a moment and decided it might be a little far-fetched and said the same to Elisabeth, then they both chuckled in agreement.

By half past two they were ready to leave for the visit to their secret place and then to Miss Violet's cottage. In short order, Abernathy was between the traces and harnessed and John was helping Elisabeth into the buggy while Rose came out with a hamper of treats for Miss Violet. They thanked her and John quickly stowed it in the box behind the buggy. Then, he took the reins urging Abernathy forward and they accomplished the drive to their trysting place and in short order they were closing the stable door on Abernathy and heading for the house.

Elisabeth produced the key and they opened the door and entered. Then, as soon as the door closed behind them, they fell into each other's arms and continued in that pleasant pursuit until they remembered that there was more to come. Hand in hand, they made their way to the large bedroom and, as always, they removed the dust covers and prepared their bower with bedding from the clothespress. Then, she sat on the bed and told John it was her turn to be masterful and he came and stood in front of her as she disrobed him, beginning with his coat, which he then folded and placed on a chair by the bed; returning to allow her to remove the next article of clothing --- his shirt. He folded it as well and placed it on the chair, then returned for him to remove his trousers and folded them, too, striding back in only his smallclothes, stockings and shoes.

She was wiggling with anticipation by this time and boldly ran her hands over his body with only his under clothing left on it. As she did so, the bulge at his groin grew larger and began to throb and push against the cloth like a tent pole might, but she left that untouched for the moment, preferring to arouse his passion until he could bear it no more and took her clothing off as quickly as he could manage.

Finally, she removed his smallclothes and directed him to remove his shoes and stockings himself, but to do it facing away from her so that she could fondle his bottom and perhaps reach around him to hold his staff. Eagerly, he complied and was rewarded with her small hand reaching between his thighs and to the front to fondle much more than his bottom.

When he was entirely naked, he stood up, legs still apart and slowly she withdrew her hand, fondling him all the while, and told him to turn toward her. When he did, she could see that his totally erect staff was pointing upward toward her, asking a question if she dared answer it. John looked at her lasciviously and said, "Now it is my turn….."

Scrambling further up on the bed in mock terror, and giggling all the while, she let him pull her to him by her feet, then remove her skirt, jacket, camisole and pantalets as quickly as a man can without tearing them off. He pulled her to the edge of the high bed and putting her legs over his shoulders as he stood leaning against the side, he entered the hot, wet recess between her legs as he stood there, gently at first, then with wild abandon, listening to the sounds she made as her passion was fulfilled and finding his own rising to a peak beyond his dreams as his body reacted to the sound of her voice and the heat of her passion.

In and out, forward he surged then retreated, pleasuring her as he pleasured himself, bringing the pitch of her voice higher and higher until she began to giggle uncontrollably and he knew he could let go and allow himself to feel the peak as well. With a few more thrusts his body began to jerk and he had to lock his knees to keep them from buckling with the force of the ejaculation he experienced. He leaned forward over her until their torsos met and he took her breasts in his hands and held them, nipples between his second and third fingers near the knuckles, and squeezed them between his knuckles by rubbing his fingers together. Each time he did it, she jerked as though she were trying to buck a rider and he could feel the contractions within her squeezing his manhood in the same rhythm as he was squeezing her nipples. Then, he put his lips to one and found that suckling brought on the same response. Being a student of medicine and curious, he wondered if his own nipples had the same sensitivity and, pinching one, he found that they did, though he had no female organ to contract.

Meanwhile, Elisabeth was still basking in the glow of their lovemaking and everything he experimented with gave her pleasure, so she lay there and let him play.

Eventually, he climbed up onto the bed with her and lay there holding her, while thinking of all of the years that lay ahead of them, God willing. They would travel to America to settle his inheritance and for him to show her its natural wonders. Perhaps they would travel to other places as well, he mused.

At that point, Elisabeth rolled over to face him and said, "Much as we would like to stay here forever, we still have Miss Violet to visit."

"Yes, we do," he answered, holding her close and raining kisses on her face and causing her to laugh. Ah, how he loved that laughter.....

Soon, they were dressed, the bedroom was put to rights, and Abernathy was pulling the buggy in the direction of Miss Violet's cottage. They covered the distance in a mere twenty minutes and, hearing the buggy coming, she had let Spot out the door to greet them. Abernathy whinnied at the spaniel as he raced toward them in greeting and Spot turned and raced alongside of his friend the rest of the way to the cottage.

Abernathy stopped in front of Miss Violet's door without being prompted, waited for his passengers to alight, then pulled the buggy to the verge where the grass was growing, green and tender, and began to graze. Spot went along with him to smell him and lick the salty sweat from his face and legs.

Meanwhile, Elisabeth and John were beckoned inside by Miss Violet and John brought the hamper from the buggy in and put it on her table. "Why, what is this?" she asked, surprised.

"Oh, a bit of love from Cook," Elisabeth answered, then asked, "Did you enjoy the wedding?"

Their friend lit up like the noonday sun at the question and began chattering away. Elisabeth had to hold up her hand and say, "Slowly, slowly, else I cannot understand a word."

Miss Violet smiled and began once more, "It was the most wonderful day! The company was dressed so elegantly and the service was beautiful. The girls were a paean to beauty and their husbands were utterly enchanted by them."

It was Elisabeth's turn to smile at her friend's exuberance and she said, "Yes, it was quite wonderful and I feel no shame in saying it, for I was not included in the preparations. The girls, Lydia Balfour, Richard and Aunt Daphne did it all."

"It must have been a nightmare of preparation with all of the events you said they would have," Miss Violet replied, "I could never have done it."

"I do not know where I would have found the patience for it," Elisabeth said, bringing packages out of the hamper as she spoke, "I was put out that she sent all of the children to the Dower House for luncheon on Wednesday without advising me of it, but then I thought of how much I did not have to do and I was able to let the annoyance leave me," then added, "It appears that Cook has sent you some calves foot jelly, tarts, lemon curd, a small ham, a packet of tea and vegetables from the Martin farm."

For the next hour and a half, John listened to them discuss the wedding and all of the activities prior to it --- Fete, dinners and The Ball --- over tea and biscuits. Elisabeth also told her friend that both Dr. Walford and Richard had asked for her hand in marriage in the space of two days and that she had sent them away gently.

Then, she asked John to tell Miss Violet of his news and he obliged. She was so happy for him and for Elisabeth as well. They asked her not to share what they had said with anyone and, as always, she agreed.

After one last cup of tea, they bade her good evening and made for the door. Spot, on hearing their footsteps left his friend, Abernathy, and came running to the door to see what was happening. Abernathy turned to look, also, then bent his head to crop the last clump of grass within reach without being forced to move. At that moment John reached the buggy and led him to the door so that Elisabeth could alight. Twilight was upon them and it would be nearly dark when they reached home, so they made their farewell short and, after hugging Miss Violet, they hurried to the road and home. Spot, having lost his friend to duty's call, followed Miss Violet indoors and lay by the fireplace, knowing that she would light it soon and talk to him while she prepared their dinner.

Knowing there would be oats when he brought them home, Abernathy hurried his pace and there was still enough light to see the drive as they walked to the house after they had given him his reward and brushed him.

They walked around to the back and washed up in the rain barrel, then went in through the kitchen door to find a towel to dry their hands. "Ah, here they be, the weary travelers!" Cook exclaimed when the door opened. Seeing them holding their hands away from their clothing, Rose jumped up from the table where she was folding napkins to find them a towel.

Once they were dry, they asked whether dinner was ready or if they should visit in the study and Cook answered after lifting a lid, "I think only about five minutes more so best be the breakfast room."

They wanted to stay in the kitchen with the lovely smells coming from the stove, but they complied and sat there with knees touching, waiting for Rose to bring dinner to them, and relaxing in the mellow glow of their lovemaking and their visit with Miss Violet. Small bits of conversation occurred, but for the most part they were silent, simply enjoying the nearness of the one they loved.

True to Cook's word, dinner was on the table in little more than five minutes. She had prepared split pea soup, a ham and noodle casserole, mixed vegetables with a creamy cheese sauce, and flakey rolls with butter. Elisabeth and John paused a moment to inhale the wonderful odors before eating, then began with a bowl of soup before they went on the rest.

Between spoonfuls they chatted --- somehow, the act of eating was a stimulant for conversation and they talked through the entire meal about many things: Miss Violet, the boys and the newlyweds, but their conversation centered mainly on their own state of affairs and whether they should wait until Christmas or marry sooner. There was also the important consideration of John's inheritance and whether he should leave for America soon, consult a solicitor first, or pursue some other course of action. By the time the meal was done, they had come to the consensus that they needed to marry soon and the rest would fall into place. To this end, they would go into Tring on the morrow to consult with the church pastor.

For dessert, Rose brought them lemon cake with lemon curd and sour cream spooned over it and a pot of weak tea --- Cook believed that tea always went better with lemon than did coffee, but she made it weaker than usual so that it wouldn't overpower her delicious offering.

All was silence as they savored the delicate flavors and the subtle affinity of tea for lemon.

When they had finished they migrated to the comfort of the study; their special room. In the comfort of each other's company, Elisabeth worked on her accounts and John read a treatise on diabetes, occasionally making comments on the condition and the perspective of the author to Elisabeth. It was late when they finished and the cocoa Rose had brought in at nine was long gone. They decided that it was time to seek their beds if they were to go into Tring on the morrow and parted in the entry hall with an embrace and a lingering kiss --- until they heard the kitchen door open and knew that Rose was coming to clean up. John took Elisabeth's hand and said a formal goodnight as Rose came into the entry hall, then left for the kitchen to snag a few tarts in case he was hungry as he read himself to sleep.

"Are you going up now?" Rose asked Elisabeth.

"Yes, Rose, it has certainly been a long day," she answered.

"That be the truth," Rose agreed and went on into the study to fetch the cocoa tray.

Elisabeth ascended the stairs with the feeling that she was floating on air --- they would be married earlier than Christmas.....

ᥱChapter 32 – Another Weddingᥲ

Elisabeth awoke the next morning feeling that there was something important about to happen, then remembered, as she became fully awake, that they planned to speak to the pastor about their intent to marry. Her excitement rose and she threw back the coverlet and washed herself, then dressed and went down to the breakfast room. To her amazement, she found John already there, reading a book, of course, and awaiting her.

"Do you never sleep?" she asked.

"Of course I do, but not as long as some people," he answered, with a smug smile, eliciting a deep, throaty chuckle from his beloved.

Rose entered at that moment and said, "Ah, you're here! I'll be back in a trice with the platters," and true to her word, she was. The plates had already been set, so she needed only bring in the hot covered dishes: one of meats and shirred eggs, another of breakfast pastries, toast and French toast, and kippers in their own small covered dish, lest they lend their odor to the rest. As Elisabeth and John were filling their plates, Rose returned with a pot of steaming coffee and a pitcher of thick cream.

"The piece de resistance, Rose, is Cook's coffee --- so rich and dark and fresh --- and she never boils it or heats it too long," John said. I can't remember having it so well prepared or tasty in America!"

Rose glowed --- she had a compliment for Cook, who would be blissful and singing all the day once she told her. It was always a nice feeling for her to be able to help the people around her to be happy and joyful and she hurried away to the kitchen to bring her friend this tidbit of joy.

Elisabeth smiled and said to John, "You know that you have given her a gift for Cook, John."

John grinned at her and replied, "Isn't that what life is for?"

She nodded and answered, "Yes, it is, and you have learned it at an early age, my dearest love."

They sat there eating their breakfast in a haze of love and appreciation of the goodness of their chosen one, each wondering what they had done right to deserve this beautiful relationship. Finally, they remembered that they had a pastor to see and questions to ask in Tring and they must do it all before clinic hours that afternoon.

When Rose came in to see if they needed anything more, Elisabeth was already putting on her wrap and asked her fetch her everyday bag from the bedroom. While she waited, John went to hitch up Abernathy and was coming up the drive when she stepped out the door. He gave Abernathy a 'whoa' and pulled him up directly in front of Elisabeth, then jumped down and went around to help her up, but in truth he had no need to, for the stoop was a good eight inches high and easily served as a mounting block for her.

When they were both ensconced in the buggy, he made a clicking sound and shook the reins. The old horse had been alive long enough to know his cues and made for the road. When John pulled on the left rein and guided him to take the road toward Tring, he picked up his feet, knowing that there were many trees in that direction and also that he sometimes got treats from the children they encountered. Most of his trips in that direction were to church and he didn't know this was no Sunday with children running around the churchyard carrying tidbits in their pockets.

However, his instincts had been right --- they were going to church.

Tring being only a bit over a mile, and the church on the far side, they arrived in less than half an hour and sought out the pastor. Seeing a gardener outside, Elisabeth asked if the pastor was there and he said, "List'nin' to choir practice he is, ma'am, in the church."

Her smile was so beautiful when she thanked him that his being responded and was joyful the rest of that day.

She and John continued to the church and began to hear the strains of music as they neared it, then walked inside and were greeted by the full glory of the human voice singing a cantata. Near the front with his back to the choir loft, they could see the pastor attempting to feel the effect this particular work might have on the parishioners that Sunday and they had a moment's remorse at bothering him, but pressed forward nonetheless.

They stepped in front of him, lest they startle him from behind and Elisabeth began to hum along with the music. This nearness of the sound brought the pastor into awareness of the present and the space directly in front of him and he opened his eyes, but was not startled at seeing them there.

"Hello, Elisabeth," he began, then continued, "What brings you here this fine day?"

"May we have some of your time privately?" she asked.

"Of course, of course," he said and led them to the rectory for a chat.

Once they were all seated, he watched and waited, then queried, "Is there something you wished to discuss? Perhaps a donation for the poor?"

"It is rather of a personal nature, Pastor," Elisabeth began, "We wish to be married and had planned for Christmas, but it is likely that John will need to go to America and we would like to be married before that, though we had wished to have the children present and they are all away at the moment."

The pastor thought for a moment and proposed a solution, "Did you know that civil marriages have been allowed since the Marriage Act of 1836? Why not have a civil ceremony as soon as the banns have been posted at the register's office for fifteen days and then a church wedding when it is convenient for all of your family to be in one place?"

Elisabeth and John were dumbfounded with the logic of his idea. It would work. Both shook his hand, saying 'thank you' over and over again, then returned to Abernathy and the buggy. John ran back inside to ask where the register's office was located and hurried back to the buggy to steer Abernathy to it by the most direct route.

In a matter of a few minutes, they were seated inside the small office, preparing to register their impending marriage. Elisabeth had not brought her birth, baptismal, or marriage certificate, but fortunately the registrar knew her and could verify her birth and first marriage, as well as her husband's death, by his own knowledge of the events, but was able to look them up as well and verify the dates for the form he must fill out.

Fortunately, John carried his papers everywhere he went, being a foreigner, and was able to produce his birth certificate and paperwork showing his travel and entry into England and the dates --- even the ships he had traveled by.

It took a little over an hour for all to be researched and the papers filled out, but the notice was posted that day and, after it had been up for fifteen days, they could be married there by the registrar.

They left feeling as happy as two birds when the snow has melted and the sun is shining through the clouds to disperse the gray of winter.

Remembering that it was an infirmary day, they knew they must hurry back home to eat and to share their news with Rose and Cook, for they expected they would want to serve as witnesses, and twenty minutes later they were pulling into the drive and heading for the stable. Elisabeth went up to the house to see how the lunch preparations were coming along while John unhitched, lightly brushed, and fed Abernathy, who had not even broken a sweat.

Meanwhile, Elisabeth asked after the preparations for lunch and finding that it was only ten minutes in the offing, she went into the study to wait for John and her wait was short. When he came to the study, she cold see that he had washed his face and hands after tending to Abernathy and asked if he was ready to eat.

"Of course, my love," he answered, "Must get our nourishment for the task ahead!"

She smiled indulgently and at that moment Rose came to tell them that lunch was awaiting them in the breakfast room.

As they ate, they spoke of the wedding day, which would be October 8th at the earliest. Fortunately, the registrar could marry them on a Saturday morning if they desired it and, knowing that from that day forward they could share a bed, they felt sure that they would most certainly desire it.

When they had finished their meal, they asked Rose to bring Cook into the study for they would like to see them both. Rose went to fetch Cook thinking that they wanted to compliment her again and Cook washed her hands, took off her apron and patted her hair into place, then followed Rose into the front of the house.

Elisabeth and John were seated in the study and asked them to take seats as well. Then, Elisabeth began by saying, "Rose and Cook, we have a very important announcement to make and we want you to be the first to know after the registrar. We, that is John and I, plan to be married in two weeks by the registrar in Tring, probably on October 8th, and we would like you to be our witnesses."

Both of the women sat there stunned for a few minutes, then Rose spoke up and said she would be honored and then Cook pulled at Rose's sleeve and whispered in her ear, "I would rather prepare their first meal as man and wife, but I'd wager that Miss Violet would be that happy to do it."

Rose told Elisabeth and John what Cook had said and they thought it was a wonderful idea. Cook's greatest love was preparing food and it would be her special gift to them, while Miss Violet, who was her friend and theirs, would have the honor of signing the register along with Rose.

Rose looked up at the clock on the mantle at that moment and exclaimed, "Oh dear, 'tis nearly a quarter 'fore two and you had best be leaving for the infirmary!"

Elisabeth nodded and all four of them stood --- Rose and Cook left to attend to their respective tasks and Elisabeth and John to walk to the infirmary.

The infirmary was busier than it had been for awhile for the changing weather was beginning to bring out coughs and sniffles, especially in children, as the nights became cooler and leaves began to fall and dry, then decompose as the rains and mists dampened them. The sweet smell of their decaying sugars was on the air, but molds and fungi fed on those sugars and some were more sensitive to their spores.

Five o'clock finally came and they left for home; their work only just completed. They were tired, but it was a good tired, for they had accomplished much. As they walked John put his arm around her and held her close to him for a moment, then relaxed his arm so that they could walk with a better gait, rather than lurching from side to side like a drunken sailor.

When they arrived it was still light, but the air was beginning to be quite cool and they wore coats into the garden to sit on their favorite bench and enjoy the twilight as night fell upon them. Sitting there, they felt so enchanted, almost as thought this were a holy moment in time, and Elisabeth said, "John I would like to come to you as a pristine bride, but I cannot for I have married and borne children….." then hesitated.

John broke into her pause to say, "My dearest love, that is no matter to me."

"I know that," she averred, "But, it matters to me and I have not been pristine for you since we met. May we wait until our marriage, may I have this fortnight, to become a blushing innocent, pure in deed, for you?"

John smiled at her and squeezed her to him, then replied, "You may have anything your heart desires, my love --- only, I hope that you will not be too demure after the wedding night?"

She grinned at him with a twinkle in her eyes that spoke volumes, but said not a word, and his lips came down on hers hungrily, but with the utmost gentleness in spite of his passion.

Their days passed slowly at times with no visits to their secret place, however they visited Miss Violet, who was very excited over their news, and she consented to be their witness in place of Cook, agreeing that the lady would be far happier in the kitchen making their wedding dinner. She asked if they planned to have a reception and they were of two minds over this, the first being that they liked their neighbors and friends, but the second that they felt that it was not fair to celebrate without the children being there also and they explained that John, and perhaps Elisabeth, might have to take a trip to the United States. This excited their friend further and she asked many questions of John about his inheritance, his family and the country of his origin.

He told her that he had been in more than one part of the continent and had been born in Michigan, but his father's family had come from England originally, immigrating through Canada in about 1810, then down into the United States in about 1820. His cousin, George, who had been much younger than his father and born of his great-uncle's second wife, had stayed in England longer and only immigrated through Canada a few years back with his young son of the same name, but he had passed through it quickly, meaning to farm in Michigan, after hearing of the rich farmland from John's father.

He explained that his inheritance was coming through a sister of his mother and that it was at least a goldmine. Her eyes grew large and she whispered, "A goldmine?"

"Yes, Miss Violet, a goldmine," he said, "But I have no idea how much, or little, gold is in it! I will have to wait until I talk to the attorney in America."

"Oh, a goldmine will always have gold in it," she said, "That is why they call it a goldmine and not a coalmine."

Elisabeth and John chuckled at what they thought was wit, but then they realised that she was serious and, looking at each other quizzically, decided that in point of fact what she said was true and nodded.

When they finally left for home, they gave her many hugs and reminded her how happy they were that she would be their witness, then faded into the dusk along with Abernathy and the old buggy.

A few days before their marriage, a letter arrived from Gerald Massey. He first gave his condolences, though very late, over the loss of Dr. Gray, then, apologized for the confusion over his small book and explained that he had called one day the year before when, apparently, she was not to house. He wrote that the maid had shown him into the study to wait when he asked for the doctor, probably surmising in error that he meant Elisabeth, and even brought him refreshment. He waited, but as the time passed he left to attend to an appointment in Aylesbury and was unable to return on that visit to the area, for he had other speaking engagements pending. He had left the book on a desk in the study and supposed that it was shelved by someone who was tidying up.

Elisabeth and John replied, thanking him for his condolences and for clearing up the mystery, while asking him to notify them when he would be speaking again in the vicinity for they would be pleased to hear his talks on clairvoyance and mesmerism.

Finally, the day of their wedding arrived and, as agreed, Joe arrived to pick up Elisabeth and Rose with his wagon and leave his wife to help Cook with preparations for the tiny wedding party. Meanwhile, John went to fetch Miss Violet and meet the party at the register's office.

By ten all were assembled and the wedding performed without much ado. The groom kissed the bride and everyone clapped, then Rose and Miss Violet signed everywhere the registrar told them to sign and, after he had made a duplicate copy for them to present to the attorney in America, it was back to Elisabeth's house for the reception. While they were few, they were all people who held very special places in the bride's heart. There would be a more formal wedding eventually but, for now, this one would serve its purpose.

Cook had outdone herself and was in her glory over the enjoyment of her creations. The French cookbook had given her many ideas and not one of them failed to please the assembled company.

John led a toast to her culinary acumen and all toasted her, then clapped. In her own right, she received as much attention as the bride and never batted an eyelash at accepting it as her due. And in all truth, she was quite an accomplished chef, only so very aware of her humble origins that she would probably never prepare food in any grand house.

The party lasted for many hours, but farm folk tend to seek their beds early and Joe and his wife left before dark, taking Miss Violet with them and would leave her off at her cottage so that the newlyweds would have time alone together.

When it grew dark, John began to yawn and Elisabeth soon understood the hint. After asking Rose to leave a tray in her bedroom, lest they be hungry during the night, they waited in the parlor for her to carry it up before they retired for the night. Once she had done that, Elisabeth went upstairs to her bedroom to change into her nightgown and John followed about twenty minutes later. He knocked at the door and heard her voice call out for him to enter, then opened the door and closed it behind him before looking at her. She was sitting at her dressing table in a beautiful nightgown of white lawn trimmed with lace and tiny rosettes of pink satin, imitating rosebuds. She looked so beautiful sitting there that his heart leapt within him and he stood there transfixed for some time.

Elisabeth smiled shyly and asked, "Are you not pleased to see me thus?"

"Oh, yes. Yes I am," he replied, still at a loss for words. Then, suddenly, he found his tongue and added, "Oh my dearest, I love you so, but not only for your beauty, for that may fade with time. I love you for your spirit, your inner being, the glory of your soul."

She sat there wondering how she could say anything after his remarkable words, then realised that the best answer would be to reflect his sentiments and said, "I love you in this way also, John, and I will never stop."

Looking at her seated there, watching him in the mirror, he felt he must come up behind her and put his hands on her shoulders to see both of them reflected there, a married couple at last. Then, as he touched her shoulders and let his hands slide down to cup her breasts, he knew that he must lift her and carry her to the large four-poster bed and consummate their marriage soon, very soon.

Elisabeth felt it, too, and she stood, dislodging his hands, and turned to face him, giving those hands better access to her attributes. This prompted John to take her in his arms and kiss her passionately, which brought his manhood to full erection and, feeling it stiffening between them, she let her hands drift from his shoulders down his back to his buttocks and lightly squeeze them, then let her fingers tickle them until he could take no more and began removing his clothing, thankful for the fire in the grate.

She stood there watching jacket, shirt, trousers, shoes, stockings, and then smallclothes disappear onto a chair and finally saw him as she loved him best, a nude as beautiful as any Apollo, only with darker hair and made of flesh, in particular one bit of flesh which was now standing straight out as though taking aim at her --- and, indeed, it probably was.

John stood there admiring her beauty, but aware that she was looking at him as well and his manhood throbbed and became harder and broader with this awareness. Finally, as he walked to her, it bobbed a bit as though seeking to effect entrance to her hidden place though its own efforts. The thought was erotic, as was his naked body and she felt a slickness beginning between her thighs, where she wore no pantalets. She rotated her hips from side to side, then in circles to release the tension that was building and waited there passively in every other way, for him to come to her and to touch her in the ways she liked to be touched and in the places she favored his touching.

The tension rose as he slowly crossed to her, teasing and tantalizing, and she cupped her hands under her covered breasts and lifted them toward him as though offering them to him as a gift. John walked slower still, then turned and stretched as an athlete might have in the Coliseum of Rome, showing his attributes off for the ladies and, in those times, for the men as well. John continued flexing his muscles, moving his hips suggestively, touching his manhood to draw her attention to it, then thrusting it forward and gripping his buttocks to squeeze them rhythmically and thrust his hips forward slowly time and time again. He enjoyed having her watch him and wanted to watch her do the same, but first he had to remove that nightgown.

Holding out his right hand, he curled his first finger, beckoning her to come forward. Elisabeth slowly walked the short distance to him, making him wait, as the throbbing within his erection continued. When she reached him he saw the tie at her neck and undid it, pushing the thin cloth away from her shoulders and down her arms until the entire garment slid down to become a puddle on the floor. She had been naked beneath it and had become as free of clothing as he. He slid his hands across her silky skin lightly, causing her to jerk as little shocks went though her body. He reached around to her back and let his hands rest lightly on the top of her buttocks, then cupped them in his hands, letting his fingers tickle the edge of the cleft between them and working themselves lower to the place where buttocks and thighs meet at the top of the leg the, finally, he pulled her closer using his forearms while his hands never moved. Then, he shifted a bit so that his right hand could reach below her buttocks and slide between her thighs to feel the juices dripping from her hidden recess, that warm, dark place so filled with sensation, which was making her hips rotate and alternately move front to back. He felt for the opening and, upon finding it, let his longest finger slide in on her wetness, only to hear her gasp with the welcome shock of that invasion. She began to moan, low and with a breathiness as he moved that finger in and out, simulating intercourse and pleasuring her, while his own member pushed against her belly and made her want that inside of her, too.

Finally, she touched his groin and moved her hands to the staff hard enough to make its own entrance on her belly and held it as his finger went in and out of her. She squeezed it with a rhythmic pulsing and his hips began to sway from front to back as well. When he could take no more, he threw her gown over the plush carpet in front of the fire and she lay on it as he fitted himself between her thighs and entered her, filling her completely, and within a few strokes felt her hips jerk and then tense to clench his staff as he ejaculated hard and long.

He tried to hold himself up so that the weight of his torso did not press her down, but his release had been so strong that his muscles failed him and he lay atop her unable to move a muscle.

After some time, he rolled away and lay next to her with an arm across her waist. In a little while, he began to squeeze her breasts again, playing with the nipples and suckling them, causing all sort of delightful sensations between her thighs and inside her belly. Feeling the juices that were dripping from her opening, he put two fingers inside of her and slid them in and out a number of times. She moaned again and he moved himself to kneel between her legs and suckle there as well. She began moaning and whimpering louder, though she was trying to control the volume, and he continued to suckle at that lower 'nipple' so like a miniature hidden penis until she began to have a hard orgasm, then slid himself into her as it was at its height and kept her ecstasy at its peak until he ejaculated a second time and lay down with his face in the furry mound between her thighs, licking and sucking that little nipple gently to keep her at that peak. Finally, he abandoned his Herculean effort and, carrying her to the bed, tucked her and himself into it, then promptly fell asleep.

Elisabeth slid her hand down to her femininity and felt the juices they had made. She slid her middle finger a few times lightly across the little nipple he had suckled and thought, no, you have had enough and are almost to the point of being sore. Tomorrow will be another night.....

❧Chapter 33 – A Trip to America!❧

The days grew shorter and the nights longer, though Elisabeth and John had little to complain about in this circumstance, for it meant that they spent more time wrapped in each other's arms. They enjoyed the falling leaves of autumn --- the orange, the red, the pink, the yellow and the brown --- and they made love in what was now 'their' bedroom, for John had moved out of the rooms over the stable.

They had consulted a solicitor in Salisbury the Monday after their wedding and he wrote a letter to the legal firm, which had notified John of his aunt's passing, asking for more particulars: specifically whether John would need to return to the United States in order to claim his inheritance and sending a copy of the marriage license signed by the registrar. Six weeks later the solicitor received news in the form of a letter offering more details about the estate and the bequest,. with a letter of credit made to John's name for two thousand dollars enclosed as well. Impressed,, the man journeyed to Elisabeth's house from Salisbury as soon as he was able, for he knew that they were anxious for more news.

When John read the letter, he understood that the attorney in America preferred that John return to claim his inheritance, but also to examine the firm's handling of it these many years, so he might see that they did well in managing the responsibilities his aunt had entrusted to them. The goldmine, itself, was in another state --- Georgia --- and they felt that he would need to journey there to evaluate the progress with ore extraction, for these things are not a matter of chance, but of assessment, planning and the selecting of honest workers.

John read the letter and listened to the solicitor's opinions, then turned to Elisabeth in a jocular mood and said, "It seems that I must return, my love. Would you care to go exploring?"

She laughed, then realising that he was in earnest, she replied, "It would depend on when that would occur but, all the same, I would like a little time to consider it, John."

"Fair enough," he conceded, "Though I feel it best to leave early rather than when the weather becomes foul."

"I agree," she said, folding her hands, a signal that the meeting was over, "There is much to consider, my love, but I will make my decision within the week."

He nodded and agreed that he would wait that long, but added that he dare not tarry any longer, for he felt that the tone of the letter indicated that there was some irregularity at the mine or they would not have suggested that he inspect it.

Then, it was Elisabeth's turn to nod her agreement at his interpretation of the reference to the mine and she said, "Perhaps you have the truth of it --- they may not feel competent to inspect it and they want you to take the burden away from their scope of management and perhaps show the workers you are no absentee landlord. Either it is that, or they want you to risk your life and die, leaving the whole of it in their hands."

"Now that makes me feel good!" he said, grinning at her.

"I did not intend to worry you, John, but not everyone is trustworthy and it is well known that barristers often mishandle the estates of their clients. It is reprehensible, but there you have it," she answered.

A little annoyed at the aspersions cast upon members of his profession, although they were after all colonial members, the solicitor stood up at this point, suggesting that it was time he took his leave of them, for he had tarried some time in discussing the matter. They thanked him and Elisabeth paid him immediately, lest they leave for America before he presented his bill.

They continued to discuss the trip after he left, but John was true to his word and didn't try to sway Elisabeth's decision. It must be hers and hers alone.

Then, John reread the letter and said, "Hold on, I thought that the goldmine was out west --- maybe California --- but it's in Georgia. That's in the South."

"Does that make a difference," she asked.

"Only that it would be a longer trip and it'll be shorter and faster with it on the east coast --- imagine traveling all the way to California! We would spend a lot of time in our cabin!" he answered, with a grin.

She grinned back at him and said, "In that case, I can make my decision immediately. We shall leave directly after Christmas. I had some trepidation after the Arctic disaster last month, but I feel that all will be well if we wait until later and since we don't have to get there quickly that should suffice."

John wanted to bite his tongue for he was eager to speak face to face with the attorneys, but he decided that half a loaf was better than none and let it be her way.

That afternoon was a busy one at the infirmary, sniffles and all the cuts and bruises from bringing the harvest home..... They were tired and not only from the work, but from the interview with the attorney as well. Cook's efforts were appreciated after all that had occurred.

The following day, as they breakfasted, a letter sent by Emmaline Roberge was delivered by a courier. She was visiting in Aylesbury and would arrive with her maid, a coachman and footman, for a visit on Saturday and stay until Sunday afternoon, when they must be on their way. Elisabeth read it to John and said, "The men can stay in the rooms over the stables and the maid in one of the empty servant's rooms in the attic, but we shall have to clean out one of the girl's rooms for Emmaline, though perhaps she could use Papa's old room across from the study," then as she read further, "Oh, and she says that she will return to us for a night on December 21st --- before Christmas --- and she says something about a house party at Richard's."

"I wondered what that room was used for," said John, "But, I never asked."

"Papa was not too steady on his feet before he died and we were afraid that he would fall, so we outfitted a room on the main level for him," she answered, realizing that they would have only two days in which to make the rooms ready and plan meals.

When Rose came in to see if they had finished, Elisabeth advised her of the visit and her plans for accommodating the guests. Rose nodded her agreement and went to summon Cook.

Elisabeth was once again made aware of the dedicated staff she had when Cook entered, already thinking in terms of French cuisine..... "Four meals, Ma'am --- four. Two lunches, dinner and a breakfast. That will be an easy task. You just rest your mind."

And, Elisabeth did exactly that, for she knew of Cook's prowess in the kitchen and asked her to tell Rose she wanted to begin sorting out the bedrooms as soon as possible.

When Rose returned to the breakfast room, Elisabeth was ready to begin with the cleaning and changes --- first with the room her father had used on the ground level, then with Caroline's room, which was across from hers and John's.

John carried armfuls of clothing into Catherine's room from Caroline's as part of his contribution and then went off to make the bedrooms over the stable hospitable and lay in a supply of wood for the fireplaces. Joe and his sons had seen to the supply for the house, though.

Rose saw to one of the spare servant's rooms in the attic and made it hospitable with a fresh dusting and clean bedding.

When Emmaline arrived on Saturday, all was in perfect order and she chose the room downstairs, just as Elisabeth thought she might and, in order to be available if her mistress needed her during the night, Emmaline's maid was content to sleep on the divan Elisabeth's father had always kept in the room, lest he wanted to lounge. It had been handy for Elisabeth to sleep on when Papa had been declining, she remembered.

The lunch was perfection --- Cook was in her glory and all was haute cuisine by the book --- and afterward, they visited in the parlor for many hours while John read in the study.

Emmaline asked if they planned to visit the United States and Elisabeth told her of their visit with the solicitor.

"Excellent," said Emmaline, "You will enjoy it!"

"I have only just told John that I would go, but we shall not leave until the day after Christmas," the younger woman added.

"Good, good, one should be with family at Christmas --- or at least good friends. So his goldmine is in the south. It will be an eye-opening experience for you, my dear."

"Everything in a foreign country will be an eye-opening experience for me, Emmaline."

"Yes, yes, that is true, but this is different and do not be surprised if you stay much longer than you had planned. It is, after all, a new country and very exciting and developing as well. You will be sailing into New York, I presume, since you say his attorney is in the vicinity, so perhaps you will visit the college at which Elizabeth Blackwell received her degree: Geneva Medical College. Though, I must say, the winter weather there is abysmal."

They went on to speak of the task that Emmaline planned to set her to and how she wanted it carried out. Having his inheritance and becoming a doctor as well, John would become a person of consequence financially and socially and this would aid Elisabeth in her future role. Emmaline spoke at length about making connections with people of like mind and nurturing those relationships that they might be brought to do good things for her protégés via scholarships, opportunities and introductions. She mentored her current protégé all afternoon and after the French dinner as well.

John read on Saturday, but the next morning he sat with them and listened to Emmaline's ideas. He agreed with them and was glad she had chosen his wife to carry them forward.

Mid-afternoon, their guests left and they were alone again. John looked at his wife and said, "Would you care to go upstairs?"

"Yes, but I believe I'd like a nap before dinner. Are you tired, also?"

"Only a little, but I'll go up with you --- who knows what it might lead to?"

They slept --- almost until time for dinner --- but, then he awoke his sleeping princess with a kiss upon her mouth. Then, he slipped under the covers and, mouth to that haven between her legs, he kissed and suckled it, waking her more fully with her hips thrusting forward toward his mouth and moaning, "Ooooohhh, ooOooOoohh-h-h." He never stopped until she had felt her body shake and shudder three times. Then he slipped into her wetness as if it had been greased and rode her until she shuddered again saying, "Oh, John, oh John, oh Jo-o-hn-n-n."

When he rested himself atop her afterward, he felt her hard nipples against his chest and pinched them with his fingertips, making her contract around him again and again.

Finally, they knew they must go down to dinner, for Cook would be frantic if she had to hold it too long, and they rose, washed themselves, and dressed for the evening meal.

Cook was indeed gratified that they had come down, for she had continued her French theme and they were treated to a soufflé as well as other bits of French cuisine.

Over cocoa in the study, they discussed the day of departure and John suggested that they purchase their tickets in advance. He felt good about the Collins Line and their ships usually had businessmen, merchants, and professional men traveling on their ships, he had been told, when he worked for his passage to England. He told her to discount the accident to the Artic, for any ships can collide in the fog --- it was no mechanical failure or fault in the design.

She felt better about the condition of the ship, but the part about the fog did little to bring her peace of mind. Then, she had the thought that everyone dies at some time and she would rather die in John's arms than live without him and all was well in her mind. She knew that Emmaline would see to her sons and the Balfours would see to her daughters. There was nothing more that she had concern over.

The days passed swiftly and Elisabeth and John packed their trunks for the voyage, for they wanted no last minute distress, especially since they would have company the day before the family wedding they were beginning to plan for the chapel at The Hall.

Soon, the boys would return for the holidays and Richard would send grooms over with their horses. Perhaps Rose's groom --- Elisabeth and John discussed that and thought they might suggest that Rose and her groom marry and take the rooms over the stable or, perhaps, they would want to work one of the small farms she owned. That is, if Richard was able to let his groom go..... so many things to consider..... so many people's lives intertwined..... However, in good conscience, they must let the servants speak for themselves first, for some employers would not agree to their servants marrying without their permission or until their contracted time was served and they didn't know how Richard would react. He was quite fond of his horses, after all.

They discussed the issue of who would take care of things while they were traveling for it would be, at the least, many months before they returned. Ultimately, they decided to have George collect the rents and Martin see to the welfare of the tenants without a man on the property.

When they had come to this decision, they visited each tenant and apprised them of their plans to assure that things went smoothly in their absence. They were congratulated on their marriage on every side by the tenants and sat down to tea or coffee with each and every one to tell the even more exciting story of John's inheritance. Somehow, the romance of owning a goldmine is a thing which captures the imagination of people the world over and these were no exception.

In this interim, they also visited Richard and asked if they might have a wedding in the chapel and he readily agreed, once he realised that they had already wed and there was no chance at all for him in that quarter. They told him of John's inheritance, as well, to reassure him that John had not married Elisabeth to secure her holdings and that they would be traveling to the United States directly after Christmas on a ship of the Collins Line out of Liverpool. He treated John with far more respect once this was made known to him, though not exactly due to a love of money, but respect for those who were the captains of industry due to possessing it.

A few days later, the brides returned and unexpectedly broke their journey with Elisabeth and John, spending three nights in their childhood residence before making their way to take up residence in their own homes. Luckily, though, the armfuls of Caroline's clothing had been returned whence they came and the brides' husbands were well contented with their sleep.

They arrived just before supper and Cook quickly pulled the rest of the roast out of the pan, as well as the potatoes and carrots she had planned for the following night, then found some onions from the larder and made a thick, satisfying, creamy onion soup from a recipe dating back centuries in her family and added spicy baked apples to the jam tarts already on the menu for dessert.

Elisabeth and John took them to the parlor while the additional dishes were prepared and began to question them about their travels.

Elisabeth asked of Quentin, "Tell us of your adventures on the continent," and he was happy to be drawn out, that he might shine and tell his mother-in-law of the places they had visited.

Her daughters watched, with admiration, her skill in making him the conversationalist as she was given detailed descriptions of the cities in France they had explored: Le Havre, Rouen, Paris, and more.

Quentin waxed quite eloquent in his recounting of their visit to the beautiful Jardin des Plantes de Rouen, for he was quite the horticulturist, and he mentioned that Joan of Arc had been burned in Rouen only in passing. Elisabeth smiled and he continued his lecture on plant life with interjections from time to time coming from his wife and sister-in-law.

Elisabeth was fascinated and told him so, which made him light up as bright as a sunbeam and the twins looked at each other and nodded. Ah, their mother was a one!

Before long, Rose announced that dinner was ready and the three couples migrated into the dining room, being too many for the breakfast nook.

The dinner continued much as their conversation in the parlor, only the meal slowed it down and allowed others to shine as Quentin had done. The girls brought up the topic of clothing and the Paris fashions --- many of which had come home with them, for their husbands were men of substance and wished their wives' attire to reflect their position in society. They promised to show Elisabeth everything the next day.

John, too, practiced Elisabeth's method of allowing the travelers to tell their tales and found that he liked them all --- and well he should, he thought to himself, for they were now his daughters and sons-in-law. For a few moments that took him aback and then he took a deep breath and allowed the role to settle on him as the meal progressed.

After dinner they spoke only for a short time, having begun their day early in Winchester where they had stayed with friends of the Balfours. Then, before decamping to their bedrooms with their husbands, the twins agreed to return and spend the Christmas holidays at the Balfour family property near to The Hall in order to attend Elisabeth and John's wedding in the chapel.

The following day, in time for the noonday meal, Justus and Gerald returned from Oxford in the coach Richard had sent for them with George following on their heels by train the day after. Gerald hitched up Abernathy to meet his brother at the station in Aylesbury and brought him home, completely filling the house with the energy of youth.

Hearing their voices, Elisabeth truly felt the holiday spirit.

She and John had written to the boys of their marriage and the reason for a civil ceremony, but now told them that they would have a second ceremony in the chapel for family on December 23rd, since that had not been possible in October. For the girls, however, their marriage had been news --- being in transit almost three months themselves and full of their own adventures, Elisabeth had decided not to write to them. She had not yet mentioned her decision to go to the United States with John, either, and brought that up when all of them were there, giving her reasons for the trip and her arrangements for the tenants almost as soon as George had arrived.

They were all quite surprised to hear of John's inheritance --- most especially the goldmine, for gold has a peculiar fascination for people. They asked him question after question, but all he could tell them was that he would write when he knew more.

That night, as they lay in bed, he said to Elisabeth, "I hope it's not a played out mine, if only for their sakes. It would completely lose all romance!"

She chuckled and answered, "If so, we'll have to buy them some gold so that they don't feel cheated of the romance," the continued, "John, might we visit Geneva Medical College while we are in America?"

He looked down at her and said, "Of course, my love --- I had planned to do exactly that. Besides, you will want to travel to the falls."

In her innocence, she asked, "Which falls would that be?"

"Why Niagara, of course," he answered, with a lopsided smile, then took her into his arms and began to kiss her deeply and insistently, feeling her response and his own there under the covers. They made love slowly and fully, savoring every moment of each sensation, lingering over the appreciation of naked skin and silky flesh caressed by their hands and culminating in mutual gratification and satisfaction. And, while it lacked the tension of the garden bench, the silk sheets and warm fire offered much to recommend them.

The Balfours left on the 16th, promising to return in a week for the wedding and Christmas.

Meanwhile, Elisabeth and John continued to pack and make lists of instructions and the young men visited their friends and enjoyed the entertainments of the season.

Richard stopped the day after the twins left on his way into Aylesbury and took lunch with them. Elisabeth, never one to miss a fortunate turns of events, broached the subject of the groom and Rose and asked if he would have anything against them marrying in the near future and the groom taking John's work with the tenants on --- at least until they returned.

"No, not at all," he answered, "He has asked my permission to wed and I gave it, though I had assumed he would remain with me."

"Perhaps it could be a loan?" she asked.

He chuckled, then said, "I could not say no to you, Elisabeth," finally unbending from his hauteur and becoming the better man for it.

"Friends?" she asked, extending her hand.

"Yes, of course," he answered, taking it.

He sensed that his brother's children would be fruitful and multiply and he would have the joy of seeing their children in his old age even though they were not purely his own. He had loved his brother, George, and was glad that he had been able to sow a healthy crop of Hastings to carry the name forward.

It was at this point that he mentioned his friend, Emmaline Roberge, saying that he received a note from her saying that she would be arriving at their home on the 19th and would come with them to The Hall on the 22nd.

"Oh, thank you, Richard," Elisabeth said, with excitement in her eyes, "She is one of my favorite acquaintances."

"Yes, she is a very special woman," he answered after a moment's pause, "She has done many good things."

Elisabeth nodded her assent.

When she closed the door behind Richard, John took her into his arms, though it was mid-afternoon, and asked if she would like to go upstairs. She looked up at him, searching to see if he was feeling insecure, then, seeing his grin, she knew he was just being fresh. She loved it, though, and allowed herself to be led up the stairs and into their bedroom for an afternoon "nap". And, quite a nice nap it was, once they had expended their energy in other pursuits.....

Two days later, Emmaline Roberge's carriage pulled into the drive and the lady herself alighted and was escorted inside. The bedroom downstairs was ready for her and her maid would sleep on the sofa as before, lest her employer need help in the night.

Emmaline began her instruction of Elisabeth almost immediately and they spent nearly two full days closeted in the study, but for meals. Elisabeth was given to know that the way had been prepared and those who knew of Emmaline's work now knew that Elisabeth would continue it when the older woman crossed over or was no longer able to hold the reins of her endeavors.

The younger woman took copious notes, knowing that she could forget some of the details during her trip to the United States. Finally, on the 21st, Emmaline departed for The Hall and Richard's doings and Elisabeth set aside the notes and the copy she had made in order to concentrate on her preparations for the trips --- the first to the Dower House and the second to the New World. Excitement was brewing inside her along with a bit of trepidation, for the latter was a serious undertaking and, despite John's brave words, she found it difficult to completely forget the sinking of the Arctic with all on board.

℘Chapter 34 – Family Gathers℘

The early morning light was blocked by the heavy drapes, drawn to hold the winter cold at bay and when Elisabeth drifted into awareness, she could still make out the sleeping form of John next to her. She snuggled close to him for warmth and fell back into a light sleep with the comfort of his body against hers, thinking this is how marriage should always be.

Later, Rose knocked and then entered to set their tea tray on a table, pull the drapes aside and stoke the last embers of the fire with a bit of oversized kindling to take the chill off of the room. She left them to their own rising and went below to prepare the breakfast room.

The morning light filtered through the open drapes and Elisabeth, then John, bowed to its insistence, leaving the bed to don dressing gowns and have their tea together at the small table. They didn't linger, knowing the day was to be a busy one and soon made their way down to breakfast ahead of the others.

It was pleasant having that time alone before the intensity of youth made its way into the room and jostled their serenity with noise and conversation. Without a word spoken, they served each other from the platters Cook had provided and Rose came in with a tray of toast just in time to pour the coffee. Even she sensed the atmosphere and didn't mar it with words.

By the time the young men arrived, Elisabeth and John were ready for the challenge of interacting with others and discoursing over any topic, but the late arrivals seemed a bit subdued and George didn't arrive until the meal was nearly over. It seemed the party they attended had gone longer than usual.

Elisabeth teased them, saying with mock seriousness, "I certainly hope that you've nothing on your dance card for tonight. I would be disappointed if you slept through my nuptials tomorrow."

Sheepishly, they all looked at her and vowed they would be awake and in attendance.

She laughed, knowing that they would be at Richard's dinner party along with herself and John, and the mild tension abated as they realised she had been teasing all along.

At that point they found their tongues and began to ask all at once what the plans were for the wedding and the holidays, required Elisbeth to remind them that she could only hear one at a time.

George looked at the other two and they stopped talking in deference to his position as eldest. He then asked the questions and she outlined the plans for the morrow as well as what she knew of Richard's plans for the holidays ahead, watching them nod their approval of the plans.

Her wedding was to be a less formal affair than that of the girls, with only family and a few guests in attendance and a sit-down luncheon indoors as reception. She thought for a moment of how she looked forward to wearing the blue ensemble she had worn to the twins' wedding and then went on to say that dinner that evening would consist solely of the family and house guests.

There was to be no Hastings ball this Christmas, for a number of families were already opening their homes to the youth and she gratefully anticipated a quiet Christmas Eve with those family members and guests who did not plan to venture out, especially Emmaline. To all that she said, her sons nodded approval. They had been invited to a Christmas party, which would include a midnight mass in the private chapel of the host, and knew they would return on Christmas Morning just in time to open their gifts, eat a bite of breakfast, and fall into bed. Meanwhile, Elisabeth and John would return home after the Christmas breakfast at The Hall to celebrate a holiday meal with Cook and Rose, while the boys would journey back to Little Tring the morning after, on Boxing Day, to see the newlyweds off at the Aylesbury station. Richard was providing them a coach to return home and for the drive to Aylesbury on Boxing Day.

"I do believe you have it all, Mother," George said, with a smile, when she had finished.

She laughed and advised him not to be pert with his elders lest he come to a bad end.

George took the admonishment well, knowing it was tongue in cheek, and asked when they were to leave for The Hall.

Elisabeth looked at John and asked, "How long would you say, dear?"

He cocked his head to one side as if pondering, made funny faces, pursing his lips and screwing his face up while nodding a bit, then suddenly looking upward, as if having an inspiration, he said, "As soon I can hitch up the buggy."

The boys chuckled at his animation as well as his answer and Elisabeth tried to keep a straight face, but finally gave way to the laughter welling up within her and joined them in their mirth. As she laughed, the knowing passed through her mind that this moment never could have happened with their father, for he was a far different man, with a love of the drink to a greater extent than most and a certain melancholy with occassional rages which seemed to attend it. With what she knew now, she wondered if he had suffered from diabetes mellitus. The thoughts lingered for a moment, then John made some inane comment and the guffaws round the table pulled her from the momentary reverie into the now and brought her own laughter to her ears. Her entire body feeling the laughter of the group, she knew that this was living --- finally they were a complete family.

The banter continued for awhile longer, then Gerald and George went to the stable to hitch Abernathy to the buggy and Justus helped John carry their bags down to the entry hall and then out to the buggy when it arrived. The boys would follow later on horseback and should arrive in time for tea at the Dower House, though Elisabeth warned them they might take tea at The Hall depending on Richard and Emmaline's schedules and the number of guests he expected.

Finally, John shook the reins and Abernathy knew it was time to leave. He made as though to turn right, but John swiftly pulled on the left rein to let him know his error and things went well from that point on, for he had a good memory and knew that they were bound for Tring or beyond.

The entire journey was spent in a glow of happiness, a residue of the laughter and cameraderie over breakfast and they fairly beamed with the light of their pleasure. Even Abernathy seemed to step lighter and livlier, his feet seeming to fly over the road.

They arrived at the Dower House before lunch and took the time to unpack and direct the staff as to the pressing of garments, then lie down for a rest before the meal. The warm fire at the hearth made them drowsy after their jaunt in the brisk air of near-winter and they quickly set aside any thought of making love for a good rest.

When they awoke, dressed, and went down to luncheon, they found that Richard and Emmaline had sent word that they would join them for the meal as none of the other guests would arrive until teatime or later and shortly after, the awaited pair arrived in a pony cart Richard had saved from his own childhood --- with, of course, a younger pony. Apparently, he reserved it for special occasions and a visit with his friend Emmaline was always a special occasion.

He helped her from the cart and into the house and the four of them ate at one end of the long dining room table in order to minimize the difficulty in making themselves heard by Emmaline.

The conversation was brisk and interesting for Emmaline would have it no other way. Her thoughts were on politics and medicine, science and social issues --- all the domain of highest intellect and greatest need for a bettering of the world as they knew it and as it must be to go forward successfully.

Richard agreed with her on every point she brought up, though she did not bring up women as doctors or politicians. She should have stood for parliament had she been a man, for she knew her audience in every venue and spoke to their wants and needs, while usually failing to mention that hers were broader based or more far-reaching.

Elisabeth and John were keenly aware of her gift and her discretion, but said nothing to alert Richard to it and fell into the sort of conversation that she directed, aware of and entranced by her mastery of the art. They found that they hardly noticed what was set before them when they fell under the spell of her wit --- so adroit was she with language.

Somehow, conversing with her elevated them and brought them to see things differently, more in the light of social equity, fairness, and good for all being a prerequisite for good to exist for the country. Her philosophy was not exactly socialism, rather more a blend of a few socialist themes with human rights and the obligation of those who have much, whether it be goods or brains, to see to the nurturance of those who have less and bring them to a point where they can have more, produce more, and be a more effective part of the system, whether that be leader or follow. In short, she was an idealist with a golden tongue and the means to move her protégés along, which is not a bad thing.

As the dessert was served, she brought the topic to their impending trip and told them straight out that they would have a good voyage and that more would await in the United States than they anticipated. When asked how she knew that she answered, "I have consulted Gerald Massey's wife, the medium, and she says it will be so; that this ship, The Baltic, will never sink. She also told me that there is more than one gold mine coming to you and they are in different states."

All three of her companions looked at her in amazement and John blurted out, "But the attorney said one, I'm sure of it."

Emmaline smiled and reassured him, saying, "I have never known her to be wrong, my dear."

He drew a deep breath, let it out with a 'phew' and said, "Well then, let us hope that they are both productive."

They all toasted with their coffee to that statement and were silent for a time over the tasty blackberry trifle.

They lingered over the end of the meal, having enjoyed the company and the discussion too much to want it to come to a close, but finally Elisabeth asked if they would like to stroll in the walled garden for a bit and Emmaline answered that the flight of stairs at The Hall was exercise enough for her, then gave Richard a look which clearly said to him, 'drive me back' and he said, "I think it is time we were going so that my guest can have a nap before dinner. You will dine at The Hall, I hope?"

Elisabeth read John's look and said, "Yes, Richard, we would be delighted to sup with you. I believe that the boys will join us at tea, but they said that you had asked them to stay over with you."

"Yes, I did," he answered, "I have things to tell them and enjoy having them about me whenever I can. They are growing into fine young men, Elisabeth --- a credit to you and my brother and also our heritage. I hope to impart more knowledge of that on this visit for Christmas is the time for family, after all."

"Yes, Richard, it is," she agreed and saw the others nodding in affirmation.

After seeing Emmaline into the pony cart, John escorted Elisabeth into the garden. Both wore wraps against the cold air of the day, but the sun and the wall contrived to warm the air and prevent the wind from doing its worst, so they grew warm as they strolled and opened their wraps to allow the heat to escape, then sat on a bench to gaze at the last of the autumn flowers in the beds beneath the trees, some now bare of their leaves and stretching skeletal limbs to the sky as if imploring the sun to return. They were still sitting there engrossed in the beauty of nature when the boys arrived and came out to call them to the parlor for tea.

Tea was light --- finger sandwiches, slices of cheese on crackers, various biscuits and tarts --- for dinner would be earlier than the usual at Richard's gatherings and served in the dining room, but left on the sideboard for latecomers and those who felt like partaking of a bit more of the holiday fare during the evening. In all, he planned on having the Balfours senior, the twins and their husbands, Emmaline, and fifteen of his aunts, uncles, and cousins, if they all arrived, plus Elisabeth, John, and the boys. It appeared that they would be twenty-eight for dinner and the evening's entertainment.

They enjoyed another stimulating conversation and by the time they had finished visiting, it was nearly time to dress for dinner, so the boys hurried out the door and onward to The Hall.

When they had left, Elisabeth and John also went to their room to dress. Without Rose there, she was glad of his help with her dress and coiffure. Her gown was in the artistic style and made of a rich, deep green velvet --- a tribute to the season --- and John wore a black jacket with velvet collar, black pants, white silk shirt and a vest of dark green brocade. When they had finished dressing their finery, they stood before the mirror and proclaimed themselves a handsome couple to be sure, then laughed at their antics. Then, with warm wraps against the cold, they walked the short distance to The Hall and were shown in.

They found that nearly everyone had arrived and most of those who were staying the night were in their rooms dressing for dinner. Only two cousins were yet to come, but they had been positive in their acceptance.

After they had shed their wraps, they wandered into the parlor where Richard greeted them warmly. Two of the boys were already there and Justus entered on their heels saying, "Your dress is beautiful, Mother."

She turned to him and said, "Thank you, Love. You are very stylish, too."

He smiled at the compliment and blushed slightly --- Justus, the youngest, had always been her sensitive child.

At that moment the twins saw them and came over to show Elisabeth their Parisian fashions and compliment her on her dress. Justus, sensing that he was de trop, eased away silently to another group of relatives who were discussing the Russian defeat at the Battle of Inkerman in the Crimean War. War was not his favorite topic, but neither were Paris dresses.....

Not long after, dinner was announced and they all proceeded to the great dining room. Most of the guests being relatives, the male to female ratio had not even been considered when invitations were sent out lest someone feel slighted for lack of one, however such considerations were not necessary among relations, for all were known to each other and there was no need to let each woman shine toward her dinner companion. In point of fact, the talk went in every direction --- from side to side and across the table as well, though at first there was little spoken as they enjoyed their first choices from the lavishly appointed sideboard.

Richard's kitchen staff had prepared the traditional holiday dishes, but he had ordered in more exotic fare as well and his guests were well pleased with the offerings. Their silence was his gauge and it was giving him a good idea of his success.

Only when they were eating their second plate of food did conversation begin to have a little more volume and less lag time. This was music to Richard's ears, as was the complete silence when the dessert had been served and all were savoring the rich, creamy custard within their miniature éclairs and the berry trifle on the plate alongside them.

Soon after, the men departed for their cigars and brandy leaving the women and young people to socialize or play cards for a few hours before they sought their beds. John excused himself from the cigars and brandy and stayed with the group playing cards. Elisabeth visited with Great Aunt Daphne and a few cousins who were curious about John and advised them of the impending trip to the United States, which piqued their interest further. She was hard put to answer their questions, for her knowledge of the country came only from her reading and what she had heard from John. Eventually, though, their interest waned and they went on to other subjects without her having disclosed the gold mine inheritance.

At least, she thought, they are sensitive enough to avoid speculating in front of the twins' mother or mother-in-law on the subject of how soon there would be little Balfours…..

Mrs. Balfour took the reins of the conversation with a near dissertation on the months her sons had spent on the continent with their new wives.

She made it interesting, but it seemed to Elisabeth that it would have been better coming from the youths themselves. Then, remembering how she had needed to draw them out, she conceded the point in her thoughts that perhaps this was the only way the relatives would ever hear of the adventures.

Eventually, the men returned and conversed for awhile, but she and John excused themselves early, pleading the need to rest for their wedding on the morrow and made their escape to the sound of good-natured chuckles and a few whispered comments about young love.

They walked back to the Dower House somewhat slowly in spite of the brisk air, John's arm wrapped around Elisabeth and her leaning into its comfort. The next day they would be married in the church before kith and kin; another sealing of their bond of love for all to see.

Strangely, they felt no need to express themselves physically that night, though the opportunity was ever present. There was a peace inside each of them, due partly to the ceremony to be conducted the following day, but also somehow a part of the evening with family. John's presence had been acknowledged and accepted graciously by them all, even his once-rival Richard, and this lack of conflict or rejection bred in them a serenity they had not expected.

They fell asleep in each other's arms, snuggled together as close as a pair of puppies, and each drawing warmth from the other as well as giving it in return.

They slept.....

✑ Chapter 35 – Yet Another Wedding! ✑

A maid from The Hall had been delegated to help Elisabeth dress unbeknownst to her and the girl finally tapped at the door when it had gone ten o'clock, waited for a moment, then tapped again. Hearing the call to enter, she brought the tea tray and set it on a small table and opened the heavy drapes to expose the light streaming through the windows. "'Tis for certain a beautiful day, madam and sir," she said, "Will you have your tea abed or at the table?"

"Oh, I think at the table," Elisabeth said, looking at John for confirmation. He nodded and she slid out of the bed, donned her dressing gown and brought him his own.

Going to the tray, she lifted the lid of a chaffing dish and added, "They have already buttered the toast and it smells delicious. Now, up you sleepyhead and we shall eat, for we are to marry in little over an hour."

The maid tried unsuccessfully to stifle a grin upon hearing this pronouncement and hurried from the room as a chuckle began to get the best of her as well.

Elisabeth laughed, saying, "See, my love, we are amusement for the staff!"

John, caught up in her mirth, let a low chuckle escape from his own throat and had wafting odors of the tea tray not promised much, they would have forgotten to eat and continued laughing for some time. However, the tea awaited and it was, in truth, excellent and quite ample. Elisabeth suspected this bounty meant that they would forego a regular breakfast owing to the early luncheon reception immediately following their wedding.

After they had eaten and John finished dressing, the maid returned to help Elisabeth dress and to arrange her coiffure. Meanwhile, John waited in the parlor downstairs for her to join him. His wait was not very long, for she knew that they had slept later than they intended --- fortunately, the wedding was to be performed in the chapel on the estate.

A few minutes walk brought them to the chapel and the guests entering to be seated. Once inside the vestibule, John went forward with George, Gerald and Justus, while Catherine, Caroline and their cousin, Viola Stillwell, waited for the signal to precede Richard who, as head of the family, would escort Elisabeth to her groom.

They picked up small bouquets of hothouse flowers which had been placed on a table in the vestibule for them and began the walk to the altar when the pianoforte could be heard. "Now, step and stop, step and stop," Elisabeth reminded them, then took Richard's arm and waited for the strains of Felix Mendelssohn's Wedding March.

When she entered, all stood up and turned to watch --- somewhat reminiscent of her first wedding. She had been on her father's arm that time and tears threatened to fill her eyes when that thought came, but she held them back. Richard was all that was gentlemanly and delivered her to the altar and John without mishap, then answered, "I do, as head of the family," when the minister asked who was giving this woman in marriage. He then sat in the first row next to his aunt Daphne.

The wedding went forward without mishap and soon they were joined in the eyes of the church as well as in the law of the land.

The pianist played a brisk recessional and all exited the building, stopping to congratulate the happy couple as they made their way to The Hall for the luncheon reception.

John and Elisabeth, having stood in the receiving line, brought up the rear along with her five children and their cousin Viola. Emmaline chose to walk with them, for she was rather slow, but Aunt Daphne had gone on ahead with Richard in the pony cart to assure herself that all of the preparations had been completed to her satisfaction.

The guests had waited until the Bridal Party arrived before beginning to eat and after the minister said grace, they pushed the group to the head of the line at the sideboard. John and Elisabeth made certain that Emmaline was seated near them and brought her a plate as well. Richard had placed the bride and groom together at the head of the table, for it was their special day, and Aunt Daphne and himself at the foot.

The company was a merry one and the conversation lasted for many hours until finally all removed to other rooms to visit, or play cards or other games. Justus deserted them for a few hours to study and a few hardy souls went for a walk about the grounds to settle the rich meal, but Elisabeth and John were not among them.

Finally, when it was nearing the hour for supper, Elisabeth saw the sideboard being prepared once again and she asked Aunt Daphne if it would be proper for them to decamp to the Dower House and recoup for the seasonal festivities the next day, December 24th. "Why of course," Aunt Daphne said, "Many newlyweds leave within a few hours for their wedding trip and you have quite a journey in store for you in a few days time. Rest!" and then, with a twinkle in her eye, she added, "If he allows you to....."

Elisabeth bit her lip to keep from smiling, but the older lady had an eagle eye and little escaped her notice.

Thus it was that they made their escape to the Dower House and their bedroom. Richard's servants prepared them a basket filled with delicacies for later --- as though there were no food in the Dower House kitchen --- and a footman carried it while they walked arm in arm to the privacy of their nuptial bower.

When they entered, he took it to the kitchen so that a kitchen maid could prepare the plates and serve it to them on a tray in their bedroom. "Tell them to wait an hour," John called after the man as he and Elisabeth were ascending the stairs to their room.

Elisabeth heard and smiled a secret smile, well knowing what he had on his mind.

As soon as the door closed behind them, he turned the key in the lock lest a servant come knocking and enter prematurely, then helped her to remove her wrap. He knelt to start a fire in the fireplace before he turned back to help her to remove her beautiful gown, then saw that she had already removed her hairpins and jewelry, leaving her long hair loose about her shoulders; a regal mane.

He brought her dressing gown against the chill, though the heavy drapes had been pulled together once the daylight had fled and the room was not so terribly chilly --- certainly nothing like a Michigan winter..... Enough, however, to make her nipples stiffen, he noted, as he helped her out of her clothing and into the thick, warm dressing gown, quilted with down filling lest she take cold. He brushed his palms lightly across the stiff bits of flesh and felt his own flesh harden in response.

Elisabeth felt weak in the knees when his hands touched her so seemingly inadvertently and a shaft of lighting surged through her femininity presaging the bolt she desired. He led her to a chair and asked her to be seated while he divested himself of his own hindering clothing and began to undress --- appearing to be perfunctory, but all the while calculating each move and each posture to arouse her further.

He walked to her still wearing his smallclothes, knowing that she wanted to see more, to lay eyes on that shaft which was pressing against the fabric and causing it to protrude forward --- he knew this to be so, for she was wriggling within her dressing gown, unable to sit still in the chair for even a moment and scarcely able to remove her eyes from that vision of what she desired to feel within her throbbing body.

He held out his hand to her and pulled her to him, allowing her robe to fall open as she rose and, holding her in his arms, he knew that she could feel the hardness between them against her belly. His arms encircled her and he pressed her to him, hands on the small of her back, then slid them lower to cup her buttocks and lift her so that she was higher and closer to the rigid shaft. She drew in a sharp breath as she felt it --- so hard against the softness of her belly and then firmly pressed to the hair of the mount between her thighs.

She leaned her head back and tried to breathe --- the shallow shuddering breaths told him that she was ready for him and, setting her feet back on the carpet, he ascertained with his fingers that she was indeed flowing with welcome.

In one swift motion he scooped her into his arms and laid her on the coverlet, removed his last piece of clothing and mounted the bed, then lay between the thighs of his Elisabeth.

She pulled her knees up, exposing herself to his groin and, as though his manhood had prehensile abilities, it found the scabbard within her and entered, drawing a gasp from her throat. No gasp of pain or dismay this --- it was energy meeting energy, passion meeting passion, and a woman so ready for his entrance that she whimpered at the ecstasy it brought.

John slipped in and out of her flowing juices, knowing that this would give them more time before the real fireworks began, before the friction became so strong that neither could delay the ultimate moment --- that merging into each other's being and becoming one in the flesh as well as the heart --- and when the fireworks began, she lifted her hips against him and he pushed himself forward into her as deeply as he could manage while his own fluids spurted forth and his hips jerked with each spasm of his release.

Early on, Elisabeth experienced a number of orgasms far smaller and less spectacular than his, but gratifying all the same, and then, as she felt him pushing against her, the sensation brought on a spasm which tightened the muscles of her secret recess as though they were a clamp seeking to hold his semen within her --- a force of nature attempting to recreate itself by holding in the seeds of new life.

He sifted his weight to his left arm and with his right arm he reached for a breast and squeezed firmly, pinching the nipple between his second and third fingers and rubbing them together. She moaned. Good, he thought, for he could feel the pulsing of her muscles around his softening member and it brought on another small round of spasms in his hips.

Elisabeth felt the contractions and, in some part of her mind, knew them for what they were: a reaction to suckling which causes the muscles of the vagina and womb to contract and eventually revert to their normally small size after birth. However, the sensation was also entirely pleasant when there was no birth involved at all and she savored it, her hips jerking at times with the force of the contraction.

John rolled to his side and slipped out of her, then used his discarded smallclothes to hold back the tide of his juices flowing from her furry mound, but also began to suckle at her breasts and pinching whichever one he was not attending to with his lips. For a medical student this was a good lesson in the anatomy of the female body and all its capabilities --- and he pursued his studies avidly until his wife cried out her release.

Finally, they spoke. John asked if she was ready for dinner and she answered, "More likely for sleep, but I'll eat with you."

As though on cue, a few minutes later the maid tapped at the door and John quickly donned his dressing gown to open it, admitting her and a tray to the room.

"I brought up your plates, but if you prefer I can take them to the dining room," she said.

The newly married made eye contact and John answered, "No, here will be fine. As you can see, we were relaxing after the long day."

"Oh, yes, sir," she replied, placing the meal on the table near the window drapes, then continued, "Is there aught you would like to add to your meal? Perhaps I've forgotten something."

Looking at the offerings, he queried, "Is there no dessert?"

"Oh, yes, but it should be served chilled so the chafing dish is on the empty birdbath in the garden staying cold!"

He laughed at the image of the chafing dish atop the birdbath and both ladies joined in with his mirth for a moment, then the maid excused herself, saying, "I will bring it up in half an hour or there 'bouts if it suits."

"That would be perfect," Elisabeth replied and the maid departed, leaving them to their meal.

"Our first meal alone together now that we are church-blessed and sanctified," John observed.

"One of a multitude," she answered, beaming at him as though he were the sun and she, but a mirror, reflecting his glory.

❦Chapter 36 – Christmas Eve❧

It was nearly noon when Elisabeth stirred and wondered how much of the day had passed. No maid had come with a tea tray, so surely it was early, she reasoned, reaching for John and finding him not. She sat up abruptly in bed, wondering just how late it was, then crawled over the coverlet and found her dressing gown, for she had been completely naked beneath the covers.

She opened the drapes and sat in a chair while, slowly, the memories of the night before percolated up from her memory and brought an enigmatic smile to her face: the smile of a woman well pleased --- more than once. She stretched, much as a cat would, flexing all the muscles which had worked hard the night before as the memories of their love-making replayed in her awareness. The mere thought of the intensity of that night brought a reaction to her body and she found herself squeezing her breasts and pinching her own nipples, just to feel the sensation in her nether regions, when a tap at the door stopped her and, after securing her robe, she called out, "Enter!"

The maid entered with a tea tray for her and said, "'Tis gone noon and the men are returned from a ride, ma'am. Would you be taking the meal with them or shall I bring it you?"

"Oh, dear," Elisabeth fretted, "So late and me a slugabed! Whatever will John think of me?"

"I doubt he will think ill of you ma'am, for he asked me to leave you sleep until they returned. Did the cold of the dessert upset your stomach?"

"No, it was merely a long day," she answered.

"They'll not be dining until our cook is ready, and she said it would be half an hour at best, so you've a bit of time to sip your tea and nibble toast before you dress if you've a mind to come down," the maid suggested.

"Of a certainty I will dine with them. Is it my sons?" she asked.

"Of course, ma'am," the maid replied, then added. "'Tis as though they be his own sons, if you don't mind me saying it, for they look up to him as to a gentle father."

This pronouncement quickly brought a smile of pleasure to Elisabeth's face, for it was her greatest hope --- that her children would love John as she did --- and she nodded her agreement.

Pleased that she had struck a chord, the maid left for the kitchen, lest the cook be calling her to help in vain, and Elisabeth drank her tea and ate a little of her toast.

After a bit, John came up to their room and offered to help her into her dress. She showed him the one she planned to wear --- green in honor of the season --- and with but a minimum of frivolity, he dressed her as well as any maid could have accomplished. She arranged her hair with his help and he selected her jewelry --- pearls, for he claimed she was his 'pearl of great price' --- and, when they had finished, he escorted her to the dining room where the young men were already seated. With her sons, two of their Hastings cousins and John, they were seven at table.

The Hastings cousins were intrigued by the impending visit to the United States and asked John as many questions as they could conceive. He answered those he could and promised that the others would be answered upon his return.

The last time Elisabeth remembered there being as many questions as she had heard in the last three days was when she was a child --- and doing the asking! That thought brought a smile to her face as her father's face came to the forefront of her memory. How tolerant he had been, she thought, and reminded herself to always be so in regard to others.

She had learned over the last few days that Richard arranged to have a midnight service in the chapel where she had been married, leaving the following morning free for the early family breakfast he had planned --- and, of course, the gifts….. Those who were able would stay for Christmas Dinner in the afternoon and quite a few would tarry through New Year's Day.

As she mulled over these thoughts, she realised that she had been asked a question and apologised for wool-gathering, then asked George to repeat it. and he complied. "I was wondering how late you are staying here on Christmas Day, Mother."

"Only for breakfast, George, for we still have many things to do. Your uncle is lending us a coach for the return home and the journey to Aylesbury. The three of you will ride with us to the station in it on Boxing Day and the groom will return it to Richard after taking you home. At that point you may stay at home, return to Richard's or fill your social calendars," she said with a teasing look on her face.

The men all laughed --- her sons with a bit of embarrassment, for they had attended many balls and parties over the past year.

She looked at them indulgently with her head tilted a bit to one side and said, "I will miss all of you when I am traveling in the United States --- never think it otherwise." She paused for a moment, becoming very serious, and then, after a glance at John, added, "However, this is a journey which we must undertake for many reasons."

Her sons nodded their understanding for they knew of the inheritance, though they had no idea of the far-reaching agenda which was being written between Elisabeth, John, and the hand of fate.

They spent the balance of the afternoon visiting, with Elisabeth taking the measure of the Hastings relations and finding them intelligent and articulate. She wondered if perhaps these were more of Emmaline's protégés and found herself assessing them even closer: they were fine young men and good scholars as well; both students of botany.

When it was time to assemble for dinner at The Hall, they made a merry party walking together and laughing heartily. As they neared it, they began to sing carols and the words traveled far on the crisp air, bringing figures to the windows facing the drive. The door opened as if by magic when they reached it, for their voices had announced their presence in advance, and they entered to be enchanted by the decorations which had been added to the entry hall.

Relatives appeared from the parlor and drawing room to greet them as they removed their wraps and urge them to continue singing, but they begged off, deferring it to the post dinner hours as a means to while away the time until the midnight mass.

Mollified by the promise of a songfest later, the music lovers drew them into the parlor just as dinner was announced and they all departed together for the great dining hall. Richard took the head of the table this time, being head of the family as well as host, with Great Aunt Daphne at his right and Emmaline at his left. Conversation was sure to be brisk at that end of the table, Elisabeth observed!

She and John were seated across from each other mid-table and every now and again their eyes met and they smiled at each other, for their great adventure was soon to unfold.

Considering that they had all been together for a few days, the conversation was fairly animated --- having stayed at the Dower House for the better part of the day, the fresh faces were welcome and the same luncheon topics could be touched on, for some of the young people would leave immediately after dinner for a house party. At breakfast, they would provide plenty of news as they recounted their experiences at the party.

Those who remained sang carols and intermittently played cards, rotating partners so that none were paired consistently with weaker players for long, lest boredom set in.

Finally, the hour grew late and the wassail bowl was running low --- time to go to the chapel for the midnight service and thence to their beds. The minister, who had been visiting all evening with them suggested that he perform the service in the great hall rather than in the unheated chapel and not one voice disabused him of the notion --- for a number were elderly and valued their comfort and their health.

Thus it was that he performed the mass in the great hall and they sang to their hearts' content. Elisabeth and John left soon after and hurried to the Dower House and to their bed. The servants had attended the service in the great hall and enjoyed a cup from the wassail bowl as well, but they had returned to their posts and the fire had been lit in Elisabeth and John's bedroom and the maid, who had been awaiting them, said, "I'll go to the kitchen and fetch the warm drinks that our cook has prepared for you. To be sure, 'tis cocoa, but I'm certain sure that she's added a bit of something heartier to keep you warm."

And, when she brought it, they found that she had the right of it, for cook had added a bit of rum to the pot and it sat warm in their bellies as well as their mouths.

The warm liquid put them to sleep before they could finish it all and they slept soundly as a litter of pups.

⅏Chapter 37 – Christmas Day⅌

It was early when the young people returned from their party to eat breakfast and open gifts and they awakened Elisabeth and John as unashamedly as they had dragged her from her bed of a Christmas Day when they were children, saying, "Come, Mother, Father Christmas has already been and gone."

John smiled, remembering his own days as a child in the not-so-distant past and Elisabeth, watching his reaction, surmised as much. Soon they were dressed and left for The Hall and Richard's festive breakfast.

It was early --- little past seven --- but all were assembled for the sumptuous breakfast and their gifts. Conversation was brisk and the meal passed quickly, for all anticipated their presents --- the ones they would give as well as the ones they would receive.

When the last crumb had been eaten, the young people fairly flew to the shoes by the hearth in the great hall and found their gifts from Father Christmas, but also discovered gifts from their parents and other relatives ranging from crocheted slippers and knitted scarves to toys, dolls, fishing poles and more --- depending on their ages and inclination. Some of the adults exchanged gifts as well --- mostly books and handkerchiefs with handmade lace, but the twins and their husbands brought Richard a number of cases of fine wines from France in appreciation of his providing lodging for so many of the guests at their wedding --- to say nothing of the ball.

Watching, Elisabeth saw how touched he was and realised that he wasn't such a bad sort, just a man who had made her feel chased and that had been more a reaction to him as though he were his brother --- her husband, George --- trying to come back from the grave and rescind her freedom from an arranged marriage.

At that moment, she felt the firm pressure of John's hand on hers and was able to banish the memory of that feeling of being chattel as she allowed his love to wash over her being, reminding her that she had made her own choice of a husband this time and need never feel less of a person than he.

The family lingered for a bit in the great hall and finally she and John rose to decamp and make their way to Little Tring and the adventure which would begin on the morrow. They took their leave of each person --- almost like a receiving line --- and wished them well for the season and the year to come, expressing their hope that all would return for the next Christmas.

When they had only Richard left to bid good-bye, they thanked him for the wonderful family gathering this had been and for their wedding as well.

Elisabeth said, "Richard, you are an even finer man than I had thought and I thank you for all you have done. I will bring you a gold nugget from the new world to attest to your merit."

Richard smiled and bantered back, "As good as gold, eh? Now that IS a testament!"

She laughed and shook her head from side to side, chuckling low in her throat at his wit, then answered, "Ah, Richard, there must be some reward for virtue."

He answered, "Yes, and my virtue extends to not only lending you one of my coaches tomorrow, but sending your daughters with it to see you off at the station."

Elisabeth was startled and pleased. She squeezed his hand, which she had been holding, and managed to say, "Thank you Richard, thank you," her voice almost catching with the emotion she was feeling.

Soon, they were out the door and into the buggy which had been brought up from the stables with their belongs already packed and stowed in the box on the back by the staff at the Dower House. Abernathy whinnied his greeting to them and Elisabeth gave him a pat on the neck before letting John help her into her seat. Abernathy needed no prodding to begin the journey home, merely an 'okay, boy', a tiny shake of the reins, and he was heading down the drive.

Alone again, they were on their way. There was an excitement, a tension, for this was a new path they were anticipating and this day would be their last day at home for some time to come.

Aside from their feelings, the journey was uneventful --- someone passing would never have known the monumental issues that were being considered in their minds.

Elisabeth was wondering how her children would fare without her there to help them and John wondered how Elisabeth would fare on the journey and what her children, their children he reminded himself, would do in their absence. He expected that the boys would go to their uncle for advice and comfort and the girls to their husbands, but he felt that he and Elisabeth should give them some direction in the matter before they departed and, in that frame of mind, he determined to have a talk with her when they had a free moment.

It was not too long by country standards before they reached their destination and were greeted by Rose and Cook at the door when they stopped to unload their baggage. Each gave them a hug and said, "Merry Christmas!" before helping to bring the bags into the house.

Here, Elisabeth thought, she felt so much more at home. Perhaps it was her father's spirit infusing the house, but it was also as though Rose and Cook were family --- nurturing like a mother and sister --- the mother she never knew and the sister she never had.

She and John slipped upstairs quietly to gather their gifts for the ladies and came down again, arms filled with packages. It had been a chore to keep them secret, but they had managed, for Rose did not feel so easy, yet, about going into the closets even to hang clothing with a man's jackets about and they had been able to stow the gifts deep in a closet.

When they presented them in the parlor, Rose and Cook were startled to see the bounty of their packages and Cook began to dab at her eyes with a corner of her apron. Elisabeth and John told them that they must open them right then in front of them, for that was the gift they were receiving --- the joy of watching them be surprised. The pair looked at each other, hesitating a moment, then began to open ribbons and slide paper off of the boxes.

For each, there was a new pair of shoes and two new dresses --- one for everyday and one for church. There were silk flowers enough to decorate a number of hats for each and boxes containing new nightgowns and shifts. Each was gifted a new handbag of tapestry with beading and most importantly, for winter had just begun, a new coat of thick wool with a capelet to keep the winds at bay. With each new gift, their eyes grew larger and larger and Elisabeth and John smiled.

When they were near the end and seemed overwhelmed, Elisabeth said, "You see, my dear friends, I will not be here for Rose's wedding and I must see her go to her husband with more than the clothing on her back and you, Cook, must look pretty, too, if you are to stand up and witness for her."

They went to her, putting their arms around her and giving a look to each other, and said in near unison, "Thank you, Miss Elisabeth," as though she were still a girl.

Tears rolled down the cheeks of all three of them as John watched, touched by the scene himself, for he had grown fond of the two ladies also. Then, Cook jumped back exclaiming, "Oh dear, me oven!"

In a trice, she was sailing down the hallway toward the kitchen with Rose in her wake. After a few moments, though, Rose returned to say that the dinner was saved and nothing even slightly burned, though it was a close call. Elisabeth and John breathed a sigh of relief --- she, that Cook wouldn't feel badly, and he, that that there would be no need to pretend that dinner tasted all right. Thus it was that the dinner was being served in the breakfast nook moments afterward. Elisabeth had insisted that they have the meal there for the lighting was better than in the kitchen and they were too few for the dining room. Indeed, Rose and Cook felt more comfortable eating there as well.

Cook had opted for duck rather than the popular turkey, Aylesbury being famed for their ducks, and had roasted two braces of them with all the trimmings --- potatoes and other vegetables --- in the same pan. Inside, they were filled with a savory dressing rich with herbs and nuts, while she had prepared plenty of side dishes against the possibility that the boys might come home for a meal and baked enough for a regiment.

As they ate, Elisabeth hoped that the boys would stay to lunch after they saw her and John off at the station the next morning so that the bakery would not go to waste or be eaten stale by Cook and Rose. With this thought in mind, she said to Cook, "If the boys fail to stay, please give some of your bakery to our friends and tenants lest you and Rose feel compelled to eat it stale to avoid wasting it altogether."

"I will, that, but I have a feeling that those young men will have plenty of room for the sweeties," Cook answered with an indulgent smile.

Elisabeth had to agree with her --- they certainly had a sweet tooth, each and every one of them, and with the girls coming as well, they might take breakfast there. She did not mention this to Cook, however, for fear it would instigate another frenzy of baking and they would be faced with the same problem of an embarrassment of riches.

After the meal, they enjoyed coffee, with Cook opting for tea, and Elisabeth broached the subject of Rose's betrothal. Rose told her that all was well, Richard had agreed to allow her groom, Seth, to marry her in January as soon as the banns could be posted --- either in church or at the registry office. He would continue to pay Seth's salary and allow him to remain at Elisabeth's where he and Rose would live over the stable, while the Bishops were abroad, just as John had. He would send a horse with him so that he could ride alongside when the three of them went to church or to travel back and forth to Elisabeth's properties and oversee them for her. All in all, things were falling easily into place.....

By the time they finished their meal, dessert, and chatting, it was already close to five o'clock and Elisabeth commented that dinner would be best to have sometime after seven and suggested that a tasty soup and tea sandwiches would be a welcome supper after their breakfast and dinner feasts. Cook nodded her understanding and said, "More packing now, eh?"

"Yes, we have much to accomplish yet," Elisabeth replied and, looking at Rose, asked, "May I purloin your helper for an hour or so to help me with the last of my packing?"

"Of course you may!" answered Cook immediately.

Elisabeth took her hand and squeezed it, saying, "You are a jewel, Cook. I know it is an undertaking to prepare such a great deal of food and then be compelled to wait for help with the dishes, but I do need her and, if you would like, you may come and keep us company --- only change that apron lest you soil my silks."

Cook looked down at her apron, which she had forgotten to remove for the meal and blushed, then looked up at Elisabeth and saw her smile and knew that no offense had been taken. She laughed at herself and said, "That I will, ma'am, in two shakes of a lamb's tail!" And, true to her word, she met them upstairs wearing a clean apron in only a few minutes.

Two large trunks were being packed, as well as four valises. Even at this, they were taking a minimum of clothing, for they could purchase anything they needed once they had reached New York City in mid-January.

Though they were to be in first class, one valise would be filled with wool blankets lest they be in short supply and the weather colder than anticipated. Cook helped by folding these and packing them, then sitting on the valise while Rose closed the latches and locked them. One done!

Afterward, she sat in one of the chairs and talked as they packed, commenting on the beautiful dresses and keeping the flow of conversation and camaraderie from lagging. Elisabeth needed this chatter to allay her fears over the trip and to remind her of the close relationship she enjoyed with them, for in a way they were far more like family than retainers.

They finished about half past six and Cook left for the kitchen and preparations for the light supper, then Rose followed her down the stairs. Elisabeth sat in a chair and looked at the baggage wondering if someday people would stop wearing such a lot of clothing and travel with one valise. What nonsense am I thinking, she told herself, then chuckled and followed her helpers.

Hearing the activity on the stairs, John emerged from the study just as her foot left the bottom step and asked, "Are you done, then? Is it supper?"

She laughed, then answered, "Yes, my darling. Cook is already preparing our repast."

"Good!" he replied, "In spite of that wonderful Christmas dinner, I could eat a whale!"

Again he was treated to her tinkling laughter and felt a warmth grow within his heart at the sound. He took her into his arms and held her close, feeling the joy in his heart growing and spreading to every part of his body. He felt as though he were floating in the air, so light did his being become, and the only thought running through his mind was: she is mine forever.

Elisabeth stood there, enveloped in his embrace, savoring the moment of communion, of oneness with her love, and knew that this was what she had been waiting for these long years. Her heart was filled as his was, with joy and more.....

Seeing them, Rose carried the soup tureen into the breakfast room on tiptoe, though her shoe squeaked and gave her away. They held the embrace for a moment longer, then followed her into the room for supper and Cook came down the hall bearing a tray of sandwiches and soup bowls.

❧Chapter 38 – The Journey Begins☙

Rose knocked on the bedroom door early. Elisabeth heard the sound and asked her to enter, then whispered to John to wake up until he finally roused from slumber. A good thing we went to bed early last night, she thought.

Meanwhile, Rose put a tea tray on the small table and lighted the lamps from her candle. It was still dark outside, but would be dawning shortly and their breakfast guests would be arriving soon to take them to the station an hour and a half away. Their train was for eleven, but by the time all was stowed aboard their coach and removed at the station, with travel time between --- as well as breakfast --- they had decided it was a better idea to leave by nine o'clock.

Elisabeth went to her bath and John followed, using the same water and enjoying the lavender scent of it. They helped each to don the clothing they planned to wear for breakfast, knowing they would do the same again just before leaving, for their travel clothing was far heavier than that which would be worn indoors.

Completely dressed and ready for breakfast they descended to the dining room and were surprised to find all five of the children and Justin and Quentin there already. They had brought the Balfours' larger coach with seating for up to eight and Rose's Seth was acting footman. Her sons had ridden their horses over and Justin and Quentin would ride two of them to the station to allow Elisabeth's children to ride with their mother and stepfather in the coach.

Once those arrangements had been explained to her, Elisabeth asked, "Shall we dine?" She was greeted with a chorus of 'ayes' from all directions.

Cook must have stayed up all night, she thought, when she saw the sideboard. It was filled with chargers of everything imaginable to tempt the pallet of a hungry man. Cook had outdone herself.

The young men, including John, filled their plates over and over and even the ladies ate heartily, for Cook had a reputation of excellence and it was honestly earned.

The coachman and footman had brought everything down the stairs and loaded it onto the coach as well as in the boot for the journey and, by nine o'clock, the coach was on the road to Aylesbury, it's team of four straining at the bit to be on the high road with the heavy load.

Meanwhile, the coach's occupants settled into conversation about Elisabeth and John's trip and all of the instructions she was leaving them. Richard had offered to support the boys in any way they needed while she was gone and she informed them of that --- also, that Seth would be acting in John's stead as rent collector and overseer of work done to improve the properties. He would turn over the monies collected to Richard, who would see that Cook and Rose were paid and had ample to run the household. He would continue paying Seth, but his board would be her responsibility.

When the boys were away at school, they could leave their horses in the stable at home rather than bringing them to The Hall and he would feed, groom, and exercise them as well as Abernathy.

They would, of course, be able to stay at the house if they were not in school or at Richard's if they chose to.

She repeated more than once that this trip might possibly be a year or longer, hoping to set it in their minds, for she felt that it would indeed be at least that.

Finally, having said all that she had need of saying, she relinquished the conversation to her children and they all began to chatter at once.

She held her hands up until they all stopped and she said four little words, "One at a time!"

There was silence for a moment and then, one by one, they began to speak alternately and order reigned. She let out a sigh of relief and leaned back against the seat to listen to their voices for the last time until her return to England. It almost brought tears to her eyes to think of that, but she was able to stifle them and maintain her composure. As she sat there, she committed the sound and what they said to memory to replay in her mind when she missed them. John watched her and surmised what she was doing with that gift of intuition he had where she was concerned.

The trip to Aylesbury passed in this manner, with her interjecting bits of conversation into theirs from time to time and the five children carrying the bulk of the responsibility. It reminded her of when they were children and traveled --- only the voices were lower in the boys now and softer in the girls.

John took her hand in his, knowing that she would have trepidation until they alighted on terra firma in the New World and let his warmth and confidence permeate her. The strength of his hand calmed her and set her being at peace as always. Ah, John, she thought, I waited so many years for you to find me.....

The ride to Aylesbury was a bit shorter than she had thought it might be, but she had not counted on having four horses to pull the load.

As it was, they reached the Aylesbury Station at twenty minutes past ten and with plenty of time to check their baggage. The coachman and footman unloaded it all onto a cart provided by the baggage clerk and Gerald and George pushed it to the baggage check window to have it tagged, then returned with the receipts for John.

They stood and talked while they waited for the train to arrive and board, not quite knowing what to say at such a time in the way of most people who are seeing someone off. They actually wanted to be going with their mother, but each knew that it would alter their current course immeasurably and she had supported their choices and helped them on their paths, so they were being brave and releasing her to her path and her journey, hoping inside that all would be well.

For her part, she wanted to gather them into her arms --- even Justin and Quentin --- and carry them off with her to America to share the experience with her and John, but she knew that they had things to do, an education to achieve and, in the girls' case, husbands to build a life with and, she hoped, children to bear and to raise as time passed.

John watched them and felt the tugging emotions of them all as clearly as though they were his own emotions and his own children by blood. He had always been this way --- one who could feel what others felt. He knew that this would help him as a doctor and from Elisabeth's descriptions of her father, he suspected strongly that he had had this ability as well.

As he listened to their conversations, he let his mind wander to the trip and the excitement that Elisabeth was soon to feel, an excitement that they would share.

When the train arrived and people began exiting, they knew it would be time to board momentarily and walked in the direction of the platform as a group.

When they found they must wait to board, Elisabeth took that opportunity to embrace each of her children and whisper in their ear that she loved them, holding each as if it were the last time.

John shook hands all around and then came the boarding call and they entered their private compartment in the carriage and sat by the windows in order to wave to their children. And, as the train slowly and ponderously left the station, that is exactly what they did.

A few miles up the track, they sat there talking of all of the things they would do when they reached the United States and Elisabeth suddenly said, "John! I forgot!"

He asked. "What did you forget?"

"I forgot to write again to Gerald Massey and encourage him to visit us in America!" she answered.

John smiled indulgently and took her into his arms. He loved this woman very much and he looked forward to a lifetime of years with her.

For the moment, however, they were bound toward the greatest adventure of their lives, one which would impinge upon everything else they did, both now and later, and form their existence as they would never have thought possible.

He kissed her eyelids and she smiled, then raised her lips to be kissed as well and snuggled against him to feel his warmth as they sped along the track toward the north --- and the Baltic --- with the secret of their love unveiled.....

The threads of fog were dense enough to form a fabric of sorts, screening everything with its veil and preventing even the wavelets from being easily apparent. Without the sound of their slapping against the hull, one could have thought that the ship glided on a sea of glass.

To the young woman standing on the deck, the throaty call of the foghorn seemed eerie and melancholic. She shivered, then pulled the collar of her coat closer and snuggled into its warmth.

It brought memories --- memories of another time, a time when she was not alone, and she rode the wave of that remembering, basking in the glow of its warmth and joy.

They were young, she and Franz, and on their way to France. It was 1936, the days of The Great Depression were beginning to wane, and their families had sent them to Europe for their honeymoon --- and, being in business, to take a first-hand look at the economies.....

Ah, their fathers, the consummate businessmen.....

Enough of that, she thought! Back to their precious time together on board their ship of dreams..... She remembered, so vividly, his hair blowing in the wind on the deck when he'd forgotten his hat. She offered her spare scarf, but he'd invoked the rule of men vs. women's clothing and refused. He didn't catch cold, though --- the steamy encounters in their stateroom saw to that.

Her mind pondered that for a moment, wondering if she could handle the memories of their love-making, then shelved them for another moment --- in favor of feeling his arms around her, warming her from outside instead of from within. Ten years..... Ten long years..... At times, it seemed like a hundred and, yet, sometimes like a minute. He felt so close when she thought of him, that she half-expected to turn and see him standing there with that tender look in his eyes and the slightly lop-sided smile he got when he saw her.

As the memories began to raise themselves, she became oblivious to the fog and let them filter into her awareness. Ah, here was the first night on board their ship.....

Walking up the gangplank was the beginning of their adventure. After waving to the friends who had made the journey to New York to see them off, they giggled at their aloneness and beat a hasty retreat to their stateroom. She remembered how the scent of the flower arrangements was almost overpowering, but, in their youthful excitement, they ignored it completely. She could see the exquisite peignoir set she had brought with her and relived changing into it in the bedroom, while Franz waited, with anticipation, in the sitting room. Finally, he came and knocked on the door to see if she was all right. Then, when she opened the door, just stood there staring at her. Even her beautiful wedding gown hadn't evoked this response.....

It was as though he had been struck dumb --- or maybe he felt that the beauty of the moment was too precious for words to mar it.

Finally, he took her hands and led her to the bed, then seated her and knelt to take each slipper off of her feet. There was something about him holding her feet in his hands that had made her go all soft inside and, suddenly, there was a fire in her private parts that made her wriggle and shiver. Remembering it, she shivered again --- or was it the cold breeze?

He stood, then, and began to disrobe slowly, tantalizing her by taking his time in folding each piece, though he probably was only trying to allay his own nervousness. With each moment and each piece he removed, she became more aroused. When he finally stood her up again and removed her diaphanous, marabou-trimmed peignoir, then lifted the hem of her negligee, she felt faint with the heat radiating from her body.

Passionate Pursuit - 1946